motherhood at the end of the world

Jesse M Harvey

paperback-978-1-956344-02-8

hardback- 978-1-956344-03-5

e-book- 978-1-956344-05-9

audio book- 978-1-956344-04-2

Editor: Bill Thompson

Cover design by: Books by E M Garner

Proofreader: Chezney Carrier

Publishing House: Mighty Mama Mouse

Illustrator: Carla Porterfield

Pen Name: Jesse M. Harvey

*Dedicated to **Springlea**, who believed in me and gave me the spark of hope I needed to start this journey. I promised you, I would see it through to the end. To my family who never let me break that promise.*
*And to **Bill** who made me write it over and over until it was good.*
And to all those who joined me on this journey and made sure that the book received the introduction it deserved.
Thank you all so much. My heart is so full.

also by jesse m harvey

Scythia Protostar: Book one of the Dark Stellar Legacy.

'Deadly Sweet Rolls' - found in: Curves and Magic- Big Swords, Big Adventure, Big Women.

contents

"Science fiction is really Sociological Studies of the future, things that the writer believes are going to happen by putting two and two together."
    Ray Bradbury.

COMPOSITION BOOK
100 Sheets / Feuilles
9.75 in x 7.50 in (24.7cm x 19.04cm)
Recipe Book
SCAVAGE LIST
ALWAYS: SOAPS!
Asprin & Meds
Bandages & bandaids
Antibiotic creams
Sanitary Pads
Diapers (Cloth!)
CANDY
Baking soada
Flour. Rice. Beans

one
tuesday, 10:36am

SO NO SHIT, there I was, standing on the double yellow line in a deserted street. Bits of trash chased each other on the wind, swirling and falling, then spinning off again.

I was holding my breath. *Any second now.* I waited for aliens to come out from behind the burned-out buildings. I scanned the area behind me to make sure no zombies had crawled up on me while I wasn't looking.

The street was just about to wake up and come to life again. In a moment the music would play, and the next scene would start. It was about that time in the movies when I should meet a new character, or some horrible monster should attack. I waited, but there was no music, not a sound. The lack of noise set my teeth on edge. The city should have been alive with horns honking, dogs barking, cars driving, people on phones, and the background hum from the power lines. Now it was just the sound of trash in the wind.

Since the soundtrack had failed to appear, and I had been lied to by years of apocalypse movies, I chose to hum the music myself. I was of the firm opinion that there should always be theme music.

I made one last scan of the area as I shifted the shotgun on my shoulder, trying to make my backpack sit more comfortably. I needed to keep moving. It was only midmorning, but time slipped away quickly on these supply runs. I pulled up my sleeve to look down at the watch on my wrist. I didn't like to be away from the kids for so long. I needed to be more careful of my daydreaming; it was way too easy for me to get lost inside my own head. It had always been dangerous for women to be out alone, and the end of the world had only intensified that problem.

I was at a small strip mall in the village of Shadowbrook. It was stylized and decorated to look like an old hamlet. The buildings in the area kept with the theme of a small country town. The main square had a little park, a gazebo, and a fountain. I had been here before, for a lovely little county fair. Now it was all just decorations for a ghost town. This so-called village was about a five- to ten-minute drive from downtown proper. Geographically, however, it was up a steep hill and over a river valley that included a brook. It was a nasty trek on foot, and there weren't any working cars after the light storms. For most people it was too far a distance to go for supplies. That meant it was safer for me. The likelihood of someone else coming here for supplies was low. People were still tearing apart the stores in the city, fighting over the supplies nearest to them.

There was a steep learning curve to this scrounging business. You figured out quickly where to look, or you starved. Best-case scenario, you wasted your time. Worst case, you ended up dead. You couldn't just go to the supermarket anymore.

Last word from Wally World was that a group of heavily armed men had taken over management. Several gangs had made attempts at hostile takeovers, but the young entrepreneurs were brutal and had managed to hold on to the property. A week later they had posted advertisements. They were going for competitive pricing and they wanted the world to know they were open for business. A whole ad campaign in handmade posters and wall graffiti had appeared quickly to let everyone know that they would "barter and trade anything with anyone."

I wasn't eager to find out what they wanted to trade. Most of the big-name stores had already burned down or been looted. The other stores would be under new management soon. You needed either a lot of people or a lot of guns to shop at those big stores now. I had neither. I had never liked shopping at big-brand stores anyway. I'd always believed in shopping local.

The first day of storms must have been terrifying in the city: blackouts, communications going down, speakers screaming, lights exploding, half the city catching on fire, and then looting. I had heard stories from some of the other survivors back at camp. The riots that had followed had ended a week ago, but I knew it was still just the beginning. Some people were mistaking this lull as a sign that the worst was over, and everything would go back to normal soon. People in general are stupid, self-serving, and short-sighted. That equals dangerous, so I avoided them when I was alone. They would soon realize the truth when the lights never came back on, when no one showed up to fix the phones, no FEMA, no National Guard. That was when they would finally understand that no supplies or aid were coming. When that happened, they would panic again, with good reason.

Upstate New York is full of rivers, creeks, deep ravines, washouts, hills, and heavy woods. It is a topographical nightmare for any kind of logistical purpose. One blocked freeway, and no one was going to move till spring. Summer was quickly giving way to fall. I didn't have the luxury of waiting to see if the government had the ability to make it to us before winter arrived. There were people counting on me. I wasn't going to let them down by being stupid and hopeful.

There is a rule in nature, if you don't have fangs and claws, then you need to be quick and clever. Since I didn't have an army, I had to be smart. I had to be a mouse. Why a mouse, you might ask? Consider this, everything eats mice—wolves, dogs, birds, cats, and some other rodents eat mice. However, mice just keep going, making their homes, raising their young, and facing all the dangers of the world. If a mouse could do it, so could I.

So that's what I was, a mama mouse foraging for supplies for the nest. In ancient times humans were hunters and gatherers. Some of the community would hunt for animals, but most of their needs were met by those who foraged for food. That's what I was doing. I supposed some people might disagree. They were allowed. It's a free country. Well, at least it used to be, when it was a country. When the world turned back on, they could send me the bill. Until then, I had mouths to feed and little ones to care for. That's why I was up with the sun, hiking up steep hills and fording creeks to get to the out-of-the-way places. A mother had to do what a mother had to do.

I had hidden my bike and wagon behind a burned-out truck at the end of the street. Then I sat behind that truck for half an hour to watch for people. I put the U lock around the wheels of my bike and set up a string of hidden bells so that if anyone tried to cut the chain, the bells would jingle. It was as close to an alarm as I could manage.

The only competition for my personally hummed soundtrack was the wind. My internal radio was set to random, and I was currently humming a nursery rhyme my son loved. *"Are you sleeping, are you sleeping, Brother John, Brother John? Morning bells are ringing, morning bells are ringing. Ding dong ding, Ding dong ding."* It was official, my movie would have the weirdest soundtrack ever.

I checked my gear one last time and then moved toward the old-fashioned buildings. They had pretty gingerbread moldings on the edge of their roofs. The whole area looked like it could have been pulled off some German Christmas postcard. This strip mall must have been remodeled in the last decade or so because it hadn't burned up with the older buildings. *Congratulations on meeting quality code regulations!*

The Shadowbrook Plaza was a typical one-block residential shopping center. There were five small shops and one larger corner store that faced the intersection. It was styled into old colonial buildings set close together instead of just one long building. The landscaping was still neat, just starting to show a little growth from the last mowing. The parking lot looked like it did every day. It could have been any quiet morning. The buildings were perfectly intact—no burns on the walls, no broken glass on the ground. It looked like the rioting mobs hadn't wanted to run uphill. Angry mobs don't really think things through. When you take a large number of poor, desperate, angry people and scare the shit out of them. Then show them that the people who are supposed to have authority aren't around anymore, *pop*! The crowd snaps. They forget that the rich don't live downtown. They live removed—far up on the hills in these silly little decorated villages, in the huge houses with long driveways and big fences to keep all those dirty, angry poor folks out. The people attack the icons they can see—the department stores they can't afford, the banks that don't hold anything for them.

Then the mob eventually runs itself down, and all you have left are tired, angry people and a bunch of burned buildings. The wealthy continue to live in pretty gated communities like this one. Oh well, it wasn't my job to sort out that mess.

Aren't I a cheerful one? Yeah, but a good philosophical rumination about the nature of riots is a great way to avoid thinking about how fucking creepy this place is.

My heart was pounding. *It is just the sound of trash in the wind,* I told myself. I switched my song to something else. Before I even realized it, I was humming Michael Jackson's "Thriller." *Thanks, brain. That is so not helping. Focus! We have a job to do.*

It was time to see what had survived the end of the world. Today's mission was soaps, specifically shampoo. Camp had sent me with our usual huge shopping list, but the main objective was soap. There were a bunch of people who needed to clean their clothes and themselves. The camp was starting to smell. My hair was so filthy that my scalped itched. I couldn't believe how dirty everything had gotten in just a few weeks. Even the kids were complaining about wanting clean clothes.

The first store was a secondhand shop for fancy clothes. I pulled out my small pocket journal, where I recorded the address and name of the store and what it appeared to have. Next to that I made a little mark. The next store over was a beauty salon. I continued my journal entries. The salon was one of those places that did hair, nails, and even facials. God, I missed pedicures, not that I'd been able to get those often. They were a luxury that my part-time student worker gig didn't allow. The next entry was a store that looked like a tax place, or maybe an investment firm. "Office supplies" was what I wrote in my notebook. Every place could be of use at some point. I might need pens or maybe some of the wires from the computers and lamps.

For the next two stores, I would need to come back with help if I was going to do much with them. The first was a little hole-in-the-wall eatery. It looked like they did burgers and fries. Next to that was a little auto parts place, not a body or repair shop but a store that sold parts. It was locked up tight. They had a pulled-down cage gate on their entrance. They weren't messing around. I would need a couple of the boys from camp and some bolt cutters to get in there. The parts would be worth the effort.

The reason I had come all this way was at the end. The Shadowbrook Corner Mart was a mom-and-pop shop. It had been around for thirty years. It was a little grocery mart and pharmacy with a little bit of everything a household might need, standing strong for generations. At least that's what it had said in the yellow pages. While everyone else was looting their local supermarkets, I had grabbed the yellow pages and found places in the nicer areas. I was betting on the nicer neighborhoods not having flipped their shit yet.

Time for a crash course in foraging 101:

Lesson 1: Be smart about where you go to look for supplies. Do not go where everyone else goes. The strong are going to go for the big stores. The scared and weak will band together and wait till they absolutely *have* to go, and then they will look at places that are closer and easier. When scouting for locations, look for small, hard-to-get-to places. If you need supplies, you don't need to go to Target. Dollar stores have a lot of the same items as big stores. Gardening stores have many of the same items as Home Depot and, as a bonus, none of the guys with the guns.

Lesson 2: Look for ingredients. Stick to evacuated homes and restaurant pantries for food. Restaurants won't have fresh stuff, but they will have surplus they keep stored in pantries. Don't ignore the ingredients. They will feed you longer and with more variety. Of course, not everyone wants a hundred-pound bag of rice.

Lesson 3: Dig outside the box. I got the idea from squirrels. If you don't want one hundred pounds of rice, fill up a separate bag and stash the rest. Whenever I found more stuff than I could carry, I looked for a good place to hide it, either at the original location or in other buildings. For example, I planned to stash a good portion of things from the corner store at the nail salon, because people wouldn't search a nail salon for food.

I got to the door of the corner store. The street was unreal, like a movie set. It was perfect stillness, waiting for someone to yell "Action!" Then cars would drive by, and people would suddenly start walking around. I felt like I was caught in between moments of time.

I looked down at my watch; the little hand was still marching forward. I let go of a breath I hadn't known I was holding. I fought the urge to shout out into the stillness. I wanted to start singing and dancing in the street. I wanted to do anything to break the awful stillness around me. I gave some serious thought to the opening songs from some of my favorite musicals. *Talk about disso-ciative behavior. It's one thing to hum your own theme music; it's another to choreograph a dance number.*

"Keep it together, girl. Quiet is better." The sound of my own voice broke the strange spell in the air, and I was able to breathe again. "A musical opener would be way creepier." I started humming again. Humming was perfectly normal behavior. People hummed all the time.

I turned back to the door. The store was closed up neatly. When the power went out, the people must have simply locked up and gone home. There was a sign on the door that read, "Sorry for the inconvenience. Closed. Please come back again."

Now for the part I didn't like. Breaking and entering still felt wrong and weird. I pulled out a small tack hammer. Without alarms or cops, the only thing stopping someone from entering was a thin sheet of glass and a few locks. I hit the glass next to the door lock. There was a sharp cracking noise, and the tinkling of falling glass echoed in the empty air. I carefully reached in to undo the locks. I had a wire hanger I used to undo the latch from the top of the door, and this slid the door open.

Jingle!

I froze at the sound. When I realized it had come from directly overhead, from a set of little silver bells hanging from a fancy hook at the top of the door, I laughed and took a second to get my heart out of my mouth. I slipped through the doorway and gave my eyes a moment to adjust to the dimness. I listened just inside the door.

To be honest, I was waiting for that weird moan, waiting for that creepy, clicking teeth noise and the shuffle of a stiff walk. I knew they didn't exist, but it just didn't seem like a proper apocalypse without zombies. Maybe this was my mind's way of dealing with all the trauma. I guess some part of my brain was trying to say, "Hey, see, it could be worse."

Yes, I realize how weird and morbid that thought was. *See, the world is shit, but at least there aren't dead people running around trying to eat you! Yeah, go, me—way to stay positive!*

"Hello?" My voice sounded dry and cracked. I swallowed and tried again, aiming for a cheerful tone. "Survival of Man donation collection service. Anyone in?" Yes, I know, I know, but it sounded better than UNICEF or Avon calling. Silence was all I got in return, so no zombies. *Oh well, maybe next time.*

The inside of the store was also done in the old-timey style. It was supposed to look like a Woolworth or something from the 1910s. Things were on wooden shelves and in wooden barrels. I loved it. It was adorable. Thank God it had updated wiring. Otherwise, with this much wood, the place would have gone up like a match in the electrical fires from the power surges. I was grateful this place was intact; the last two places I had tracked down had been a bust. One store had burned to the ground. The other mom-and-pop shop had been run by a very ornery elderly couple with a matching set of double-barrel shotguns to keep everyone on best behavior. They had decided to ride out the chaos in their store. I liked them, and they had given me some diapers and baby formula in exchange for some fresh apples. I figured I could trade things with them in the future. Now I might actually have something to trade.

I moved slowly among the shelves. It seemed this place was part grocery, part household goods and knickknacks. There was even a small pharmacy in the back. Nothing was broken. I reached out to touch one of the shelves and saw my filthy hand against the clean, neat display. My throat tightened at the sight. Tears burned my eyes as my stomach knotted. I wanted to walk out and leave the store as perfect as I had found it. I thought about all the places that had been thrashed, picked clean in the wild violence of those first few days. My tears dripped dirty water onto the floor. I didn't want to do that to this place. The owner's pride and love were on display on every cute, clean, tidy shelf. It felt so wrong to touch them with my dirty hands.

I paced the aisle three times while I tried to get over my senti-mental ideas. It was hard to break all those years of right and wrong, rules and discipline that had been instilled in me growing up. I knew my father would understand, but that didn't make it easier to take things. I thought of my kids and was able to push my feelings aside. I would always do what I had to for them. Always.

I got a large shopping cart and, with as much gentle respect as I could, started taking items off the shelf. I diligently wrote down each thing I took and how many. Stupid, maybe, but this was how I dealt with the morality of it. I stopped at the magazine rack and looked at all the pictures of celebrities and models. Were they like me, wandering around looking for supplies, realizing credit cards didn't work, money was just paper, and you couldn't eat gold and jewels?

I turned back to the household goods. I switched to humming Jimmy Buffet's "I Don't Know" and swung down the cleaning aisle. I grabbed jumbo packs of soap. I dumped an armload of dish soap, laundry detergent, and two big jugs of bleach into the cart. I added a couple hard-bristle scrub brushes and some rubber gloves. If the clothes were going to get cleaned, they would need to be done by hand. I went to personal care and picked out shampoo and conditioner, including Head & Shoulders and the no-tears kind for children. I picked up a bunch of combs and brushes, fingernail clippers, toothbrushes and toothpaste, and toilet paper —you could never have too much TP.

Lesson 4 is very important: Never take more than you can carry—hence my rule about setting up stashes for later. It will slow you down and wear you out. It will make it easier to track you and take your stuff. Remember, if you're dead, you can't use the stuff you have gathered.

I was gathering for a large number of people, and I was pushing the weight limit. I would have to come back here to gather up the things I had hidden. I used things in the shop to make my stash packs. I spent time filling up bags with items I knew would be important later: diapers and tampons. I went into the pharmacy, pulling out the list from the nurses back at camp. They were short on a lot of supplies, so I did my best to find the urgent items and drugs that I thought could be useful. I put those in my backpack since they were so important. If I had to ditch the soap, I wouldn't lose the most precious cargo. I didn't take all of anything. I made sure there was some left of each item. Someone else would eventually come looking, and I didn't want them to go empty handed. I picked out a couple of things for the kids and packs of socks. The last things I grabbed were chocolate bars and as many packs of smokes as I could fit, along with lighters and all the packs of matches I could find.

The last thing I did was diligently put up a notice on the counter. It was a document from the army, saying that the items taken had been taken with government approval, and everything would be reimbursed when order had been reestablished. This made me feel better about taking from people, and now if anyone came in behind me and looted the owner would be covered.

It was almost 2:00 p.m. when I finally finished hiding what I couldn't carry in my wagon. I ate a couple of protein bars and drank water from my canteen, which was really a jug on a strap. It was a long ride back to camp and past time to leave. At least most of the trip would be downhill. I tied a tarp over my little red wagon and made sure my hitch was secure before I climbed up on the sturdy hybrid street bike. I made my way down the main exit of Shadowbrook Village.

The days were getting colder now as the last of summer surrendered to fall. I was glad for the chill. It would have really sucked to do this in summer heat. The only beings that noted my passing were the birds. The trees were packed with them—crows, starlings, sparrows; it was impossible to tell. They didn't sing. They just sat watching in silent vigil.

Nope, that's not creepy at all. Not one little bit.

I hummed old show tunes.

two
tuesday, 2:07pm

I FOLLOWED the curved road that circled around the park, in the town square. As I came around the other side of the loop, I saw the cracks in the facade. The illusion of movie set perfection vanished as I stepped beyond the camera line. The pleasant view was ruined by the debris left behind from the evacuation. A stack of suitcases and bags sat underneath the covering of the bus stop, as if waiting for the next pickup. Trash was piled up next to the bus sign. There must have been weight restrictions. They left so much behind. To the right of the bus bench, at the corner of the square, was a large sign awkwardly zip-tied to the wrought iron fence.

"Evacuation Point" was plastered in big mismatched letters across the top of the sign. Under these red stickers were instructions for evacuation and preparation: where they were going, what people needed to bring, and what was not allowed to be brought. The instructions were printed on regular printer paper and had been given a makeshift lamination job with clear packing tape. Times were handwritten on the sign in Sharpie. I couldn't help but wonder how far they'd gotten. Had they actually made it out? I looked over the instructions; they were similar to the ones I had seen before. They all talked about heading to smaller rally points before moving on to the fairgrounds for the final evacuation, which would go to one of three places. The closest was the Army Base at Fort Drum.

Of course, it would be Fort Drum. If we had known that, we wouldn't even be here. If I had just turned the other direction we could have headed straight for the base. But no... I wanted to go home. Good Call Marlene.

The image of that first sign filled my vision as I became lost in the rain of my memories. The rain had been so heavy that I'd almost hit the road blockade. It was just a wooden barricade across the turn-off road leading down to the small mountain town near the campgrounds. The sign had been painted on the wood: "Road Closed, Evacuation." I'd had to slowly back up our little RV to take a different route down the mountain.

"I'm sure it's just a precaution because of all the rain. Don't worry—there is a gas station further down the road. We can call for a service truck there to get your truck up and running again," I had said to Silas Sumner, or Grandpa Si, as we had begun to call him. He was from the next campsite over. Albert, my husband, and Silas had become fishing buddies almost immediately. His grandson, Jeremiah Levison, was sweet, and my kids liked him. When he had let me know his truck was dead, it had seemed natural to offer a ride. My cell phone had been dead for the last three days, so we had to take him to the nearest service station. It wasn't very far down the road from the turn-off. It was a small gas station, with a shop and a garage.

The heavy rain made the early afternoon sky seem closer to nightfall. The kids were asleep by the time I pulled onto the small gravel driveway of the station. There was just enough light to see in the twilight created by the afternoon rain. I pulled up and parked at the gas pump. As I opened my door to climb out, the hairs on the back of my neck stood on end. The smell hit me first; burnt plastic and rubber. The credit card machine was melted, with bits of wires exposed. The display screen was cracked and charred black.

"Honey," I said in a small voice as I pointed at it through the window.

Albert didn't respond; he was staring hard out the passenger-side window. Finally, I noticed that the store's front door was smashed, and in the ambient light I could see that the inside of the store looked ransacked. We all sat in silence for a long heartbeat.

It was Grandpa Silas who finally spoke. "Just keep driving, Marlene. We don't want any part of whatever this is." His voice was low and almost growling. He was like an old hound with his hackles raised. This only amplified my worry. I knew he was probably right, but I couldn't bring myself to begin driving again.

A little voice in my head just kept whispering until finally I had to say it aloud. "What if someone is hurt in there?"

Grandpa made a little noise in his throat and got to his feet behind us. "Stay here and keep the engine running."

Albert joined him in exiting the RV, and they walked slowly toward the store. The rain hid the sound of their footsteps. I waited in the camper with only the sound of the rain. They seemed to take a lifetime to come back. Every horror movie I had ever watched haunted me. I was finally able to breathe when they returned.

"There is no one in there we can help," Albert said as he took a towel to his rain-soaked head.

I knew he worded it that way for a reason. I didn't ask him to clarify, but I knew.

"We will keep going until we find a working phone or a sheriff's station and can report what we saw up here. So just keep driving and get us off this mountain, hon," Albert said, resting a hand on my shoulder.

I nodded and began driving eager to do just that. That wait in the rain had been terrifying. I had just wanted to go home, to be safe.

How were we supposed to know that the mountain was the safest place we could have been? We had no idea what waited for us once we left the Adirondacks. We didn't know what had happened to the world. For us there had been strange and beautiful glowing lights smeared across the horizon. For two days we had watched in wonder as green and red ethereal lights did their ballet across the sky. We hadn't thought it odd that our phones had died. We knew a magnetic storm that caused the Aura Borealis could do that. It hadn't worried us when we'd had to crank-jump the RV. It was old, a relic from a cousin's father who had rebuilt it. We hadn't even stopped our camping trip until the rain came in. The stream we were next to swelled and started flooding our area.

At the base of the mountain there was an exit. One direction led back towards home, the other pointed further north to Watertown and Fort Drum. If I had known, we could have just gone to the fort. If only, if only... My Daddy always said if only was like trying to sweep the desert, exhausting and pointless.

It wasn't until we reached the freeway that we realized something was very, very wrong. There were so many dead cars on the road. The telephone poles looked like burnt matchsticks. There were scorch marks from the freeway lights to the cars and concrete below. Our little hand-cranked radio picked up nothing but static. We drove until the RV ran out of gas and then had to walk the thirty miles to get home.

Too bad home turned out to be a pile of burnt rubble, the bitterness of the thought snapped me back to the present. I adjusted my position on the bike seat. *Knock it off, Marlene. Don't think like that. Be glad you are all safe and the kids weren't in the middle of that insanity. Houses are just buildings. They don't make a home. Family makes the home, and yours is safe. Be grateful.*

It had happened again. I had gotten lost in my thoughts. I was a sitting duck when I did that. I had to work harder to keep myself in the moment. I took a deep breath and started pedaling again. That camping trip had probably saved our lives. I didn't want to think about what could have happened if we had been home when the solar storms hit. I was not sure I would have been able to protect my children in the chaos that followed.

Motherhood was a tough gig even in the best of times. In the days before modern convenience, motherhood had been dangerous and time-consuming. Between housework, meals, and child-rearing, being a mother was an all-day event. That was why people lived together, and women formed communities to help each other. It was quite literally something everyone worked together to accomplish. Motherhood was even harder now that there was no built-in community. People were going to need to relearn all the obsolete ways of doing things.

The disaster had made things harder but simpler for me. Now every day was about survival. Every chore had a purpose and, if done well, a tangible reward. I didn't have to avoid bill collectors. I didn't have to worry about our utilities getting shut off. I didn't have to worry about some exhausting part time job. I didn't need to collect cans to have enough money to put gas in the car to make it to work. Albert didn't have to work a job that he hated and that hurt him, just too still not have enough money at the end of the month to pay all the bills.

All those problems had gone up in smoke. From a mother's perspective, the changes were not that big. The biggest issues were still the mom questions: What will my kids eat, what are they going to wear, how am I going to keep them clean, and where are they going to sleep? All very simple questions; but those questions can get hard to answer. The solutions are where the changes really showed.

I had learned some very valuable truths growing up dirt-poor in the Southwest. First: Time moved on its own. It would not slow down or hurry up for anyone. Second: The newer something was, the more likely it was to break. And third: It was always better to learn how to do things the old way first. These truths I carried with me all my life. Strangely it gave me a slight advantage now that most tech that was newer than 1990 was fried.

Our camp was lucky—we had some old folks with us. They were still filled with piss and vinegar, as my daddy would say. They weren't able to go on supply runs, but not many people would go anyway. Not that I blamed them. After all the fires, looting, and riots most didn't feel safe leaving the camp.

Lesson 5: Security is a double-edged blade; it can cut both ways. When you are all alone, you don't have to worry about someone betraying you or screwing up: But it also means you don't have any support. If you have people, that means they will support you. The drawback is you have to also provide support back. Handle security with care and be ready for when you cut yourself.

There was only a small band of us brave foraging mice willing to scurry out for supplies. Finding parts to cannibalize was a top priority. Yesterday's shopping trip had been to a small pawn shop. I had been looking for tools and wiring. The power surges had killed anything with small wires or filaments. I had found a couple of neon bulbs and fluorescent lights that were still functional. Albert had been an electrician in the navy and was helping to get the power on.

Everyone was desperate to get the lights on. With sunset came nightfall, and with nightfall came all the old stories crawling back to life. Conquering darkness had been one of the great achievements of humankind. We had taken it for granted. Now groups worked all day collecting firewood to keep the night at bay. I counted myself among them. Deep down, everyone was afraid of the dark. I never foraged after dark. I always began my trips as close to dawn as possible. I figured bad guys stayed up late. My bet was they slept in late too. A secondary benefit to getting started early was that I was done sooner.

Today I was running late. The wind was picking up. It was going to be chilly for the rest of the day. Leaves were beginning their change already. It looked like it was going to be a short autumn. It was bad enough that the dark came earlier every night, but it would be cold soon too. Central New York winters were no joke. If help didn't come before the first major snowfall, we would have to hunker down for the winter. I thought the little house we had decided to stay in was good enough if the worst happened.

Most of the houses I passed near Shadowbrook were still nice, tidy little homes, with big lawns and nice porches. Some homes even had storm shutters closed over their windows. There were old groves of mature trees towering over and shading the street. These were homes that had been in families for more than one generation. It wouldn't be long before they were those scary houses with ivy crawling over walls and bushes hiding the door. I know, a happy ray of sunshine—that's me! The area must have actually followed the recommendations from the CDC, or whoever it was that issued those safety guidelines for storms. Not that many people could have followed the instructions even if they wanted to. How the hell were you supposed to ground your house anyway? Or disconnect from the power grid? I barely knew were the fuse box was at home.

I rolled gently down a hill along a side street that would lead me to a small footbridge that crossed a stream. It flowed down from further up the hill behind me. I was on guard, so my vision caught a flutter of motion to the left. I stopped. Two long lines of crisp white sheets were fluttering in the breeze. They were hung neatly on the line to dry.

Suddenly, I was five-year-old me in a pale-yellow sundress, barefoot, with a giant smile, my brown hair in long pigtails like handlebars on either side of my head. I was racing full speed with my arms stretched out as far as they could go, just barely able to touch both sides of the row at the same time. Singing out with as much force as I could muster, I flew between the rows of still-wet white sheets flapping in the brilliant hot sun of summer, feeling the wind cool as it passed through the wet cloth. Nothing smelled like sun-dried sheets.

It had been a long time since I had seen sheets hung out like this. I found myself pulled up to the fenced yard, listening to the sound of them. Wet sheets make a funny little sound when they flap and snap in the breeze. It is almost impossible to describe. Soon they would be billowing out like flags, but for right now they still had their heavy ends to weigh them down.

It didn't occur to me right away how creepy I must have looked. I hadn't had a proper shower in over a week. I was in my foraging gear, which was basically a hodgepodge of clothes I had found with extra pockets: military fatigue pants, a utility belt with little pouches, a fisherman's vest with all its little and large pockets, a fanny pack, and a backpack. I also had on a military coat with pockets along the arms and a pair of work boots that had a hidden pocket. Even my cap had a little pouch inside. I was the queen of pockets. My hair was dirty and pulled into a rough ponytail. Not to mention I was also carrying a shotgun over one shoulder. I wouldn't blame someone for not liking me at first glance.

However, I had been thinking about five-year-old me, so I had forgotten how I appeared. So when a woman appeared from between the rows of laundry pointing a handgun at me, I didn't really understand at first. All the same, I held up my hands and gave my best "don't shoot me—I'm nice" smile.

"Sorry, no harm meant. Just admiring the sheets," I said.

She gave me the look that answer deserved.

"It's just been a while since I have seen clean sheets. I didn't realize I had missed them so much. When I was a kid, we used to hang them on a line. I was just remembering how I would drive my mom crazy by running through them when they were hung. Up and down the line I would go singing for all I was worth." I was rambling.

In my defense she did have a gun pointed at my face, which was enough to make anyone ramble. She might be a very nice lady, but dead was dead. If a nice person gets scared and shoots, you are still as dead as if a bad person pulled the trigger. There was no law out here. It was just like the Wild West waiting for the lawmen. She didn't know if I was dangerous or not, but right then I knew she was.

"I was just taking a break. I will be on my way. I am on my way home to the little ones." I hooked my thumb toward the road and slowly lifted my hat. I showed her the picture I had tucked into my cap. It was a photo of my children dog-piling their dad and laughing.

She looked at the photo for a moment and lowered her gun. "What do you have in there?" She nodded to the wagon as she put the gun in her laundry basket.

"Soaps, different kinds of soap. Some household goods, a little food." I motioned to myself. "I am looking forward to being clean."

She gave me a small smile. "Yeah, I had to work all day to get those sheets clean."

She looked back at the big house. As the wind blew the sheets out of the way, I saw a group of women standing on the porch. Most of the ladies seemed slightly older than me, but there were a few younger ones holding babies.

"You should move your lines." The suggestion popped out of my mouth without my thinking about it.

She returned her gaze to me with an arched brow. "Why?"

"It stands out. It lets people know someone is here. It would be better to have them in back where no one can see, so no one thinks to stop here."

"Yeah, I guess so. We'll do that when this group is dry." She held out a hand and smiled. "My name is Margie."

I wiped my hand and shook hers. "It's a pleasure, Margie. I'm Marlene." I put my cap back on. "Hey, I am planning on coming this way a couple of times. If you guys really need something, let me know. I will see if I can find it for you. We are up at the rally point a few miles away. We are waiting, hoping the army sends someone."

She gave me a funny look. "Well, we're good. The boys should be home soon. I am not too low on anything yet. But Grams has a big sweet tooth, so if you find any candy, let me know."

I smiled and held up a hand. I dug around in the packs till I found the right bag. "I got Jolly Ranchers or peppermints."

She took the peppermints. "Thanks. Be safe out there." She smiled and walked back toward the house. I looked up at the little patch of sky I could see through the trees.

"Well, big man, I hope you are watching out for this bunch. I'll see what I can do on my end." I am not overly religious, but since my only true knowledge is that I don't truly know anything, I figured it would be safest to assume that there was someone keeping things moving along.

After a few more empty blocks I reached the bridge that crossed over the runoff canal for the stream. It headed out of the neighborhood and into the valley. The little footbridge was overgrown with moss. I couldn't tell if the canal was human-built or just a natural formation that had been reinforced. The bridge looked to be made of old square stones but still formed around the curves of the hill. I crossed slowly to listen to the sounds of the water passing underneath me.

I was born in the Chihuahuan Desert at the junction of Texas, New Mexico, and Mexico. This place was once called the great pass of the South. For the unfamiliar, here is a little history for you. The middle of the United States consisted of vast open tracks of flat land. The plains ran until they hit a wall of granite called the Rocky Mountains. Historically, if you were a seasoned, trained, and hardy mountain explorer, then this was an exciting challenge. For everyone else this enormous and dangerous mountain range was what separated them from the West Coast of the nation. There were two passes that could be traveled by horse, foot, or wheels to reach the golden West Coast of America. One was in the north and was difficult and completely closed off during the winter, as the Donner party discovered. The other and the more traveled was in the south. It began at what is now the pointed tip of Texas. The city that was built there is called El Paso, which means "the pass"—not creative but descriptive.

Modern-day El Paso is a sprawling city. It is arid, windswept, and very hot. As soon as you step out of the concrete and adobe city, you see the rolling hills of desert scrub brush and in the distance the frightening majesty of the Rockies. The sky is vast and a shade of blue I have never seen anywhere else. It looks like the place adventures begin. Oh, how I missed my sky. Here the sky was clogged and cluttered with gray clouds or hidden by trees.

I grew up in that uncompromising heat. Rain was a special occasion that was celebrated. Myths were written about the sacrifices that had to be made to bring the precious rains. Rivers were proof of divinity and the love of God. Wells and springs gave true value to land. Symbols of wealth included fountains or outdoor displays of water. I didn't know if I would ever get used to how common water was here. It was everywhere, just lying around. The people here always complained about the rain. No one understood the flowing miracle that passed unnoticed below these little stone bridges. No one understood why I was always so happy on rainy days or why I never carried an umbrella.

What was the price for all this wealth? Everything was wet, damp, thick, soggy, or moist. It took forever to get anything to dry. That included the air itself. When I first moved to central New York, I was sick for the first six months as my body tried to figure out what to do with the air. It took three rounds of bronchitis before my lungs acclimated. The world was shades of green. There were forests tucked between houses. The landscape was winding and rolling, and tall trees hid everything from sight. However, the air was hardly clean; the pollen in the air looked like golden dust storms. I was always relieved when fall and winter hit. I liked the snow; it was cold and crisp and made the air so clear that it would burn my lungs. I enjoyed the cold taking my breath away, though to be honest I missed my sand. I missed my scrub bushes and cactus.

I stopped halfway across the little bridge. I looked down, trying to see if I could spot signs of fish. This was Albert's home turf, and he was quite the fisherman. He had told me what to look for, but I was still never sure I was doing it right. After a moment I gave up and just looked out at the surface of the water. There were gentle ripples spreading across it. I suddenly realized there was no sparkle. There was no light dancing off the water. I frowned as I looked up. Sure enough, the gray of the water reflected the gray above it. What little sky I could see was dark and gloomy. The cool but pleasant day had shifted to a damp cold as the sky built up its force.

In my hometown, when it was going to rain, you could taste the water in the air. I loved getting caught in the rain. The problem here was how to get dry afterward. I had to be careful; I couldn't afford to get sick. We did have an army medic and a retired pediatrician at camp, but the best option was still to not get sick in the first place. The rain was powerful, beautiful, and something to respect. It could bring life or death. It was a threat I took very seriously.

I checked my watch and took out my folded paper map. The next leg of the ride could go one of two ways. My original plan had been to take some back roads crossing a few personal farms and a big estate property that followed along this little stream. The problem with that plan was that most of the trip was unpaved, which meant the ground turned to mud when it rained. My rig was prone to getting stuck, especially when it was fully loaded. The first time that had happened, my kids had been riding in the wagon. It had been really scary.

The second choice followed the paved roads and crossed the main street, Salina Street, close to downtown. It would be faster and paved, so the rain wouldn't affect the wagon. It was the major metro area, by the university. I hadn't been there since before the storms. There could be damage to the road, or there could be people. The dangers were different but still very real. I had to choose. I could either brave the weather, hoping to avoid the calamity of mud, or try my hand at the main street and hope it was all clear. On the plus side, Salina Street would cut hours off my time, and I could probably make it home before the heavy rain set in.

Downtown had become a dangerous place, but then so had everywhere else. Fear spider-crawled along my spine. I pulled my hat off to peer at the picture of my children. All these supplies wouldn't help them if I was dead. I looked at the stream and the unpaved trail I had used to ride up here. It would be a slow and hard ride home even if it stayed dry enough for me to not get stuck. The supplies also helped no one stuck in the mud. The wind picked up and began tugging at strands of my hair. If I didn't get home sooner rather than later, I was going to get wet, and that was for certain. Death from pneumonia or from a bullet made no difference. Dead was dead. The bullet was uncertain. Even if there happened to be someone on the street, that didn't mean they would hurt me or that I would even see them. If the rain started, getting wet was unavoidable.

So be like a mouse, quick and quiet, and hope the cat is not around. My daddy always said that if you had to go through hell, you shouldn't waste time complaining. If you were quick and quiet, the devil might not notice you. I just hoped the devil had better things to do today. I checked my new route on the map and headed down toward Second Avenue.

It didn't take long for the scenery to change from large lawns and parks to the burned-out shells of old colonial-style houses. Most of them had been converted to rental duplexes with a nice old-school look. All the lots were smaller and squeezed close, to make tiny city houses. Without working fire trucks, most places had simply burned. If this whole damn city weren't waterlogged, the entire place probably would have been nothing but ash. Some of the houses were just black piles on stone foundations. On some others, only the roofs or sides had been damaged. It was a giant's broken and burned jigsaw puzzle.

Lesson 6: Don't fear the dead. Burned buildings were just the ghosts of past tragedies. You didn't have to be afraid of them. It was the ones that hadn't burned that you needed to be wary of.

The buildings made of brick were damaged but stood firm, a testament to the bricklayers who had built them. I felt eyes watching me from those burn victims. No faces peeked from the windows, but the hairs on my neck stood on end. The air still smelled like wet smoke and burnt wood. I had to weave along the road through debris. I approached Fire Station 3. The red bricks were charred around the edges. The fire truck sat just outside of the station. It was completely useless. All its flashing lights and shiny chrome were blackened and scorched from the electrical wires burning out.

The wrongness of the place left a knot in the pit of my stomach. I rolled to a slow stop. There was something off here. I studied the scene for a moment, trying to figure what was out of place. My skin felt clammy. My mouth was both dry and clogged. I wondered if animals felt that sometimes. Did they get an unexplained sense that something just wasn't right? Did it suddenly hit them and make them freeze in their tracks?

In case I was being watched, I pretended that I wasn't looking, that I had stopped for something else. I forced myself to take a drink from my canteen. I didn't want anyone to know I suspected a trap. Paranoid much? Yes. Yes, I was.

The wind held its breath. Nothing. My mental theme music had stopped playing.

All of the quiet amplified the sound of my shaky breath. I was sure it was from the exertion of pedaling my bike. I sucked in a deep breath through my nose and tried to calm down. The silence was so loud. The echoes of the past still lingered in the air, mixed with the scent of smoke. The fear and panic clung to the ashes and soot staining the scene.

I started pedaling past the big red fire engine. As I came around to the driver's side, I saw the body of a firefighter lying on the ground. His face was turned away from me, and his helmet hid his hair. His body was wrong. He was all swollen up, like a human-shaped balloon. The normal slopes and curves were distended, and his flame-retardant clothes looked stretched, as if he were over-stuffed with lumpy fluff. I stared with morbid curiosity.

Fear clawed up my throat when I realized his clothes were shifting. Some unknown horror was moving around weirdly under his clothes, making the fabric quiver and wiggle.

My rational brain assured me he was dead. He was laid out on the concrete in a strange oozy puddle, with his limbs at funny angles. It looked like he had fallen out of his seat when the door opened. His exposed skin was blackened and not at all human. My gut tightened so hard that I was worried I would pull a muscle as whatever it was squirmed around inside his clothes.

I was twenty feet from him when the wind shifted and the smell hit me. This wasn't the smell of a dead animal. The smell was something all its own; nothing else compared to it. I had imagined that dead humans would smell like rotten fruit or maybe rotting meat.

We do not.

We smell completely different when our bodies rot. It was sticky. It was cloying. It clawed and crawled its way up my nose, trying to reach down into my throat so I could taste it. I felt my stomach heave at the strange, sickly sweet, rotten, coppery smell. This was a whiff of death.

Animals don't like the smell of their own dead. I think humans are the same way. This wasn't just something dead. It was terrifying death. It was human death. A primal instinct inside me said, *this could have been you.* That instinct screamed danger, but my brain was stuck in sick fascination. I had seen bodies from a distance, but I had never been this close before. I had stayed with the kids and kept them away. The idea of actually moving away occurred to me about a heartbeat before I saw something squirm under the blackened skin of his exposed neck.

If it breaks through the skin, you can see what it is. Sometimes I am really worried about that part of myself—the other self. You know the strange other. We all have one. It's the one that makes you peek during the bloody scenes in horror movies. The one that makes you look at car crashes or poke dead things with a stick. Mine seemed more present than most people I knew. It had made it easy for me to dissect that frog in high school. It had convinced my mother that I was going to be a scientist and my father that I would get into trouble.

The flesh pulsed. Whatever it was broke a tiny hole through the surface, and its pale greasy body worked its way out of the blackened flesh of the dead man's neck. Its tiny, wiggling body writhed for a moment. It gyrated slowly, turned, and dug its way back in.

Maggots, he is full of maggots. Though the sight was revolting, I sighed in relief as the curiosity was satisfied.

The man was slowly rotting in the rain and sun. He should have been past this point of decay, being exposed like this. Maybe the heavy fire-retardant clothes had kept the bugs away for a while, delaying the decomposition. Maybe a looter had come up and opened the door to the fire truck with the intention of digging around in the cab, and the body had fallen out. Something had delayed the process. My brain flipped through the strange facts of human decomposition I had learned from too many late nights watching real-crime TV and reading detective novels.

He shouldn't be here. He deserved better than this. My brain, always ready to make things worse, tripped over the thought. He shouldn't be here. If he had died at the same time the truck was hit by the electrical storm, why had the other firemen left him there? The mystery of it overrode the grotesque display of natural decay. I moved forward.

I saw more bodies inside the station. The three of them were spread out in the firehouse. These bodies were less, well, juicy than the one outside. I stood there for a few heartbeats while I tried to come to terms with what I should do. The less rational side of me said to just keep riding. I couldn't shake the feeling of wrongness, the sense that something was going on just out of sight.

Maybe it was paranoia or too many movies, but something was screaming "Trap!" My brain whispered, wasn't that body a little small to belong to a firefighter? Didn't it seem like these bodies had been placed instead of falling randomly? Of course, I couldn't tell anything more than that they were human and they were very dead. *So much for all those nights watching crime shows.*

That's when I saw the crows watching me. Not just one or two crows but entire trees full of them. Every tree I could see looked like it was filled with black wings. I hadn't noticed them before because they weren't making a peep, just sitting there silently watching. Alfred Hitchcock would have loved these birds. Mother would have said, "That's not just a murder of crows—it's a massacre."

Lesson 6, expanded: Don't fear the dead. The dead can't shoot you; the living can. Stealing from living people was a good way to become one of the dead people. Searching dead people was super gross but a lot less lethal. I wanted to leave, but there was some incredibly useful stuff in there, and it didn't look like anyone had been here yet. Now was the time.

I tied a bandanna around my face to help keep the smell out of my mouth. The big garage doors hung open, and most of the smell had escaped. The bodies inside the garage had black leathery skin. It stretched them unnaturally, turning them less human. It was less scary that way. They became movie props or Halloween decorations. There was still a clinging smoky smell to the air, though I couldn't tell what had burned.

I thought this scene might have to do with the solar storms, but I had no idea what an electrocuted person would look like two weeks later in a garage. Either way, whatever the cause of death, I tried to avoid touching them. I had been studying to be a historian, not a forensic anthropologist. I was interested in dead people in only an abstract way, not in an up-in-my-face kind of way. I walked back where the firefighters' clothes were hung on the wall to put as much distance as possible between me and the bodies. I took two of the fire axes and their first aid bags. The food in the fridge would obviously be spoiled, so I didn't bother opening it. They had canned goods in the firehouse kitchen, and I took as much of that as I could fit in my wagon. I also took the toolbox I saw sitting on a table in the garage. I carefully marked my map and filled out my little notebook about the place.

In the break room, a roster sheet was posted on an information board. I pulled out one of my official papers and tacked it on the board. I wrote all the names from the roster and all their shield numbers in my notebook. I walked around and saw the neatly made beds in the back. The blankets went into the wagon. The sheets, I used to drape over the dead, including the one outside. I went to drape him first, mostly for my own sake. I looked for his shield number, but I wasn't willing to turn him over to find it. I shouldn't leave a sign that someone had passed through, but these people had deserved a better end. I took a moment to whisper a little prayer of passing.

As I began covering the bodies inside, a thought popped into my head. The bodies inside the garage weren't wearing any of the gear. One guy had on sweatpants and a gray hoodie that had become horribly stained but had no insignia. A little voice in my head whispered, didn't firemen have uniforms or something? How had that guy died? He was right in the middle of a wall, and there was nothing near him, no scorch marks or anything. He was just sitting up against the wall. I frowned and looked around again. Only the guy outside had boots on.

No badges or bags or wallets. There weren't any over by the clothes racks either. I moved to the smaller of the bodies and winced as I gingerly checked his pockets. Nothing—no wallet, no keys, nothing. Didn't firefighters have to be ready at a moment's notice?

The eeriness was too much for me. If this was a trap, it seemed someone had sprung it before me, and I didn't want to be here when someone came to reset it or check it. I placed the sheets over the other bodies and moved outside. I mounted my bike and pedaled as fast as I could out of the area. The dark glassy eyes of crows watched me the whole time as the wheels on my little red wagon creaked in protest.

three
tuesday, 3:28pm

MY FATHER WOULD SAY, "Marlene, now is not the time to cry. Now is the time to cowboy up and ride on." That's what I did. I got back in my saddle and pushed my pedals. The damn cart was heavy. It wasn't long before I had to cross Saline Street.

Have you ever noticed how things get so loud when you're alone, when you are doing something that might not be the safest? It was like that now. I was doing my best to focus on getting home, but my wheels suddenly began to squeak. Had they always squeaked so loudly? How had I never noticed before?

I focused on pushing one foot, then the other. Every sound caught my attention—the birds flapping their wings, the wind picking up and scattering leaves, the squeak of the wheels, and the jingle of my coat. They seemed to dominate the air. Each one filled me with dread. My mind conjured childhood monsters to stalk me; imagined enemies swarmed and surrounded me. I looked down and saw my knuckles turning white as they gripped the handlebars. My heart throbbed painfully in my chest and then leapt upward into my throat. It lodged there making it almost impossible to breathe. My chest burned. My wheels suddenly bumped over the curb, bouncing me hard against the seat, and air rushed into my lungs. I had made it to Saline Street.

I pulled up behind a large van that was parked next to a brick wall. It created a little box to hide in. I needed to stop before I passed out. Panic attacks were a bad thing. I focused on filling my body with air and pushing it back out again. I counted backward in my head as I pulled oxygen in. Once I could control my breathing, I was mentally able to beat my fears back into their dark little corner. I sacrificed some of my water to the cause of calming down. It helped. The wind caressed my face gently. It was cold and crisp and felt good, but it reminded me of why I was in a hurry.

The sky was dark, heavy, and ominous. The wind was colder than it had been earlier. I could almost see steam rising off my skin. I wiped my face down and was rolling the tension out of my back when the sound of voices startled me. A mischievous conspiracy between the breeze and the brick surfaces of the street echoed the words to me. The voices seemed ethereal, and it took me a moment to find them from my little lookout.

There were two men down the street about a block or less. Their words were muffled. They wore dirty one-piece jumpsuits. The smaller of the two men was scratching viciously at his arms as they talked. He was thin, lanky, with a light scruff of a beard. His hair was short, patchy, and wheat blonde. The idea of a scraggly farm boy popped into my head, or an itchy scarecrow.

The other was bigger in every way by comparison. He was taller and broader. The man's muscles must have worked out because they had their own muscles. He seemed very intimidating. He had tattoos on his neck all the way up and around his ears. His head and face were completely shaved and deeply tanned. He looked like he had been outside forever. His hand was big enough to cover my whole face. He was effortlessly carrying two large duffel bags that looked close to bursting. The skinny scarecrow was struggling under the weight of just one. They turned toward me as the wind blew on them. They were pulling out a beat-up pack of smokes.

"I don't know, man ... I don't trust them," the scarecrow said.

His movements were jerky and sharp as he pulled out his cigarette. He was a wind-up toy that was wound too tight. His face was taunt and pinched as he put a smoke to his lips. It took him three tries to get it lit.

"You don't have to trust them. Just do as you are told until it's time to move on," the tattooed giant replied. He waited for the scarecrow to take a drag from the smoke and then calmly plucked it away to take a turn himself. They continued this way for about half the smoke before a third man came out of the building and took the cigarette himself. He also carried two bags, but they were much more compact.

"All right, that looks like everything. Come on, you two." His tone made it clear that he expected them to obey without any question.

This third man was long and lean. His hair was coal-black and cut shaggy around his face. He had the darkening shadow of a couple days of scruff on his cheeks. He paused as he scanned around, taking a long pull from the smoke. His eyes stopped and seemed to be staring right at me. I froze. Like a rabbit spotting a predator, instinct told me not to move. I held my breath. I tried to stop my heart from beating, anything so that he wouldn't see me. His eyes were bright blue. Even from this distance, I could see them. He was not pretty-boy handsome; he was too hard around the edges for that. He brought to mind those lean, hungry wolves featured on wilderness documentaries. In my wilder days, I would have bought him a drink, flirted with the danger, and then gone back to the safety of my friends. The moment stretched on unbearably. It seemed to last forever but it couldn't have been more than a few seconds. He finally let out the smoke slowly through his nostrils. The wisps of smoke trailed after him as he turned and headed down the street, away from me.

"Come on, you two. You don't want to get wet, and I see rain coming. The boss is waiting," he said over his shoulder, and the two men followed.

I relaxed once I realized he had been looking at the clouds rolling in. I didn't move until I couldn't see the men anymore. Then I pushed my bike and wagon away as quickly as I could. I didn't want to be spotted by those men.

When the wolf man had turned towards me, I had noticed something. He had numbers stenciled on the chest and across the shoulders of his coveralls. They were prison inmate uniforms. I added a note to my journal: "Prisoners on Salina Street."

As I moved out of the downtown area and headed southwest toward my old neighborhood, the claustrophobic cluttering of tall buildings broke up, finally giving me a view of the sky. Everything around was in black, soggy, smoky ruins. Here the damage could be utterly understood. It was so complete that it belonged in some terrible fairy tale. The devastation went on a good mile or more. Buildings had been turned into heaps of blackened ash and soot, down to the old foundations built a hundred years ago. Sturdier houses still had some of their inner iron frames or stone supports standing. These remaining skeletons' reached their twisted, ghastly, blackened fingers up to grasp at the rainy sky.

The road was empty here, making it easier to pick up speed. My wheels stirred up the ashes, leaving a heavy cloud on the ground trailing behind me. I pulled my bandanna tight around my face, but the smoke still seeped into my mouth.

It had taken two days for the fires to burn themselves out. The heavy rains had helped keep the blazes contained. The streams and ravines with their sharp drops and soggy beds had kept the fire trapped in this valley. The poorest sections of town had gone up like kindling. Even if the fire trucks had been running, I don't think it would have helped. All those cheaply made houses, stuck close together, had never stood a chance. The story around camp was that evacuations had started about three hours before the storm began. The power lines just couldn't take the juice, and fires started about halfway through the first day of the solar storms. Telephone poles became torches, lampposts exploded in lightning, and anything that wasn't able to handle the heat melted or caught fire. There had been some kind of explosion from the local substation and power plant. No one really knew what had happened, since communication had been the first thing to go down. People with megaphones ran around organizing the evacuation. With every story I heard, I was more grateful to have been up in the Adirondack Mountains. Albert thought the reason we had been so protected from the magnetic fluxes and power surges on the mountain was that the mountain's mineral deposits created their own magnetic field, and the power would have been grounded. I remembered the glowing smears of light dancing around the sky in greens and reds. I had thought we were seeing the northern lights or something, but Albert had assured me we were not far enough north for that.

I passed by a fire hydrant that somehow still had water to give. It was not the powerful geyser it should have been, but it still gushed, like an artificial spring. It was making a small river down the road. I could see where it had formed a breaker for the fire, at least for a while. Now it made a weird clean spot in all the black.

A car that someone had parked illegally in front of the hydrant was still sitting pretty. The water now rushed over the hood of the car and kept the soot from blackening the paint job. It was a beauty, an old deep green four-door 1960s Impala with a V-8 engine. It was one of those classic muscle cars. I stopped and just stared for a moment before I started to laugh. Someone's assholery had saved this beauty, but no one was going to be able to come get her anytime soon. I knew the Impala wouldn't start. None of the cars could; the starters were burned out, if not the complete electrical systems. Fate was laughing at me, so I laughed too. This was my dream car, saved from fire, but I couldn't get it started. The story of my life. *Hey, Marlene, here is that thing you have always dreamed of. Oh, look, but no touchy. It won't work for you anyway. Yeah, funny, very funny.* I pulled out my notebook and noted the car's location, just in case.

I glanced at my watch and saw that time had marched on while I wasn't looking. I pedaled the flat paved road, an easy ride for once. My mind drifted into daydreams of riding horses across a great field. I imagined my gallant steed galloping across the charred landscape, my armor shining, my lance glinting in the light. I was always the hero, the knight to the rescue. Today I was returning to my village with magic potions that would save the people from some terrible evil. I was lost in my little mental fiction as I hummed the *Excalibur* theme and charged my wheeled steed up to the top of a small hill. The crest of the hill was at the edge of the burn scar, about a quarter mile from the road that would take me to our camp. I pedaled as fast as I could. My heart pounded so hard I thought it would burst. Sweat rolled down my cheeks as I huffed and puffed like a little steam engine. I reached the top and crowed like a conquering hero, both hands raised in the air. The elation of reaching the top filled me with a sense of happiness. Yay for endorphins! Physical activity is a great way to fight off depression, you know.

The wind blew across me, cooling the sweat and heat from my neck. I pulled down my bandanna, and for a moment the smell of ash was pushed away. I took a deep breath, sighing in relief. It was heaven.

Then the smell attacked me. It was that sickly sweet, horrid, stomach-tightening smell. It crawled into my nose and down my throat. It stuck to my tongue, making me gag. I choked. I tried to spit, but the heavy breathing had made my throat dry. Coughing made my sides hurt. When the gagging and coughing subsided, I fell silent as I looked around with dread, trying to figure out where the smell was coming from. It didn't take long. Not too far from where the black scar of the fires ended and the green grass of life began again, there was a ditch that looked like it had recently been dug. I slipped off my bike and tried to stay up as my legs wobbled.

I would like to say I was wobbly from the exertion of the bike.

Yes, I would like to tell you that. I didn't know how long they had been there. It had been long enough for the bodies to turn putrid.

I had seen photos of terrible things, like the mass graves from the world wars and the Holocaust. I had even seen more recent footage of battles in burning sands and photos of the dead or maimed. Photos were not the same as seeing it in person. Not even close. What I saw wasn't like in the pictures. It was people, but at the same time it wasn't. They were all put in a line, one after another, some stacked on top of each other. Some looked burned; some didn't. I don't know how long I stared, but in my mind, they just became a jumble of pieces. I managed to hold it together until I saw a little pair of bright pink boots. I recognized the brand from Target. *My daughter has a pair like that.*

The boots' bright, cheery color stood out against the black and grays of rot around them. The color of those boots set off a synapse in my brain. It fired through memories of the day I'd bought them and of her wearing them to the playground. I saw her dancing in the living room in them. I saw her walking with her brother down the street. Then my brain continued backward to the time I sat in a movie theater watching *Schindler's List*, to the little girl in the red coat. I would not classify the sound I made then as a human noise.

I became aware of the sound about the time I had finished puking in the grass next to my bike. It seemed like a cry, a scream, and vomit all trying to escape my mouth at the same time. I only managed to vomit. The rest seemed trapped inside me. I didn't look again. I couldn't.

My daughter had those same boots.

four
tuesday, 3:57pm

I WAS PEDALING before I knew it. I didn't stop until I got to the base of the hill of our camp. The hill rose at a 45- to 50-degree angle, so I took a moment to get my breath. This was the toughest part of the trek. I knew that by the time I got home, my legs would be aching and trembling, and that would continue for hours. My first trip out had put me down the rest of the day. I was getting stronger every time.

Before riding away, I had taken a moment to mark the location of the mass grave. I didn't want to accidentally go there again. I would see if someone from camp could do something proper for them. Someone had put them there. Finishing burying them was the best we could do. I sat on my bike for a good ten minutes, looking out behind me, resting and waiting. I watched for any sign that someone had followed. The sound of rolling thunder was all that greeted me.

The hill, which was more like a little mountain, had four roads to the top. Two were meandering things going up a gradual slope. The other two were straight shots up the hill on either side. Each road had lookouts about halfway up the hill so that we knew who was coming. The hill was large and fairly level at the top. Thick undergrowth and trees covered every undeveloped spot. The rain chased me to the hill's first plateau, where there was an old flower shop, a gas station, and a pizza place. All of them had been cleaned out of supplies.

I stopped at the gas station and called out, "How now, brown cow?"

There was a laugh and then the reply: "The rain in Spain stays mainly in the plains."

We couldn't remember what the reply in the movie was, so we just mixed and matched. My smile helped my face relax as I saw Grandpa Silas step out of hiding. He was the older of the two armed men who appeared out of nowhere. He was grinning and shaking his head at his younger counterpart.

Jeri looked genuinely confused. "I really don't get what you're talking about. What cow? And the rain is nearly here, Grandpa," he said with a serious face. I about died. He was such a great straight man for the comedy duo.

"You're too young to get it. Youngsters missed out on the good stuff, huh?" Grandpa Silas said the last bit to me as they stepped over to me.

I hadn't seen them at all initially. It was eerie how good at that they were. I nodded in agreement, feeling much lighter now that I was with them. I liked Grandpa Silas and Jeri. I had long ago decided that Grandpa Silas was the toughest son of a bitch on the planet. If someone were to make a man out of gristle and then fill him up with vinegar and give him a knife for a tongue, a backbone made of solid iron, a heart of gold, and a gut full of sand, then you would have Grandpa Silas. I loved him like my own grandpa. Jeri was a handsome young guy who was learning how to be a tough man. He was thoughtful and quiet. To me they had become family. Having them with us had probably saved our lives.

Silas and Jeri were staying in these three buildings on the south-face lookout. They kept watch there, and since I knew this road best, it was the side I used most often. Si refused to live in the main camp with the army boys. He said he preferred to take his own orders. He worked with me and some of the folks at the camp. I wasn't sure about his reasons, and I knew he would not tell me if I asked. I was just grateful. I pulled out two king-size chocolate bars and two packs of smokes. Both men grinned as they got one of each. Some people were easy to please.

Grandpa Silas looked up from his prize, smile still in place, and said, "You know, someday soon the lieutenant isn't going to let you go off willy-nilly. He's already making noise about camp security and such." He tapped his pack against the heel of his hand and unwrapped it. He pulled open the top, extracted one of the perfect little sticks of death, and lit it with quick, smooth motions. He had the urgency of a longtime addict. Some inner tension eased out of him as he pulled in the first drag of smoke and blew it out again.

It made me feel better to see that this helped him. Obviously, quitting would have been better, but for fuck's sake, if it was the end of the world, have a damn smoke. If I could, I would have been sitting around drinking margaritas at noon. Now I wished I had spent more time doing that. I was sure that eventually people would figure out how to fix everything and the world would turn back on. Humans were nothing if not persistent. I just hoped we wouldn't run out of smokes and chocolate before then.

"Of course, I told him that we couldn't do without you crazy folks willing to go scrounge for the rest of us. The hunters don't have time to be searching rubble," he added after letting his nicotine set in. Silas pulled the cigarette away from his face, giving the glowing tip a loving look. He was talking about the handful of us who left camp each day looking for supplies. There were about five or six of us who did it regularly. Grandpa Silas had organized a different group who went hunting in the wooded areas. That meant our camp had hunters and foragers. Silas was a hunter, and I was a forager. He snorted and shrugged. "Not that the brass listens to an old man like me."

I didn't say much; I wasn't supposed to. It was our ritual.

"Well, I will try to keep clear of him, or at least try not to piss him off."

In the weeks that I had known Silas, we had produced our own little greeting ritual. He always warned me about someone or something. Then he talked about how he had dealt with it or spoken to them, not that they listened to him. It was like talking about the weather. He would ask after the children if they weren't with me and promise to come up a bit later with something special for them. I would thank him and make sure he knew we were expecting him before I headed off.

Right on cue, Silas nodded and said, "Well, how are the little ones? We will stop by with some rabbit we caught earlier for you."

I smiled at him and nodded. "I look forward to it!"

They were reliable as the ticking of my watch. It was our little bit of normal. It was our way of keeping sane. Jeri would not speak until the very end, when he would say, "Be safe, ma'am".

Even though Grandpa Silas was a fully loaded PTSD marine, he was a straight shooter, literally in fact. He had gotten out of the corps twenty years ago, but the corps was never getting out of him. He had been so intense the first time we met. Albert had been so happy when he met Silas by the water as they were fishing. They had spent hours discussing angling and lures.

Even though I had been a bit wary about Silas at first, he'd quickly won me over. I was a sucker for when those military boys called me "ma'am." The first evening he had visited us with Jeri, we were all sitting around the fire when little Victor had a bad dream and started to cry. I was in the middle of some other task, so I was slow to respond. I went to look, and there was Grandpa Si, bouncing my little boy on his knees. It just melted my heart.

Jeri was so quiet that at first, I thought he might not be able to speak. Then I came across him singing with Zyada as they played cards by the camper. He was easygoing and even-tempered. Jeri didn't like hunting, but he was a heck of a fisherman. Albert and Jeri got along well. They would fish and chat for long periods of time. It was on the third day that I'd found out more about them. Jeri's mother had passed away from cancer in the spring. His parents had been divorced, and his father wasn't coping well. So, he had gone to live with his grandfather on his mother's side. The trip was supposed to have been a bonding experience for them. At the time Jeri had been worried, he didn't think it had been going well.

But I'll tell you what, there is nothing like the apocalypse to bring a family together.

"Thank you, ma'am," Jeri said about the candy and moved to head inside the gas station.

"It looks like you're clear. We'll throw up a signal if anyone follows you," Grandpa said as he moved to stand in the door to smoke.

"Thanks, guys. Appreciate it. Don't forget to come get some dinner later," I said as I adjusted my seat to start pedaling again.

"Stay dry, ma'am," Jeri said with a shy lift of the corner of his mouth, which was as close to a smile as he ever gave me. He was more standoffish with me than with Albert. Maybe I was too much like his mom, or not enough like her. Either way, I tried not to push him.

The two men disappeared, going back to their job. Again, I couldn't see them at all. I wasn't sure if it was because they were that good, or I was that bad. It could be like when I try to spot fish in a stream. I have no idea if I am doing it right. In the desert I know what to look for. If they were jackrabbits in a mesquite bush, I would spot them nine times out of ten.

For a kid who wasn't into hunting, Jeri had the hidden part down really well. I was glad they were our lookouts. I gave one last wave to the men I couldn't see and forced my tired legs to start pedaling again.

The road continued up the hill past a large cemetery on the left side of the road. Something weird and strangely helpful about the hill was the cemeteries. The hill was covered in several large graveyards, some of which were hundreds of years old. All along one side were slopes of tombstones and cracked stone pathways. Even away from the main graveyard, smaller graveyards popped up all over. Since there was almost no metal to heat up, there had not been flames here, and the cemeteries had helped to work as a fire-break. Most of the hill was undeveloped due to a historic site from the War of 1812. One of the major battles had been won here. There was a lot of dense forest area and underbrush. You might think, *Hey, forests burn, right?* Well, when it rains something like every other day, forests stay really damp. Trees don't really just combust on their own. The sides of the hill consisted of steep drops into gullies and crags and ravines from snow and rain runoff. There were dozens of little streams and brooks all year round, feeding into the canals below in the valley. The roads up here were steep and easy to monitor. There were houses and shops that were still in one piece even if they were not working. We had found a huge wild berry patch and animals in the thicker parts of the trees. There were pods of deer that came in, and the creeks and streams led to bigger places to go fishing. It wasn't quite the post-apocalyptic hell-scape that movies portrayed, but there was plenty of death and mayhem out there. I was all for Mad Max-ing it across the desert, but since we were in central New York forestland, it just had not worked out like I had planned.

For the most part, it seemed the slopes of the hill were nothing but graves and forest, with homes and businesses popping up around the edges like mushrooms. That was until you reached the top. I thought I'd read somewhere that the hill was just over a thousand feet high. That didn't seem like all that much until you had to pedal a fully loaded wagon of shit up the damn thing. The top had been developed more since it was extremely level, like a little hat perched up at the flat tip, a cluster of shops and homes all bunched up with a community college.

The college had been designated as an evacuation rally point by FEMA because it had a large gravity-powered sand filter system that had been completely unaffected by the power surges. That meant clean water and working sanitation. The campus had large flat open areas, such as parking lots and a lacrosse field, for tents. That made it easy to process refugees and handle logistics of the evacuation. We had repurposed most of what the college had left behind, taking over the sections of campus that weren't too damaged. The big reason our hill was important was the bizarre shiny death spike pointed at the sky. The community college was outfitted with some super nifty neat-o laser-thingy radio tower or communication relay. The Army Corps of Engineers had determined that this was "the optimal option for reestablishing communications in the area." This translated to twenty-seven smart techie guys in fatigues and pistols trying to rewire and configure a burned-out radio tower and to me pedaling all this shit two billion miles straight up. Albert and I had decided to stay here because we thought we could help the army boys get things working and get ourselves evacuated to someplace safer.

I finally made it to the top of that last rise and rolled around the curve of the street, toward the makeshift perimeter gate that had been put up. It was constructed of fencing and debris we had collected from the area. The gate was manned by two people at any given time. I was in luck; today the gate guards were my two favorites, Davis and Fredricks. They were a pair of army boys who seemed to be joined at the hip. I had never seen one without the other.

"Hey there, Mouse. Looks like one serious haul today. You want me to get someone?" Private Davis said as he looked me over.

Sweaty and tired, I was practically shaking by the time I slid off the seat. "Hell yeah, I do! This shit is heavy," I panted. I took some time to drink and catch my breath.

Private First Class Fredricks stepped up to look in the wagon. "Holy shit, Mouse, you got everything but the kitchen sink in here." He looked up and grinned a little. "It's like Christmas." He let out a high-pitched whistle and waved at someone.

I made sure to pull out my toll fee, as I called it, just a six-pack of Coke and a can of chewing tobacco. I didn't really need to bribe the gate guards, but I figured I was cultivating good service. Another pair of guys who worked the gate, McManning and Williams, were assholes. Every time I tried to go through the gate, they would hassle me. They would ask all kinds of questions, go through my things, make sexist comments, and in general just piss me off. I did my best to avoid them. They worked the afternoon duty on the gate. Yet another reason to go to work early. Fredricks got his soda, Davis his chew, and they were all smiles.

A young, fit private ran over in response to Fredricks' whistle.

Fredricks nodded to the bike. "Hey, you help her get this stuff brought home or wherever it needs to go, and then you're done here for the day."

"Got it," the private said as he went over to the bike and got it rolling. We hurried down the road toward the college, chased by big fat raindrops.

Before the street turned into the college, there was a corner lot. A small house was tucked away in the trees at the back of the lot. It was along the edge of the campus property but hidden from view. It had been evacuated before Albert and I arrived. We had quietly taken up residence there almost two weeks ago. It was a lovely single-story home with a rustic cabin vibe. Having been relieved of my heavy load, I ran ahead of the poor private. I ducked under the cover of the wraparound porch, managing to soak only my outer layer. I probably should have felt a little worse for the private, but I was the old lady. That young gun could handle a little rain. He wasn't made of sugar. He huffed and puffed, pedaling the heavy bike to the shelter of the back garage. He was red-faced and panting as he dismounted.

Stamina is not this kid's thing, I thought. It did make me feel a little better about myself that I had managed to bike all the way back. The last few weeks had involved serious physical conditioning for me. I stopped myself from laughing as the private made sure the brake was set and looked at me. His clothes were drowned-rat soaked. He looked like he might weigh a hundred pounds if he had rocks in his pockets. How had this kid made it through basic? The army must have changed some standards somewhere along the way.

He saluted me smartly and asked politely, "Is there anything else, ma'am?"

He was so baby-faced. He was freaking adorable! I wanted to pinch his cheeks. Somewhere out there was a mother who was just so damn proud of him that she drove people nuts. I almost cracked up thinking about her.

"Private ... Fowler, how old are you?" I said, inspecting the name badge on his uniform.

"I will be nineteen in two weeks, ma'am." He gave me a bright smile. He had freaking *dimples*.

I tried to do the math in my head. I had to do it twice. Math and I were not friends. It didn't add up—with enlistment, training, and secondary schools, he should not be in the field yet.

Private Fowler laughed, spotting my mental math struggle. "I received special consideration because I graduated high school two years early and had parental permission."

I was impressed. "Two years?"

He beamed with pride and a big smile as he puffed up a bit and stepped up onto the porch with me. "I am an engineer, but LT wants me to do more PT." He motioned to the bike. "Obviously, he's right. That was really hard." He picked up my backpack and headed into the house.

I grinned at his back. *That's someone's pride and joy right there.* I imagined what Victor might be like someday. I knew he would be a mountain of a man at least. He was practically a tank now. If I could manage to feed him as he got older, he was going to be a giant.

In the mudroom, I had just managed to get out of my top layer of wet gear when I heard it—a mash-up of high-pitched, excited squealing and laughter, then a series of grunts and the thudding of excited little feet racing toward me. I smiled as I braced for the incoming attack.

It was my youngest, Victor, the first domino. It didn't matter if I had been gone ten minutes or eight hours. He always greeted me the same way, at a full charge. He would run as fast as his little feet would go, screeching his battle cry as loud as his lungs could blast. He would fling his entire body weight against me. That was a serious amount of force considering that he was bigger than any other two-year-old I had ever seen. Once his older sister realized why he was running, she squealed and joined him, giving her own high-pitched "Mommy! You're home!" Because of their three-year age difference, they arrived at the same time and attempted to knock me over and hug me to death. Their excitement was contagious, so my stepson, Nathan, who was the oldest at twelve, followed behind them and hugged me too. This was one of my greatest joys in life. I dreaded the day they no longer came running when I arrived home. Those who have never experienced this level of enthusiasm at their return have missed out on one of the happiest things life has to offer. However, all this made it impossible for me to sneak into the house.

Albert sat up from where he had been abandoned while playing with Victor. "Yep, I'm chopped liver over here now that Mommy is home." He grinned as he slowly rose. He tried to hide his pain as his bones and joints popped and snapped, but I knew better. He never really could disguise his groans. He had gotten pretty smashed up in a boiler explosion while working as a technician in the navy. He had nerve damage and permanent injury to his knees and his right hip. He had served on a couple of security details, but mostly his job had been to run around making sure the ship didn't blow up. Considering how old that ship had been, it was a tough job. That had been over fifteen years ago. We had met as he was being discharged. We had known each other for ten years before we started dating. He was smart, tough, brave, and honest to a fault. He was my rock.

I finished hanging up my coat and gear by the door before hefting Victor onto my hip. *God, he gets heavier every day.* He had been a big newborn, coming in at almost nine pounds. He had been wearing size 2T before he reached eighteen months. Now he was almost as tall as his older sister. He was going to be the *big* little brother. We thought he might become a football player, if football was still around by then. His head was covered in dark brown curls and swirls. He was made for being happy, all big brown eyes and chubby cheeks. He was mama's little teddy bear.

Zyada was five. When she was born, the whole world had gasped in surprise at such a pretty doll-like baby. I remember the nurses whispering and getting distracted because she was so cute. That cuteness had not faded; she was still as beautiful. Only now, she also had that wonderful awkwardness of a preschooler. She had long, rich brown hair, bright eyes, and a huge smile. She was a bit of a drama princess and far too clever for her age. She was a great talker and had a huge vocabulary; the real trick now was getting her to listen. She reminded me of those beautiful baby fawns, full of awkward grace. She got that from her dad. He was tall and lean. I was short and curvy.

Nathan was like his dad, all arms and legs and thin as a beanpole. He had just started hitting that pre-teen phase where you can begin to see glimpses of the adult they will become. I had a bet that he would grow to be taller than his father. He was a smart kid; however, he was a bit of a soft touch, quite literally. He didn't like to use his strength for anything. He seemed to exist mostly inside himself. I worried about him the most. He had always been a sensitive kid. He had a gift for numbers and figuring things out. He was inventive and loved taking things apart.

I didn't know what was going to happen as our three kids got older. They were all amazing, and I was terrified. Victor was strong and happy, Zyada was beautiful and clever, and Nathan was intelligent and empathetic. I used to dream about all the things they would grow up to be. Now it was more like nightmares. Now they were targets.

I used to be amazed at Zyada's beauty. Now it filled me with dread. Being beautiful had major drawbacks. Women throughout history have been fought over, kidnapped, or killed. We were going to have our hands full keeping her safe. I was only a tiny bit less worried about Victor. He was going to be tall and strong. Men like that were forced to fight and were punished if they didn't. Nathan was so smart but easily pushed into things. Each one of them had weaknesses and vulnerabilities that worried me.

My hope was that they would learn to take care of each other. If they worked together, they might be all right. I just wanted them to have a chance to grow and live healthy, happy lives. Life wasn't about to get easier for anyone. I had to focus on the problems I could solve.

Some people were certain the lights were going to come back on. They would say "It was the modern era—there was nothing to worry about. After all, we had airplanes and space shuttles. It wasn't the Stone Age. You just needed to be patient; relief was on the way." However, I couldn't stop thinking; *what if the rest of the world is just like us? Everyone waiting for someone to fix this.* As my daddy would say, "Hope for the best, work for what you need, but always plan for the worst." Maybe the government would fix things; maybe they wouldn't. Even if they could, how long would it take? How were you supposed to survive in the meantime? I couldn't afford to be the person who expected the best and didn't prepare. My children couldn't afford for me to think that way.

Albert walked over and kissed me on the top of the head. A warm content feeling bloomed inside my chest and helped chase the darker thoughts away. He always seemed to know when I needed one of those. I leaned into him, and for just a moment, everything was OK. He was my still pond, my gentle breeze, and my happy place.

This was it—this was the why, the reason for everything, the fear, the worry, the hard work, and the pain. This moment made it all worth it. Zyada was already telling me all about what she had done that morning. Victor babbled at me at the same time. I turned toward Albert. He was tall enough that my head only reached his shoulder. I am a short 5'2" on a tall day. Victor held on tight, Zyada squeezed me around the waist, and I rested my chin on Al's chest, letting it soak in.

The private cleared his throat awkwardly. I had completely forgotten he was there.

Zyada shouted in excitement at the wagon, and just like that, I was forgotten. She was headed to the doorway, leading her brothers by half a heartbeat. We were able to stop them on the porch. They were content to stand at the railing, arms outstretched to touch the rain. Albert and I pulled on our rain ponchos and ran out to where the bike was parked in the detached garage. Along with the private, we quickly sorted through the supplies. We put the stuff we were keeping under tarps or on the porch to be taken inside. Nathan and Zyada helped carry the containers and items into the house.

The house itself was small, two bedrooms with an open kitchen and living room setup. The size was one of the reasons we had decided to stay here. The home's most important feature was the functional wood-burning stove in the middle of the living space. Not only was it set up to allow for cooking, but it also provided heat to the rooms in the house. The smaller size of the house made it easier to heat. It even had a small cold room, a "root cellar," as my mother would have called it.

September was almost over. Summer was still hanging on, but the cold snaps were harsh. Once fall arrived, the snow would not be far behind. Without cars, trucks, or snowplows, we were one bad snowstorm away from being stuck here for months. Albert and I were figuring out how to get through to spring. It wasn't fun, and it wasn't easy, but people needed to realize that things weren't going to be easy for a very long time. The young had the benefit of stamina and youthful resilience. They could run or fight all day. Albert and I didn't have the knees for that. Preparation and planning were the only choices we had. We had to think ahead if we wanted to survive. That meant thinking about winter and, more importantly, planning for the people who *didn't* think about winter.

It was just like the fable "The Grasshopper and the Ant." The grasshopper didn't gather food for winter, and when the snow started to fall, he realized that he was going to starve. What did the grasshopper do? He went to the ant. In the kids' version my daughter was taught in school, the ant saved the grasshopper, and he learned his lesson. In the version my grandmother told me, the ant said no, and the grasshopper died, hungry, miserable, and alone. There was a big difference between humans and grasshoppers: humans don't tend to handle starvation with dignity or restraint.

My grandfather had talked to me about his disaster plan once. He'd said, "Plan? What plan? You only need to know two things. One, where is your shotgun, and two, where are the Mormons?" He said the Mormons were supposed to keep a year's worth of food in their homes. Since I didn't want to shoot Mormons, I had to plan on ways to keep others from shooting me and taking my stuff.

Hence, we had decided to work with the army boys on their radio tower and stay within the perimeter line. Every male in my family going back three generations or more had served in the military in one fashion or another. The service members include my brothers, older and younger, my father, my grandfather, my great-grandfather, my father-in-law, and my uncle-in-law. Hell, even my mother had worn combat boots for a while. And I had married a military man. If you spent enough time around the military life, you learned about it, including the long watches and the even longer deployments. You learned all the bad and good things about it. You learned to love the men and women in it and hate the fighting. Eventually, you come to understand the sacrifice, the courage, and the desire to serve these people possessed. I choked up every time that flag was lowered and when taps were played. Nothing broke my heart more than flags over coffins. People who weren't part of a service family saw memorials of the wars, and maybe some felt awed or horrified by the number of names on the walls. However, to me the memorials represented our fathers, brothers, mothers, and sisters, our husbands and wives. Those names were flesh and blood. It made sense to me to help the army. The world was chaotic and uncertain now. For Albert and me the military was familiar and comforting. We saw uniforms, and they weren't strangers; they were family.

After we finished sorting out what was staying and what was going, I brought Private Fowler inside to warm up. Zyada brought him a towel, and we gave him a bowl of soup. I took a moment to just be there with my family. I smiled as Zyada diligently told Victor each item we had brought in and then allowed Nathan to put it away. Once the crayons were found, she was off to color, the game completely forgotten. Victor followed, eager to be a part of whatever his big sister was doing. So, we boring adults took over the chore. The last thing to do was to deliver the rest of the supplies. Then we could get ready for bath time, and tomorrow would be laundry day. Oh, the excitement was overwhelming.

five
tuesday, 5:10pm

DADDY HAD EARNED A BREAK, and I could tell the rain was making his joints hurt. I left Nathan to help clean up and bundled Victor and Zyada in their rain ponchos and rubber boots. With their little hands tucked tightly into mine, I led them back outside. Private Fowler and I unhooked the bike from the wagon handle. The wagon was lighter now, and with Private Fowler there to help pull, there was no need for the bike. The walk was a bit winding, but it would be good exercise for the kids, and it was easier on my legs. It was never a good idea to do a heavy workout and then just stop moving. That was a fast way to get cramps. The slow walk there and back would help cool down my legs.

The breeze was cold but gentle as it carried the fat raindrops in a widespread around us. The children squealed and jumped in the puddles. I let them play. It was nice to watch them laugh, and besides, it was bath night; it didn't matter. The rain was more like a pre-rinse anyway.

We followed the driveway down to the quiet street and took the gently sloping sidewalk toward the main campus. The welcoming signs at the entrance read "Visitor Parking." The sidewalk ran along the large, paved parking lot. It flowed in a smooth, natural way toward the buildings. Over the sounds of the kids laughing and splashing, I could hear the clank and rattle of the empty flagpole. It stood atop a lovely, landscaped mound with stone benches positioned in a way to allow the flow of foot traffic to swirl around it. A wide-open area created a welcoming and open visual.

The buildings beyond the flagpole formed an L-shaped corner. The long side held the athletic center. It was deceptive in appearance. The front was low and looked as if it were one story. However, it was built down and consisted of three floors and was much wider than any of the other buildings around it. It held a large gym, indoor basketball courts, an indoor track, and an arena. Just behind the mammoth structure was the outdoor lacrosse field. In the corner were the administration office and the student center. The short part of the L included the technology center, bookstore, and campus bank. The structures were still standing, but there was a lot of damage on the inside. The large white pavilion tents FEMA had been using were missing from the open area in front of the building doors.

"Hey, what did they finally decide to do with those tents?" I asked Private Fowler as we switched off so I could pull the wagon for a little while.

"Oh, they got moved to the main quad across the bridge. The last of the civilians were finally able to be sheltered in Dorm A. The fire damage wasn't too bad in that one. We also finally got the perimeter fence up around the campus. It's not much, but at least it's there now."

We entered the large glass doors of the gymnasium, where the supply center had been set up. The chill followed us in. The huge open area made temperature control impossible. The arena had been a bragging point for the campus. The structure was compact and elegantly designed. It was two different buildings fused together. It was built down the side of a ravine with three levels. The entrance we had used was on the top floor, which from the outside looked even with all the surrounding buildings. The left side of the split was the gym, where the exercise machines and weights were kept. This floor also held the two indoor basketball courts. The lower floors on the left side had classrooms, lockers, and exercise rooms with and without wall mirrors. As you moved into the massive right-hand side of the building the floor dropped away revealing the indoor arena and track. It was designed as an indoor playing field with AstroTurf, and a running track looping around the outside. Bleacher style seating surrounded all of this, rising from the bottom floor to just under the third floor. On the top floor there was the ticket office and a large concession stand along the wall. A railing kept you from tumbling down to the floors below and allowed for a wonderful view of the events. Stairs and a long ramp provided access down from the top floor. The elevators were currently not functional. The natural slope of the hill made it possible for each floor to have an exit to the outside. Behind the building was a large parking area as well as an outdoor lacrosse field.

I took the wagon down the ramp to the indoor field. The whole area was organized madness. Tables and shelves from all over campus had been brought in and set up. They were divided into sections that made no sense to me. They were labeled so that foraged items could be categorized and prioritized in a way that I didn't even try to understand. Every surface was packed with items that had been salvaged. The whole thing reminded me of a beehive. The people buzzing in complex patterns as others keep dropping in more items.

Zyada took Victor's hand and ran with him down the ramp. Then off they went to race along the outside lines of the track as fast as they could.

I did make an effort to rein them in. Honest, I did. I even used the big voice. That froze them in their tracks for a whole two seconds. They both looked at me and made a big show of slowing down and moving carefully. They made it about five feet before they started running again. In general, they were careful, so I didn't worry too much. I did make sure I could see them at all times, mostly just to prevent them from climbing on anything. Victor was a climber. It didn't help that the second they were spotted by the army boys, they had at least one or two playmates, who were desperate for an excuse to goof off. Once the military got involved, I decided to admit defeat and let them play.

I arrived at the starting line of the racetrack. The army had decided to put the check in desk there. Maybe they thought it had a certain ironic flair. According to procedure all collected items had to be carefully documented and recorded. I assumed that was because somewhere in Washington there was a bean counter who cared how many rolls of toilet paper I gathered. My guess, it was for reimbursement issues. I didn't know if the US government was ever going to compensate these shops, but at least there was a record. Hey, think positively, right?

I shifted around a tall section of shelves and spotted Corporal Cera Baltimore working at the intake desk. I ducked back a little and tried not to groan. She didn't like me. OK, to be fair, I didn't like her either. To me she was one of those petty bureaucratic tyrants you found working in crappy office jobs. They knew they were just middle management, and instead of trying to reach higher, they used whatever petty authority they had to make other people miserable. However, that was just my opinion; she was quite liked by some of the other civilians. There is no accounting for taste, I guess. I had been fired from many office jobs because I could never figure out how to get along with those people. I knew most of the problem was with me. I was an arrogant know-it-all who walked around like I owned the place. I behaved as if I did not have to follow "procedure." Those words had been written almost verbatim on more than one office disciplinary form.

"Hey! You kids stop running over there! You're not supposed to be here!" She stood up from her table.

My nerves went jagged around the edges from the shrill echo of her voice. I felt my mommy hackles rise, and I stepped into view, pulling the wagon behind me as I went toward the desk.

"Hey, Sales!" she shouted toward me. Her voice grated on my ears.

"W-w-whoa! I got this!" Logistics specialist Alonzo came out from one of the other sections at a speed-walking pace. "We don't need no cat fights in here. I'll take this, Baltimore." He took her place at the desk and smiled at me. I felt the muscles in my cheeks relax into a smile. He gave me a secret wink. "Ma'am, I've told you before about bringing them in here ..." His voice was stern even as he peeked over his shoulder to see if she was gone.

"I am sorry," I replied, trying to sound sincere. The moment Corporal Baltimore was out of earshot, he shook his head. "Eh, don't sweat it. She can get bent. I like it when they come in. They're cute and don't cause no trouble. So, what we got today?" he said as he came around to help me unload.

He was a painfully thin young man. He looked like he was wearing his big brother's clothes. Dark red-brown curls were beginning to grow out slightly and appear at the top of his military haircut. His eyes were a warm brown, and he had a big smile that gave him dimples on either side. "Alexxuryo-azeuri" was stenciled on his uniform jacket where his name was supposed to go. I couldn't pronounce it, not even if I was really drunk. That was just his last name, and not even the whole thing, just the first and last part with a dash in between because his full name didn't fit. He answered to Alonzo or Mouthy, on account of his prolific and creative vocabulary.

We emptied my cart: soap, soup, TP, bandages, bleach, and sundries. I turned in only four of the cartons of cigarettes. I had tucked the rest away, hidden in the root cellar. I didn't feel bad since Mouthy recorded only two of the four cartons I'd brought in. *Ah, the joys of reciprocity.* One of the bottles of booze was recorded. Private First Class Turner came out to collect my inventory and winked as he wrote down the numbers. Even though he could clearly see the discrepancies he stuck with Mouthy's totals. Mouthy seemed to have a team within those working in the supply department. Baltimore was a stickler for all the rules and regs, but Mouthy and his little crew were about getting things done. That was why I stuck with Mouthy. I knew that these were shady dealings, but that meant I had more leverage. I would rather work with someone who was a bit more flexible.

I took a moment to pull out my notebook. "Got some good news. There were some good locations this time. I found a car parts store and a pharmacy that seems mostly intact," I said as I put the medicine on the counter. "I also found a fire station and picked up tools and a couple uniforms."

Mouthy beamed. "That's great, just great. We're using flame for everything, so these'll be a help. The infirmary is always needing something. The next thing they're asking about is rubbing alcohol or anything they can use for antiseptic and syringes. I also got some requests in for copper tubing, baling wire, glue, baking soda, and nails. Specifically nails. I don't know why screws won't work, but they said it had to be nails. Apparently, they think this is a hardware store or something." He grumbled as he leaned on his elbows, marking off things that I had found from his huge list of items. "Considering how much bullshit the LT gave about civilians working salvage, he sure likes to add to the list."

I shrugged as I added the new items to my list in my little notebook. He had moved on to the quiet mumbling that meant he was done relaying information and was now just leaking words, so I spoke over him. "I suppose I could consider this job security. Anyone else volunteer yet? I could point them to a couple places."

Mouthy smirked and made a gesture. "Nah, the other civvies don't wanna go off the hill. They're doin' pretty good picking it clean, but ain't no one crazy enough to go as far as you."

I flipped him off with a friendly smile. "Did you just call me crazy?"

He laughed and nodded. "Damn straight. You're a full nutter.

I ain't complaining. You're my kind of nut. Any news from the world?"

I sighed, and my mind flashed back to the mass grave. "Nothing good. Found a poster saying that the fairground is a FEMA camp. But that's old news. Fire Station 3 was completely unmanned, and it seems someone was trying to clean up around the valley. There is a makeshift mass grave." I marked the map he had set out on the table. We used it to show where we had already searched and for promising sites to return too. I had tried hard to keep my voice level and calm, but Mouthy was a perceptive bastard.

"Shit, Ms. Mouse. You a'ight?"

I shook my head a little and took a deep breath to keep calm. "Yeah. I saw some other survivors. Looks like the blatant rioting has stopped. But most people seem to be staying indoors. I spotted some prisoners downtown. Looked like they were salvaging too."

Mouthy frowned. "You talked to them?"

I shook my head. "Hell no, I avoid everyone when I am out there. Saw them from a distance. They didn't see me." Mouthy nodded as I continued speaking. "Did that hand crank I found work for the emergency radio?" I was as eager as anyone else to get some news from the world.

Mouthy nodded. "Oh, we got some static. We even heard someone using a little ham radio. But he just seems to be someone who's played a little too much of that *Fallout* video game. He kept talkin' about how this is all a left-wing liberal coup trying to take over the country with the help of Satan's army no less." He fixed his uniform a little. "I wonder ... do you think Satan's army has any openings? I know a great supply guy."

A laugh escaped me, though I knew it really wasn't funny. "I thought at least with no news, there couldn't be any fake news. To tell you the truth, I am glad there isn't any of that political BS from social media all over the place right now. People have been so on the brink. If someone starts that shit right now, after all this ... I think this country would tear itself into pieces."

Mouthy smiled at me. But it was a strange smile, like I was a little kid talking about Christmas or something. "You think it hasn't already?"

I gave him a serious look and shook my head. "No way. You're still here. You are still wearing the uniform. As long as we've still got you guys, the country is still here." I gave him a smile. "There are a lot of people willing to fight to keep this place together. Just because the extremists are the loudest doesn't mean they will work the hardest."

Mouthy puffed a bit with pride and smiled. "All right, that's enough out of you. My wife will get jealous. Just focus on today, Ms. Mouse. Tomorrow will sort itself out." He nodded and started pulling some things from the shelves he had set aside for me. This was the normal we had found: I went salvaging for other people, and he made sure I got what I needed.

Mouthy had started the Ms. Mouse nickname for me. It had spread quickly with the other service men. They all love a good call sign. Mouthy said it was because I was small, cute, and very good at scurrying around with no one the wiser. I had my suspicions that my husband had given him the idea, but I still liked it. Mice are very brave critters, like I mentioned before. They are tiny furry creatures, and their only real defense is being quick, clever, and hard to notice. So how is it that something so very vulnerable is able to find the will to keep going? Seriously, take a moment to consider what it takes to face those kinds of odds. I had always thought that Mrs. Frisby was the bravest soul. She was the mouse from *Mrs. Frisby and the Rats of NIMH*, written by Robert C. O'Brien. I had always felt connected to that little mouse facing all those big dangers, just to save her family. Though I might have turned out a bit more like the shrew.

Anyway, Mouthy wasn't the kind of person you warmed up to. You either loved him or hated him instantly. He was like a younger brother. He made me laugh, and he adored my children. Victor laughed every time Mouthy said his name. His accent was really hard for me to place. Mouthy sounded like someone from New Jersey pretending to have a Brooklyn accent. He said he was from Long Island, but really, how the hell would I know?

"Oh, I put in a good word with the tech boys. They are gonna talk to your old man 'bout his idea." He winked. "Told them he was smart and could be really useful, being an electrician back in the day."

I gave a smile. "Thanks. I really appreciate it. Did you send Jacobs by to help with the firewood?"

He nodded as he spoke to someone over his shoulder. Somehow, he always seemed to be having more than one conversation at a time. "Yeah, I hope it helped a bit."

"Oh, it did. It's hard to get all the chores done and take these trips."

Mouthy signed some papers and handed them to someone behind him. It was just something he was able to do—have a conversation with two people, mutter something on the side, write down something else, and then yell at someone across the room. It must be so loud inside his head.

"Well, that's why I send these lazy bums over to help out. Cause we need you out there. You're really good at this. You manage to find a lot more than most, and your notes really help."

To be clear, I am paraphrasing this whole conversation. Mouthy used three times as many words. I will try and give you a better look at how he talks. It's just hard to catch all of it.

"It might be a few days before we can get some guys together to do the digging, but we will take care of those bodies." He sighed and leaned in closer to look me in the eyes. "You sure you're all right?"

"I'm fine ... Just glad the kids weren't with me."

He winced at the thought, glancing over to where they were playing. "Yeah, no shit ... Well, get going, or I won't ever get these lazy bums back to work." He put my rations in the wagon: flour, salt, jars, and cans, as well as a few things wrapped and tucked in the back.

He turned toward the junior privates, his voice getting louder but not much deeper. "OK, OK, OK. What? What is this? Is this work? You workin'? Nah, ya not. You're playin'. Playin' ain't workin'. If ya need me to explain the difference, I can, but no. No, no. This ain't work. Get ya lazy bums back ta work, ya lazy bums." It was like he had so many quotas to think about. Maybe there was also a spoken-word quota he had to meet—a high one.

I helped our exit by heading toward the door. "All right, the mommy is leaving. Zyada, Victor, come on, or Mommy will have to leave you here." There were little shouts of "Wait!" as they came thundering after me.

The rain was falling faster now, in smaller chilly drops. The children hid under the tarp in the wagon, giggling at every bounce. I took the bumpiest route home. It was important to find the little joys in life. What sound was lovelier than children giggling in the rain?

Once we arrived home, there was the noisy business of getting the children and supplies inside. Then there was the noisy task of stripping off wet outer layers and warming up by the fire. Soon they were settled together under a blanket eating nuts, and Nathan joined them. Then came the hard work. Every big pot we could find was filled with water and put on the woodstove to heat up. I was very thankful for the chopped wood. It would take a bunch of wood to keep the fire burning while we heated up enough water for everyone to bathe.

While the water heated up, I set some coffee to brew. I didn't care if it was the end of the world. There would always be coffee in my house. One of the things I'd found were tins of coffee and powdered creamer. Coffee wasn't hard to find; after all, there was a coffee shop on every corner. I had a cup of dark roast with creamer and two cubes of sugar. We had powdered sugar, but that was strictly for baking now. I took a sip and started making dinner. I put some potatoes in a small pot with just enough water to start them cooking. In a little bowl I mixed flour, salt, sugar, and baking soda. After mixing the powdered milk with water, I added that too and made some biscuits.

Into my pot of potatoes, I emptied a can of carrots, peas, and corn, including all the water from the can, and started the pot to boil. I added a bit of cornstarch, salt, pepper, and brown sugar. Grandpa Silas had brought us some deer meat. It made a great stew. As the food cooked, I started carrying half the pots of steaming water to the bathtub. They filled the tub a few inches and steamed nicely. I tested the water to make sure it wasn't too hot. We had a few pots sitting in the room steaming as I got Victor stripped and into the tub. Zyada joined him since they were both young enough that it didn't matter. I scrubbed them vigorously, washing hair, toes, noses, and elbows, until the water was cold and dirty. Then we used some of the warmed-up water to rinse them off. Albert had already refilled the pots and set them to boil by the time I was getting the kids dry, dressed, and wrapped up to warm by the fire. Albert had also made sure the biscuits hadn't burned—because he was an awesome husband, and we were a team!

We worked together to fill the tub and refill pots. Nathan had his turn to scrub, with some mild supervision from Dad, who helped keep the candles lit and the warm water coming. I spent some time towel-drying the younger children's hair and making sure they were bundled and warm in clean clothes. Afterward, I gave them both biscuits to eat as I heated more water for Albert. Nathan took his turn drying in the warm spot in front of the fire and got into his clean clothes. I served dinner while Albert took his turn in the bath. The stew was good, and even Zyada didn't complain. She had once been a very picky eater. There had been a couple of hungry days for us at the beginning when we couldn't find anything. Since then she had eaten what was put on the table.

It was so strange to feel glad that she had overcome something like that and heartbroken at the same time because she'd had to.

I did dishes and cleaned up the kitchen while I waited for my water to finish heating. After Albert got out of the tub, he brushed Zyada's hair while warming up. Teeth were brushed, and the little ones were tucked into bed. We made sure everyone was warm and dry. We all slept in the same room on three mattresses pushed together on the floor. Nathan slept on one side, then his dad, then me, and then Victor and Zyada. It was easier and safer this way.

Albert read to them as I took my turn in the bath. I cheated. I brought one pot into the bathroom, and after stripping, I lathered and scrubbed. I stood in the empty tub to rinse the soap off, letting it drain. Then Albert helped me put in the rest of the water so I could soak until the water was cold. It helped with all the aches and sore muscles.

He kissed my head and smiled at me. His smile was wide, tired but pleased. I held his hand silently for a moment, looking at my suntanned hand holding his dark mocha fingers. I called him my mocha latte and he said I was his vanilla crème. Shut up, I know how it sounds. I didn't care, and he liked it. We were just corny.

He was my super-geek and their awesome science dad. He was always working on some invention or another. We had hundreds of tiny pocket notebooks that he had filled with his notes, equations, ideas, and diagrams for things I had never heard the name of. I won't lie; it wasn't easy to love someone who lived so much inside his own head. I often wondered if Albert Einstein's wife had felt like that. It must have been hard to play second fiddle to the string theory. But when he was here, he was worth the wait.

Anyway, we didn't have time for that now. We all had our jobs to do. None of them were easy. It was back to basics, and basics were backbreaking and time-consuming. Albert never complained. Even with all his injuries, he just pushed through it. We didn't say anything as I sat in the tub; we just held hands for a few minutes before I dragged myself out of the chilly water. I wrapped up and headed to the kitchen. I quickly dressed in my warmer sweats and started prep for the next day.

Tomorrow was laundry day. It would be an all-day affair, so I refilled the pots on the stove. It would help keep the air warm and make reheating easier in the morning. Albert was already asleep by the time I started brushing out my hair. It was only slightly damp when I braided it tightly so it would remain tangle-free. I banked the fire so it wouldn't go out on us in the middle of the night or burn up our pots. I made sure toys were picked up and put away.

Even before the storm, Albert had always been asleep by nine. I was the night owl. We weren't exactly exciting. I stood in the doorway listening to my family sleep.

That was when they arrived. Once the candles were blown out and the chores were done, they slipped in. In the peace and quiet of evening, they came. At first, it was just a hitch in my breathing, a tightness in my chest. I stepped away from the sleeping room and stood in the glow of the fire. It did little to keep the darkness at bay. Like wraiths, they haunted me. They stole into my eyes to dance behind my eyelids, these monsters. My own little horrors.

I saw the little pink boots positioned at funny angles in putrid filth, only this time, they were on Zyada's feet. The glow of the fire blurred as tears filled my eyes. Pain seeped into my body as I tried to force the thoughts away. Maggots squirmed out of Albert's face just below his beautiful brown eyes. *Air*. I had to breathe, but someone was squeezing my chest from the inside. I could taste metal on my tongue as I tried to suck air.

An empty stroller with a little lonely teddy bear ...

I bit my finger hard enough to bruise it before that image could take hold of me. I had to wrap my arms tight around myself to stop the trembling. Tears ran uncontrolled down my face. I gasped for air. I couldn't even scream. There wasn't enough air in the world. My body was frozen as I fought to remind myself that the images weren't real, that my babies were sleeping in the other room, that we were alive. I didn't need to borrow someone else's pain. It can be nearly impossible to think rationally when you are afraid.

I didn't realize I was kneeling until I felt a little hand touch my shoulder and grip tight. I looked, and there was sleepy-eyed Victor holding on to my shirt. He started to fuss. It wasn't a loud cry or a squeal, just his grumpy sleepy noise. His voice was so little that it was almost just a grumble, not quite words. It was enough. It was as if a switch had turned on. With just a flick he flooded the world with light and banished the darkness. He chased the monsters away, and the air returned. I was able to take a deep breath and forced myself to calm down. I didn't want to scare him. I wiped my face with my sleeve and carefully pulled in air and let it go in a slow, even breath. I shifted and pulled him close and rested my cheek against his curls. I snuggled him as I rocked him and hummed softly in his ear. He gave me his sleepy smile, the most beautiful thing in the world.

"Fear is a sickness. It spreads from person to person. Some people, it kills or scars. Some people sniffle a bit but just get right back up. No one is immune to it, Pookie," my father's voice whispered from my childhood bedside, after a nightmare.

"But you're never afraid," I whispered with the confidence that only the very young had.

"Sure, I am, Pookie-doodle. The world is full of things you're supposed to be afraid of, but it's just like having the flu. You sniffle, cough, take your medicine, and get over it. Not much time to waste being sick." He petted my head and waited for the question he knew was coming.

I didn't disappoint. "What medicine is there for when you're scared?"

He rubbed his jaw as he pretended to think about it. "Well, the only medicine I know of is a hug, a kiss, and a little bit of courage."

So of course, I got my hug and kiss. He tucked me under the covers. "But what about my bit of courage?" I asked.

He smiled and winked. "Ah, Pookie-doodle, you've already got that. It grows a little bit each time you face your fear."

So I took my dad's advice. Victor got a snack, I got a hug and kiss, and the two of us got into bed. He cuddled up close and kept the monsters away. I was asleep before my eyes closed all the way.

wednesday, 7:22am

Laundry Day

VICTOR WAS OUR EARLY RISER. He was more reliable than any clock I had ever owned. He was always the first up. Lucky for us, he was happy in the morning. We would take him into the front room so others could sleep. Back when the lights were still on, he would watch cartoons and play with quiet toys until everyone was awake. He still got up that early, and we still took him to a separate room, but now, with no TV to keep him occupied, he sang his happy songs and played with his cars. How he loved his cars. He sang to them every morning. I hummed along while I made breakfast.

Now let us take a moment to think about all those wonderful gadgets we took for granted. For instance, our beloved man Mr. Coffee. Oh, how we mourned him. However, hope was not lost; there was still coffee at the end of the world. Even without the wonder of electricity, my house would still have the elixir of the Gods, for I had the amazing device that had come before Mr. Coffee. Behold the percolator. Basically, it works like this: the water is on the bottom, the grounds are in a filter in the middle, and a tube goes through from bottom to top. When the water heats up on a stove, it bubbles up through the tube and out the top, in a process called percolating (hence the oh-so-clever name. Sorry, it has nothing to do with perking you up in the morning). Then the water trickles through the coffee grounds, and *poof*, you have coffee. Now I had heard of a way that cowboys used to make coffee too. They boiled water in a pot and dumped in their grounds. The grounds would start floating and then slowly sink to the bottom. When the coffee was as dark as the cowboy wanted it, he cracked an egg into the pot. The egg would spread across the surface and cook in the hot water. It would then sink and capture all the grounds at the bottom of the pot. The coffee was extraordinarily strong, but here is the hard-core part: cowboys used to *eat the egg*! I imagined that was one seriously caffeinated egg. Cowboys might have done that for a long time, but yuck. Besides, it was hard to get eggs now. How many chickens did anyone see in the city? Guess what, folks? Chickens were really far away.

Eggs will remain good for about three weeks if you can keep them cool. If you ever need to check if an egg is good, put it in a pan of water. Good eggs, about a week old, will lie evenly at the bottom. Two-week-old eggs will float a little with the end slightly tipped down. Three-week-old eggs will float with the tip pointed up. Bad eggs float at the top of the water and *should not* be eaten. Also, if I had eggs, I wouldn't waste them on coffee. One egg could make a loaf of bread or noodles. So much protein and good stuff in a tiny little shell. There were few things on this earth more perfect to be raised and eaten than chickens. Chickens could eat just about anything, and they laid a lot of eggs. Further, you could use every single part of them. They even ate their own eggshells, and it made them have better eggs! Baking required a lot of eggs. I guess the point I was trying to make was I missed eggs.

This morning it was fried potatoes, more biscuits, and fried slices of tinned ham. I mixed up some Tang for the kids and some powdered formula for Victor. He was still little enough to take it well. We had the huge canning pots already on the stove. The heat from the stove was intense. I tied a bandana around my forehead to keep sweat out of my eyes and gathered up our wash. Albert finished his coffee and hung up some clotheslines. The sky was clear, and though it was still cool, it felt like it was going to warm up. It was just at the beginning of October, and we had some warm days left.

Laundry by hand was exhausting, time-consuming, and back-breaking work. It could take days to get things soaped, scrubbed, rinsed, and dried.

First thing you had to do was heat the water. At least we still had the convenience of working plumbing. That saved us from having to haul water up from a river. Next, you took the dirty clothes and soaked them in warm soapy water. You stirred it up and then took out an article of clothing, scrubbed it with soap, and rubbed the fabric against itself. If it was really stained, you used a scrub brush. This part of the process took a *very* long time. One of the best inventions ever made was the agitator washing machine. Before that, there were washtubs and manually cranked wringers. The particular item that I wished I had was a wash-board, a large board with a section of metal bumps or ribs to rub clothes against. It helped cut down the time a person had to spend scrubbing. Unfortunately, I had not been able to locate one. So, I was doing it the hard way: with my knuckles. I took a little of the cloth in one hand and some of it across the other and rubbed them vigorously together. Not so hard, right? Yeah, super easy. Now repeat two or three hundred times or until your knuckles are so raw that you are leaving more stains than you are removing.

If the rubbing wasn't bad enough, most laundry soaps were extremely harsh on skin. It important to remember these soaps were designed to cut through grease, fats, dirt—basically every-thing. If the work was done correctly; by the end of laundry day, a person's hands were chapped, red, sore, and ready to be chopped off at the wrists. It might hurt less that way. There was a secret to saving your hands: butter, olive oil, lanolin. These were nature's skin savers.

After scrubbing the dirt out, you had to remove all that soap; otherwise, your clothes would be hard and scratchy. You had to wring them out, which basically involved twisting the cloth up as tight as you could, to squeeze all the water out. Then you put them in hot clear water to soak and wring them again. There was a reason that depictions of historic laundresses showed large, burly women without corsets, with rumpled hair and sweat pouring off their red-faced cheeks. This work was hard and hot and required a great deal of strength and stamina. The last step was hanging the clothes up to dry. It was very important to make sure your line was taunt and strongly tied. Clothes are very heavy when wet. The line needed to hold, or the clothes got dirty, and you had to start all over. This was where the verb "clothesline" came from. If you ran into one, it *really* hurt. You must securely pin the clothes up, stretched out but not too tightly, or the shape of your clothes would be ruined. My mother had taught me a trick: about halfway through the drying, you went back through and flipped the clothes to dry the other direction. That way your clothes didn't lose any of their shape. How long this even took to explain shows why laundry day was a *day*, not an hour. That's why washing machines were so wonderful.

I had Victor stir the bucket of dirty clothes and soapy water. Zyada helped me rinse and squeeze. She got to use a rolling pin. Nathan assisted his dad with hanging the clothes. Then with all that leftover soapy water, we scrubbed the floors. Might as well, right? Then we all had more biscuits and ham. At the end of the work, my back hurt, and my shoulders ached, but as I stood there looking over the line of clean sheets flapping in the breeze, the sight made me happy. I could smell the difference in the house and from all of us. It was a great feeling. There was something so satisfying about being able to see the results of your hard work. It was so nice to have a problem and be able to fix it. I sat on the porch listening to the clothes as they flapped gentle in the breeze while I smoked.

Grandpa Silas came and picked up his laundry and dropped off a couple of rabbits as payment. Jeri brought Zyada a wooden whistle and Victor a carved wooden dog. For Nathan, he brought a book he had found. I delivered clean bandages to the infirmary. The infirmary helped everyone, so I paid them forward. Albert always talked about specialization and utilization, but normal folks just called it barter. Our labor was traded for theirs. Grandpa was a hunter, Jeri carved, and some of the privates chopped our wood.

Welcome to the most basic form of economy. According to my cultural anthropology class, we would likely be defined as a "band" of peoples because we were small in number and had no agriculture. We were formed of individual family units that could split apart if resources became slim. There might be some debate, though, because we did have a leader, the lieutenant. Though technically we weren't soldiers, it was safe to assume that martial law was in effect. If we wanted his protection, we had to follow his lead. That possibly made us a tribe. I hadn't bothered telling anyone that. Everyone was still in the nation mindset. Also, no one would really care; I was sure I was the only anthropology geek here.

I found the situation rather odd, humorous but odd. In the past I had been considered weird, eccentric, and geeky because I was old school. I paid for a manual typewriter when everyone else was trying to get the new iPad. I wanted an old transistor radio or the old rotatory phones when everyone was trying to get cars that could talk or text for you. My inability to integrate, sync, download, upgrade, input, compute, decode, or connect had made me an outsider. Now it was precisely because I was so archaic that I was much better equipped to handle the sudden changes we all faced. Life, am I right?

It's amazing how fast you fall into new routines once all the distractions are gone. There were no more TV shows to watch, no social media feeds to check, no more Netflix to binge, no more nine-to-five or traffic jams, and most importantly, no more bills to pay. Suddenly, the poor were free of all debt and expense. Think of all that money lost, the electronic debts, stocks, bonds, and wire transfers—*poof*, up in smoke. As if Bonnie and Clyde had come back for some great revenge. Maybe there was a hidden bunker where the computers were keeping a record of debt and wealth. But none of that mattered now; all that information was pointless if no one could access it. Money was just paper—and not even useful paper. It didn't burn well, and you couldn't use it for writing. Now that the mighty dollar was useless, all that energy previously used to chase it could be used for other things. The pressures were still there, but they were completely different.

I was relaxing in the afternoon sun when Nathan came out and said, "Is it OK if I wear this nice shirt to the meeting tonight, Mom?"

For a moment I had no idea what he was talking about. Then it came back to me—the regular "briefing" we had to go to. I supposed for the kids it was just a weird get-together that all the grownups did.

"Sure, honey. Wear whatever you want. Just try to keep it clean, OK?" I answered with a smile.

Nathan nodded and headed back inside. I finished my smoke and slowly got up. Taking off my apron, I made sure I wasn't too filthy and brushed my hair. So much for no longer caring about what other people thought. I could practically hear my mother telling me to fix myself before going into public.

Albert had just finished getting Victor into shoes, and I made sure Zyada's hair was brushed. These might have seemed like dumb things to worry about, but it kept the kids in their routine. It helped reinforce personal grooming, which was important for health. We made it out the door rather quickly for us and headed down the winding walkway toward the campus. Albert and I walked with Victor between us, each holding one of his hands. Zyada and Nathan walked slightly ahead.

We moved at a slow and easy pace. The afternoon sunlight was beginning to fade, but it was still pleasant, with a nice breeze chasing leaves. I smiled up at Albert as we strolled. I tried to pretend it was any other day.

"I chatted with Mouthy while I was in supply today," I said, pulling Albert out of his own head.

"I don't think it is physically possible to not have a chat with Mouthy. Ever. He never shuts up." Albert gave a half smile.

I rolled my eyes and sighed. "It's nice to find someone who talks more than me. Anyway, he said he talked to the techs, and they should be coming by to see if you can help. I let him know you were in the navy. I told him you used to work electrical—I didn't know the name of your job, but I knew it was with batteries."

He grinned and shook his head. "I did a lot more than just work on batteries."

I smiled back and shrugged. "Well, you can tell them all about it when they come and talk to you. Just try to be helpful, OK?"

He raised an eyebrow. "Of course. What are you so worried about?" He looked at me with concern. "You have been really tense today. Is it about the briefing?" He turned slightly and strolled us along the walkway, giving us a few more minutes to talk.

I took a deep breath and tried to relax my shoulders. "I am just worried about some of the changes the LT is putting in place. The FEMA people were practically useless here, but they didn't try to control things. What if he tries to force us not to go salvaging? What if he won't let us stay in the little house and forces us into the dorms? The longer we go without receiving news, the more desperate people will become. I don't know if this LT has what it takes to keep this place from imploding. There are so many what-ifs." I was speaking to fast, and it all spewed out in a rush, but I did feel a little better.

Albert grinned and leaned over to kiss my head. "Take a breath. It's OK. That's my love, always thinking. I know I was in the navy, not the army, and there are differences, but the system is basically the same. Their mission is the radio. They aren't here to run a refugee camp. The only reason there are so many people here is because FEMA wasn't able to evacuate everyone. They are Army Corps of Engineers; they are different than standard army. It is their job to figure out how best to adjust to the situation." He was very relaxed as we moved closer to the auditorium.

I took a deep breath and shook my head. "I have just heard some rumors that he is going to announce a bunch of restrictions tonight."

Albert gave a snort. "That's because FEMA isn't here anymore, so people are being paranoid. If he has any brains at all, he will put the restrictions in slowly, so no one notices. That's how you take control of a group." He gave his best evil villain laugh.

I gave him a withering glare. "That is not funny."

"Yes, it is. See? You're smiling right now."

I was not. OK, maybe a little.

We could see other people heading into the auditorium. Our children took off at a run to join with the other kids playing in front of the big doors. This was the third one of these briefings we had been to. They had started before we arrived. The FEMA personnel had begun them to help keep everyone informed. When the unit of army engineers arrived, they had joined the briefings. Now that FEMA had left, the LT would be taking over. This was his first briefing. It would set the tone for everything. We were all waiting to see how he would choose to run both the briefing and the camp. Theories floated around, varying wildly. Worries and doubts stalked around this camp like a hungry cat. There was nothing to be done but wait and see.

Albert held open the door for me, and we herded our children inside. The auditorium could house everyone easily and had a built-in stage. The windows were cut out high up on the walls and set at such an angle that in the late afternoons, the stage was lit up. It made the stage perfect for those who were trying to speak. Their voices projected easily even without a microphone. The first meeting had to be held outside at the tents. There had been over two hundred people in attendance. Now we were less than half that. There were somewhere around seventy-five adult civilians now and twenty-six army engineers. So there was plenty of room to spread out inside. The civilians that were still here were those who couldn't make the evacuation on foot. Those people who were too old, too injured, or with small children had remained behind.

The communication networks had cooked during the storms. Everything from radios to satellites had just fried. It seemed the more complex the machine, the more damage had been done to it. Once the cars stopped running, nothing moved really. Supplies and evacuations had to be done on foot. By the time the storms had stopped, there was no way to communicate between the FEMA relay stations. The only information anyone had was what they had heard last on the emergency broadcast system or had seen on signs and fliers. Those fliers were what had brought us here. When we arrived, supplies and personnel had already been whittled down due to people heading out on foot. By the time the army engineers came for the radio, I had already started salvaging for supplies.

When the army boys had arrived, you would have thought they were a famous boy band from the way people ran to crowd around them. So many people just expected them to have all the answers. I think many people took it hard when they realized that evacuation was not why they were here.

It was during that first meeting with the LT and the man in charge of the FEMA people that the rumors had started. The FEMA fliers said that Fort Drum was one of the final evacuation points. A handful of police officers had offered to traverse to the army base, taking all those willing and able. People were convinced that to stay was to sit and wait for disaster. We knew that the National Guard base next to the airport had burned. A plan was eventually settled on. Anyone who felt they could make the trip would pack up what they could and make the walk to Fort Drum. In theory, it was a thirty-hour walk to the base. The average walking speed of a person was between three and four miles per hour. If they went slow and covered only two miles per hour for six to eight hours a day, the trek would take two or three days. They would let whoever was in charge at Fort Drum know that we needed help here. Six days ago, they had left. They had packed up what little they had and headed out. It was a crazy plan to me. I wanted to tell them it was a bad idea. I had almost spoken up when a woman with a little five-year-old had been among those wanting to leave. Thankfully, the head officer had told her she couldn't go. The trip would be too much for a little boy. I was so relieved that I hugged the man. His name was Officer Manus. The woman's name was Ronda, and her son Tyler played with Zyada. I watched the group leave from the top of the hill. Victor rested on my hip, his little boy hand waving his goodbye as they walked away. As of yet we had received no word from them.

This was the fear and doubt that was prowling around our makeshift fence. Why hadn't we heard anything? Had they made it? Had they abandoned us? What if they hadn't made it? Why? What was our plan? Did we just keep waiting? These were the questions that lurked in the eyes of people gathered at the auditorium. That was why it was so important for the LT to help calm the crowd.

I never said anything to anyone, but I had felt a tiny bit relieved when the group left for Fort Drum. There were several issues with a crowd like that. They were young and confident that they knew what was best. When was the last time you talked to someone in their early twenties who was willing to wait patiently for the right time for something? Perhaps that isn't a fair stereotype. But it felt accurate in the circumstances since they'd decided to walk close to ninety miles because they didn't want to wait here. That wasn't the only reason I was relieved. It might be true that there was safety in numbers, but only if you could feed everyone. A person could be reasonable, but in large numbers, people were stupid and dangerous. I had worked in the food service industry for several years. I knew how unreasonable some people could get if their food wasn't on time or perfect. Now tell those people there isn't food at all. It wouldn't take much to turn them into a mob. If a mob of that size had turned on our squad of military men, the latter wouldn't have stood a chance.

Albert and I had taken seats in the back so he would not bother anyone if he had to stand and stretch his back. The group of children that ours had joined were playing inside now. An area had been set aside for them. There were half a dozen children besides mine here. Two were infants, one girl named Sarah and a boy named Vahid. They were, of course, little darlings. I loved babies.

Sarah's mother was a very shy woman named Alice, whose husband was our resident paramedic, Michael. He would have gone to the National Guard depot, but he wouldn't leave her behind. The walk would have been too far to go with such a little baby. Vahid's mother was a very outspoken woman named Samara. I had liked her instantly. She had a lot of gumption, as my mother would have called it. Samara had no idea where her husband and family were. They had been visiting a sick aunt about a hundred miles away. They might as well be on the moon. Alice was breast-feeding, but Samara was having trouble. I knew that because she had asked me to bring back baby formula for her. I did as often as I found it, though I had found little handheld breast pumps for both women too.

I had met them both on the same day, our first day at the camp. The FEMA coordinator had put all the people with chil-dren in one building. It was big and open, with each person assigned a little cot to rest on. It was impossible not to notice them. Alice was crying, and Michael was arguing with Samara. Their respective babies were in full-blown meltdowns. The adults were not far from having their own.

I was, am, and will forever be a meddler. It didn't take me long to figure out what was happening. After a few angry gestures, I noticed the single diaper lying on the table. I probably shouldn't have laughed. I couldn't help it. Here were two adults, one in a business pantsuit and the other in some kind of medical uniform, about to get in a good old-fashioned fistfight over one diaper.

"*What*? You think this is funny?" It was Michael who turned on me like an angry dog. He was at the end of his tether. His wife and baby were bawling, and all he wanted was to fix the problem.

"Yes, as a matter of fact, I do." I smiled at Michael and shifted Victor over to my other hip. "You look like a cherry tomato. And seriously, I think that woman over there is going to stab you. I would be careful. She looks tough."

They were both watching me as I stepped between them and walked over to the table. I pulled one of the receiving blankets from the neat pile stacked there. I laid Victor down on the table. He wasn't potty-trained yet. That was something we were going to have to figure out along the way. I pulled down his pants, and the plastic bag that his little legs were sticking through crinkled. It was just a little plastic shopping bag from a grocery store.

"What the hell is that?" Michael looked over my shoulder. His voice was still heated but was down to a simmer instead of a boil.

"It's his new plastic pants. I had others, but he outgrew them." I untied the plastic handles I had tied around his waist and then unfastened the safety pins that secured the cloth diaper. I took the whole thing off him and wiped him clean. I folded the receiving blanket and put his butt on one end. I folded it over him and secured it with safety pins. Then I pulled out a new plastic bag. It had two holes neatly cut in the bottom, where his legs would go through, and I used the handles to tie the bag around his waist before I pulled his regular pants back up. I turned and smiled at my little audience. They stared like I had just performed a magic trick that bordered on miraculous. It was fun to see someone realize how completely ridiculous their situation was.

Michael quickly shifted his posture, and suddenly, he didn't look like a red-faced football player. He was actually sort of slim and baby-faced. He blinked and looked at Samara as he mumbled some apology, looking ashamed. Samara looked upset and not easily appeased. She nodded and then also apologized. They had their awkward moment, and then suddenly I was looking at the biggest pair of blue eyes I had ever seen. Her eyes were huge in her face. She was young and had the happy, exhausted look of a new mother.

Now Alice was a wonderful lady, but half the time I wondered if she was secretly an evil superspy. She was just too ... sweet, too innocent. No one was really that nice or naive or wholesome. She was that character in a movie that no one thinks is real.

"Wow, I never would have thought of that. Can you show me how you did that again?" Alice was from a midwestern town that you couldn't find on maps. Her mama had died when she was young, so no one had shown her this stuff. Alice had been a home-coming queen and the sweetheart of Michael, whom she had married right out of high school. He was the football star who had earned the scholarship that had gotten them out of the little town in mid-west nowhere. Because of course they were.

She told me all this in the time it took me to change her little girl's diaper. She gave the story to me in just the sweetest accent. It was all bright sunshine and lemonade made with honey. I don't even mean that sarcastically, which is the weirdest part. She was a teaching assistant finishing up her courses to be a full-time teacher. If I looked past the accent and small-town girl demeanor, I could see a thinker in those blue eyes. In my overactive imagination she was really a secret superspy, in deep cover waiting for word from high command.

Samara was a confident woman who didn't say much as she changed her son's diaper and looked at me for a long moment. Her countenance was very steady and serious. Her voice was much lower than mine in octave and resonance. It had a slight accent I couldn't place. It made me think of faraway places. It was a voice made for storytelling. I could listen to her talk all day.

"What happens when we run out of blankets?" She motioned to the pile.

"You just clean the ones you use. If the supply really does run out, you make them out of sheets or T-shirts, whatever you can find. In some places they just don't wear pants. Don't worry. Women figured out how to get by without Pampers for thousands of years. We are smart ladies. We will think of something."

We had become friends after that. Albert had introduced himself and backed up some of what I had been telling them. He showed them how to use the arms of a T-shirt as the legs of a diaper and a few other tricks he knew.

Thump! Victor charged into me with a running start and nearly knocked me out of my chair, yanking me out of my thoughts. Laughing hysterically the whole time, he squirmed to get away from me. I grabbed him and tickled him.

I took him over to where the children were being corralled, to play with some found toys. The other kids ranged from four to twelve. There were a couple of teenagers here, but they were with the adults. Pretty much anyone over the age of thirteen was being treated like an adult. There was an eleven-year-old girl helping with babysitting, along with her fourteen-year-old sister.

We milled about with the other people as we waited for the meeting to start. We had brought muffins to the potluck, which I had used two of my precious eggs to make. We had also brought some of Albert's ground and charred dandelion roots, to share as coffee. All the food was stacked neatly on tables in the back, away from the stage, so people could mingle. The meeting would start when the light hit the stage and would go until everyone was done or it was getting dark. No one wanted to waste candles on these meetings, so once it was too dark to see, the meeting would stop.

I was the only one with a watch, so I was the only one who knew that it was almost four now, and the light hit the stage around four thirty. I kept the watch private. It was as old as the man who had given it to me. The leather band had grown soft with age, the glass face had a crack, and the edges had become discolored. However, the hands still moved steadily in their circles. The second hand, a faithful soldier, continued marching on. It was probably the only working timepiece in a hundred miles, if not more. I wasn't sure why this old-timer kept ticking. Every other clock I had found was stopped dead or burned out. The inscription on the back claimed it to be of Swiss make from the 1940s. I wondered if it had been worn by someone during World War II or in any of the wars after that. Where had it been keeping track of time for so long? How long would it keep track of time with me? So far it had been with me for two weeks.

I had been trying to set up a sundial. Did you ever have that stupid word problem in math class, the one where the goal was to figure out how tall the stick needed to be to calculate the time? Let's just say I was struggling. On my third attempt to solve this riddle, a man approached me. He walked slowly and leaned heavily on his cane. He smiled when he reached me. His face was more wrinkled leather than skin. At first, I thought he was wearing a mask. There were two crystal-clear green eyes peering out at me; like some young man was trapped inside a face that wasn't his own. I could almost see him hidden in the folds of himself. He handed me the watch and whispered in a rusted voice, "Time doesn't matter to me anymore, but it seems it still matters for you." He patted my hand and shuffled away. I was lost in the moment and forgot to ask his name. I would never forget that particular shade of green in his eyes. I had not taken the watch off since. But I kept it hidden in my sleeve. I just wasn't sure how people would react anymore. If it wasn't something you could share, then it was best not to flaunt it. People got worked up over almost anything during times of stress. I could only imagine what would happen if someone found a working phone.

Albert nudged me awake as the meeting started. My special ability was being able to sleep almost anywhere. All the physical stress and worry left me tired all the time. Now the trick was to stay awake when I sat down. I hoped I wouldn't fall asleep as often once I was more used to all the physical work. I looked around, blinking back into the world. It looked like everyone was here. All the army guys were sitting up front, except for whoever was on watch duty.

For anyone not familiar with the military ranks and chain of command, here is a basic run down. There were twenty-seven military personnel in total. The lieutenant was the top rank for our mini-base: Lt. Eugene Roberts, a.k.a. LT, Lt. Brick, or if you are feeling particularly sassy Bobby the Brick. He was... a brick. Shocker, I know. We are so inventive with our nicknames. I don't mean to say he was stupid, because he was very intelligent. What I mean is that he was shaped like a brick or perhaps built out of bricks. He was all hard edges and sharp angles; even his hair was cut square.

Then there was the senior sergeant: Senior Sergeant David Adams. I was fairly sure this man was made of carefully woven bands of cable wire that had then been lightly covered in strips of gristle. He was tall, but it was more accurate to say he was long. His arms, torso, legs—everything had a stretched, taut look to them. His hair was white, even his eyebrows. His face was always clean-shaven. I didn't know how he was getting shaving supplies. In my imagination he used an old-fashioned straight razor, just to frighten the young troopers. Either that, or he just intimidated his facial hair into not growing. The scuttlebutt among the troops was that he had been in the service for over thirty years, which no one could prove, of course. Usually, at the twenty-year mark the military encourages retirement. At the thirty-year mark, they forced the issue. According to one of the riflemen, Adams had managed to stay in service because he once had been the sergeant to a now four-star general who pulled strings for him. Another said it was because he scared the reenlistment clerks so bad that they just kept reenlisting him. Either way I wasn't going to ask him.

Under the senior sergeant there were three middle sergeants: Emanuel Gomez, Peter Franklin, and Mathew Douglas. Mouthy affectionately called them the three wise men. "Not so much because they're wise, but because they always show up after all the yelling, screaming, crying, pushing, shoving, and labor is done," as Mouthy put it.

The next level down in the ranks can get a bit confusing. Private First Class Mouthy answered to Sergeant Gomez, whom he called an administrative sergeant. The administrative sergeant had two admin NCOs (noncommissioned officers) or senior corporals, referred to as junior sergeants. And each junior had two enlisted men (privates, private first class, corporals, etc.). The other two sergeants, Franklin and Douglas also had two NCOs, or juniors, but their NCOs had three enlisted men to order around. Different people from the corps were trained in different areas, such as engineering and mechanics. Mouthy was actually a specialist in logistics. He had been assigned specifically for this mission and wasn't always attached to this unit. There was a specialized radio technician and a couple of dual-schooled people. There were four riflemen, and they were not specialized in any technician training, so they usually did the patrols and heavy lifting. This was a technical crew, so there wasn't a single combat specialist here. Everyone had gone through basic, though, so they all had combat training. Basic training made them better than any one of us civilians. It was easy to forget and to feel like the army was guarding us. It was an illusion we used to feel safe. This helped when you were trying to ignore the fear that lurked outside.

I had never been the town hall meeting type; I tended to zone out. This was different since it was the first time Lieutenant Brick

—or Roberts—was running the show. He stood up in front of the crowd and raised the hand that wasn't holding his clipboard.

"All right, folks, simmer down please," he said.

I grinned. His accent was so Texas. It felt like home to me.

"This being our first briefing, I feel we should get everyone up to speed. As many of you already know, I am Lieutenant Eugene Roberts, in command of Second Platoon. We are with the 414 Army Corps of Engineers, deployed from the North Atlantic Division out of Whitney Point." He rattled that off with the ease of repetition. I knew it was important and told us all kinds of things, like whom he answered to. However, I had no idea how to find any of that out. It always sounded so official when they gave that information, though.

He didn't bother waiting for anyone to process what he'd already said; he just continued his speech. "Here is what we know. Just over two weeks ago, we suffered through major geomagnetic storms. These solar storms caused massive infrastructure damage. This company was deployed to establish a relay station to help reconnect essential communication. Getting the radio tower operational is our primary objective. However, I want to assure all of you, we will do everything in our power to make sure you are secure and are evacuated as soon as possible."

He paused and looked out across the crowd. The tension was very heavy in the quiet room. "I know you are scared. I know you want the lights on. I know you are desperate for news about what is happening out there. The truth is we have very little information about what is going on out in the world. But I can tell you what is happening here. We got the facilities working so that we could get people into the dorms and out of the tents. We are working to restore power, so that we can get the lights on. It is a slow process. Even if we get power, most if not all the light bulbs we have found are completely burned out. There is no quick fix here. But there is good news."

He smiled and nodded to a few of the people in the front row.

"Due to some very hard work, we were able to get a hand-crank powered ham radio operational. Using Morse code, we were able to connect to our command and report in. We were able to receive some limited information. We will keep you updated."

It took a few minutes for the rush of comments and questions to die down. I was impressed. I had seen the damage done to the electronics when I was looking for wires. I was stunned they had managed to get anything working. Never underestimate the Army Corps of Engineers.

"I helped Daddy do it," Zyada mumbled to me.

Albert shushed her with a wave. When he scanned those around us, there was more worry on his face than would normally follow a mild disturbance by a child. Either he was overreacting, or he was reacting to something I didn't see.

"As of now we have been sending communication through a series of relays and shortwave radios. They aren't military but they are all we have been able to make contact with. This is how we sent and received our intel". His voice was even and calm as he continued. "Fort Drum took some damage but is still operational. We have brought them up-to-date on our status, and they will be sending out a supply convoy. We have told them about you, and they are looking at a number of contingencies. The commander there has assured me that he will do everything he can to get you to a safe location as soon as possible."

Ninety miles away would have been an hour-and-a-half drive last month. Now it was a trip to China.

"In fact, they have already sent a supply convoy headed to us, a group of five large trucks and two jeeps. They should be here no later than the end of this week. Even if they have to clear some roads, it shouldn't be much longer."

The room filled with noise as people cheered, shouted, and hugged. A couple of people closed their eyes and looked to be praying. The overflowing energy in the room seemed to vibrate my very skin. I felt myself smiling as I looked up into Albert's face. The energy on my skin turned into icy fingers. He wasn't smiling. He was staring hard, his face tight. I followed his eyes to where he was looking. He was staring at Lieutenant Brick.

Lieutenant Brick didn't smile either. He watched the crowd, his face unreadable. I looked around at the other soldiers. None of them were smiling. Some looked at papers in their hands or stared up over our heads, but not one of them was looking at us. Everything in their body language screamed, "We have a secret!" A shiver ran through me. Brick had said they told Fort Drum about us, but the FEMA people should have already reported that when they arrived at Drum? So what happened? I flashed back to the dead bodies at the fire station and the men in prison jumpers on Main Street. I took Albert's hand. He forced a little smile for me and squeezed my hand.

The sergeant whispered in the ear of the LT, who nodded and waved a hand. "Folks, hey... people!"

Everyone settled down at once, eager to hear more.

"We have a lot to do before they arrive. Everyone is going to have to chip in. I know you are all civilians, but until you are evacuated, or relief arrives, I am going to need you all to work together." There was a rousing thrum of agreement. It seemed that Lieutenant Brick knew what he was doing after all.

It didn't take long to pass out new assignments. Everyone was happy to be of assistance. All the jobs were broken up into smaller tasks. We were put into groups to be headed by one of the enlisted. Those of us in charge of acquisitions were now to work in groups of at least five individuals, and there would be three groups. Our job was no longer limited to people who volunteered. People could be assigned to do it. However, it also meant that now we could be told where to go and at what times. We could haul more together; from places we had only scouted before. We would be given areas to clear in a grid. Remember lesson five, security and people are a double-edged blade.

It might have been my imagination, but I could have sworn I

felt the lieutenant's eyes on me when I was given my group assignment. I felt my hackles rise. I didn't take well to being hedged in. It wasn't that it was a bad plan; I just didn't like being forced to do it. The assignments were finished quickly. The lieutenant closed by wishing everyone a good night and telling us to get some rest. He turned sharply and walked off the stage.

No one asked any questions, not a single one. Everyone was happy to just accept the good news. I didn't ask either. Even though I had one in my throat. I still felt the coldness on my skin. There were so many missing pieces. I glanced around and saw that the soldiers were smiling now, talking to everyone. Even Lieutenant Brick wore a smile. Everyone wanted to enjoy the food and good humor. So, I kept my questions to myself. There is no faster way to make enemies than to tell unpopular truths. This meant I had to shut Albert up before he said something too. He was far too honest for both our sakes.

I pulled Albert close and whispered in his ear. "I saw it too. We will talk about it later. Just try to smile for now. Don't scare the kids." I kissed his cheek. He nodded to me, hugging me tightly. His smile would have fooled almost anyone. We kept right on smiling through the small talk and potluck. We didn't say anything as we took the kids home.

We went right on not saying anything about the situation while we finished the last chores and got the kids into bed. When all the candles were out and the children were asleep, Albert and I sat in front of the glowing embers of our evening fire. The air was warm in the dark room. It was an unspoken rule: we didn't scare the children. Some people believe that kids are weak and fragile, and we have to protect them. We didn't believe that. I knew that kids had survived the Great Depression, the Industrial Age, the French Revolution, and World Wars I and II. They might suffer, but they survived. Children were resilient if you raised them that way. But that didn't mean I was going to be the one who ruined

Santa. I wasn't going to take away the idea that Mommy and Daddy could keep them safe.

The world would eventually do that all on its own. As they got older, they would understand that the world wasn't fair or just or even very nice. However, I was going to let them hold on to magic for as long as possible. They didn't see Mommy cry, and Daddy was big and strong and would protect us all. Albert sat with his arms around me, looking at the glowing light. His voice was soft, barely there over the crackle of wood. People tend to whisper in the dark. I believe it's a holdover from our ancient ancestors, when we had to be wary of nighttime predators.

"It reminds me of when they would change heading on the ship." His words tickled the hair on my head. I tucked my head under his chin and stroked his forearms softly.

"Whenever it would happen, the officers couldn't look people in the eye. I remember the first time I realized it. One night we were headed to Australia, and the next morning none of the officers would look me in the eye. I realized what had happened when I reported a malfunction in the number one gyro because it read northeast heading instead of south." He shifted, placing his cheek against the top of my head.

"It could just be that he doesn't have the info. Maybe he doesn't know if the evacuation group made it to Drum." I whispered back. "If they are using Morse code, it could be hard to send specifics. If the trucks already left, maybe it's because Manus and the others reached the base. It's the military; they are always very need-to-know. Maybe he just didn't want to make promises that he couldn't keep." I tried to sound upbeat and certain.

"There are plenty of ways to give the intel with Morse code. I am so pissed. No one asked. It was like they were perfectly fine not knowing. That's why he led with the news about the trucks. I think there is something else. It felt more like there was something specific he wasn't saying. Whatever it was, it must be pretty bad. I know that look. I have seen it before, when I was still in. It's like they don't want to tell us the ship is sinking." He squeezed me tight, and I felt him shiver in the warm room.

This was something to remember about marrying military men: there would be moments like this. These were the moments when you just held them. You didn't say anything; you didn't move. You just held on and tried to squeeze their broken pieces back together. All vets handled their past differently. Some handled it fine; others not so well. PTSD was different for everyone. I turned slightly and wrapped my arms around Albert. I shifted my weight back and forth, so we rocked slowly. His whole body seemed to vibrate with tension, his breathing was uneven, and his skin was clammy. I hummed softly. It wasn't any particular song. It might have been something I had heard before or something I'd pieced together from different songs. I just made sure it kept time with us rocking, for as long as it took; you couldn't rush these things. I knew the moment had passed when his skin stopped feeling cold and he started moving himself to our rhythm. He brushed my hair back with his fingers. I kissed his neck and relaxed against him.

"It is going to be OK. We will find out what it was they weren't telling us, and we will handle it. We'll figure it out and make the best of it. We always do," I whispered against his neck.

He laughed softly at my little mantra, the same one I had used when he had lost his job and when I had found out I was pregnant, the same one I had used when we'd had to fight the courts and his ex for custody of his son. In one crisis after another, it was our magic spell. It helped get us back up when life knocked us down. This time it helped us get up and go to bed. He was asleep before he hit the pillow. I drifted off to the sounds of my sleeping family.

seven
thursday, 8:15am

First Baking Day

LIKE LAUNDRY DAY, there would now be a baking day. Baking was not something you wanted to do every day. Even if you could find premade bread somewhere, it was probably moldy by now. Preservatives kept bread good for a while, but the bread sitting at the store had already been on the road for over a week before arriving. With as wet as this place was, things molded fast. I was going to use a makeshift brick oven Albert had put together. If it worked, we could show other people how to build them.

The tricky part for me was the little external gauge we had for temperature. I knew it wasn't very accurate. However, I had a watch. That meant I could time it. I had prepared regular-sized loaves and two smaller mini loaves. I put the mini loaves in as a test. The sun was shining, and the air was nice and cool, which made sitting next to the hot little oven rather pleasant. I hoped the army boys could get one of the bigger ovens working. After one loaf undercooked and the other turned into a blackened brick, I managed to produce about six loaves of warm, steaming goodness. My heart breaks for anyone who has never had homemade, hand-kneaded bread.

Bread making was one of the things in life I was truly grateful to have taken the time and effort to learn how to do. The first and foremost was learning to read. Don't laugh—I struggled with it as a child. I had to work hard to overcome my dyslexia. One of the truly defining moments in the shift from humans' wretched existence to better civilization was literacy of the populace. The second-most important thing I had learned was how to use a firearm. Making bread was in the top ten, along with how to waltz, milk a goat, and sew. I had made cheese once or twice, but I was going to have to get a book on that. See, the reading thing never stops being useful.

Back to the bread. There were fresh beautiful loaves cooling on the counter. I was particularly proud of these loaves because they had come out that perfect golden color. They had risen nicely and smelled amazing. They were a rich, heavy loaf of white bread, not like that junk in the store. This bread was a meal. This was the kind of bread where people could eat one slice with butter and be full for the rest of the morning. I called it my butter and honey bread, because that was all it needed.

I cut slices and set them aside to cool for Victor and Zyada, who had been prowling impatiently for a taste. We were all quietly munching slices when the first visitors arrived. Some of the men had smelled the bread on their way to their stations and had come over to see what was cooking. I cut them a taste, and they headed off happily. After them, it was Alice, the baby, and Samara and then a whole passel of kids. Before long, I was down to just three loaves. I started stonewalling people and making apologies about having only a little left. I had to give that speech about fifteen times before it was late afternoon.

If there is something I have always known about people, it is that they are nice as long as you give them what they want. Once you don't, they stop being nice real fast. The only way to make them not nice faster is to give what they want to someone else. Then they get downright mean. That is why I was not surprised when a group of less-than-nice people marched up the little path to our home, army in tow. About fifteen people in total were harassing Lieutenant Brick himself on the way to our porch. Three of the women I had turned away grumbled and shuffled, along with their husbands, behind Lieutenant Brick. An annoyed-looking Mouthy was also grumbling as he rushed ahead to reach me before anyone else.

"I had nothing to do with this bunch of bitches whining," he assured me as he arrived. "I mean, no disrespect—the bitch-husbands is bitches just like the bitch-wives. Bitchin' is a verb, ya know? It means to bitch, to gripe. A person that bitches is a bitch. So they's all bitches."

I was sitting in a rocking chair that had come with the little porch. I was using the outside afternoon light to sew up some of the tears in my pants. Victor and Zyada were napping. Albert was resting his back, and Nathan was sitting on the porch steps, reading a book. Nathan sensed the hostilities coming and went inside without being told. The boy had good avoidance instincts. The angry horde stopped at the bottom of the steps. I didn't get up as I continued my stitches. I knew how this game was played.

Tamping down my annoyance, I looked up and gave Lieutenant Brick a pleasant smile. "Afternoon, Lieutenant. What can I do you for?" I said it like a lady in an old western movie, when the sheriff had just rolled up. I let some of my Texas drawl seep out.

The lieutenant gave me a little sideways smile. He caught my drift and stuck his thumbs in his belt buckle. "Well, ma'am, seems we have a bit of a disturbance here."

I finished my line of stitches and tied it off while he spoke. "My, my, that's a right shame. What seems to be the problem?" I tucked my needle away, just barely stopping myself from adding "Sheriff."

"Hoarding! You're hoarding supplies," one of the angry women said from the back.

I heard Mouthy grouse as the scent of the bread hit him. "Damn. Maybe I'm a bitch too."

I raised an eyebrow. I had expected to be accused of this at some point. After all, Mouthy and I were working a bit different than everyone else. Getting to play by different rules made you a target for this sort of thing. It just seemed early to me. After all, fresh supplies were on their way. I had figured things would have to get a lot worse before people started noticing that my kids weren't going hungry or that we still had certain supplies. People resented whoever still had what they had already used, or if they at least appeared to. I set my sewing to the side and slowly stood up, looking down at them.

I knew reciprocity was on the shady side, but fuck it. I was the only one who had been willing to take the risks of salvaging. My risk was a benefit to everyone here. I forced myself to maintain a pleasant smile and slipped my hands into my pockets to hide my clenched fists.

It had been a mistake for them to stop at the bottom of the stairs. That left me on higher ground. It literally let me look down at them. Body language and position are very important to winning an argument. I leaned casually against the post at the top of the steps. I waited to see if anyone else had anything to say. People in the back looked angry but unsure. Mouthy looked genuinely pissed as other people spoke up.

"Lieutenant, these two have been sneaking in supplies and hiding them so they don't have to share with everyone!" She was gesturing angrily at Mouthy and myself. I didn't know her name, but I had seen her around. "We all have to help each other. Everyone has worked together. No one should be exempted from cooperation. Here she is squatting in someone's home, looting wherever she wants, and keeping whatever she pleases."

I gritted my teeth; she was really on a roll. It was like watching a scene from a propaganda movie. I kept my face calm. I knew any reaction would only feed the beast. I had a feeling that public shaming was kind of her thing. I had seen this sort of thing before, where if the victim of such an attack put up any resistance, it only proved they were deserving of the attack. Circular logic like that had been allowing persecution for centuries. The names and causes changed, but the methods seldom got updated. Why change what works, right? She genuinely believed she was in the right. I wasn't struggling like everyone else, so I must be cheating. That was, of course, just her perception, but perception makes reality. She didn't know and probably would not have cared about my reality. I was scared and tired. My body hurt like a son of a bitch. I would never be able look at pink boots again, but she could see only her side of things. Therefore, there was no point in arguing. I had to keep telling myself that in my head—because I swear I was about half a heartbeat away from making her eat my shoe.

"Can't you smell it?" She turned back to Lieutenant Brick. "Lieutenant Roberts, when was the last time *you* had anything fresh-baked? They didn't bother to share with anyone else. They didn't even help anyone figure out how to bake for themselves. The rest of us are standing in the soup lines and trying to cook over little fires and makeshift grills!"

She wagged her finger at me. If I had been any closer, I would have grabbed a hold of that finger and given it a twist. "It's not right!" she shouted. "You should be ashamed!"

I watched the people behind her nod along and parrot her words and actions. It was like something out of an old horror movie. It was strange to watch people get this worked up over loaves of bread. The smell of bread had a primal effect on people. Everyone recognized it. If you ever doubt the power of bread, think about the French Revolution; they didn't start beheading the rich when they ran out of cheese. The Romans didn't appease the masses by giving away wine at the gladiatorial games. All that these sheep were missing were pitchforks and torches. That thought kept me from telling them all to just kiss my ass.

"Ma'am," Albert addressed the woman from in the doorway as

he arrived on the scene. He was holding his back. He didn't step all the way out but instead leaned against the door frame. He was trying to hide the pain from either his hip or his knee. "Where were you and your husband when I was building that oven?" I could hear the resentment in his voice. He used his angry but polite tone. He was too honest for this fight. Anything he said, she would just use later to bad-mouth him. I put up a hand and smiled at him. I had this.

This woman had made a mistake. She had jumped the gun. She did not know me well enough to bring this to my door. The disparity between people wasn't big enough yet. There were many recipients of the things I had brought back. Resentment wasn't high enough yet to overcome my good standing. She should have waited. This was a common mistake. I kept to myself, so perhaps she was under the impression that I was shy or introverted. I was neither of those things. Most people were not good at confrontation. They didn't know how to hold their ground and argue a point without insult or anger. Honestly, the art of the argument was really being lost. Dueling with words was one of my little brother's favorite games. We had been very competitive as children and sparred regularly.

It was entirely possible that this was all about her being upset that I had refused her invitation to attend the church group and that my muffins had been well received at the briefing. Some people were just petty. But raking me over the coals was not enough for her today. She had to drag Mouthy along with me. And that, ladies and gentlemen, was unacceptable.

"That Alonzo is in on it with her too," the woman said. "He handles her supplies personal, making sure she gets the best. He always takes care of her before anyone else." Her expression turned to one of scandalized outrage. "Maybe she has been taking care of him as well. Who knows what kind of arrangement they have?" She spat out the insinuation, the words dripping with contempt.

Her tone and expression made it clear what she thought. I

heard Albert groan behind me. I couldn't tell if it was because of the accusation or because he was standing for so long.

Mouthy decided he'd had enough at that point. "Hey, wait a minute there, lady. Let's be clear about one thing—I don't need to use supplies to get tail. And she doesn't need to make any special deals to get what she needs. She's better at the whole salvaging thing than most of the others combined. I get what I need from her. When your old man got sick, it was *her* that brought in the meds. She doesn't get first pick; she gives everything she don't need to everyone else. She don't need supplies from us. So why don't you just shut your—"

"Private!" Lieutenant Brick barked.

Mouthy's mouth shut so fast that his teeth clicked together. He snapped a sharp and well-practiced salute to the LT. For a moment, I actually believed he was a soldier. It was weird. The woman wasn't looking at Mouthy now. She was staring directly at me. It was a long piercing look before she turned indignantly to the LT.

Sometimes I think about that moment. I want to say that deep down I knew something was wrong. I feel like I should have sensed something off about her. I should have seen the hate inside of her, felt the blackness. But honestly, she just seemed like an entitled upper-class ultra-right-wing nut. That's the problem with true sociopaths; they seem just like everyone else. I have no idea why I became her target or what I did that offended her. Maybe nothing. In the end, it doesn't really matter. At the time I had no idea what kind of creature was standing at the bottom of my stairs. If I had, I am not sure what I would have done.

Since I didn't know, I pushed down all my anger and irritation. I kept a smile in place and played the game. "I understand—it's frustrating that we don't have everything we are used to. We're trying to figure out a way to make more bread. It's a lot of work to build an oven, even when it is very small. We were waiting until we knew the design would work before showing people how to build one. We were really hoping to get the big ovens operational. Making bread is a serious effort. We would need a half dozen ovens and people to work a whole day to make enough bread for everyone—even if we had the supplies." My years of customer service in the food industry had taught me a few tricks for how to deal with entitled upper-class pricks. She was using indignation and insult, so I had decided to counter with patient condescension.

"Well, since it worked out for you, are you going to share?" called an annoyed voice from the back.

The woman snapped a look at the man. She knew that cross talk would give me an advantage.

"Absolutely!" I assured him with a smile. "We are happy to share how we did it." Looking back to the LT, I added, "We are happy to help the group."

The crowd nodded and shifted, and I knew I was gaining ground. I really shouldn't have been so smug.

There are moments in life when you learn very valuable lessons. This was when I learned to be very careful with what I said to older men in uniform. Brick wasn't exactly old, but he was older than the other soldiers, probably five to ten years older than me, and you didn't get to be a man of rank and age without learning a few maneuvers. "Old age and treachery will win against youth and exuberance," my mother would say.

"That's good to hear, ma'am. I'll have Mouthy here make the necessary arrangements, and you can set up wherever you need to. I expect there to be fresh bread by the end of the week."

My smile suddenly felt painfully stretched and uncomfortable on my face. I looked at Mouthy, who looked as confused as I felt. "Wait, what?" was all I managed to get out before clever Lieutenant Brick turned to Mouthy.

"Make sure Mrs. Sales has everything she needs," the lieutenant said. "Get the ovens built close to the kitchen. Until further notice, Mrs. Sales will be in charge of providing bread and assisting the mess." The sly bastard looked over his shoulder at me and gave a wink. "Thank you so much for your generous offer to help your fellows, Mrs. Sales."

I managed to keep that uncomfortable smile on my face until Lieutenant Brick turned to the angry woman.

His voice was stern as he addressed her. "Just so we are clear, up until this very moment, Mrs. Sales was not required to provide anything to anyone. Maybe you haven't fully comprehended the situation here. This is not a refugee camp. She is not employed by the US government. She does not work for you. No one here has to give *anyone* anything. This is not a discussion. Either ask nicely or fend for yourself. I am not here to settle your petty squabbles. I assume, Mrs. Kerns, I won't be hearing any more on this subject. " He nodded once and turned on his heel, heading away from all of us.

She didn't respond, though I had a feeling she would have a few things to say when she got home. It didn't occur to me to care all that much. I had a few choice words I wanted to throw at the departing Lieutenant Brick myself. I had absolutely no desire to be the bread maker for this group, especially after this little display. Didn't he have a clue how long it took to make bread? I winced when I realized I was clenching my fists so hard that I was leaving marks in my palms.

As he followed after Lieutenant Brick, Mouthy handled the task of cursing the departing people with expertise. "Good thing you were here, Lieutenant. I would have had to call her a cunt. I know I am supposed to be nice to the civilians, but I just can't stand useless stupid bitches that complain because you're doing them a favor." He wore a satisfied smile as he trailed after his lieutenant, who didn't respond. "Cunt or twatapotamus? Can't decide which. Either way, she needs to plug that leak in her face-hole." I imagined that his one-sided conversation would last the rest of the evening.

Scandalized gasps and murmurs followed the crowd as they dispersed without looking at me.

I sat back down on my porch and lit a smoke as I tried to do the math in my head. How much bread did a group of this size need? After a few puffs, I stopped. I hated math, and it was just making me more aggravated. I started thinking about where to find all the supplies instead. I took out my little notebook to make my lists. *Just enough for a week*, I told myself, *because then the trucks will come, and everything will be taken care of.* Yeah, I didn't believe that either.

As Albert set down a note in front of me, I smiled and hugged his arm. Written on it was the list of ingredients for one hundred loaves of bread, with scaled quantities. I hated math; Albert loved it. Teamwork made the dream work.

I checked out my little notes about things I had found. All the items on my list were within a half-mile radius. There were a lot of little restaurants around the campus. Although almost all the perishables were either gone or rotten, the supplies and nonperishables were useful. People took things like canned goods and packaged foods; not many thought to take yeast, flour, or baking soda. I also had found a big case of canned peaches. Like I said before, scavenging has a steep learning curve. Everyone grabs the easy stuff. People in desperate situations don't think long-term, so they go with quick, easy, and portable. I looked at it the same way I did shopping. I had to think, *what can I get that will make more than a single serving or just one meal?* The person who takes the time to think ahead is the one who won't be hungry when all the little bags of chips and cans of soup are gone.

So later on that day, I went around and met up with my newly assigned group of gatherers. That's what I called us, because "scavengers" sounded, well, awful. Were we buzzards or something? When I was a kid, a bunch of friends and I had thought it would be cool to call ourselves "the Scavengers." My family had moved off the farm and into a cramped duplex in a barrio, which in the Southwest was a poor neighborhood, filled mostly with those of Hispanic descent.

I was twelve and didn't really understand that my family was poor. My brother and I loved our new neighborhood. We loved all the abuelas that would pinch our cheeks and put little candies in our pockets. It didn't seem weird to me that the neighbor who babysat us after school was a stripper. We just liked that she had a friendly pit bull to play with. She taught us how to play gin and hearts. We liked that her boyfriend was a big, tough bouncer who had stopped that gang member from beating up our friend's older brother. We were young and truly carefree; it was before smartphones, before emails, before computers.

However, even then we seemed to understand that danger was close. Gang violence got worse every year. We traveled in groups to and from school so no one got jumped. We never went very far from our street without someone. Like baby gazelles in the savanna, we seemed to sense that lions were just waiting for us to step too far away from our herd. We decided to make our own gang so that we could protect each other. Little geniuses, I know. We were "the Scavengers" because we searched for things to recycle or repurpose and sell for money. Oh yes, we were little adventuring entrepreneurs. We did everything from looking for quartz and arrowheads to braiding friendship bracelets and doing odd jobs for people in the area. We were actually pretty well known in our little corner of the world.

What did we do with all this scavenged loot? Well, we would gather all our money together, and then we all would walk down to the little convenience store three blocks over and buy as much ice cream or sweets as we could afford. Yep, that was our big payday. In our defense, it was like 102 degrees most days in the summer, so seriously, all you wanted was an icy pop. Then we would sit under the only tree in our neighborhood and play whatever we could manage in the heat.

Though I remembered the Scavengers with fondness, it still sounded like something a twelve-year-old had come up with. For the current situation, "the finders" or "the gatherers" was better in my opinion. Other people seemed to prefer "finders." This sounded like something chosen by a teenager. God forbid someone think us uncool. It did sound better than looter, I guessed.

Back to the point: I gathered up my assigned team of finders. We had coordinated a bit before now, though that had been nothing formal. We just didn't want to search over an area someone else had already worked. I stopped by the places where they were camped or shacked up. I gave them my plan for the bread. Since everyone wanted fresh bread, they were eager to get started on finding supplies. One of the ladies even offered to help with baking, if she got to pick her own loaf. I didn't have a problem with that.

It was important to understand the value of things, especially favors. Maybe I would make that Foraging lesson number seven. I hadn't decided yet. It was nice to have people to talk to, though it was hard to work as a team. It was a bit like trying to get a bunch of cats to focus on the same thing at one time. When we came across some chocolate tucked underneath a big industrial-sized bag of sugar, we had to take a moment and discuss how to handle it.

We finders were a special breed. We understood that material possessions were only as valuable as their function and their perceived value. Even though this was generic baking chocolate in those weird little cubes, it might as well have been Aztec gold. It was precious and cursed.

"We split it evenly and keep it for ourselves." I will not name who said what, to protect their identity.

"And if someone finds us with it? No way. People are already weird about us getting better stuff than the rest. You saw the people going after Mouse. Now she has to work double duty."

"We could just leave it here and come back for it later. Or just forget we even saw it." We had already counted the bars, only seven.

"How about we don't?"

"Don't what?"

"Don't split it—just take it to be used in the kitchen for everyone. That's baker's chocolate; it's not very good on its own. It's not even sweet. We take it back, and we make something special."

There was a long silence as we all considered this altruistic idea.

"Yeah, like cupcakes. I love chocolate cupcakes."

"Yeah, and I think the kids would like it. Everyone agree?"

There was another long pause. Then, with a ridiculous amount of seriousness, we all nodded, though we quickly covered up this moment of generosity.

"If we find any decent candy, we are just going to eat it on the spot."

The suggestion received enthusiastic agreement. This seemed to make everyone feel better. A special breed were we. This little moment of democracy seemed to do something more than make cupcakes; it bonded us.

Suddenly, we weren't five stray cats. We were "the Finders." I didn't realize it at the time, but that was the moment things started. The Finders served as the beginning of our tribe, the new Scavengers. Just like when I was a child, there was a sense of looming predators just at the edges of our little world. For now, we kept the darkness at bay with our little flicker of hope.

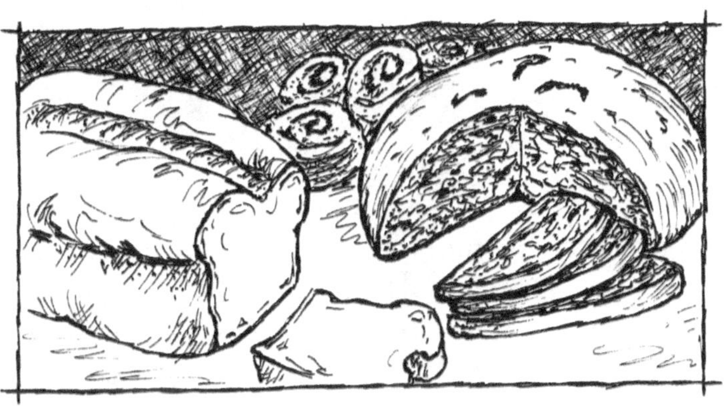

eight
saturday, 7:10am

Official Baking Day

A HOW TO GUIDE ON baking bread: Ingredients, blood, sweat, tears, and flour. Instructions: pain, work, more pain, more work. At least that's how it feels. Bread is like hope. It can be warm and wonderful. It can grow stale and brittle. It can sustain you even if you have nothing else. It's *not* easy to create. However, once you have begun, you always wind up with more than you expected.

Bread became vilified in recent years because of carbs and gluten. People failed to realize how important bread really was. Baking bread is hard, time-consuming work. Throughout most of history, bread was a major source of a person's nutrition. It was full of grains, carbohydrates, and even protein. A person could survive on bread and water, without much else. In many points in history bread was all that was available

Mouthy proved able to work miracles. The day after the baking chocolate was recovered, I found myself in the most surprising location. A kitchen workspace that had been cleared for me. Three men wearing aprons over their uniforms were scrubbing everything vigorously, working hard to prepare the kitchen. I will tell you, nothing makes you feel more powerful than having young men in uniform scrub a kitchen clean for you. Three ladies from the retirement village, Viola, Barbara, and Sharon, had come down, though one was here only for company and to give her recipes. Viola's arthritis made it impossible for her to work. The women were old but still very sharp.

We sat together, poring over my mother's ancient cookbook, one of the few possessions I still had. The pages were old, yellowed, and frayed. The cover had been repaired repeatedly. Notes were written in the margin, and I had little cards to mark my favorite places. After a bit of debate about how much bread each person should get, we finally decided that a one-pound loaf per person was adequate.

My recipe was set up to make four, one-pound loaves. I started working the math out on a piece of paper, but the ladies did it all in their heads. Never underestimate old ladies. We decided to make the bread in batches of twelve, because we had only three bowls big enough to handle all the ingredients. We were doing a rising loaf, so there would be a lot of kneading involved. It was hard work to manhandle twelve pounds of dough.

First measure your lukewarm water and add your sweetener. Then mix in your yeast. Then just leave it someplace warm for a while. You are looking for the cloudy water to bubble. The more bubbles the more active the yeast.

We set the first massive bowls to rise—lukewarm water and honey mixed with yeast. We had decided to use honey because sugar was more widely needed in other recipes. We let the yeast bubble and germinate for fifteen minutes before we added any flour. Then we used beaten eggs and powdered milk. Eggs would give the bread more substance, and powdered milk would give it a smoother texture. We used a mix of all-purpose flour and whole wheat.

Next comes the hard part: add half the flour and stir for one hundred beats. That might seem easy, but you aren't dealing with cake mix here. It will have the consistency of thick, slick mud. It is important to stir a hundred beats or until the top of the mix was shiny, your arms burn, and it feels like the muscles in your triceps and biceps are going to tear themselves off the bone. When you have reached that point you know it is time to set it aside to rise.

We set the bowls in the warm spot near the ovens with a wet towel over the top to keep the draft off. We had to let the dough rise for forty-five minutes. Once again, my watch played an important role here. Next, we took our rising monster of dough and added oil, salt, and more flour.

It is particularly important to *not mix* your dough at this point. Don't stir! Fold in the next set of ingredients, gently pulling the mud over onto itself from bottom to top. It is important not to tear the mud apart. It will stretch as the gluten develops. That is how the bread will get fluffy.

After we folded in the oil and flour and salt, we let the dough rise *again* for sixty minutes. Then we punched it down. Yes, that is exactly what it sounds like. We pushed a fist into the dough knocking the air out of it. The ladies called it kitchen violence. I called it stress relief. Once we had the first round of dough out on the counter, we washed the bowls. Then we set out the next batch of yeast and honey-water to bubble. We all took sections of the dough and began to knead it. During the times one batch was resting or rising we would work on the next batch.

Do not fear punching your dough and squishing it. Give the area where you are going to knead the dough a light dusting of flour. You will want to work it until the dough gets a nice, smooth elastic texture. It will take a little time to get there so be patient. If you want to add things like nuts or raisins, now is when you would do it. You will be looking for the point where the dough holds a shape and doesn't stick. Finally, you cut it into separate one-pound parts. Then shape the pieces, cover again, and let them rise one last time for fifteen minutes. I usually put small slits across the top of the loaf at an angle, so the crust doesn't split.

We did not have proper loaf pans. We had to use the schools

big flat baking trays. We decided to make our bread in a rough log shape. We wanted it to be easier to slice the bread for sandwiches.

If you have loaf pans, make sure they are oiled before putting the bread in. Any oven safe container will function. The bread will just be whatever shape it was baked in. You may have to adjust cooking temps or times, but it will still bake. An egg wash should always go on right before the loaves go into the oven. Bake a one-pound loaf for fifty-five minutes at 350 degrees. It should reach an internal temperature of 200 degrees. I look for a deep, dark golden-brown color for the crust. There should be a hollow thump sound when you tap the bottom of the loaf. You are supposed to let it cool before you try and slice it. I always fail at that. It just tastes so good warm and steaming.

Word to the wise: never get punched by a baker. They lift heavy dough and giant bags of flour all day. Those guns are *loaded*! Power lifting builds bulk, but the high-tension repetition that baking requires builds a wiry tone. Bread baking is long and back-breaking work; it takes patience and timing. This is why bakers don't do anything else but bake.

We had to do this over and over. It took all day even with six people working. With twelve loaves per pass, we had to repeat the process nine times. Somehow we got it done, a pound of bread for each person. A big loaf like that should last at least a couple of days. We had started in the morning and had loaves cooling by noon. People were already starting to circle the kitchen like hungry birds. The smell brought them in. Kids played right outside. Some of the army guys came by to bring us lunch. They decided to "help" keep track of the loaves.

It was going to take well into the afternoon to get all 108 loaves made. By noon, everyone was sweaty, talking, and laughing, and before long, we were singing. I think it was Viola who started it; she was sitting by the warm ovens with this tiny smile on her wrinkled face. As the first loaves began to fill the air with the smell of baked bread, she just started.

Viola's voice was soft and fragile like aged lace. It fluttered at first and drifted in pitch but was so beautiful and light, that before long we were all singing with her. I wondered if she was thinking of other kitchens and other women from a long time ago. People kept singing, coming up with songs they knew from the radio or from childhood. By one o'clock, Viola was asleep in her chair. Barbara and Sharon were so tired that they just sat and sipped tea. Other volunteers had taken their place. Albert brought Zyada and Victor by, and they visited with us and the old ladies before joining the kids out front.

By three in the afternoon, Grandpa Silas had set up a grill in the yard by the ovens and was slow-cooking meat. Jeri came in and quietly sang with us and helped lift the heavy loaves onto the cooling trays.

By five, we had begun passing out bread. Others had joined the cookout by the ovens, setting up tables and bringing side dishes and drinks. The large loaves were warm, golden and smelled wonderful. There was one for each man, woman, and child. I was so tired and sore by the time the sun set that I let the others finish up and mostly just supervised.

I watched people as they picked up their bread. The reactions were amazing. Some said thank you; some said things like "God bless you." Some came and took the bread with a look close to shame and resentment in their eyes. One woman started to cry. It was such a strange experience for me. In my mind I knew bread was important, but I had never witnessed anything like this. It was simply bread, and simultaneously it was so much more.

Right when the cooked venison was being passed out, we brought out the chocolate cupcakes. The kids lost their damn minds. You would have thought we had suddenly appeared at the Magic Kingdom from the way these kids screamed. Everyone was smiling. Even Old Man Harris got a cupcake and gave me a wink. I will admit, there have been few moments in my life where I have had as much satisfaction in completing a task. I had just fed the whole camp. I might have cried a little.

Someone was playing a guitar. People were dancing, some sang. Other people grouped together talking and laughing. Suddenly, we were like a true little town. All the things that we typically used to separate ourselves from each other were surpassed by a bridge made out of warm bread. It was like magic.

I leaned my head on Albert's shoulder, exhausted and sweaty. "That wasn't so bad. Actually, it feels good to make so many people happy," I said as I smiled up at him. I took one of the pain pills I had found, though I knew I would have only the one. They were too precious to waste on body ache.

He kissed me and rubbed my aching shoulders. "So you're not mad you had to do so much work?" he said softly against the top of my head.

I groaned as he found knots in my shoulder blade. "The work was hard, but no. I don't mind. Honestly, I liked it. It was like work for the soul or something. Remember, once I told you that cooking for others is like praying to me." As I talked, I dropped my head low to stretch my neck.

He laughed a little and worked on my lower back. "Think you prayed enough for one day?" he asked teasingly.

I laughed a little but mostly just groaned and melted as his hands worked out some of the pain. "Yeah," I said thoughtfully. "It reminds me of something my dad said once." I looked at my children playing with the other kids. "He said if the end comes, and government collapses and society fails, build a community. People need people. People are your greatest threat and your greatest protection."

Albert was quiet for a while. "That's a much better plan than your grandpa's idea about Mormons. Your dad is a smart man. I am sure he is fine, Marlene." He kissed my neck and hugged me tight. He always saw what was beneath my words even when I missed it. I felt something inside my chest quake. I refused to think about it. No, I wouldn't even let my thoughts wander in that direction.

I had kept myself from thinking of my family spread out across the United States. There was so much we didn't know. Everything I had heard was secondhand. People talked about the last news broadcast or radio announcement. We knew that the storm had continued for three days. We knew it had been felt all over the globe. However, we also knew that some places there was barely any damage. Just like in the Adirondacks. There might be places that hadn't been touched at all. Until we got the radio tower working, nothing was certain.

I had to stay positive. Dad was alive. He was in his basement bunker in Spokane, Washington, right now. He was tough, hard, and gnarled as old buzzard jerky. Some stupid solar storm wasn't going to be the end of him.

I could just imagine Mom, sitting on her porch in beautiful Hilo, Hawaii. With her iced tea grumbling to herself, "Oh, now they have a reason not to call, but what was their excuse before?" Mom was just as tough, and she was on the big Island. Of all the places to be during an apocalypse, a tropical paradise didn't seem so bad. She was fine.

I couldn't let myself worry about them. They were all just fine. My older sister had traveled all over the country on her own as a personal chef. She was probably staying with some super wealthy family and their kids right now, making gluten-free waffles or something. My older brother, the techie guy, was most likely mad as hell because his equipment had been fried. It was also just as likely that he was well on his way to rebuilding it out of old parts. My little brother was probably the best off out of any of us. I mean, he was a naval officer on a submarine. Those subs must be shielded against this sort of thing.

I had no way of reaching them, and I couldn't go looking for them. I had to believe that they were all fine. What else could I do? Any other thoughts I shut out or shut down. It was the only way to stay sane really. I couldn't afford to think about brothers I couldn't help, a sister I couldn't save, a mother I couldn't hug, and a father I couldn't run to. There would be a time to think about them, to worry and panic about how to reach them. That time was not now. I hated that they were so far away, that I was so helpless and in the dark about them.

I didn't realize I was weeping until I heard Zyada whisper.

"It's OK, Mommy. I will kiss it and make it better." She kissed a bandage on my hand. I had gotten burned on the ovens earlier in the day. Her gesture helped pull me away from the black hole of my thoughts. The painful flutter and quake in my chest eased, and I was able to breathe again.

I wiped my face and smiled at her. "Thank you, sweetheart. I am much better now," I said, putting a kiss on her forehead. I let out a breath and shook my head as I spoke to Albert and myself. "I am sure they are all OK. We're made tough in my family. It will take more than this to do us in. Seriously, there isn't even a zombie outbreak. It's just not an apocalypse without zombies ... but it's better to just think of here and now. When communication gets restored, we will find everyone. Right now, there is no point in worrying about something we can't do anything about." My voice was even and strong by the end of my little speech. I almost believed it myself.

Albert gave me his little grin and gently bonked his forehead against mine. His voice was soft but warm as he spoke close to my face. "There she is. I was wondering where my little mouse had gone. I was worried all this singing and community-building was making you all mushy. I should have known better. It'll take more than some group picnic to make you go soft. It's all right. We will figure it out. We always do." He rubbed his nose against mine.

"We always do," I said, repeating our mantra.

The mood remained pleasant and cheerful late into the evening. Backyard Tiki torches were lit as the sun set. For once the darkness didn't seem so frightening. People stayed late into the evening. I was practically asleep on my feet by the time we went home.

The next day, the mood of the camp was downright cheery. People walked around smiling and saying hello to each other. The children played in the open grassy areas in front of the college gymnasium, playing with balls someone had found. Everyone seemed to be outside, enjoying the sunshine.

The ladies from the prayer group were making lemonade from real lemons they had found. I will admit it was some damn fine lemonade. I went outside with the kids and let them run and play with everyone else. It was nice to do nothing. I was so sore from the last few days I just found a comfy spot and sat there. I watched and sipped lemonade.

Victor was so happy to be able to run and play chase. He often got tired of holding Mom's hand. Zyada was my little star, but Victor was my rock. One had me looking up; the other kept me rooted. Watching him run still put my heart in my throat, out of fear he would fall. I knew he would. But he needed to learn that falling was OK, that scrapes and bruises weren't the end of the world. These were important lessons for kids and parents. That didn't mean the sight didn't make me flinch every time, just like when Zyada cried to get her way. Parents have to stick to their no. That doesn't mean it's easy. It doesn't mean that you don't sit in another room later and hate having made them sad or that you don't want to just scream. It can drive any parent crazy.

So why do it? For the music that makes mothers and fathers forget hardship and love their offspring—for the timeless music of laughing children. It may come from being tickled or from splashing in bathtubs, digging in sand, or chasing after a ball. Every parent knows it, the sound of true joy, that infectious wonderful sound of a baby's giggle, a toddler's squeal or kids laughing in hysterics. It squeezes your heart, and you don't even realize you're smiling. It is the sound that makes all the tears and whines disappear.

Today that sound had the power to change the world, at least for a little while.

We were all content to pretend the world was fine and sip lemonade, playing with borrowed soccer balls and Frisbees. Those of us who had finished our work at least. Some of the adults even started talking about what they were going to do when they got to the refugee camp. I didn't go that far. I stayed in the moment. I didn't think about what would happen when the trucks came; I focused on the music of my children. It was too beautiful to waste on thoughts of tomorrow.

I tried to play soccer with all the kids, including the teenagers. But I was sore and slow. I still chased the ball up and down the field. Well, mostly I chased the little kids and rolled in the grass. Mouthy put together makeshift bubble blowers from wire. Even Albert came out and had some fun. He helped make pinwheels for all the kids.

Albert's pinwheels hadn't started out as toys. Remember how I said he was always working on one project or another? These pinwheels were a model of some kind, maybe a wind trap. I had no idea what he was doing. Which was the normal state of things with his projects. I think it was supposed to be like a windmill that lays flat and points up. He was making a little prototype to see if it would work. The breeze would turn it, but not very quickly. When he stood up to kick a ball back towards the kids, he accidentally leveled the pinwheel toward the breeze. It spun very quickly, and the kids completely forgot their ball. Next thing we knew, they were all making pinwheels or running around like crazy.

A little before sunset, we ate dinner made of leftovers from the day before. Albert and I bathed the kids and put them to bed. We made love in the front room after the children were asleep. The day had been filled with the last bits of summer. It was like late-harvest berries, full and bursting with sweetness. This warm day had probably been one of the last of the season. The days were getting shorter, and soon fall would be headed into winter. It had been a perfect day. There hadn't been many perfect days even before the lights went out. I was exhausted when I hit the pillow. I should have slept straight through until dawn.

So, when my eyes suddenly snapped open in the middle of the night, I was a bit peeved. I was sore, and I knew I needed my rest, but I couldn't fall back asleep. For whatever reason, I was on high alert. I sat up and looked around the room. All the little ones were accounted for, and Albert was snoring. I slowly got up and went to get myself a glass of water and a bite of bread. The air was cooling, so I checked to make sure the fire was banked and the house was secure. Everything seemed in order as I sipped the water and paced. I finally decided to have a smoke and pulled on my housecoat. I slipped into the shadows of the porch. Covering the match from the breeze, I struck it and relaxed into the chair. I looked out toward the empty road as I blew little smoke rings into the moonlight.

I nearly jumped out of my skin when a deer leapt past me and ran down the hill. It disappeared into the light forest behind the house. There was a lot of wildlife in the area, but I had never been this close to a deer before. One deer turned into a whole pod running downhill past the porch. I watched a couple of does gracefully float through the air past me and some young bucks leap across the yard. I saw a few little fawns wobbling as they followed. The largest buck stood on the edge of the yard and watched me. His antlers were massive, and in the moonlight they seemed to be jagged daggers reaching for the sky.

In just a handful of heartbeats, they were gone, as if they had never been. I could have dreamed the whole thing, but I checked my smoke, and it was still burning. The glowing ember hadn't even moved down the cigarette. I had never seen anything like that. There weren't deer where I'd grown up.

I stood up from the chair, listening to the night sounds. I leaned on the porch rail and looked up at the night sky. It was overflowing with stars. With all the power off, the light pollution that had kept them hidden was gone. Jewels glittered across the black velvet above, filling the night with starlight. I ended up having more cigarettes than I'd meant to, watching the tendrils of smoke curl into the starry sky. The magic of the view stayed with me even as I curled up under my blanket.

Just as I began to drift off into sleep, my eyes too heavy to keep open, a voice in my head whispered, *but what were they running from?*

The next day, I was waiting to get my bandage changed at the infirmary. Albert had insisted that I get a "professional" to look at it. Since the burn was on my right hand, my dominant hand, I couldn't really bandage it, at least not well. I was waiting for the army medic to finish stitching up one of the guys who had gotten hurt. One of the machines they had been trying to restore had shorted and shocked him so bad he had flown back and hit a fence. He had a nasty slash over his eyebrow, but he was going to be fine. Supposedly, it was a good sign because it meant that electricity was being conducted. Honestly, I was enjoying the quiet of the waiting area. I had been working hard and watching the kids for a couple of days straight. I was happy to sit there and work on my Sudoku puzzle while waiting for the medic. I was about halfway through when we heard the awful noise.

A horrific screeching sound exploded into the quiet, followed by a blaring horn, a crashing boom, shouts, and then screams. I don't remember setting the puzzle down. I don't remember running outside with the medic. I don't remember any of that.

However, I will never forget the look of that military truck as it bore down at us. I will never forget the dust and dirt filling the air. I will never forget the pointed guns as marines seemed to explode from every orifice of the vehicle like some horrific clown car. Blood was everywhere, a stark splash of red against the tans and browns of dirt. Everyone was shouting as bloody men helped even bloodier men out of the vehicle.

I don't know how it happened, but soon I was helping carry a stretcher. Then I was helping cut off clothes and applying pressure, then holding equipment. Before I knew it, I was cleaning wounds, helping the few medics and the one pediatrician perform triage.

Ages earlier, when I was still young and just out of high school, I'd had some crazy idea that I was going to be an ER nurse. I went to school for almost two years. I was almost done when I saw my first patient die. I was helpless; there was nothing I could do for him but hold his hand and be with him when he passed. I wept and prayed. When an older nurse told me to hurry up because other patients were waiting, I realized that there was no way that I could emotionally survive being a nurse.

I couldn't be a nurse not because I didn't care, but because I let myself care too much. When I say I "realized" in that moment, I mean that I flipped the fuck out and turned into a sobbing mess and had to leave then and there. It would take a while before I understood that I didn't have the fortitude for nursing. I still carry that with me. I feel like what I learned as a nurse was the most valuable education I ever could have received. Nurses are superheroes.

Because of that training, I could handle a crisis. It was having nothing left to do, no way to help, that tore me apart. I had never regretted being there for that man; I just didn't want to do it again. But that training was part of what led to my helping with these wounded men. It wasn't because I wanted to do it. I moved into action because it was a crisis. I could hear my mother's voice whispering in my ear, "You don't stand by. You step up. Even if all you do is apply pressure and talk to the person, you *do* it". Between that and my training I didn't have a choice I stepped up.

I did many things. I took vitals, helped with stitches, and dressed wounds. It was all a mad rush. Like when you hold your head under water; you could only really focus on the next breath. It was crazy how much of my education and training had stayed with me. I even had to do things I had never trained for in the first place. It was well after dark when the last soldier was finally resting as comfortably as we could manage. I knew we had lost two, but thankfully I hadn't seen it.

I felt dizzy when I finally sat down in the chair I had been in before. I saw my puzzle. I saw a blood-stained hand try to pick up my pencil. It frightened me. It was something out of a horror movie. Then I realized it was *my* hand. I barely made it outside before I started puking in the grass. I don't know how long I sat there shaking before Michael patted me on the shoulder and handed me a bottle of water. He didn't say a word. When I was able to look up at him, he just nodded as if he understood and helped me get to my feet. I didn't need to explain; I didn't need to be embarrassed. He understood. I went and cleaned my hands and face. I helped with one last set of rounds and shook the hands of the rest of the medics. They looked as tired as I felt.

"I'll be back in the morning," I said, and I patted Fisher, the retired pediatrics doc, on the shoulder.

"Get some rest. You did well," he said back to me. We smiled in that way exhausted people do when they don't know what else to say.

The walk home felt long and hard. I would barely remember it later. No bed had ever been softer or more inviting when I finally crawled in. I didn't stir until the sun came in the window. That's how I got my new job at the infirmary.

nine
tuesday, 9:08am

THE NEXT DAY, Albert took the boys and headed over to the main building. He wanted to see what he could find out about the wounded soldiers. I decided to take some of our personal supplies to the infirmary. After working in there, I felt responsible. It had been terrifying how fast we had gone through antibiotics and bandages. We tried to be frugal, salvaging anything we could for reuse even boiling and drying bandages. I was afraid we were going to run out of everything.

Today was all about maintenance care. Zyada came with me. She was only five, but she was great at following instructions and helping. She fetched and carried small items and helped wash and rinse. She held patients' hands and talked to them. That was as important as cleaning wounds and stitches. I was so proud of her. She didn't flinch away or whine about the work. I helped strip beds, bathe patients, and look for infection, wash wounds, and change bandages. I checked IVs, gave meds, and performed a dozen other tasks. For some of our patients it was more important than others to monitor their dressings. Seeping wounds had to be changed regularly.

Zyada found herself a chair and sat with an unconscious blonde soldier. He had been shot twice. One shot was in the leg and the other had cut a deep gouge in his side. We were worried because he had lost so much blood. He was showing signs of infection. His side wound was swollen, the edges an angry red. He had a fever, and his skin was clammy. I had brought antibiotics for him. Dr. Fisher, the pediatrician, came in and helped make sure the meds were administered. He made sure the wound was cleared. He didn't say a word, just nodded before he continued on his rounds. He smiled at Zyada and gave me a nod before leaving.

Zyada was talking to the unconscious man. It seemed to be a story she was making up on the spot. She was using a quiet voice and leaning near his ear. Her voice seemed to settle him, so I let her.

When I was finished and had updated his chart, I looked at Zyada. "Do you want to finish your story, or do you want to come with me?" I motioned to the door.

"Mom! I am just getting to the good part!" She gave me an exasperated look.

I kissed her head. "OK. Finish and then come find me, or wait in the front room for me." I left her, leaving the door slightly open.

The work was hard but important to keeping people healthy. I kept at it. It wasn't like when I had been in training. There were seven patients and none of the right supplies. Our charts were handwritten notes and checklists. I kept a log of when things were done and always wrote down the time. The watch became the hero of the day! At some point the medic, PFC Mark Louis, noticed it and put it to good use. It helped with the dosage and timing of drugs and heart rate.

It was amazing how lucky we were. We had the paramedic Michael, the retired pediatrician Dr. Fisher, and the army medic. There was a marine medic with the group that had come in on the truck, but he had been hit in the leg and was resting. He would be up and able to help in a couple of days.

It was about lunchtime, so I started setting up the lunch trays. The food had been made by the prayer group ladies. I had begun to think of them as the Ladies of the Circle. They had cooked whatever had been donated. It was old-school chicken soup, with bread. I had some for lunch too. It was good, not as good as my grandma's, but then no one's ever was. The downside was that soup was a pain in the ass to deliver. I had a big pot of the soup on a covered wheeled cart along with empty bowls and dishing it out in the rooms. That way it didn't slosh all over the place. The process was slow to say the least.

I heard voices when I came to the room with the recovering marine medic. His name was Dakota, but that could have been a nickname. I won't lie—I snooped. Military personnel were secretive. You had to snoop to know what was going on. If you weren't willing to pry into other people's business, then you just didn't want to know bad enough.

"How fucked was it?" It was PFC Louis speaking.

"My ass is still sore kind of fucked. We had three trucks to start out. Not just any trucks either, the kind of shit you see in hot zones, armored and tactical. We even had Special Forces riding shotgun for us. We had the personnel in the middle of the line, with food up front and equipment loaded in the Deuce taking up the rear." Dakota's voice sounded tired and frustrated as he continued. "It's a good thing too. They trapped the road, with a fucking pit. Food truck took a dive headfirst into the hole. Then we started taking small arms fire. I think we lost the two driving the food truck. The two riding in back came with us, but I heard one of them didn't make it." There was an unspoken question in his voice.

"Yeah, he had a massive chest wound. We did all we could, but we don't have a lot to work with here. We lost him." Louis sounded very somber.

"So who attacked?" That was Lieutenant Brick. I hadn't known he was there until he spoke.

"You don't know?" Louis said quietly, maybe to Brick. I couldn't tell through the door.

"No, not really," answered Dakota. "Could just see a bunch of hostiles in makeshift gear running around. I saw one guy wearing a football helmet. They looked like B-movie rejects. They chased us and tried to shoot out our tires. Dumbasses didn't know that a Deuce and a Half has solids. But when the lead truck crashed into the pit, they swarmed it like fucking ants." He sounded grim.

"That's when we got separated. As the carrier took off in a different route the rest of us loaded into the Deuce with the equipment and rolled out. Honestly, I thought they would have made it here before us. The Deuce was designed to take all kinds of punishment, so we just plowed through a building and gunned it. We had one hell of a driver. I was in the troop carrier when the lead went down. A bunch of us jumped out to grab the guys from the first truck before the hostiles overran them. It was like those food riots we had overseas," Dakota said quietly.

Brick sighed and spoke with resigned calm. "People are people; they're going to do what they have to, especially down in the valley where you drove in from. The fighting there has gotten bad. Ever since the fires burned themselves out, the survivors have struggled to find food. People are terrified and are forming little bands. Some work together, but there have been some violent groups. We are just thankful you made it, son. Get some rest. We need you back on your feet," Lieutenant Brick said kindly.

He had never mentioned any trouble in the valley before. Maybe this was one of the things he had been trying not to say before at the briefing. I thought of Grandpa Silas, talking about Brick's complaints about me leaving the camp.

"Let's hope the carrier shows up," said Dakota. "We aren't much in the way of reinforcements. Most of the combat specialist were in that one. I guess it was good luck, though, that the sniper and his spotter decided to ride with the equipment, and I pulled out two guys from the food truck." Dakota sounded apologetic.

"Good job. It's more than we were hoping for," PFC Louis said.

I backed up, just in case the LT decided to leave the room and counted to fifteen before stepping up to knock. After an acknowledgment from within, I opened the door to bring in the tray. There were polite greetings and thanks for lunch before I headed off to the next patient. I kept a pleasant customer service smile on my face. The information slowly steeped in my brain. It wasn't that I didn't trust the military. It was more that I knew them too well to blindly follow them. The military will do their job to the best of their ability. The thing to remember is that their job isn't protecting people. Their job is to defend the republic, not individuals. They are not public servants. They are the sentinels at the gates. They will defend this country. Individuals needed to be prepared to defend themselves.

The camp was quiet. I walked across the empty quad where the massive army truck had nearly plowed into the infirmary building. My feet stopped at the stains on the concrete. There were massive black scars left behind where the tires had screeched to a halt. Brown stains led toward the building, like someone had been running with leaky paint cans.

I took a few breaths as flashes of bright crimson blinded me. I counted to five in my head before I opened my eyes. I watched the wind rustle the tops of the trees. The weight of it crashed into me. The fear and despair I had managed to keep back threatened to roll over me. Thoughts raced around in my head.

There were so many unknowns. How bad was the damage out there? If these were the trucks they had sent from the base, did that mean we were cut off? We knew there were places with power, but how many? What could drive people to attack a military convoy instead of asking for help? If the convoy had been attacked, what did that mean for the people here? Would the military even try to send an evacuation? Was there anywhere to be evacuated to? Were there even any refugee camps? Did this mean the group that had left camp before hadn't made it after all? The questions I had refused to think about over the last week swirled around in my brain. I knew it was panic. Panic was the first thing you needed to learn to control in a bad situation.

Air in, air out. One. Two. Three. Air in, air out. One. Two. Three.

It was hard to swallow; my throat felt dry. My arms trembled, and I tried to hug myself tight. There was a coppery taste in my mouth as I forced air in and out of my lungs, in through my nose and out through my mouth. I slowed my breathing and focused on what I did know. I knew that some places had been hit worse than others. I knew the soldiers had been sent here. That meant they had received orders. Those orders had come from someone higher up. That meant there were people in those positions to give orders. It meant there was still a chain of command. It meant there was still a government to serve. It meant that there were still people working to put things back together. As long as there were people to rebuild, the world wouldn't end.

Don't panic, I told myself. *You can't do anything if you panic.* I reminded myself of this over and over till all the questions disappeared into the air I blew out. I lifted my head, squared my shoulders, and started my feet moving again. The truck was parked inside the supply area in the gymnasium, to be off-loaded. I wanted to see what new equipment had been sent our way.

It wasn't time for another briefing, but everyone who could make it was there. I found my children coloring with the other kids in the makeshift day care area. Since they all seemed content, I went to find Albert. He was talking with some of the army boys, so I didn't interrupt. No one looked pleased about anything. The whole place buzzed with speculation. Anyone not talking worked to unload and sort the equipment from the two-and-a-half-ton truck.

The army guys had set up a perimeter around the truck with waist-high wooden barricades. My dad called them horse benches. They had four legs and a strong back you could rest heavy objects on. Normally, you would use two, spread apart, and lay wood between them to form a table. Here the army had them standing end to end around the truck to keep the crowd back. This setup wouldn't have stopped anyone, but it was a visual deterrent to show where they wanted people to stand. Like sheep, everyone stood right next to the fence and watched the uniforms unload crate after crate.

It was good that we weren't hungry. There was no food in that truck. Well as far as I could tell. All the crates were hard cases. They looked like drab little olive-green squares and rectangles. Different codes were stenciled in white across the sides. Military camo didn't look like the camo from the movies, with blotches and smears of browns and tans. The newer uniforms looked almost foreign to me with their strange pixelated digital squares. This pattern allegedly worked better than older versions. Even the black combat boots were different from my dad's. It unnerved me.

Once when I was little, my father had shaved off his beard, and I couldn't recognize him. He had suddenly become a stranger. I didn't want to let him hug me, and I cried until he turned and sang "You Are My Sunshine" in his deep rough voice. That's what these uniforms were like for me, a figure I should know but somehow, they didn't seem quite right.

The truck was painted in that strange new style of camo. I don't know why it wasn't just brown or gray like the cargo. Watching the soldiers unload it was like watching a weird game of Tetris in reverse. All the crates were similar colors, so it was strange to see them slowly broken into dozens of smaller pieces. The soldiers then stacked them in some undecipherable order that only Mouthy understood. I drifted at the edge of the crowd till I could move closer to the cab. Everyone was watching the things coming out of the back of the truck, so eyes weren't on the front. The barricades weren't manned, so I stepped around one and slipped up to the truck. I walked calmly around to the passenger side and climbed in, closing the door behind me.

No one even noticed. If you walked around like you belonged

somewhere, people didn't really question it. The military guys were still understaffed, so they were too busy to notice. I quickly looked through the glove box and under the seats. I found a map of the area with a route marked out. There were symbols and letters written on it. I quickly copied the map into my notebook with as many of the symbols as I could. I wrote down the frequency the communication radio was turned to, the mileage of the truck, and even how much fuel was still in it. I found an extra key under the gas pedal. I left it there but noted that too. I didn't touch the gun that was holstered next to the stick shift. I scanned some papers, but they didn't make sense to me. I thought they might be a manifest, but everything had strange designations or crate numbers that I didn't know. I scribbled down a few of these notes but not all.

I put on the marine hat I found on the driver's seat and slipped out of the truck. My feet hit the floor, and I shut the door. I came eye level with a strange mark in the metal. A deep indentation, about a finger's length, was gouged into the armor plate, charred and black. It took me a moment to realize that it was a bullet scar. I ran my finger along it in fascination. I expected my finger to come back smudged and black, but the burn was set into the metal. I became aware of the damage that the truck had endured. The black spots seemed like part of the camouflage. It was like one of those trick paintings. Now that I could tell what the damage was, I understood. The black spots looked like cheetah print mixed in with the rest of the paint. There must have been over a hundred of these spots, too many for me to actually count.

For a moment my imagination took over, and the sounds of gunfire and men shouting echoed through my head, as if the trauma from the battle had absorbed into the metal and spread up through my finger into my brain. The fear, the adrenaline, and the anger seethed under the paint. I had a metallic taste in my mouth as I pulled my hand back. I heard voices coming closer, so I moved away. I made sure my pace was relaxed and easy. I walked back the way I had come.

I am not going to pretend that I don't enjoy being sneaky. I do. I imagine everyone gets a thrill from moving with stealth and managing to go unnoticed. I don't like stealing, but there is something distinctly satisfying about getting away with something. No one even noticed the hat.

Well, at the time I thought no one had noticed my sneaking. I had no idea that this mouse had been spotted scurrying about. Never a good thing for a mouse.

I had a little swagger when I left the truck and went up to stand next to Albert. He was still talking power inverters. I would like to tell you exactly what Albert was talking about with the technicians. The truth was that I had no idea. There were words I recognized, but that didn't mean I knew what they meant. I spoke geek, but not electrician physics quantum-engineering geek. I was a history major, not a science major. That was a different side of the brain.

Albert summed it up for me later. They had been discussing what it would take to convert the power from the generator into the power grid. The generator was a huge metal rectangle that looked like a massive Lego brick with switches and levers on it. This was how I understood it. Imagine a portable mega-water tank that had one spigot and never ran out of water. Awesome, right?

The problem was the spigot was like a fire hose. That made it hard to fill up a cup or a canteen. There needed to be a separate container for it to pour water into, so that the flow could be controlled and used effectively. A second tank took the pressure and included control valves. The valves would allow the water to be spread around. I had no idea how anyone would accomplish that with electricity. This was the reason why I baked bread, rather than fixed batteries.

Albert and the technicians were still in an excited debate about capacity converters, or output or input or hertz or something, when Lieutenant Brick called for everyone's attention. He stood on a platform set up on the left side of the stadium. My first thought was that he looked worn. I had known him for only a few weeks, but he had always seemed so precise in his angles. Right then, he seemed less precisely cut and more jagged-edged. His face had a little bit of stubble, and there were dark circles beneath his eyes. His shoulders were so taut that his movements looked rigid and stiff. Lieutenant Brick was calm as he lifted his clipboard and faced the crowd. He stared out over the small group of humanity and searched for something. A thought filled my head: he was worried.

The people settled immediately. Even my own little chatterboxes were quiet. There was a heavy tension in the silence. I felt my nerves stretch; my skin was suddenly a size too small, and my hair itched. It was so quiet that I swore I could hear the ticking of my watch. His voice startled me when it boomed out over the crowd.

"This is what we know. This was the convoy that was sent to us. We could not be given more details over the shortwave because the connection can't be secured. With the convoy I have received written orders. Our instructions are as follows: to establish a secure and reliable radio relay hub, to fortify and hold this position, and to assist the remaining refugees and those seeking aid as best we can without compromising our first objective. We have to be prepared to hold this position without relief for an indeterminate amount of time."

He stopped there, waiting. It didn't take long for the news to sink in.

"Wait, what?" someone to my left said.

"We have to stay here?" a woman said in a raised voice.

The next person was even louder, and this only escalated. By the fifth person, their voices were a cacophony of panicked questions no one could understand.

The lieutenant didn't move, not our Brick; he just remained in position, all hard edges and uncompromising angles. He waited stoically as people realized that no parade of trucks was going to arrive and whisk them to safety. The illusion was gone. There were tears and angry shouts, denials and accusations. I went and picked up Victor, who was covering his ears. Some of the smaller children had started to cry.

The sergeant stepped up and barked something incomprehensible. The words didn't matter; his voice was deep and sharp enough to cut through the noise. Once the crowd had settled back down, our stoic lieutenant continued to speak.

"I know all of you are upset. There is nothing I want more than to see you all to safety. However, I have my orders. I will help all of you survive out here until help arrives. It's still warm, but cold weather is on its way. We need to prepare for the winter now, so we survive until spring."

"You really think the power will be down that long?" an uncertain voice asked from the crowd.

"We know it will. According to the intel I received, things are ..." Brick took a moment to select his words carefully.

In this moment of silence, Mouthy's voice carried out across the crowd: "A shit show?"

Brick's jaw tightened as he impaled Mouthy with an angry glare, who just smiled in return.

"A mess," Lieutenant Brick continued. "There're places far worse than us. Maybe it was the topography of the land, the composition of the soil; the scientists aren't sure. But some places were hit harder than others. What that means for us is that we were lucky there was anyone who had supplies to give us. With this generator we'll be able to run lights, radios, heaters, and utilities. It'll be tough, but we'll make it through, if we work together. Now let's just deal with the here and now. Otherwise, we won't have a then and there to worry about."

Lieutenant Brick stepped back, and the sergeant stepped forward to speak.

"Everyone, get some rest. We will start setting up duty rosters tomorrow. Everyone who remains here will work here." The sergeant's voice was calm and even encouraging. It scared me a little. It was so different from his normal surly attitude. It reminded me of old science fiction movies. Remember, authorities are only ever encouraging when things are really bad.

I found myself clutching Albert's hand. I didn't want to stand there anymore, but I didn't want to be the first one to walk out. Patience was key. Never rush when you're worried; you will just make a mistake and miss something. When you're nervous or scared, move slowly, deliberately; be certain it is safe before you dash.

Grandpa Silas stepped forward, and in his usual charming way, he spit out of the side of his mouth and practically snarled at the LT and the sarge. "So we're mushrooms now? We supposed to just pretend that an army convoy didn't get jumped on its way here, and there ain't a bunch of boys bloody on beds at the doc's office?"

Oh shit, I didn't think about that. I realized that in the moment, I had forgotten all about the questions around who had attacked the convoy or why. *Very clever, Brick.* He was trying to control what we were upset about, to keep control of the narrative.

There was a muttering of nervous agreement as everyone looked between Silas and Brick. The whole room turned into a middle school playground, with a circle forming around two kids about to fight. The lieutenant looked at the sergeant for a moment and then stepped forward.

"Yes, the convoy was attacked, most likely by gangs or other criminal elements that are no longer being contained by law enforcement. I can assure you, steps are being taken to fortify this camp and increase security." The LT's voice was respectful but held a sharp edge.

I knew that tone; it was a tone that said, "Stop talking, or someone is going to make you stop." Grandpa Silas must have heard it too. He didn't say another word, but the way he spit again out of the side of his mouth said volumes about what he thought.

Suddenly, Mouthy drew people's attention away from the platform. "OK, OK, OK, OK ... Everyone line up. We gots a new ration disbursement for each of you. And we have enough for everybody." His announcement seemed to give people something else to focus on.

This disbursement wasn't food. There were blankets, boots, canteens, warmer jackets, and a bunch of other equipment. People somberly lined up to receive their packages. Some were still crying. All I could see were sheep afraid to step out of line and risk losing their protection.

I didn't move. I just stared at the empty platform and then looked slowly around the room. Grandpa Silas and Jeri were nearby. There was a small group of us standing away from the mass of people lining up for their consolation prize: Albert and me, Grandpa, Jeri, Michael the paramedic, Dr. and Mrs. Fisher, Samara, my team of finders, Old Man Harris, two exchange students from the Ukraine, and a woman named Mary-Beth. We all stood there awkwardly, connected by some force that made us different from the others but not knowing what to do with it.

"Well, that's a hot heaping pile of horseshit!" said my new best friend, Old Man Harris. There was just something about the matter-of-fact, disdainful way he said it that tickled me. He didn't say it angrily or even nastily; just there it was.

A deep laugh suddenly burst out of my mouth. I couldn't help it. Before I knew it, we were all laughing, even Old Man Harris. I knew that others were looking at us like we were crazy. I laughed so hard that tears filled my eyes. It was a surreal moment, but it helped ease the tension. Victor clapped his hands and giggled with me.

As we settled down, Samara looked at us and said in a quiet voice, "So what do we do?"

I didn't realize I was going to answer until the words were already out of my mouth. Sometimes it could be a real pain when your mouth moved faster than your brain. "We watch, we wait, and we prepare. We have to make sure we are ready when the time comes to take action." My voice came out calm and confident. Albert and Grandpa were nodding.

Mrs. Fisher took her husband's arm and leaned in. "What action are you talking about? You don't think the military are going to hurt us?" she asked in a worried whisper.

I shook my head vigorously. "No way, not these boys. We just need to understand that we are not their top priority. We are not their orders." I looked from one person to the next to see if they were really getting me before I continued. "The brass isn't worried about a bunch of local folks; they are worried about the whole country falling apart. Think about what it was like before the storms. The failing economy, the rising prices. We had protests every day. The fires in California, the floods in the South, the police violence, the misinformation campaigns, everyone distrusting everyone else. We were on the brink before, so imagine people now. Fear is contagious. It spreads fast. It makes people dangerous."

I shook my head. "People were already scared and angry. The government has big problems to deal with right now. Do you really believe anyone on the political side is going to be able to pull their heads out of their asses long enough to get something done? Everyone is going to need the military to keep this country from ripping itself to pieces."

Michael frowned and looked at the soldiers passing out bundles. "These boys care about us; they wouldn't let anything bad happen to us. I know that when it comes to it, they will take care of us," he insisted.

I smiled and nodded in agreement. "You're absolutely right —*these* boys do. But I am not talking about the guys here. I am talking about the guys they take orders from. Those guys answer to people even farther away. They have to look at a bigger picture."

Albert cut in, and I reminded myself that he had more experience with this than most of us. "Lieutenant Roberts and his boys want to take care of us, but that is not their job," he said. "Their job is the radio, and believe me, it's a super important job. These radio relays are life-and-death important. Communication is key to keeping a country together. If the military is setting up relays, it means that the other communications are fried. These solar storms must have done a lot of damage to the networks." He sighed and ran a hand through his hair. "That means we are extra baggage. We need to understand that no matter how much they want to be, they are not here for us. We need to be prepared to take care of ourselves," he said with calm seriousness.

Old Man Harris frowned, or at least I thought he frowned. His face was more wrinkles than face, so it was hard to tell with him. "It sounds like you have some ideas you're working on."

Albert and I used to stay up late arguing the finer points of zombie plans. I was not the kind of person who made a plan and stuck with it. I was the kind who prepared for plans to fail. I prepared for backup plans to fail. Contingency plans were the name of the game.

"There are plenty of reasons to stay here for the winter," Albert continued. "We help them fortify; we use them for cover against whoever is out there. We just make sure we have our own exit strategy and some idea of how to save ourselves if the army can't."

I nodded in agreement. This was usually our plan for things. I smiled at Michael and some of the others, who seemed a little relieved.

"There is no reason to rush off," Michael agreed. "Obviously, there are a lot of dangers between us and the nearest refugee camp. So we hunker down and get ready."

We all agreed to work together and shook hands. We took a moment to make sure everyone had been introduced and then joined the line to get our blankets and boots. We all shuffled quietly through the line.

As Mouthy handed me a bundle, he leaned in and whispered, "Got-ya back, Mouse."

I smiled and nodded to him as I gathered my things and my children. Albert walked ahead with Zyada and Nathan as we went back to our little borrowed house.

As I was putting things away at home, I heard Nathan asking his dad some questions. Albert answered them quietly and reassured him. We tucked the kids into bed. Albert read them a bedtime story, and once they were asleep, he put on a pot of coffee.

I lit an extra candle at the table. We pulled out the area map. In whispers over steaming mugs of caffeine, we started going over what was in my notebook. We made lists and talked about locations. Well into the night, we worked on our plans. Any mother will tell you that preparation is key. You plan for the worst and hope for the best.

wednesday, 8:30am

THE NEXT DAY, there was an all-hands-on-deck call. Everyone lined up and was given duties. It was decided that the closed-off day care would be reopened and used as a school for the children. That way, the kids would be looked after, which would free up more adults to take on tasks. Alice and Sharon were assigned teaching duty, because Alice had just started her teaching career and Sharon had recently retired from it. A handful of the teens were assigned to help as teaching assistants.

To help conserve the amount of energy we would need over the winter, we began consolidating where we were keeping things. The infirmary was moved to the student building, which was next to supply in the gymnasium. It wasn't ideal, but having them closer together would make the spaces easier to heat as it got colder. The kitchen was attached to the student building by a series of hallways that could be closed off. The kitchen would be kept warm by the ovens and didn't need a great deal of power.

People were divided into teams, some of them set to making simple wooden buildings called yurts and sheds. Some folks would work with the army guys to define the perimeter with fencing and a guard post. Other people were assigned very heavy-lifting jobs like gathering firewood. One team was responsible for weatherizing the buildings.

I figured Lieutenant Brick would use the opportunity to keep me busy and on base. I was a little surprised when I was called into the makeshift office they were using for assignments. Brick and the sarge were sitting at a desk, and Mouthy had a few guys to the side going over papers as he worked out logistics. Lieutenant Brick looked up and nodded as I came in, then returned his eyes to his papers.

"Good morning, Mrs. Sales. We will continue to make sure that you have the personnel you need for baking since that seemed to go so well. You will also have a rotation at the infirmary. I was informed you were vital to the care of the injured. I wanted to thank you for stepping in and helping." He spoke very quickly and directly, the way long-term military people often did.

I smiled and nodded. "Not a problem." I had barely said the words before he started talking again.

"I want you to know that I realize how important your salvage trips were, as well as the information you brought back. Specialist Alozerro has made it clear that you are an asset to our supply. So I want you to continue to work with your assigned team. However, for security purposes I will need you to follow some rules. We need to know where you are going and send a protection detail with you. Please, no more solo runs." He looked up from his paperwork to emphasize his words.

I can't lie. It made me feel good to know that I was needed, that my work was appreciated. This wasn't why I did it; I was doing it for my family. But the pride was there either way. Mouthy gave me a grin and a thumbs-up. I smiled and nodded at both Brick and Mouthy.

"Yes, sir, I understand. No more solo runs."

Albert was assigned to the electricians and technicians. They were to make sure the power stayed on and lasted the winter.

With assignments passed out, everyone went to work right

away. Nathan and Victor went to the new school day care, and I took Zyada with me. I headed to the infirmary to look at the rotation roster. There were more "volunteers" now, and because I had other duties, I would be on for only three days out of the week.

Zyada and I went to check on our blonde patient. His hair was so golden that Zyada called him Mr. Sunshine. She sat on the chair beside his bed. He looked pale today, and he had bright red cheeks. I checked his chart to be certain he had received his antibiotics. I changed his sheets while Zyada talked up a storm and colored pictures by his bed.

She had some colorful little plastic ponies with sparkles in their manes. She put one in his hand and played with him, even as he remained asleep. She helped me change the water while I gave him a quick wipe-down bath. She sang to him while I checked his wounds. It seemed to help. Dr. Fisher came in to look at the wound on his left side and gave a worried sigh.

Zyada looked up at him and said in a little voice, "Is he going to be OK?"

"Don't worry, we will take care of this," he said to Zyada.

She looked concerned and held his hand tightly. She nodded and whispered to Mr. Sunshine, "It's going to be OK."

We were going to have to fight the infection the hard way, it seemed. We cleaned and prepped the area. We lanced and drained the puss out of the wound. We cleansed and bandaged him back up. We had received some new medical supplies. It meant he got a proper IV drip and proper packing bandages. He was doing much better by the time I had to head off to help with other patients. Zyada decided to remain with him, coloring flowers to decorate his room.

I came back at lunch to sit with her. She had made him quite the collection of flowers, now taped to the wall. She and I sat eating sandwiches in a quiet kind of contentment.

"Mommy! Mommy!" She suddenly was squealing and pointing frantically.

I almost choked as she cried out. My heart leapt into my nose as I looked in the direction she was pointing, trying to figure out what she was shouting about. In the corner of the room, on one of the electrical outlets, was a tiny blue dot, a little lost star. It was the LED light that indicated power was running to that outlet, there to make the outlet easier to spot. The sunlight from the window had made it hard to see. I cheered with Zyada and hugged her tight. The noise brought first Dr. Fisher and then others, and before long we were all cheering and gathered around our tiny little star.

I found out later that in other places, sparks had flown, and in one instance had cause a small fire. Fluorescent lights seemed to be working in several rooms. The most important thing to come back to life was the radio tower, which crackled and buzzed. Lt. Eugene Roberts finally reached command, and we were designated Hill Radio Relay Station 37. Like magic, we were no longer stranded on the moon. We were reconnected to the world, for better or worse.

The next morning, I met up with my team for acquisitions, my finders. We met down at the main street just inside the new perimeter exit. Jeri was there. I smiled when he came up to me.

He stood next to me and leaned in to whisper in my ear. "Grandpa said to help out. We will stick with you for the winter." He gave me a little smile before moving back to check his gear. I was more than a little relieved. I knew Silas had some serious reservations about staying with anyone in a uniform. I worried he might decide to head off on his own. He would be just fine, but I knew we were so much better off with him around.

Ethan and his brother John were checking the chains on their bikes. The college had been almost completely empty between the summer break and the evacuation. Almost all the college-age kids had left on foot with the others. John had been recovering from some serious electrical burns, and Ethan had stayed with him. They were polite and friendly young men. They seemed smart and willing to listen and learn. Last but not least was Erica, a middle-aged woman who lived in the area. She was quiet but hardworking and smart. All in all, I was pleased with the group I had been assigned to work with.

I was the only one with a proper wagon hitch. Most had a milk crate attached to the back of their bike, behind the seat, and a basket in the front. We all had backpacks. As soon as supply let us, we would get to use those nifty little three-wheeled ATVs that pulled a flatbed we could load. They were solar-powered and needed a full day to charge. Today was about getting immediate supplies. We checked that our weapons were ready but stowed, that our bikes were in working order, and that our wheels were good. We checked our map again.

We had gathered together just before dawn, and the first rays of light were cresting the hill as we finished with prep. The air was cold, and there was a tiny tipping of frost on the grass, a reminder of how close we were to winter. The lighter leaves had already changed to yellow. The dog days of summer were coming to an end, and the dark green was shifting. The trees would soon catch fire with their autumn glory.

"All right, folks, remember we keep it quiet out there," an unfamiliar voice barked at us. "We don't want to make ourselves targets." This was our military escort. He had a bike, but he wouldn't be carrying any supplies. His job was strictly security, according to Lieutenant Brick's orders. I didn't recognize him. He didn't introduce himself. He was one of the new arrivals. He was armed to the teeth with scary-looking tactical gear. Even though it was kind of funny to see him sitting on a bike, he still managed to appear intimidating. His name was not stenciled on his chest, he didn't offer it, and none of us asked.

I made sure to stretch my legs and back. I had learned that lesson the first day. We weren't heading to Shadowbrook. I would go back soon, but today's mission was specific. Today was about clearing the hill. We had been given a quadrant of resident houses to search and mark so we would know if they were occupied. Each team had a quadrant. If we found people, we were to offer shelter. If the building was unoccupied, we were to mark it and lock it up. Our destination was less than two miles from camp. This was mostly for security, but we were also looking for supplies. Our lists of needs were crazy long. We needed anything that could be useful for winter, which meant basically all household goods. We were going to be busy, that was for sure.

"OK, boys and girls, let's get to work. We aren't paid by the hour," I said. I gave Jeri a wink as I pushed my pedals and started off, pulling my wagon behind me. The weirdest song popped into my head as I let gravity help pull me down the hill. I found myself humming the happy, bouncing tune of "Big Rock Candy Mountain."

It was a short ride to our quadrant, a very fancy neighborhood on the edge of the fire scar. I pulled my bike up to the front steps of the first intact house on the left. We had already discussed a routine we would use. One person would go into a house to check for occupants. If there were none, we would mark it with red, then take what we needed and move on to the next house. This first one was a nice single-family colonial house. I walked up the steps and knocked politely. I didn't hear anything. I knocked one more time before I tried the door handle. It was locked. I searched around the porch to see if there might be a hidden key. I checked under flowerpots and looked for false rocks. No luck.

I peeked in the front window and didn't see anyone moving around. Then I went and checked the back. Once again it was locked up tight. Coming back around the front, I pulled out some of the tools I had with me: a crowbar and a hammer. I made short work of the door handle and managed to pry my way in. It was musty inside. There was an ozone smell that had been trapped. There were a couple of scorched light bulbs, but most of the lights had been LEDs, and it looked like someone had gone with high-quality materials, so the house hadn't burned.

"Hello?" I called out. My voice seemed to barely disturb the quiet inside.

The crowbar was in my right hand, the hammer in my left. You know, just in case. You never knew when the world might decide there needed to be a zombie or something. Crazy, I know, but I still waited for it.

I called out a few more times as I walked into the dim house. Other than the creaks and groans of an empty house, nothing answered me. It looked like a family of three had lived here. From the toys in the bedroom, the child looked to be a boy of about ten. For a kid's room it was surprisingly clean. The extra rooms had been converted to a home gym and office. It was a nice place. Whoever they were, they kept a very orderly and neat home. Returning outside, I sprayed a red mark on the front door as neatly as I could. That way when the owners returned, they would only have to replace, or repaint the door. With the mark in place, we knew it was empty and checked.

I put the notice on the inside of the door and headed back into the house. I took a spare sheet from the linen closet. Yeah, they had a freaking linen closet. It was that kind of house. They even had a walk-in pantry, and the master bedroom had an en suite. There were beautiful quartz countertops and tiled stone floor in the bathroom. I laid out the sheet and threw things on it: canned goods, nonperishable boxes, baking supplies, spices, and every medicine bottle I could find, including prescriptions. I found a lot more of those than I thought I would. Then like some cartoon bad guy, I pulled up the edges of the sheet to make a bag and dragged it out to the wagon.

After I loaded and organized the items, I had some room left in the wagon, so I went back in and headed to the attic. It was a nicely finished attic, but there were only holiday decorations stored inside, so I moved on to the basement. In the half-finished basement I found what I was looking for: winter gear, including coats, boots, hats, gloves, and even some camping equipment. I hauled that out too.

The kitchen smelled funny, but I knew that was because the fridge had not been emptied out. I originally wasn't going to bother opening it—it would just let that horrible smell out—but I wanted to check for eggs. I held my breath, opened the fridge, and winced. Holy God in Heaven, that was bad. I snatched the eggs, shut the door, and ran outside for air. I had to check the eggs, so I found a pot and filled it with water. Out of the dozen, three were still good enough to use. I tossed the rest out in the yard. I took one more walk around and grabbed some crayons and construction paper. I grabbed clothes from the kid's closet. By then my wagon was full, and my backpack was almost there. I headed over to help with some of the other houses. We loaded up and turned our bikes around to pedal up that horrible Mount Everest. Once we arrived back at the camp we unloaded and headed back out to our quadrant.

We worked like this for a few hours. We had managed to make three full trips by 9 am. The sun was out and helped take the chill out of the air. We were on our fifth drop off when we heard that one group had found a family and brought them back instead of supplies. We made good time on our runs and by 12pm we had made eight full trips.

We had made a good dent on our lists and had found several items that were too big for us to carry but should be retrieved. For example, someone had found a snowmobile and skis in a garage. We also found a bunch more bicycles and helmets, so we brought those back. It was amazing how much got done with groups working in coordination. There was still plenty to do. Our lists were long, and there were still plenty of houses to search, but it didn't seem so impossible now. The lieutenant wanted a complete two-mile radius searched and inspected. It didn't seem like such an unreasonable request now.

We were exhausted by the ninth trip back up the hill. I knew I was going to be seriously sore after today. The hill was brutal. It would be easier with the ATV tomorrow. I was so glad it was my last trip. I set aside the few things I had collected for my family and went to drop off the rest with Mouthy.

He was sitting and looking a bit on the sullen side when I approached. He sat up and smiled at me. "Hey there, lady. Whatcha got for me today?" He leaned over the desk to look in the wagon, and even though I wondered what was wrong, I never got a chance to ask.

"Well, just a lot of canned food, and household things. Found a bunch of toilet paper and shaving razors. Lucky for us, this house looked like it belonged to a health nut, so they had a lot of dried food and one of those cartons of milk that don't need to be refrigerated. I did find something special for you boys." I pulled back a blanket where I had hidden the good stuff, revealing three mostly full and two unopened bottles of hard liquor. Mouthy smiled like a kid at Christmas. One bottle of hard liquor was recorded, and I kept the milk. After that hard work, I headed back home and made food for the kids. It was meatless chili with corn bread since I needed to use the eggs right away. The kids actually liked the milk since it was sweetened. I used it in my coffee.

Albert, who had watched the kids in the morning, ate and then kissed me on the cheek as he headed out. It was still early afternoon when I was able to take an icy rinse in the bathroom and got the kids presentable. The school was still trying to figure out scheduling, so they didn't worry about when the kids got there. Zyada and Nathan were excited to do something resembling school. They really missed it. Victor wasn't so happy about me not staying with him, but there were other kids his size and toys, so he gave me kisses and ran off squealing to play with trucks. Then I went to help in the infirmary. Even with my legs all wobbly, I could make the rounds and check the vitals.

It was impressive how much of the building had power already. The power was weak, so the few lights that worked were dim, but some of the newly arrived medical equipment could be used now. There were so many machines to repair. I checked in with Mr. Sunshine and was startled when he started mumbling in his sleep. It was a good sign as far as I was concerned. He still had a fever, but it wasn't so high now. I changed his bandages, cleaned him up, and took the dirty laundry to where we were getting it prepped. We had told the LT that getting the washers working was imperative. However, it was clear that it would be a while till those were running, if ever. Until then it would have to be laundry done by hand.

I put sheets into the large tub to soak and then the clothes in a separate tub. There was a large fire going to boil water, and huge clotheslines were hung tight to put the clothes up. I worked until it was almost 6:00 p.m. and then headed home. Then I set about prepping our stuff for tomorrow's laundry day.

When you're busy time slips away quickly if you aren't keeping track.

My next week went like this, laundry day, baking day, and then five days split between searching and working in the infirmary. Albert helped the techs, and the kids either helped with work or went to the "school," depending on whether it was open that day. In the evenings we made plans for the winter and tried to prep the house as best we could. We fixed doors and put plastic sheets over windows. My salvage group worked well together and finished our section in record time. It was a fancy area, which meant bigger lots and a lot of stuff per house but fewer houses. By the third day, we joined some of the other groups to work on their houses and complete their sections. By then we had a little ATV to help cart up the hill, so it was a lot easier. I was getting into a groove with the routine.

I headed into a cute little house on the corner. The door was slightly ajar, but that wasn't that odd these days, so I walked in. It wasn't until I was all the way into the house and down the hall a bit that I realized something was wrong. It was cold that day, with fall coming on strong, so the house was cold inside. Something tickled my nose, and my mind flashed back to the dead man in the fire truck. It was faint, but it was there: the smell of something dead.

I froze. Every muscle in my body pulled taut and still as I waited. I didn't know what I was waiting for, but I could hear the music playing. That music that seemed to be in every zombie flick ever made. I looked at the doors at the end of the hall, waiting for them to burst open and for something with only half a face to come out and try to eat me.

There was only silence in the house. I realized I was holding my breath and let it out slowly. I was trying to remember how to bring air back into my lungs when I heard a little whimper. For a moment I thought I had made the sound. Then it came again.

It was coming from down the hall to the left. *I should leave, I should run*, I told myself. I always yelled at the movie screen in these moments, things like run, leave, and don't go toward the sounds. I understood right then, in that moment, that you can't turn away. Some terrible part of you, something in your core, forces you to move toward the sound. You just have to know. Or it will haunt you forever.

Against my will, my feet carried me toward the sound. The horrific thought that it might be a child flashed into my head. My mother instincts took over. Mommy courage, I call it.

"Hello?" I didn't recognize the pinched, small, cracked voice that called out. It didn't sound like me at all.

The whimper turned into a little yip. It sounded like a small dog, or a puppy.

I stepped into a clean, neat kitchen and saw a door that appeared to head into a basement. The sound was coming from the other side of the door. I opened it up, and down at the bottom of the stairs was an adorable little half-grown puppy, maybe a husky mix. It was sitting and wagging its tail for all it was worth. There was a baby gate at the bottom of the stairs preventing it from going up the stairs.

"Oh, poor little thing, are you all alone?" I frowned, looking around. If someone was still living here, it wouldn't be great to be here when they came back. But he looked so sad and lonely, and I had a weakness for puppies. I went down to pet him and make sure he had water before I headed back out. It wasn't until I got closer that I realized how terribly skinny and dirty the poor pooch was. The basement was finished but cold. The only light down here came from a little camp lantern.

I reached out and pet the happy puppy. I looked around for his food dish. Two bowls sat by the foot of the stairs, both of them empty and bone-dry. I climbed over the gate and picked up the water dish. There was a sink by the washer and dryer, so I refilled the dish. As I set it down, he thirstily began drinking. There was an area with some newspaper down, and it was covered in dog poop.

It looked like it had been a couple of days since the paper had been changed. The smell was bad, but it wasn't just from the poop. The dog poop couldn't cover that very distinct scent of death, the sickly sweet, coppery smell that had turned into putrid rot. Just past the newspaper, I noticed a black puddle seeping out from under a door.

I found myself moving toward the door.

My own inner voice screamed, *No! Leave! Some things are better left unknown.* It said to me with disdain, *this was the moment in those movies where the stupid chick who wandered off alone got eaten or murdered. You are that stupid bitch!*

I took a deep breath, screwed my courage tightly in place, and opened the door. Beyond was something I will never forget; I wish I had left the damn door alone.

What was left of a man laying facedown was the first horror

past the door. Half his skull was gone, in some sort of chunky mess around the rest of his head. The mess might have been red at some point, but it was rotting away now, turning a putrid black-green. The discoloration this cause ruined the cheery winter pattern on his matched flannel pajama suit. The swollen body underneath the soft material distorted the shape of the reindeer and Christmas trees.

Further in, there was a body half-lying across the bed, decomposing slowly into something that seemed more like a microwaved Barbie doll than a person. The body was misshapen and falling in on itself. There were places where I could still tell it had been a woman. It took me a moment to register that she wasn't wearing clothes. The sheets had black streaks everywhere. I was pretty sure it was dried blood. There was a shotgun next to her.

Some part of my mind separated from this time and place and tried to solve the puzzle of what had happened here. Had she killed him? But then who had killed her? Why was she naked? Perhaps he had been attacking her and was leaving her for dead when in her last moment she managed to shoot him as he was leaving, but then she died after that. It was some grotesque mystery puzzle.

Even as that sociopathic little voice told me its conclusion like an evil Sherlock Holmes, the other part of my brain screamed and clawed, kicking to get away from this. My body was frozen, standing there staring at what used to be people, now rotting away. Maybe I had been holding my breath again, but suddenly the smell was overwhelming. I gasped for air and slammed the door.

The next rational thought I had come when the puppy started licking my face. Apparently, I had taken a seat next to the washer. I may or may not have thrown up in the sink. I washed my face and hands anyway. I picked up the puppy. His leash and collar were hanging on a peg next to the stairs. I put them on him and started collecting his things. We went upstairs. I turned and locked the basement door. I grabbed a blanket off the couch. I found a couple cans of puppy chow under the sink and some puppy flea and tick drops. I stepped outside and put the puppy in my wagon. I used his leash to secure him inside and continued on to the next house.

I don't know why I didn't say anything about what I saw to the people I was working with. I didn't even write it in my notebook. I guess I was hoping that when I had locked that door, I had locked up the ugly with it. There was already so much ugly.

I took a moment to close my eyes and lock the door inside my mind too. When I opened my eyes again, the puppy was looking at me with a very serious expression, as if he knew. I let out a breath and smiled as I stroked his head. "I think you are one lucky dog."

He yipped and wagged his tail.

"OK. Lucky it is then."

The air outside was crisp and sweet. It smelled of damp leaves and fall, the smell of October. Fall had arrived. It helped me remember how to breathe.

People have different views on what to do with animals during a crisis. Some think they are as important as people to save. Others think that saving them is a drain on resources and that it's hard to take care of them. I think it depends on the animal and what function they are going to serve. It didn't take long to know that the puppy was worth it. Jeri's face lit up when he saw Lucky. I didn't think I had ever seen him smile so big. He came back to the group a bit later with a huge bag of dog food and some toys. Lucky was a hit with the ladies as we rolled back toward camp. It was a hard haul back up the hill, but it was totally worth it to see the look on the little faces when I got home.

I was actually scared the kids might smother the poor little guy with all the hugs or scare him with all the shrieking. Victor was so excited that he did his little happy dance where he stomped in a circle and shrieked with his hands stretched out in front of him. Zyada jumped up and down and ran around the living room twice. Nathan squealed and almost knocked himself over. Lucky seemed as excited as the rest of them. He spun in a circle, yipping and barking as his tail wagged for all it was worth.

Everyone wanted to help give him a bath, so everyone crowded into the bathroom. We boiled water and bathed the two smaller children and the puppy together. It was a mess. But everyone seemed to love it. They all sat nicely to dry by the stove. Lucky ate and then fell asleep wrapped in a blanket. The kids ate dinner sitting next to him.

Nathan was smiling calmly, which was unusual for him. He was a smart and sweet boy. Sometimes, before the storms, he could be withdrawn and hard to reach. But when he was excited, he seemed to vibrate around the room. Now, with all that had happened, he was usually withdrawn and quiet. I knew this was all very hard for him. In the last week or so, he had started coming back to himself. I was so happy to see it.

Zyada had always been an extrovert and was a bit of a handful. Honestly, I had never minded. I liked that she was bossy, assertive, and full of initiative. I had always figured it would serve her well. After all, bossy girls will become the boss.

Victor was my little joy. He always seemed to be smiling or laughing about something. He didn't let Zyada push him around, and he was always singing to himself. If his disposition remained the same, he would be my giant with a heart of gold and sweet smile. The day's work had been hard, but somehow the night was pleasant, and everyone seemed to be smiling as the lights went out. Lucky curled up next to me. I was able to drift off easily and none of the monsters came for me that night.

It was a good night.

tuesday, 9:00am-ish

A week after finding Lucky

IT TOOK three days for Lucky to become the unofficial mascot of supply, Zyada's best friend, Victor's nap buddy, and my shadow. My father had once told me that pets were fine, but every animal should serve a purpose in a family, even if it was to be spoiled. When it came to dogs, he was very clear: all dogs should work. Lucky was turning out to be a great little worker.

The pup followed me everywhere. Whenever I dropped off the kids or went out with teams, there he was, right along with me. I was trying to train him so he could be trusted off-leash, and he was taking to it well. There were no cars to worry about; it was just a matter of making sure he didn't run off and get lost. He was content to not wander off too far anyway. He was still young, not even a full year if I had to guess. He was big for a puppy and still all paws and ears. His paws were already as big as my palm. I had thought he was a husky at first, but he was too big, so maybe a malamute. I was growing concerned about how big he was going to get. We were trying to find all the dog food we could to prepare for winter. Mouthy had given us a harness for him to wear, and

Albert had rigged up a little plastic sled for him to drag around. It was good practice since he was going to help carry stuff later.

It didn't take long for dogs to go from puppies to work dogs, but if we got him trained, he was going to be very useful come wintertime. It was best to train him now. This also gave our family something to focus on doing. He still pulled loose and ran like a crazy dog as soon as he was free, until I held up a treat or called him back. He was my new scrounging companion. I walked him with his new harness and had him drag small pieces of wood and a few rocks in his pack so that he got used to the load. I stopped at the library at the top of the hill and found a few books on training a working dog. They were very helpful. Just a general tip: when in doubt, head to the library; it is the best place to find answers. Libraries were the original Google.

It was about a week after Lucky's arrival that they managed to get the power working more steadily for the college. The technicians were setting up a grid and running power to additional buildings. They had power to the infirmary, a few of the smaller buildings, and the mobile radio station. There was gossip that they might wire up some of the surrounding houses. I thought it was just wishful thinking. Even now, certain buildings had power for only a few hours each day. They were looking for the most efficient way to use the power and restore it. They had decided the current supply area was too big to be heated, so personnel would work in a mobile station built inside the huge stadium area, and storage would be in the adjoining gyms and rooms.

The generator was strong enough to power a small county, but it was limited to our fuel supply. It was designed to assist municipalities in disaster zones. It was not designed to be the sole solution for a long-term crisis. The major issue was that wires and junctions had been completely destroyed. The technicians had to rebuild all the ways to spread the power. Even though we had the electricity it didn't solve the lighting issue. Most of the light bulbs had burst during the storm. They could turn on only the remaining LED lights. A very small number of lights had been sent with the equipment trucks. All the finders were supposed to be on the lookout for any bulb that might still be intact. The new security rules didn't make things easier. Since the attack on the convoy, it had been decided that only battery-powered lanterns or fire lights could be used outside. Those ran the length of the new fence. The people who were set up as scouts were given walkie-talkies and night scopes. I presume it was to help hide our location, or at least hide the fact that we had power.

The changes that had occurred in one week were truly dramatic. With everyone working under orders and tight observation, we had gone from a cobbled-together mass to an ordered and organized encampment. We even had a composting latrine area. I wasn't sure we needed them since we still had water flow, which Albert said had something to do with gravity sand filters. He laughed when people questioned how long the water flow would last but never really said anything about it. The military is all about contingency plans, so we dug latrines while the ground was soft. An area had even been cleared for planting in the spring. One area that had once been an office was now a dorm for the soldiers and was filled with beds.

The camp centered on the radio tower, with everything carefully encircling it in a grid-like pattern. The army engineers had even put together a radio shack next to the tower, like a little Lego brick hut. Our house was outside the perimeter fence. We were hidden in a set of trees that circled the campus. I liked it because the road was not far from supply but away from the radio. We figured they wouldn't bother getting us any power, and we were OK with that. The wood-burning stove was enough.

Our little house smelled of clean sheets after another laundry day had passed. It was three days till Halloween, and my team was setting off on a supply run. A bunch of parents had discussed what we could use to make some Halloween costumes and have a little celebration. Since winter was coming, we also discussed Thanksgiving and Christmas. We knew we would be here, so we might as well plan for the fun parts. We had seen a lot of holiday things in attics and basements, such as Christmas lights, fake Christmas trees, boxes of decorations. We had even found some nice sets of dishes. I had found a box of decorations for Thanksgiving and Halloween too. At every house we left the notification that we were working for the government and that anything removed from the house was to be returned or compensated for. I for one genuinely believed that this would be honored eventually. I would like to promise that all the finders were honest and never took anything of value for themselves, but to be fair I don't know.

I had been tempted during one of our supply runs, when I had walked into a bedroom that looked like it should be in a magazine. It had a huge super soft bed, thick carpets, and floor-to-ceiling windows with French doors that led out onto a little Juliet balcony. There was an antique French vanity with a little bench, and atop the vanity were all these beautiful colored glass perfume bottles, plus makeup and hair accessories. Next to the vanity was a tall, lacquered wood dresser, only the drawers were too small for clothes. Rather, they held the woman's jewelry and watches and other sundries. The jewelry looked like it belonged in movies. Some of it had to be fake because it should have been locked up in a safe, but there were gold chains, bracelets, earrings, cuff links, watches that were now stopped, and even one watch that was still working. There was a blue velvet box containing a matching gold and diamond set, with a necklace, earrings, and bracelet. The diamonds were mostly white, but mixed in were champagne and pink, just enough to give hints of color between the necklace and bracelet. It was so beautiful and sparkled so nicely that it was enough to make me believe in princesses again. It occurred to me that these things would be useful for trade. The world was over, true, but gold would always be gold.

The truth was I didn't want the set to trade. I wanted the set because the pieces were beautiful, and I wanted to wear them. I had always wanted something so lovely. It was like buried treasure. Who wouldn't want it? If I had taken it, I never would have traded it. If the reason had been to feed my children or buy supplies for camp, then maybe. But I had found my line. That was the difference, for me, between stealing and foraging. I moved her jewelry box to the closet safe, which was hanging open. It seemed they had had to evacuate in a hurry and had taken the things in the safe quickly, not realizing this necklace was elsewhere. I left a note saying, "Didn't want you to lose this. It's lovely."

I did take the wool jacket, mink muff, cashmere scarves, and snow gear I found in the closet. These items were things people here needed, not wanted.

I hope you can see the difference. I am not a thief. Some will disagree with me, but those people aren't here. If they have complaints or concerns, they could call my manager at 1-800-APOCALYPSE.

Today I was working on one of the large, remodeled homes, and its pantry was huge! The basement had been finished, and the owners looked like they had stocked up for a year. It reminded me of the reality T.V. show about those folks who did extreme couponing. Because of how they bought something like seven of an item at a time. It wasn't like a hoarder's house, though. Everything was neat and organized. Maybe they were a gathering station for their church charities or just always purchased in bulk.

We were using everything from shopping carts to the little ATV with the flatbed trailer. The army techs had even gotten a golf cart working, and it was towing a little pull wagon. It took over half a dozen trips from each person to cart everything up the hill. This neighborhood had basically saved us from starvation this winter. And this was the jackpot house. Their basement storage really set us up for a long time. I even carted out an entire case of baked beans to put in the trailer behind the ATV. There were a lot of canned goods and nonperishable food items. The canned goods were super important since there would be no fresh vegetables or greens all winter, and scurvy was *not* fun.

People were so excited about all the toilet paper we had found. There had been so much stuff, including canned fruit, soup, vegetables, cookies, and even candy, that everyone had decided to leave thank-you notes. We tried to make sure we didn't leave a mess, and at every house we wrote a little 'thank you' on the back of the notice from the army.

We were discussing what else to write at one house when the warmth and hope of the day was shattered by a sharp *crack!* I jumped, startled so badly that I almost dropped the jar of pickles I was holding. Lucky crouched low next to my ankle, his hackles raised. Birds scattered and took wing, cawing their displeasure. We all stood frozen, heads up and turned in unison like deer in the glen. I never realized how loud the sound of bird wings could be when so many take off at once. The crack sound had lasted only seconds, but it was loud and echoing.

Then there was another crack and another and another.

Lucky growled low in his throat, looking to the south. Everyone turned to face the same way. People responded to his signals as much as he responded to theirs.

The soldiers moved first, coming to life before the third shot was fired. They grabbed the nearest person by the shoulders and gave orders in low voices as the shooting continued. This broke the daze that had fallen over us. We became the birds bursting into motion, loading bags, closing doors, and hopping back onto bikes. Those with motors headed off last, letting those pedaling have a head start. The soldiers followed behind us at a fast clip, their weapons ready.

The gunfire echoed loudly in the distance, seeming to chase us like the barking and snapping of unseen monsters on our trail. I pedaled as hard as I could, as thoughts of bodies in the basement chased me. I set a personal record getting to the top of the hill. We arrived back at the entrance of the more fortified base and passed through the guard post where a "Relay #37" sign was posted.

Everyone was in motion, everything buzzing like an angry anthill. Suddenly, those weren't my friends at the gate entrance, smoking and waving me in. No, these were soldiers on guard and ready. They ushered us in quickly so they could shut and lock the gate securely behind us. New heavy wooden barricades had been built for them to stand behind if they needed cover from fire. They looked like heavy wooden tables lying on their sides with firewood stacked behind them, but whatever worked.

Past that gate, there was a sense of urgency. Everyone was running, not in a panic but in that busy "I have something to do, and I am ten minutes late" way. It was startling for me to suddenly see soldiers instead of my army boys. We all picked up our pace and hurried to the supply depot. It had a little office and everything now. It was built with plywood walls, roof and even a door that creaked terribly on a hinge.

Sometimes when I came to supply, I thought of the *M.A.S.H.* T.V. show. The colors were all wrong, of course, the uniforms were all tan and gray now, but the feel was the same.

I rolled my bike up to the side of the supply area. Mouthy sat next to the desk as he flipped through the papers on a clipboard. Victor was sound asleep in a wooden crate half-filled with blankets right next to him. Zyada was sitting at the desk, diligently coloring, an army hat perched on her head. It was way too big, and the only reason it didn't fall was that her hair was divided into two adorable ponytails on either side of her head. They looked like they were there specifically to hold up her hat. She smiled as she saw me and gave a squeal and a wave. The squeal was muffled by the lollipop in her mouth. Of course, she ran straight to the dog. I smiled and let Lucky go so he could get some love while I checked on sleeping Victor. His cloth diaper was dry. I knew it would soon be time for potty training. That was going to be rough with winter coming.

Now was a better time. He was using his words more, and it would be better to do it now, before it got any colder.

"Hmm, I could have sworn I already had a set of these," I said with a grin as I planted a kiss on Zyada's head.

Mouthy laughed and shook his head, playing along for a second. "Oh, I thought I got them for a steal. Turns out, I got robbed. That one eats like three marines, and this one talks more than I do." He motioned first to Victor and then to Zyada. He ruffled Zyada's head with a wink.

Zyada gave him a giant grin and fluttered her lashes at him. The grin he gave in return was so cute that I just had to laugh. She had him wrapped around her finger.

"Why are they here and not with the day care folks?" I asked, not all that worried but just surprised.

Mouthy grinned and finished something on the papers as he talked. "Well, it turns out them gunshots everyone heard were from one of our missing trucks. Apparently, they had a nasty trip here, they got chased, got lost, and then had to do road repairs. Some of the boys got pretty banged up. Long story short the ladies from the day care were needed in the infirmary. Your man Albert picked the kids up, but he was needed for some crazy electrical conversion thingamajig. I don't know. He said something about making sure the radios were working. He was looking for someone to help out. I volunteered." His hands never slowed as he spoke. "I knew this was the first place you would go anyway. Your big boy, Nate, is with the older kids in the gym, playing ball. Looks like he is coming out of his shell a little. Don't look so worried, Mama Mouse. I asked one of the older boys to look out for him. They are really trying to help him learn how to play basketball." He took a moment to yell at someone about something and then started going through my haul.

"Wow, I'm sorry. I hope it wasn't too much of a bother."

Mouthy just waved a hand as he kept working, pulling things out of the wagon and writing stuff down. "Are you kidding? I love kids. V there is the calmest baby I have ever seen. He is always happy. And Z here was helping me boss these lazy bums around, so it's been great. She doesn't take no shit from nobody. I love it."

He gave a shrug and grinned up at me for a second. "I helped take care of all my cousins. I would always get kid duty back home. There were days when I was watching like fifteen kids, and I was sure I wasn't related to half of them. Big families. So I kinda miss the noise." He stood straight again and for a moment looked very serious, which was what got my attention.

"I've had lots of help. The boys here they love 'em. And besides, I reminded the guys that you were the one who brought those bottles around. And boom! I even had a volunteer for diapers. Most of the guys here have little babies back home, so they miss them too. This makes Victor very popular. I think he might get a bunch of stuff soon. The boys here get carried away."

I took a moment to breathe and blink back the tears that had suddenly sprung into my eyes. Mouthy was stepping off to move things and didn't notice. I looked around at the faces of the folks working in supply. Everyone was smiling. Even the guy who was getting yelled at by Mouthy had a little grin on his face. I knew at that moment that these guys would have done anything to keep my little ones safe. Right then, my kids were the safest kids on the planet. I smiled a little. It was nice. It felt like when I was a kid, hanging out with all the navy guys. I stood watching people work for a moment. Victor was still sleeping, and Zyada was happy playing army clerk. I decided to take this moment of safety and do a little investigating.

I headed over to where the newly arrived vehicle was parked. A trooper carrier was much smaller than the Deuce, but what it lacked in size, it made up for in metal. It looked more like the armored trucks from the movies. The back and the top were all hard shell, and it had a mounted machine gun. There were little slit windows. The driver side was smashed, and it looked like that door wasn't going to open again. The passenger side was scraped so heavily that the metal was shiny. Someone had tried to run them into something solid.

I ran my fingers along the gouges in the metal and let myself become displaced for a moment. I was lost in the story the battle scars echoed back to me. I heard the scraping metal against metal, the shouts and shots being fired as they made their escape. There was still blood smeared in the bed of the truck. It was slowly turning brown.

I let my mind wander deep into the mental puzzle of the ambush. That word, "ambush," implied that the attackers had known where the convoy was going or where it was coming from. There was no food in this truck, no supplies, just people. It was heavily armored with a heavy gun. It was scary-looking.

Why try to ambush a scary ATV full of military men? What would be the payoff for the risk? Had they meant to hit the entire convoy? That would mean they thought the convoy would be together. That didn't make sense since the convoy had split up days ago. So was this a different group from the one that had attacked the convoy? This didn't really matter because with one look a person could see that this was not a supply vehicle. The attackers had to have known there were no supplies in the ATV.

So again, why attack? It was either crazy or stupid. *Unless, of course, you think you can win. Then you have a badass bulletproof ride, and a hell of a reputation.*

Reasons to attack a heavily armed ATV: one, their weapons and gear; two, to stop the people inside from getting to their destination; or three, to prove you could. The biggest questions were, who would want to do any of those things, and where were they now?

I was turning those questions over in my mind and didn't notice the shadow growing behind me, looming over me. I nearly screamed when I caught the movement out of the corner of my eye. I jumped and turned so quickly that I slammed hard against the truck panel. A star burst behind my eyelids, and tears pricked my eyes. When my vision cleared, I was looking right at a set of fatigues, so I looked up—and up. I finally found a pair of ridiculously beautiful dark eyes looking down at me.

My first thought was, *what kind of mascara is this guy wearing?* Hand to God, that's what I thought. His lashes were dark black and thick. It took me a couple of breaths to realize he had more face than his eyes. It was just long enough to make me seem super weird. His face was all steep angles and high planes. His nose was straight and slightly broad. His mouth was full, and his cheekbones could draw blood, they were so sharp. It was like his face had been carved with a knife.

He wasn't handsome exactly. His features inspired other descriptors, like fierce, bold, and strong. His hair was so black that it disappeared into itself. Where the light hit the strands, I couldn't see the under-color. And there was so much of it. It hung down past his collar. Since when did any military guy get to have so much hair? It wasn't just long it was thick and framed perfectly around his face.

I felt pinned by those intense eyes and realized how long I had been staring. He just stood there towering over me. His face with all its straight lines seemed somehow distant and remote but angry at the same time. He was fully geared, as if expecting to head out on mission. There was something wrong with his uniform. The shade, cut, and pattern were different. It also had different insignia. It took me a moment to realize he was a Marine not an Army engineer.

To be fair there are actually many variants in both Army and Marine uniforms. Those differences are used to distinguish rank, position, and overall job description. It was something I was aware of but since I wasn't enlisted, I didn't have all the details. I couldn't tell at first what this man's job was. However, his uniform was different enough to make him stand out from the rest of the military members here. That was until of course I noticed it. Well to be fair it wasn't so much that I noticed as I became aware of the long rifle he had slung over his shoulder: a sniper rifle.

I have no idea how long we stood there staring at each other in weird, creepy silence. Somehow, we had missed the point in the conversation where you could say an awkward hello and had moved right on to an unrealistic slow-motion movie entrance. It had been long enough that it felt wrong to speak. So I just stood there, one hand on the knot on my head, looking up at him, with my mind a complete blank.

"You should not go out tomorrow. We have to sweep the area."

It took so long for him to finally speak that I jumped when he did, bumping the truck again. His voice was just above a whisper. It had a deep-chested rumbling sound that I could almost feel. There was something different about how he spoke. It wasn't an accent but was more the way his words fit together.

The break in the silence seemed to lessen the weird tension but didn't make me feel any less awkward. I nodded in response. I tried to smile, but I knew it had to look weird. Honestly, I had barely heard what he had said. My eyes had been focused on his mouth. It was a very nice mouth.

His breath smells like peppermint. That was the thought that made me realize he was invading my personal space. When I felt the urge to slink away, I put some steel into my backbone. I realized it was just his height that made me feel trapped; I had plenty of room to move. I knew he was over six feet tall because of the relation of his head to the ATV.

I took a sidestep away from him as I said, "Yeah, no problem. Tomorrow is baking day, so I will be busy. I do the baking. Well, not alone. There would be no way to do that all by myself. That's why we had to make sure so much got done today. Its baking day and then one day till Halloween. And I have to help put up decorations. We found a bunch of decorations for Halloween." If that epic level of conversation seems terrible please imagine it a double normal talking speed. I had utterly failed at any attempt to seem calm and collected as my mouth rambled on without my consent. *What the hell was that, mouth? Just shut up! Stop talking!*

He matched me step for step as I backed up around the truck, which meant no peeking into the cab this time. The oversized shadow didn't say another word as he followed me back to the desk. Mouthy had really good hearing, apparently.

"I love baking day," Mouthy said. "It's become my new favorite day. Tomorrow we will have all those ovens working, so it should be easier for you. They will even have some fans for you. Oh, I need to let you know something. The boys from this carrier that drove in today also brought along a couple of families they found. So, we will have some fresh faces around. Good news, the techs think they can get some serious power to the grid in the next day or so. It will help as we section off the area and get more serious walls up to prepare for winter. There should be enough space for every-one, so we can all be safe inside the compound."

I forced myself to remain there, listening to Mouthy ramble on. The man continued to loom not far off. I could feel his eyes watching us. My skin felt flushed, and butterflies danced in my stomach. I made sure my eyes didn't travel back to him. Instead, I focused on gathering my little ones. Victor snoozed through it all. I fixed him a place in the wagon to ride home, and Zyada skipped along beside me as we said our goodbyes and left. I tried hard to not think about the figure who seemed to watch me as we left.

It was amazing how much more fun baking was once we had real ovens. We had moved up baking day to make use of them. We had more folks now, but when you were baking this much bread, it didn't matter. The important thing was that someone had gotten the big restaurant-size mixer working so my arms didn't break off. I didn't get to see any of the newcomers until late afternoon, when we started distributing bread loaves. They had kept to themselves. It seemed like they were afraid of us, not that I blamed them. It was hard to trust strangers even in the best of times. I knew it was hard for me. I didn't want the bread to go to waste. The ovens were in the main student kitchens, where we had baked before. When everyone gathered in the big open cafeteria to pick up their bread, the new arrivals didn't get into line for theirs. I gathered up the bread and took it to them. There were about twenty of them total. Most of them were youngsters and women. There were two teenage boys. The boys looked particularly unhappy.

"Hey, guys. Don't worry. I heard we had some new folks, so I made enough for you too." I held out the tray of warm loaves. When no one moved immediately I set the tray on a table next to where the group had gathered. Some of the wary arrivals were seated but most were simply standing around the table.

One of the ladies smiled at me while the rest looked uncertain. A little girl peeked up and waved. I smiled at her. One of the teenage boys, the one with freckles, picked up one of the loaves, and the other, who had curly brown hair, elbowed him.

"What? I'm hungry," Freckles grumbled.

Curly glared and shook his head. An old woman walked up and smacked him on the back of the head. He jerked and looked at her angrily and then lowered his eyes.

"You should show some appreciation," the woman said. "We should all be grateful. Bread is very hard to make." She might have been gray, but she seemed fit and strong. She smiled at me. "Sorry about my grandson," she said. "He don't have the respect he should. None of them do."

We shook hands, and I smiled. "I'm just glad you all are all right. We heard it was a dangerous trip."

The older lady nodded. "We lost folks. Some got left behind. But the lieutenant has agreed to send some men to go round up the rest of our families."

I nodded. "Well, how many more can I expect? I like to make sure everyone has their own loaf."

She smiled and seemed to be counting in her mind. "Well, I guess there would be about twelve or so more. We were a small congregation taking shelter. We helped the military boys and hitched a lift to a safer place. How lucky we are to be so blessed." She sighed and sat down as a few of the other women murmured amens. A few of the children chimed in with their own amen.

I was not really into church groups, but these folks seemed all right. After the initial reserve, they were very friendly. I let them know that there was a little school being set up and that two of the women in our camp were grade schoolteachers. The boys seemed less sullen when they saw a couple of the teen girls from camp.

As the camp's picnic-style dinner was served, the newcomers began to meld into our group. Lieutenant Brick was good to his word and had their families back by the end of the day. This made them much happier. It did a great deal for general morale as well.

This group's situation made me wonder how many little pockets there were. Small bands of people trying to struggle along out there by themselves. How would they survive the winter?

The LT wasted no time in getting the new men into the work routine. He used the dinner to give out new work orders. We now had guards assigned to walking the perimeter and standing at posts. The extra hands were welcome relief to the rotation.

I decided I didn't want to wait much longer. I was worried that the LT would put more restrictions on us finders. As soon as Brick had finished his talk, I gathered up my crew. We all sat sipping coffee and tea. I smiled and tried to appear casual as I spoke.

"Fredricks and Davis have gate duty tomorrow," I said. "We all know that sooner or later, Lieutenant Brick isn't going to let us go out anymore. The collection from the latest area was a big help. But we need to show him that they still need us. He thinks its best that we just stay inside the fence. I don't think he realizes how much we have to offer."

Erica nodded. "Though I appreciate the protection in general, I don't like it when stuffed uniforms tell me what to do." She was a bit of a "no uniform is a good uniform" type. Still, she was smart and careful and very reasonable. She always came off strong, but I think that came from years of being told to shut up.

Ethan and John nodded a little at each other and then Ethan said. "Well, if you think there is something worth going for, we will help."

I smiled and showed them in my notebook where Shadowbrook was located.

John nodded but frowned slightly. "It does seem a bit far. Maybe we should also scope out for places along the way. The more we find, the more we have to bring to the table."

Jeri, who had been very quiet, now whispered, "One of the boys talked about folks trading goods, like a big farmer's market. He said people were trading all kinds of things. It was over outside the fairgrounds. There used to be a flea market there, I think."

It was the most I had heard him say all week. I nodded and looked around. The others all smiled and nodded.

"I like that idea," I said. "We should check that out after we hit Shadowbrook. OK, tomorrow we head out first thing. We head over to Shadowbrook, gather supplies for trade, and see if this market is for real. If it's a bust, we can come home. Later we do a run to gather anything we left behind. While we pedal, we will mark any good places we see, to check out later. Sound like a plan?"

Everyone nodded.

I got up and headed over to Albert to tell him the plan. He wasn't exactly thrilled to have me heading out, but he nodded and kissed me. "Just be safe and come home quickly. You are taking Lucky with you."

I nodded and leaned against him.

That night, I held Victor as he drifted to sleep. He was getting so big. I wanted to enjoy holding him while he was still small enough for me to do that. He cuddled and gave me kisses and smiles. Wordlessly, he wrapped us up in his joy, his peace. He didn't know the world was dangerous; he didn't know that things had changed. I sang his favorite songs and tickled him and rocked him. We were cocooned in a world of joy. I whispered my dreams in his ear, just like I did with his sister.

He squealed in laughter when Zyada jumped into the bed with us, cleaned and happy. I tickled both of them. Before long, Lucky was in the bed, and we were all laughing and cuddling. I pulled out a book, and we read bedtime stories by a battery-powered lamplight. For a little while, we were in our own little world, safe and full of wonder. I vaguely remember Albert taking the book at some point.

Sleeping children have the power to change the very air in a room. Their dreams seep out and fill the room with quiet. I rested easy in that space until Albert woke me when it was time to leave. We had to leave with the dawn to make the distance we had planned. I kissed dream-filled heads before I left.

NO
ZOMBIES
HERE
HELP
US!

twelve
wednesday, 4:56am

Two Days Before Halloween

THE AIR WAS COLD. They sun wouldn't rise for another couple of hours. My watch said it was almost 5:00 a.m. when we rolled ourselves to the front gate.

Davis looked at us and shook his head, holding up a hand. "You know that the lieutenant wants a military escort for every forage group. I am not supposed to let you out without one." He looked uncomfortable but serious. "I am sorry, Mouse, but they have gotten really serious about it since the last refugees came in."

The team looked at me. I was about to try to convince Davis to let us slide this one time when a deep, rumbling voice spoke out of the predawn gloom.

"I'm with them."

Davis looked over at him. He glanced at me, then back at the looming shadow from the truck. The predawn light made him look unreal. He was wearing his fatigues, and his face was painted. He looked scary. No, he looked terrifying, as if he had stepped out of a war movie. He was a dark shadow come to life. My mouth felt dry. I didn't speak, but I managed a nod.

"Awesome. Let's go," said Erica as she moved forward.

I tried not to be shaken. I didn't know why everyone else was so calm about this. I felt like his black eyes were staring right at me, though I don't know why. I was a little freaked out. It wasn't that I had anything against snipers. I had met one or two before, and they had been very calm, collected guys. But this guy seemed so intense, it left me on edge. He reminded me of an electrical fence. It seemed normal until you got closer. Then you could smell the ozone, and the hairs on your neck stood up. I could practically feel the electricity crackling off him.

I should have remembered what this feeling was, but it had been a long time since I was sixteen. I had forgotten what it was like to be so physically attracted to a stranger. It was that crazy bit of chemistry. To be clear, my husband was very attractive. He was a crackling fireplace, a slow heat that filled you up, soothing and happy. This, on the other hand, was like smelling smoke on the wind in the dry grasslands. This was wildfire. It was dangerous. My mind was on survival, not on romantic drama, so I didn't really notice. Honestly, I thought he might try to kill me at first.

I tried to keep my mind on the task at hand and focused on making it to Shadowbrook. We still had a lot of things to gather, and we wanted to check out the farmer's market to see if the rumors were true. We started pedaling down the road. Honestly, I don't remember if he had appeared with a bike or if someone brought him one. We all headed down the hill in the dark, silent as we waited for sky to lighten with the approach of dawn.

Lucky rode in my empty wagon. We followed my original path down back roads and footpaths. It had been a while since my last trip, and the path looked different. The leaves had begun changing color. Deep rich greens had begun to bleach to sickly yellows or were stained the first shades of red. It was an amazing transformation. We just didn't have this in the Southwest. There weren't these kinds of trees. To me it was like the city had just popped up in the middle of a forest. Nature seemed to be reclaiming what man had built. Dirt and leaves were already taking over the footpaths through parks. The natural quiet of the world unnerved me. The only sounds that could be heard were our breathing and our wheels across dirt and pavement.

We made good time. I was in the lead since I had taken this route before. The wagon pulled a bit on my bike but didn't slow me down. The bike and wagon combo were both sturdy and wasted little effort on the winding paths of the park. We crossed a side road and headed for the bridge I had previously taken across the runoff canal, where it looked like a once naturally formed brook had been modified, with smaller streams rerouted to it. The main streets also crossed over the canal, but these side bridges were designed for walkers and people in the park. They fit the bikes just fine. The footbridges were fenced in a way that created a sort of tunnel across the water. It was a little creepy but only because I had never liked the idea of having fences over my head. It would be a short, straight shot across the bridge. I didn't even really have to slow down for it.

But I screeched to a halt when I finally reached the bridge. My brain halted as well. The bridge was still there, but it looked like something from a horror movie. For a terrible moment, my mind believed what it saw. It believed that there were babies tied to the fence. After a moment sanity returned, and I realized they were dolls, about a dozen different types and styles of dolls tied to or hanging from the fence.

Behind me, Ethan said, "What the fuck? Oh shit." Then he let out a breath. "I seriously thought for a second ..." He didn't need to finish that thought.

I was scanning around when Erica leaned forward on her bike and in a low voice asked, "Was that there before?"

I shook my head. "No. Not three weeks ago anyway."

John looked behind us, and we all started looking around. "Looks like someone has been doing some redecorating." He nodded in the direction of some benches and trees. Now that we had stopped, it was easier to see the little markings of red spray paint and piles of crap stacked up.

"Looks like we need to find a different road back," I said as I wrote a note in my book: "Baby doll gang." I looked around and unslung my shotgun. I checked the safety and load. "I will go first. This side is pretty open, so we would be able to see if they were waiting for us. It's the other side we need to be worried about. There are a lot of trees along the path."

Jeri readied his hunting rifle and gave me a nod. The Shadow, as I had come to think of the sniper, had already set up his rifle and adjusted his scope. Between those two, I felt pretty secure about crossing the bridge. I slowly pedaled down the little path.

Lucky laid his head back down as I started moving again. The wheels of the wagon squeaked. The breeze blew against my red cheeks. It was cold today, but the pedaling kept my skin warm and blood flowing. My heart pounded in my ears as the glass and plastic eyes of those empty, soulless replicas of life watched me pass. Dolls had always creeped me out. I preferred teddy bears.

Beyond them other things had been tied to the fence: a set of shoes, a string of pearls. A bunch of CDs flickered and flashed in the early morning light. I emerged from the tunnel of the discarded both a little frightened and sad. Someone had gathered up all these things that had once meant something to someone and strung them up in a lonely, gruesome display. I stopped for a moment with shotgun in hand and waited to see if anyone stepped out. I looked at Lucky, who simply yawned at me. I waved back at those behind me and motioned them forward. They all made their way through the tunnel.

We found ourselves staring at the display. John was the first to dismount. He walked up to the fence and dug out something from deep in his bag. It was his college ID badge on its nylon strap. He looped it and tied it on the fence. His face and name fluttered amid the flickering shines from the CDs. Ethan joined him and tied on what looked like a sports award medallion. Erica removed a beautiful glass-bead necklace and tied it in place. Jeri looked at them and then at me. He shrugged and moved up. He used one of the strings already tied in place to attach a little carved bird. Even the Shadow tied something to the fence, though I didn't know what was in the little bag he tied in place. I found myself smiling a little. We were placing our offerings in the tunnel, paying a toll for crossing by leaving a bit of ourselves.

It was my turn, and it took me a moment to figure out what to leave. With slow and deliberate motions, I tied my house keys to the fence. Tears stung at the corner of my eyes as I watched them flash and jingle. My heart clenched painfully as I let them go. They were all that was left of the first home I had ever owned. It was nothing but ashes now. The doors the keys had unlocked were gone. I blew out a breath and turned to the others. They were smiling, and Jeri gave my shoulder a squeeze as I headed back to my bike.

Erica smiled encouragingly to me and then looked at everyone. "It can be scary to let go. It is frightening to see what others let go of. But once you let things go, you suddenly realize how much lighter you feel. It wasn't a warning. It was a whisper of goodbye."

I thought that was a beautiful way to think of it. I wish it had been true.

We made a circle around the downtown area. Even on these back roads, one could see more evidence of people passing. Folks had figured out not to use the main road. We passed a few more parks and then crossed the last bridge before the long shot through the quiet neighborhood and up to the strip mall. The water was high, higher than it had been last time. I figured this was because of the rain. The sun was fully up now. The crows were gone when we crossed the last bridge. We rode along the residential streets, the yards overgrown now. The porches were full of leaves.

I stopped in front of a familiar house. The sheets were gone from out front, and no one was visible. I stepped off the bike and slowly walked up to the front door. My hat was off, and my gun was slung over my shoulder. I pulled out a note I had written ahead of time to Margie. I was slipping it in the mail slot when the door opened slightly. A little, clean, round-cheeked face looked out at me. The eyes were bright, and there was a little smile there. The door didn't open all the way because of a chain.

"Hi," the voice squeaked at me.

I handed the note through the opening. "Give that to Mama, OK?"

The child nodded and disappeared, and I heard the sound of little feet running on the hardwood. As I heard heavier thuds approaching, I backed up. The door suddenly shut, and then a handsome but angry-looking man yanked the door open with a baseball bat in his hand.

"Who are you? What do you want?" His voice was low but harsh. I guessed someone was sleeping.

I kept my voice low as well. "Sorry. I was just stopping by to check on Margie. I rode by a few weeks ago. Since I was passing by, I thought I would check in." I kept my hands where he could see them. "I didn't mean any harm."

He looked past me to the folks who waited in the street. Jeri had his rifle resting across his legs.

He nodded a little and looked back at me. "You are cleaner than she described."

I laughed and nodded. "I put all that soap to good use." I saw the little face peek out from behind him. "I actually brought something for your family. I didn't want to leave it on the doorstep. May I bring it to you?"

He frowned a bit but nodded. I went to the wagon and retrieved the small box of things I had brought. It wasn't much, but it was some of the important stuff.

The man frowned again as he looked inside the box. "What is this?"

"I knew there were kids here, so its basic medicine stuff—kids' multivitamins, baby aspirin. These are antibiotics."

He had set down the bat as more faces had appeared in the doorway. He was holding the box while I inventoried it for him, his expression becoming more and more confused.

"Bandages and antibiotic cream for scratches. These are instructions on how to purify your water. This is a five-pound bag of rice. Some cans of tuna and spam. Here are some waterproof matches. Crayons and coloring books for the kids. My kids wanted to make sure those got here. My husband sent this—it's a working LED flashlight. It has one of those emergency wind-up generators."

I looked up and saw Margie coming toward us. She was cradling a nursing baby.

"Good morning," she said.

I nodded and smiled. "Good morning to you too."

She looked tired but pleased. "Wow, you really meant what you said."

I smiled and nodded. "Sorry it took me so long to get back here. I didn't forget about Gramm's. I put some arthritis cream in there."

Margie smiled even bigger. "Thank you. This is my husband George."

"It is nice to meet you," I said, looking back at him.

He stood there looking at the box and then looking at me. His lips were set in a hard line, and his face was intense. I thought for a moment he wouldn't take the box. Some people thought charity was insulting.

"Liam." George said the name very quietly, and the oldest kid, probably eight years old, came forward. George handed the box to him. Liam staggered a little but held it.

Suddenly, I was engulfed in a bear hug. George was shaking. I suddenly realized that he was almost in tears. I saw Margie smile, and I patted his shoulder.

"Thank you. God bless you. Thank you," he said.

I was a bit overwhelmed by the reaction. He set me down and

held up his hands, looking behind me. I waved to Jeri and the Shadow, who had lifted their rifles.

He sniffed and coughed. "Sorry. Sorry. It's just that …" He shook his head and grabbed the box and his son in one big lift and walked back inside without finishing the sentence.

Margie shook her head. "Sorry. George doesn't express himself well. He is very grateful—and not just for the care package." She shifted the baby and began gently bouncing him. "He and some of our folks ran into problems with another group. One of his friends got hurt. It really shook everybody. It's hard to have faith in people these days. I think you've done a lot to show him that there are still good people. Thank you." She gave me a look I couldn't read. "Is there anything we can do for you?"

I shook my head. "You just keep yourselves safe, OK?" I smiled and tipped my hat, waved to the little peeping faces, and headed out of the yard.

The others looked at me and then at the house. "Why don't they come up to the hill?" John asked as I got onto my bike.

Jeri looked at him seriously and said, "Why would they? They have a home. Why leave it when they have what they need?"

Ethan shook his head. "Aren't they scared out here?"

I smiled at him. "Of course, they are. But we are scared on the hill. They have their own community. Just because we don't see any others doesn't mean they are alone." I waved at Margie standing at the door, and we all started pedaling again.

It wasn't long before we stopped at the end of the road that led to the strip mall. I didn't see anyone moving around. It was still early morning, and the road was filled with leaves and bits of trash that had blown in from somewhere. The street and windows looked dingy and empty. Now this place looked like a ghost town. It seemed as if it had been left for ages. Even now, nothing was broken or burnt, but it was hard to say if anyone had been here after me.

I didn't realize I had started humming until Ethan said, "Seriously? Are you humming that now? I am going to get that stuck in my head."

"Sorry," I said with a shrug. "This place just gives me the creeps."

Erica laughed quietly to herself. Jeri didn't look fazed. He was used to me by now.

John shook his head. "You're a strange lady, Mouse. Humming Disney tunes out here is seriously a little creepy."

I shrugged again.

Ethan looked grumpy. "Damn it, I'm never going to get it out of my head now."

We went straight to the main store. I remembered the bell and smiled as I stepped in quietly. The place looked much the same. There was a stillness in the air that suggested no one had been here for a while. My note remained where I had set it. I went and gathered smokes and liquor from the back and carried them outside. The Shadow was nowhere to be seen, but I knew he was watching us. Lucky jumped out of the wagon and followed me. We picked up more dog food and a grooming brush. Then I went to the hair salon to get the stuff I had stashed away. We loaded things we thought could be traded for goods. I grabbed as much of the medical supplies as we could fit, from antacids to aspirins. I made sure we left one of each thing in a basket at the front desk with a note that said, "In case of emergency."

Jeri looked at me and tilted his head. "Why are you leaving that?"

I shrugged. "What if someone is hurt and runs in here looking for supplies? I would hate to think I had taken it all and left some poor soul without. We aren't the only people out here."

Everyone stopped to look at me like I was crazy.

"What?" I said defensively.

Erica grinned and looked at the guys. "See, I told you. She seems all hard-core, but the truth is she is just one big mommy, trying to help everyone."

I rolled my eyes as I put the supplies in the wagon. Lucky got back in the wagon and made himself comfortable on the toilet paper.

I pulled out my map. "From what I see on this map, if we are going to head north from here, it should be on that road. It's a straight shot out of this neighborhood. If the market is where we've heard, then we take that road till we get onto the freeway. Then there are surface streets we can try, or we take the freeway till three exits down and turn west."

John shrugged and looked around at us. "Freeway would be faster, and we would be able to see easier."

Erica nodded in agreement.

"Yeah, but we would be a lot more visible as well," I said as I put my map away.

The Shadow spoke from out of nowhere. "We take the freeway. We don't slow down. We take the other roads back," he said as he slung his rifle over his shoulder. None of us even thought to argue.

We all set off again. The outskirts of the neighborhood to the north looked very different. There were a lot of abandoned cars and what looked like FEMA tents set up. It seemed they had evacuated this area, and this was where the refugees had begun their trip.

"I wonder where they went," I said as we passed the loading zone.

"It doesn't matter. It wasn't far enough," Jeri said in a quiet voice.

The remark sounded so sad and doomed that I wanted to argue, but I let it go. I just focused on pedaling. I hoped we would find something worth all this effort. I already missed my kids. It was going to be a long day.

The road opened up as we got on the freeway. The wind felt good on my face. John and Ethan raced each other ahead of us, laughing. It felt so good to just go along the flat, even surface. My mind drifted between different songs, playing them in my head as I moved in easy time with my heartbeat. Lucky leaned to one side of the wagon, his mouth hanging open. The sun was not even that far up in the sky, but it was warming up a bit, so it was a nice day to be outside. The highway was surprisingly empty. The world was quiet except for the wind rushing past my ears and through my hair.

I flew, zooming over the smooth pavement. My early morning shadow raced beside me as we headed north. My wheels buzzed as I shifted gears. In moments like this, my mind could be free, free from worry, fear, and doubts. Those things were heavy; they couldn't keep up. They would catch up eventually, but as I flew, they simply fell away. I didn't realize how much I was smiling until my cheeks ached.

Jeri was laughing as he caught up with John and Ethan. Erica grinned, and I started humming something fast and happy. I found I even had a smile for the Shadow. What was even crazier was that he smiled back. How they had ever found a bike tall enough for him, I had no idea.

For twenty minutes we just rode, wonderfully free and excited, happy from endorphins or maybe from the sunshine. We were smiling when we came to the first signs of the marketplace. We spotted spray paint on the freeway sign and arrows on the side of the road. I read the signs painted in big graffiti letters: "EVACUA-TION CENTER"; "SAVE US"; "SURVIVORS"; "NO ZOMBIES!"

We rolled up to the exit off the freeway. There was a blockade. We could see men in police uniforms standing guard, watching us. The uniforms were wrinkled and looked like they had seen better days. As we approached, two men in National Guard uniforms stood up next to the policemen. The Shadow went forward and spoke to the National Guard men.

A policeman held up his hand and waved us over. "All right, here is the deal," the officer said. "We are not taking any more refugees. You want to come into the market, that's fine. You have to have this on your hand." He held up what looked like a stamp. "If you are spotted here overnight, you will be removed. Sorry, but there is no more room."

I held up my hand. "We aren't here to stay. Just here to trade" —I motioned to the wagon—"and talk to some folks, that's all. We don't need a place to stay."

The policeman nodded and looked behind him. "Don't advertise that. Most people here don't have anywhere else to go. Unless you want a bunch of people chasing you back to where you came from, don't talk about it. Do not tell anyone where you came from."

I nodded. "Thanks for being honest." I hoped he could tell I meant it.

He gave me a tired smile. "Just doing the best I can, ma'am. Power or no, I am still a cop. Now boys, stay close your women and your bikes. Not to be sexist, but we have had some assaults. Do *not* go past the yellow fences. We police the market as much as we can, but there is less policing in the camp. There are just not enough of us."

They stamped our hands and lifted a barricade out of place. The Shadow finished his conversation with the uniformed guards, and we followed him in, riding slow down a gravel path. We could see the campfires, and a scent hit us from the east. It wasn't pleasant. Mingled together there was the smell of smoke, human waste, and cooking food. It was the stink of humanity, of too many people crowded together. Thankfully, the market had been set up in the parking lot at the edges, so we didn't have to try and navigate through all of it. People had tables or little wood booths. Some had their actual booths from farmer's markets. Others sat on blankets with things laid out in front of them.

It was impossible to tell if there was a FEMA camp somewhere beyond those yellow fences. The State fairgrounds covered more than 375 acres, there were dozens of buildings and facilities. It was connected to the local railroad line. I was confused. I expected this place to be cleaner and more organized. Is this what happened to all the people who were evacuated. There was supposed to be a rally station here. As overcrowded as it was, I could tell—it wasn't even a quarter of the people who *should* have been here.

"It's so crowded," John said as he looked at the market and at the shantytown that was being built behind it. There were nylon tents, FEMA tents, and even some actual National Guard relief tents. It looked like some people from the Red Cross were here.

I frowned and nodded. "Yeah, but there should be more people. The city seems like a ghost town. Where is everyone? There were like, what, sixty thousand people living here? There can't be more than ten thousand here."

Ethan considered that. "They can't be dead. If they were, bodies would be everywhere."

The Shadow gave a nod and said, "Trains. Old steam trains." He motioned to the south.

We could see the train station. Steam billowed up from something in that direction. From this distance it was hard to make out what was happening. It reminded me of an ant hill. It looked like they had been busy. It was good to know people were figuring things out, not just sitting here waiting to be saved.

thirteen
wednesday, 11:30am-ish

WE WALKED our bikes to where the edges of the market seemed to begin, next to some folks on blankets. We decided that we would chain the bikes together, and the Shadow would stay there to guard them and our things.

The Shadow sat down on the bikes and readied his rifle. I unhooked my wagon and kept Lucky in it as I pulled it along behind me. It was like a mix between a bazaar and a mining town. The ground was muddy, and the smell was just barely tolerable. I kept my shotgun on my back, and Erica and I stayed close to each other. We walked through the market, where people were bartering and trading. There were children, many of them dirty and looking thin, but it wasn't as bad as I had feared. A bunch asked to pet Lucky, which I didn't mind and the kids all loved. I was out of candy in no time, but I was very popular. Pretty soon, everyone knew about Mouse and her Lucky dog.

Before long I got to meet the moms of these kids. I shook a lot of hands and talked to them. A woman carrying an infant who didn't look more than three months old followed a blond boy of maybe five to my wagon. He got a granola bar since I was out of M&Ms. He seemed happy that there were bits of chocolate in the bar. Then his mother looked in the wagon and apparently saw something. She grabbed my arm, leaned in close, and whispered, "Please."

I was a little startled. "What?"

She showed me her wedding ring and whispered, "I will trade you this if you will give me those cans of formula. It's impossible to get here. I am trying to breastfeed, but I am not producing enough. And the powdered milk just isn't working for him." She was whispering in a rush, and there were tears in her eyes as she looked around. She seemed afraid that someone would jump out and attack us.

I looked at the baby in her arms and at the boy, who was petting a very content Lucky. I leaned in. "Why are we whispering?"

She sighed and shook her head. "Some things are harder to get than others. I don't have anything else to trade."

I patted her hand. "OK. I can't give them all to you. But it will be enough to get you through a little while. Do we need to hide it?"

She nodded. I took a jacket, wrapped it around three cans of baby formula, and put the bundle into a plastic bag with other items, so it looked like just a coat and gloves and a hat for the boy. She started trying to pull off her ring, and I grabbed her hand again.

"It's OK," I said, shaking my head.

She blinked in surprise. She started to cry a little and grabbed the bag. The baby started fussing, and the boy stepped over to help his mother carry the bag. He waved goodbye.

I winced as Erica gave me a look. "I know ... I know. I will stop, I promise."

She nodded. "You had better, or we won't have anything to trade." Her tone was a little sharp, but I understood.

Ethan patted me on the back and gave me a wink. "It's OK. Gives us an excuse to come again."

We continued walking. We did manage to trade some bleach to

a man who was selling dried and smoked meat. We traded a bag of flour for fresh vegetables. I traded some rice for honey. I was surprised when on the very edge of the market, we found a very neat, clean area being tended by either Amish or Mennonites. They had bread, preserves, meat, vegetables, and even furnishings. I walked up and looked at the selection. An older woman who looked stout and serious nodded to me. I smiled at her. "Good morning," I said.

She nodded again, and I noticed her very bright green eyes watched me carefully.

"I have some things to trade, but I'm not sure if you're open to it."

She looked around and shrugged slightly. "What are you trading?" Her voice was surprisingly kind-sounding, though she looked like she could chop a person to pieces with her face.

"I have salt, some spices, medicines," I said, motioning to the wagon behind me. Lucky wagged his tail.

She nodded and looked at my items. "What are you looking for?"

There were some really wonderful things here. I picked some overalls and socks and a new pair of leather shoes for Victor. These were the hardest-to-find clothes for him. I chose some canned goods and dried meats, and I almost cheered when I saw eggs and butter. The last thing I put on the pile was a small hatchet. It was solid wood with a good, strong, sharp head.

An old man came and looked at my pile. He broke into a grin when he saw the shoes. "These were made by my son."

The woman gave him a disapproving look.

"You have a son?" I responded, smiling back at him. I pulled the picture of my own son out of my hat.

He nodded. "A strong son." He looked at my pile and the items I had set out to trade. I knew I didn't really have much they needed, but I had set out the items anyway. He pulled out a heavy quilt and set it next to everything. "There, that looks about even, doesn't it?"

The old woman gave him a not-pleased look, and he nodded back at her. "Greed is a sin after all," he said, and he added a bag of raisins and a bag of apples. "We have a whole passel of grandchildren here with us. A bunch have come to tell me tales about a Mouse with a lucky dog in a red wagon who was passing out candy." He grinned. "It made them very happy. We should remember that it is children who suffer or prosper from the choices of adults." He smiled at the old woman, and she huffed but gave him a soft smile.

I tried not to grin at the unspoken communication between them, at her simultaneous exasperation and love at his overly generous nature.

"Blessings be to mothers," she said. She smiled and looked at my photo. "I see you have other children as well. There is much joy in this picture. Lovely. You are very blessed. Are they all well?"

I nodded and smiled. "Thank you both so much. The eggs are a miracle."

She nodded and helped me load everything into my wagon. Lucky had to move so there could be room. He licked her hand. She petted him gently. "Good day, Mrs.," she said.

I felt a little teary-eyed. "God bless you."

She smiled brightly. "Oh, he has, for us all."

The old couple stepped back behind their stand. The old man whispered, "Beware the Sol's Apostle." He patted my hand as he stepped away.

I nodded as I left. I had no idea what he was talking about. But I would soon find out.

We had been at the marketplace for an hour or more when we stopped by a little stand for some lunch. We traded salt and a box of baking soda for meals. They were serving hamburgers with fries on the side. I didn't ask what the burgers were made of. I knew there were cows in the area, but I didn't ask. I had water, but Ethan and John decided to try the lemonade. I got a meal for the Shadow, who was still with the bikes, and a rare-meat patty for Lucky, who also got water.

Back at the bikes, we could hear someone giving a speech and spotted a man standing on a wooden crate near the edge of the camp. I handed the Shadow his meal, and he smiled at me and nodded, sitting down to eat his food quickly. He kept his eyes on the crowd that was gathering around the crate-box speaker. I wasn't really listening to them until they started chanting: "Praise be! Praise be!" The speaker continued with what was more a sermon than a speech. The cops milled about; they didn't seem very happy with the size of the group. I started hooking my wagon back up to my bike. We all started checking our equipment, preparing to leave.

"Take heart, my brothers and sisters, for we are the chosen ones. We survived the wrath! We saw the lights of God's divine justice. He smote those that displeased him. He gave us a chance to start anew. In his mercy he did not wipe us away in a flood but destroyed the devil's chains around us so that we might be free. He has delivered us from the wickedness of the world. He has set us free from the greed and the perversion! He has shown us that we do *not* hold dominion over this world, that he is present and watching us. He will always be watching over us. Praise be to Him our God."

His voice had a distinctly rhythmic sound. He was full of energy and a kind of music. He reminded me of televangelists. I kept waiting for him to mention that the people needed to open their hearts and their wallets and give. Or when politicians really got going, they had a wonderful banter to their speeches. I turned back to my task. One thing I had learned a long time ago was not to listen to either; they both just wanted whatever was in your pocket.

We were finishing up our packing when three young people approached us. They all looked like they were eighteen to twenty.

They were surprisingly clean and well groomed. They wore light-colored clothing. The girls had little flowers tied in their hair, probably paper since it was too cold for blossoms.

"Hello, brothers and sisters," one of the girls said. "My name is Julia. This is Maria and our brother Mark."

John smiled. The girls were pretty after all. "Hi, it's nice to meet you," he said. He shook hands, and his brother followed suit.

I was busy making sure that my tires were pumped properly and that my gears didn't need to be oiled. I wasn't really paying too much attention. They were chatting about casual things, from what kind of bikes those were to the fact that they were brothers. It seemed innocent enough until I heard the girl Maria ask, "So you all rode here together?"

I looked up and saw that Ethan was smiling and nodding like an idiot teenager. "Yep, we are all here together."

She smiled brightly at him, shifting slightly back and forth in classic flirty posture. "Was it a long ride?"

Ethan opened his mouth, and I threw a bag at him. It hit his shoulder, and he jumped. He turned and gave me a perturbed look. "What? What did you do that for?"

I tilted my head and smiled at him. "It's time to go, Romeo."

He glared at me and looked at Maria with a smile. "One second." He came over to me. John also separated himself from Julia, who had been talking to him about the college classes they had been taking.

"Look, why don't you guys go on ahead, and we will catch up?" Ethan said. John nodded.

I stopped smiling instantly and glared at them. "Because that is a stupid idea. It's the idea of a teenager who is trying to get laid and isn't thinking about how dangerous and obvious it is."

Ethan looked disbelieving, but John blushed and looked back at the girls. He then looked over at the brother, who was talking to Erica. Ethan was starting to rationalize and make excuses to get what he wanted when John suddenly broke in with a whisper.

"Hey, isn't that Bobby?" he said to Ethan. "From the lacrosse team?"

Ethan looked at John for a second. "What?"

Ethan started to turn, but John stopped him. "Don't make it obvious."

Ethan turned casually and smiled at the girls, holding up a finger in a "wait one second" gesture. He turned back, looking confused. "Yeah, that is Bobby. She said his name was Mark. Why didn't he say anything? He just acted like he didn't know us."

I looked over and frowned a little. "Was he one of the people who left to go to the base?"

Both Ethan and John nodded.

"He wasn't a good friend, but we had some classes together. I was on the track team, so we sort of ran in the same circles." Ethan shook his head. "This turned weird really fast."

"We should leave," I said seriously. "Don't tell them where we are from or where we are going. Maybe he doesn't recognize you, and that's good. It's never a good thing when someone hides who they are. Whatever they are after isn't good."

"But what if he is in trouble? Maybe we should find out what's going on. I mean, we should help, right? We can't just leave."

I almost groaned. Young people, ten feet tall and bulletproof. "Look, Ethan, I know you think you need to stay here and figure this mystery out, but this is not a movie. There are real dangers out here—and real bullets. You can't just go running around like some Scooby Doo wannabe."

He was nodding and looking at me, but he was not listening.

"I can't afford for you to be reckless right now. The group can't afford that. Your brother can't afford that."

He nodded again. "I will be careful," he said as he started to turn away.

I wanted to slap him.

Erica was laughing as she said, "Hey, guys, Mark says they are having a gathering over in that field. There will be a music circle, even some food and wine. It sounds nice."

"Yeah, you guys should totally come," Julia said brightly.

Maria nodded her enthusiasm. "It is a lot of fun, and Father Jacob will want to meet everyone. He loves meeting new people."

The Shadow had finished eating and stood up. "No. Time's up."

Erica frowned and looked first at him and then at me. "Well, surely we can stay a little longer."

I shook my head and pointed to the sky. "We really need to be going, like right now," I said, trying for my best 'Mom is serious' voice.

Julia stepped over to John and smiled. "Well, if you're close by, maybe you can come back and see us after you ditch Mom and Dad."

Maria nodded again. "The fun stuff happens after sunset anyway."

I raised an eyebrow at her. "You don't even know these boys. Don't you think you're moving a little fast?"

Julia clearly did not appreciate my disapproving mom tone and gave me an angry glare. It was soon replaced by a nice, pleasant smile. "Well, of course not, but if we don't spend time together, we never will."

There was a swelling, clapping cheer from the crowd and shouts of "Amen." While we talked, the Shadow had passed out each person's packs. I had strapped down my tarp to hold everything in place for the ride home, making sure my precious eggs were safely cushioned with the quilt and clothes inside a metal toolbox. The look on the Shadow's face made it clear that no one was staying behind. John and Ethan didn't bother arguing. Jeri wasn't even looking at the two girls. He knew a trap when he saw one.

Julia looked behind her toward the crowd, and Mark (or

Bobby) looked nervous. "Well, if you can make it, then come back," Julia said. "We would love to see you there."

Maria looked at John for a moment and then smiled at Ethan.

"Who are your friends?" a voice asked from the now dispersing crowd. It was the man who had given the speech. He looked to be in his late twenties, early thirties. He was also clean and dressed in light colors. It looked like linen. That must be hard to clean out here.

The girls suddenly stopped all their flirting and took on the shy demeanor of girls younger than themselves. "This is John and Ethan and their friend Erica. We haven't officially met the other two," Julia answered.

Mark kept his eyes lowered and didn't say anything. Lucky stiffened, and I felt tension rise up in his body as his hackles raised. I instantly disliked the man. Animals were always a good judge of character. The man had a placid smile on his face. He reminded me of a polished piece of glass, smooth, sleek, and transparent. I nodded politely and finished prepping my wagon. It was my guess that this was Father Jacob, or one of his people.

"Ah, you all look like long travelers. I see you have a military man with you. But I can tell you are not with the National Guard. What base are you from?" he asked smoothly and pleasantly.

If this had been any other time, any day before the power failure, I would have smiled and chatted. The glassman had a sweet demeanor, like old-fashioned caramel. But now something in that sweetness made me worry, like the sweetness was hiding poison. My agitation only got worse as Lucky growled low in his throat. I hadn't noticed when, but the man had come three steps closer. I felt a dread climb up my legs as he looked at me. He was almost within arm's reach when the Shadow stepped slightly in front of me.

The Shadow looked at the man. "You're right I am not National Guard." he said as he shifted his pack and set himself to leave.

It was all I could do not to pull my shotgun or run.

Erica seemed to get the drift and frowned as she stepped away from Mark and over to her bike. "Well, it's time we were on our way. It was nice meeting you," she said to Mark as she mounted her bike.

John, who was already on his bike, forced a friendly smile. Ethan stepped forward and shook hands with Mark. Looking at him seriously for a moment, he asked, "Did you ever play sports?"

Mark looked just as seriously at Ethan for a moment. He smiled politely. "Maybe in another life. Not in this one. Safe journey."

Ethan nodded and climbed onto his bike. I mounted mine and shifted to make sure my gun was reachable.

"Head out!" the Shadow shouted. His voice cracked out like a whip, and we all started pedaling.

"Safe travel, friends," the glass man said.

Lucky snarled at him to show his distaste before settling down as we pulled way.

Once we were back out on the open freeway, I felt a pressure release in my chest. I didn't realize how frightened I had been until I was away from there. My arms and legs got weak, and I had to actually stop for a minute. As I tried to catch my breath and took a drink of water, the others circled back and came to a stop next to me.

"You OK?" Erica asked, sounding concerned.

I nodded and shook out my arms. "Am I the only one who feels like we just escaped something really bad? I don't know if it was that place or that preacher, but I had a serious case of the creeps."

John nodded and looked behind us. "Yeah, me too once I noticed how many questions they were asking. They were careful not to directly ask how many of us there are, but they asked, 'Are there other students there?'" He sighed and shook his head. "That was so stupid. I shouldn't have even started talking to her."

I felt bad. He was just a normal guy used to talking to girls all the time. It wasn't easy to just change the way you thought about every person in the world.

Ethan looked upset too. "Shit, she asked me what we had traded for." He cursed a bit. "I didn't even think about it. I just thought she was looking for something to talk about. So I told her."

Erica frowned. "So what?" She looked at the rest of us. "What could that tell them? What could they possibly get out of how many students are with us and what we traded for?"

The Shadow spoke calmly and quietly but ominously. "Everything's important. It could tell them if we are near campuses, if we have students or soldiers. We traded for tools, wires, and eggs, and we let go of staples like salt, baby formula, and bleach. That tells them we have those things to get rid of." He shrugged and took a moment to look into his scope behind and around us. "That tells them that we have things they want and that there are other people and children there."

Erica suddenly looked stricken and swallowed hard. "Oh no. I mentioned that I was still in my house. I think I might have said something about not wanting to leave it no matter what the fascists say." She looked upset. "I didn't think about it. I am so sorry."

The Shadow shrugged. "That's probably a good thing. It lets them know we have military presence. They will be careful not to come too close even if they figure out where we are going." It was odd for him to say so much.

"We are being followed," Jeri said softly.

"Yes, good eye," the Shadow responded.

"What should we do?" John asked.

I sighed. "Only one thing to do. We take the long way home and try to lose them."

The Shadow nodded and looked around before looking at me. "You lead. You know the way."

Everyone nodded and looked at me. That weight returned. Fear crept up my spine. I didn't want to be in charge. I didn't want to be responsible for them. I felt a fluttering of bird wings inside my center, the kind of panic that could send a person running scared. I looked at my watch and out at the road ahead. I took a moment to breathe. I pulled air into my lungs and slowly let it out. In and out. *Breathe, just breathe*, I told myself. Suddenly, I felt the warmth of the sun, and I could almost hear my little ones laughing.

Courage is doing what you must, even when you are afraid. It was never easy. I focused on calming the bird inside and listened to the theme music being played for me. Inside my head I listened to Johnny Cash singing to me about "when the man comes to town." The makings of a plan began to form.

We pedaled fast. I took the group past two exits. This put us on a downward slope toward downtown and gave us a view behind. I stopped in the shadow of an overpass and watched as a group of riders crested the hill. They were on what looked like mountain bikes. They stopped at the top of the hill. We took off again, and this time I took a congested exit. A bus had crashed into a truck, but there was enough room to pass, so we rolled into downtown.

"We have to be careful here," I said. "There are gangs and all kinds of different groups. We are going to lose them in the buildings and then head along the back paths."

The others nodded, and we all started pedaling hard. We saw the followers start after us. I stopped looking behind then and focused on where I was going. I zoomed the wrong way down a one-way street, past dead cars and burned-out streetlights. I raced down the streets past hollowed-out shops and charred bricks. Most of downtown was intact because of solid construction and good city planning.

The roads were bumpy with debris and clutter. We heard shouts, and things were flung at us as we zipped past an apartment complex. A group of very hard-looking men stood guard at a front door. They watched us pass with their hands on their guns. I took a turn to the left, down a main street that would lead to the big university. There were blockades at the end of the street. The massive stone edifice of education and higher learning stood strong against the rubble from the small shops and cafés that had been the college crowd's hangouts. It looked like this might have been a bad riot spot. We heard the shouts again in the distance behind us and knew our pursuers were catching up. I turned again sharply back downhill, hoping my cargo would make the turn as I came around from an alley to a main street. I let out a yelp as I screeched to a halt. I almost collided with a cement roadblock and a man with a gun. Our eyes met in a startled frozen moment.

It took me a second to see that this was the police building and they had blockaded their street. The man was as surprised to see me as I was to see him. His police uniform was a bit dusty and wrinkled, but he was still wearing it. The others screeched behind me. He looked nervous and kept his gun drawn.

I spoke quickly. "Sorry—we are being chased."

He looked at me and then nodded. "All right. Get out of here quickly. Be careful. Someone else might shoot you." He moved behind the blockade, and we started pedaling again. He waved us on urgently. "Go, quickly, before you are seen."

I headed down to city hall and through the main square. There were a bunch of streets in this area that curved and turned into each other like they had to follow the flow of the landscape. My idea was to lose them before we headed back along the scar. Then that route would give us plenty of view and time to make sure we had indeed lost them.

We heard shouts and gunfire from behind us, and we pushed harder. I suspected that the cop was giving us a warning. My breathing was becoming ragged, and I felt my heart hitting my ribs. Sweat trickled down into my eyes. I took a straight shot up Main. As we crossed Fifth Avenue, I saw some men step out of a building wearing the prison outfits I'd seen before. They were carrying bags and tossing them into dumpsters. They didn't stop us. They just watched as we zipped past them.

I pedaled for everything I was worth, making three figure eights around the downtown area. I suddenly caught sight of Fire Station 3. I raced for it. I don't know why exactly. Maybe because it was familiar or because the garage gate was up. There was enough room for us to duck inside and move to where we couldn't be seen. I almost crashed into the back wall while trying to stop.

We were all panting as we hid on the dark side of the garage. My adrenaline was pumping so hard that I didn't see anything inside at first. All my senses were straining to perceive our pursuers. My mouth was dry, and my skin dripped with sweat. We had been going top speed with full cargo for at least three miles. My thighs felt like Jell-O. I got the kickstand down and practically fell off my bike. Lucky got out of the wagon and sat next to me. Everyone else did the same. Even the Shadow was panting and sweating. He took off up the stairs. We all breathed heavily until we heard it, the buzzing sound of gears turning. Then we did our best to cover our breathing. We watched them come around from three different corners.

One of the riders shouted to the other, "Which way?"

The other called back, "Don't know. I lost them."

I sat motionless, my hand over my mouth forcing myself to breathe through my nose.

"We need to find them. The Apostle said we had to find where they came from."

"I know that! I didn't let them get away on purpose. Did you see what they were doing? It was like trying to chase rats in a maze. I was almost shot by that fucking cop."

The pair started to argue about what to do next and where to look. Suddenly, one of the other riders shouted, "Shut up!"

The others stopped and looked over at him. "What?" the first asked.

"Listen!" he said and held up a hand. They all listened.

We listened too. We looked at one another and strained to hear what they were hearing. I heard a tapping. It was not quite a drumming sound, but narrower and sharper, like a metal bar hitting something rhythmically.

"Shit, it's the Crazies," one of the riders whispered.

"We need to get out of here—*now*."

There was a moment of arguing as a more devout rider tried to insist that God would protect them. The discussion was cut off by a voice high and loud, screeching in a bizarre laugh: "Here, little piggy! Here, piiig!" Then there was the most obnoxious pig call I had heard since I was in Texas, followed by a howl from somewhere else.

Jeri grabbed my arm, and I twitched, clutching my shotgun. There was more banging, screeching, laughing, and hooting. It seemed to be coming from everywhere at once.

"Fuck this!" one of the riders said and took off as fast as he could pedal. Two others followed suit.

One of the riders dropped his bike, sank to his knees, and started praying. The last two sat terrified on their bikes, not sure what to do. Then the source of the sounds revealed themselves. Several were on skates and skateboards. A few were on foot, and a couple were on bikes. They were filthy, covered in soot and paint. I was reminded of the book *The Lord of the Flies* and those bad 1980s movies featuring underground street gangs. The last two riders abandoned their kneeling friend and raced off. This only seemed to excite the mob, which took off after those who had fled. One picked up the bike of the fellow who was praying and used it to chase after his companions. As quickly as the scene had filled with these wild ones, they were gone, chasing their prey with crazed abandon.

For a few moments there was nothing but the sound of the last one praying. "Praise be, he has delivered me," he said as he got to his feet.

I waited in dread for the Hollywood moment where one last

crazy remembered that the young man was standing there and came back and killed him. But the guy, who probably wasn't even old enough to drink, just turned and walked back the way he had come. I was glad.

Jeri was still holding my arm. We just sat in silence, trying to breathe. That was when I noticed. The bodies were gone. The smell that had been so heavy the first time I was here had faded. All that remained of those who had been left here were stains on the concrete, easily mistaken for grease from the trucks. Even the sheets were gone. Someone had cleaned up. I thought about saying something to the others, but I didn't say a word.

After ten minutes or so, the Shadow came back down. In a whisper, he said, "All clear for us. We go. Now."

We all mounted up and rolled out as quietly as we were able. We took a slightly more direct route than I'd planned but did a couple of loops to confirm we weren't still being followed. By the time we made it back up the hill, we just walked our bikes up the last bit of it. I didn't even take my wagon to supply. I was so tired that I just sat on my porch and let my children climb on me.

Tomorrow. I could think about all of it tomorrow. I could deal with the supplies and turn in the things we had collected then. Right now, I had no other intentions but hugging my children and not moving my legs. I know, such high ambitions and lofty goals.

fourteen
thursday, 9:15am

THE NEXT MORNING, I sorted out the wagon, separating what was going to supply and what we were keeping. I kept most of the eggs, but some were for the next baking day. I dressed Victor in his new clothes, and everyone got new wool socks. I tried out the hatchet on the firewood. It worked wonders. We put the cheese and eggs in the nonelectric cooler that Albert had built. It consisted of two large clay pots, one inside the other, with what looked like sand or rocks between them. Then we just poured water between the pots, and the evaporation kept everything really cool. It was neat. We had eggs, butter, and cheese. I made sure we had enough soap for cleaning and washing.

I decided to take Victor and Zyada with me to supply because they wanted to get out of the house for a while. Nathan seemed content with his book. Victor and Zyada walked together just ahead of me, one on either side of Lucky, as I pulled the wagon. The air was still a bit a chilly as we walked. Even though the sun was out, we needed jackets. I figured we would have frost soon. Winter snaps were very harsh here. But today it was just a bit brisk and pleasant.

Mouthy was not at the table when we finally made it into the mobile office. Instead we found one of his crew, Private Fowler.

The private smiled brightly at me. "Hello, ma'am." He grinned and waved at Zyada, who beamed at him. Victor smiled and waved hello too.

Fowler helped me unload the cart quickly, and we loaded my rations of other supplies. I was pleasantly surprised to receive baked beans, peas, hot chocolate, soup, spaghetti sauce, and dried noodles. We were given some crackers and even some broth mix.

I was planning meals in my head when Private Burgess tapped my shoulder. She nodded politely at the private behind the desk and then returned her attention to me. "Ma'am, Lieutenant Roberts would like to speak to you," she said very formally.

I nodded and pointed at my kids. "OK, let me gather the little ones."

She nodded again and smiled at Zyada, who was grinning at her from ear to ear. I chased down Victor and tugged him along with us. Zyada helped pull the now mostly empty wagon behind us. Lucky was trotting along easily, just on the other side of Victor, who had his free hand resting on Lucky's shoulder.

Private Burgess unbent enough to whisper, "They are adorable children."

I grinned and nodded. "Yeah, they really are. I lucked out."

We stopped a few feet from the office where command had been set up. The private pulled out a small photo of three boys, each one just a head taller than the next. "These are mine," she said with just the smallest crack in her voice, a voice full of love, pride, and pain.

"They are so handsome. Have you heard anything?" I said with a soft smile.

Her hand shook just a little as she kissed the photo and put it away. She resumed her military bearing and nodded. "Yes, ma'am. I haven't spoken to them directly, but it seems our neighborhood didn't lose power. They were in Wyoming with my husband and my parents." She continued walking then and up the door for me.

We all walked inside. The office was sort of a mobile

command, set up inside one of the classrooms. I didn't know why they hadn't taken an actual office space. Maybe it had something to do with wanting open space for equipment. The lieutenant was looking particularly square today. His bushy eyebrows seemed intent on meeting in a frown above his brown eyes. It was a bit distracting. I was trying to figure out how he managed to keep his uniform crisp and sharp. I thought maybe it wasn't his uniform at all that caused the creases, but just how he was shaped.

He growled at someone over a shortwave radio. At first, I listen in, but I was suddenly in a wrestling match with Victor as I tried to keep him from racing off around the room. Zyada took this opportunity to slip away. Lucky looked from me to where Zyada had walked off, tilting his head from one side to the other. I was so busy with my little wrestler that I didn't notice until I heard her cheer and say, "It's a *map*!"

"It's the map, it's the map, it's the map!" she repeated in a singsong voice. The area wasn't very big, so she was easy to spot. She had stepped over to a table to the left. It was sectioned off mostly by chairs and rolling boards. There were diagrams and charts. It looked like a planning area.

"Shit!" I said as I did my best not to drop Victor, who was squealing and shouting to be set down. "Z! Get back here!" She ignored me completely as I headed towards her.

Suddenly, my vision went completely white as pain blossomed behind my eyes. To keep from falling on my ass I squatted. I was barely able to hold onto Victor even though I had too finally set him on the ground. I was worried my nose might be bleeding. I heard Victor laughing hysterically. When my vision cleared, there was a concerned marine looking down at me. Lucky was wagging his tail, his tongue hanging out slightly. I swear he was laughing at me.

"You OK, ma'am?" I could tell the marine wanted to laugh too.

"Yeah, sorry. They are driving me crazy today." I tried to smile.

He nodded and picked up Victor. I took the opportunity to rub my face.

"That was a good hit. He has great form with that head butt." he said as he turned a giggling Victor upside down over his shoulder. "This is a seriously huge little man here."

I nodded as the pain finally diminished to a dull throb. I looked over at Zyada, who was apparently explaining to someone that she knew all about maps. A rather fierce-looking fellow was listening with a serious expression and began quizzing her on what she knew.

"Why don't we look after these two while you go talk to the lieutenant?" the big marine asked with a smile. Shifting to a whisper, he continued, "Simmons there misses his little girl anyway. He has been moping. That's the first time he hasn't seemed depressed all day."

I nodded. I was feeling a bit overwhelmed, so a break was good. I stepped back and tried to enjoy having my hands free for a while. I took a deep breath to relax. Victor was being flown around the room and carried on tall shoulders. Zyada was sitting at the map, talking about symbols and how to tell where something was. One of the female communication techs joined in, and they started discussing radios.

"Well, it looks like you have managed to completely disrupt my command post," said a gruff voice from behind a cubicle wall.

I winced and looked behind me to see Lieutenant Eugene Roberts, looking even more brick-ish, if that was possible. He motioned me into the private area.

I braced myself as I stepped in. Lucky followed at my heel and sat down. "That wasn't my plan," I said. "But it's my turn to watch them. Albert is working with some of the electrical stuff today."

Lieutenant Brick nodded. "I know. I appreciate you coming in. Sergeant Mikoto said that you had quite the adventure. It's interesting that you went so far from camp. I don't remember giving any authorization for any team to be out yesterday."

I was standing in a relaxed posture with my hands in my pockets. My brain did a little skip as it tried to place the name. *Who the heck was Sergeant Mikoto? Wait was that the sniper's name? Nope, his name is 'The Shadow'. And who the fuck did Brick think he was. Authorization my ass.* He was being dramatic, beating around the bush. It was an intimidation tactic to see if I would quake or pretend to be contrite. If he thought I was that kind of person, he was in for a surprise.

I flicked my hair back out of my face in the casual "I don't give a damn" way I had learned as a stubborn teenager. "I don't remember enlisting and signing a contract saying I have to obey the chain of command." I smiled and shrugged in a carefree way. "I guess maybe we are both getting forgetful in our old age."

He gave me a hard look. I swear, somehow those brown eyes were little squares disguised as circles. They were hard little pebbles. He stood over me, his gaze boring into mine. It was like looking at my dad, as if he could will me into submission.

If I had been ten years younger, maybe even just five, I would have caved and made my apologies. But I wasn't that young anymore. I had to be harder than Brick, scarier than the Shadow, smarter than Mouthy, and just as stubborn as Grandpa and still be able to kiss boo-boos and sing bedtime lullabies. I had to be all that because I wasn't just *a* mother; I was *their* mother.

I felt all the frustration, fear, anger, pain, and despair rise up inside me. It was cold. It helped focus me on those eyes. I didn't look away from his face. I let the solid heaviness form into steel of my own. I was not sure how long we stared at each other in this silent battle of wills, but Lucky yawned, not at all impressed with either of us.

"If you're waiting for an apology, don't waste our time. I won't promise not to do it again. I was raised better than to lie," I finally said, breaking eye contact. He was better at this than me.

The lieutenant sat down, looking away as he picked up his

coffee and took a sip. There was a smile on his face. Honestly, I didn't know if that meant I had won or not.

"I was hoping that would be your response," he said. "Mouthy said that you were fierce. I am glad he was right as usual. The world is going to need people like you."

I was a bit confused because compliments weren't really the Brick's style. "Thanks, I think. If this isn't about reading me the riot act, what is this about?" I said carefully, sitting in the chair across from his desk.

"Winter is on its way, and we aren't ready. Word from command is we should be prepared for it to be a bad one. As it happens, your ... expedition gave Mikoto an excellent opportunity to recon and visually confirm intel of the fairgrounds. You have seen the numbers down there. They are in a world of hurt if they remain in the valley once winter starts. They need to get out of the valley. We have sent word up the chain, and additional resources are being sent to evacuate them." He sighed heavily. "The railroad is operational, but there are only a handful of trains running. It's a race against time. And that's just the fairgrounds; there are a number of groups holed up in their homes or at strongholds."

I nodded, still confused as to why he was talking to me about this. He seemed to be waiting for me to respond, so I gave a shrug and offered my opinion. "If they don't have the supplies to make it, they will try to leave, right? They won't stay and starve."

He shook his head. "If they were planning on evacuating, they would have tried by now. We must look at this more realistically. Let me pose a question to you: if you started to run out of supplies, what would be your first choice of action?" His expression was solemn, and I realized what he was saying.

"Their first choice will be to get more supplies," I answered, which led me to the next step. "We have more supplies."

He nodded and sighed. "Initial command thought the city would be either evacuated or deserted. Recon tells us there are several armed factions controlling sections of the city. We have decided to send a radio to talk to a group that has been spotted downtown. The police have formed a strong foothold there. It seems they were able to hold on to some of the old federal buildings. We will be in regular communication with them, trying to help with logistics."

He adjusted his position in the old chair behind the teacher's desk. "With all due respect, Mrs. Sales, you are a pain in my neck. Several of the corporals have complained about your behavior. They don't like a civilian acting like she has run of a military command. I know you have been a military dependent for a long time. You understand the traditions and mindset here. I know you respect them; they just need to see it from you."

He took a deep breath before continuing. "You are very capable. I can appreciate that. I would appreciate it more if you could follow the guidelines I put in place for your safety. I want to allow your team to continue your gathering and reconnaissance as long as you follow the strict rules I put in place. They aren't just for your safety but also for the safety of the camp. Right now, you have the most experience in the area and have provided the best intel. If possible, I want to find other allies in the area who can help support this relay." He sounded tired.

I nodded and started to stand. "Yes, sir. I understand."

He raised a hand. "I don't want you to put yourself in harm's way. You will take the sergeant or one of the other combat specialists with you every time. *No* exceptions. Clear?"

I nodded and smiled at him. "Crystal, sir."

He nodded back. "Excellent. Dismissed." Catching himself, he smiled sheepishly. "Umm, I mean, thank you, Mrs. Sales." He stood up and stepped out of the cubicle with me. In a quiet, conversational tone, he continued, "Your husband has been a big help too. He is very smart. A little odd, though."

I laughed and nodded. "Most really smart people are, and he is a genius." I sighed. "He loved being in the service. He still thinks of himself as a navy man. It took him a long time to think of himself as anything else. I know he loves the fact that he is working with the service again." I looked at the Brick again and gave him my most serious look. "Let me make something clear to you, sir. The navy was careless with him, broke him, and then dumped him. If you hurt him or let him get hurt, I will hold you personally responsible."

He looked a little taken aback and nervous. I suspected the expression on my face was a bit scary. The lieutenant nodded. "I will take good care of him; you have my word."

I nodded and backed up. Lucky was already on his feet and heading out to where Zyada was sitting.

Victor squealed and escaped the ladies who were letting him play with radio knobs and dials. He charged me and slammed me with a hug. I lifted him up and called Zyada. She said her goodbyes and ran up to me. The table she had been sitting at was crowded. They all called goodbyes. Those poor soldiers, all wrapped around her finger. They'd never stood a chance.

Barking and happily wagging his tail, Lucky helped herd the kids, like a cattle dog, keeping his charges close together. Zyada sang a happy song as she ran from leaf pile to leaf pile, throwing the leaves into the air. Victor chased after her and squealed and cheered as they fell around him. Lucky jumped and ran around them, playing in the leaves. God, I missed my camera. The world had not ended. Time had not stopped. This was proof. Even if the power was never restored and the government collapsed, the world would continued.

In my mind's eye, I took pictures of Victor chasing his sister, dancing and laughing with wild joy and abandon in the shower of leaves she provided. I took mental pictures of Zyada laughing and smiling with love and affection at her brother's happiness. I hoped they would still find happiness in each other when they were older. The air was getting colder. I didn't have gloves on, and my hands were stinging. Winter was approaching. I raised my hands to my mouth and blew warmth onto my fingers. I heard my father's voice whisper, "Don't borrow future trouble; it will get to you soon enough."

Instead I chased after Zyada and Victor, throwing leaves over their heads and chasing them to tickle and swing them around. We crunched and collected handfuls of the golden and red foliage. We chased and played for about an hour, until hunger took us home.

fifteen
thursday, 5:47pm

ALBERT WAS NOT AT HOME.

This was odd, but I set about making dinner and getting the kids cleaned and settled. Nathan arrived home about the time dinner was ready. He was in a good mood as he told me about the friends he had made today. I listened and encouraged him to tell me all about it. I didn't mention the fact that Albert was supposed to have picked him up. The sun was setting, and the days were getting shorter. I tried not to keep looking at my watch. I focused on evening chores. Hours later, I sang the last goodnight as Lucky curled up with the kids and they all snuggled down for sleep.

They were all asleep when Albert finally made it home. I was so relieved I wanted to cry. But in that same instant I was so angry that I wanted to punch him. I can only imagine what he saw when I turned and looked at him. I knew my fists were clenched and my eyes were full of tears. I didn't say a word. I didn't want to wake the kids.

He had been smiling when he opened the door. The second he saw my face, his expression transformed into one of worry. He dropped the bags he was carrying and hurried forward to hug me. I was tense with anger when I hugged him tight. Then I started crying and hitting him. I was so upset at him. He let me hit him and cry into his shirt. He whispered softly to me. I have no idea what he said. When I could finally hear him over the pounding of my own heartbeat, he was rocking me softly and petting my head. "It's OK, it's OK, everything is fine," he whispered softly, over and over.

I finally figured out how to breathe again, and after a moment I remembered how to stand on my own. He looked at me seriously, his big brown eyes searching mine, his teddy-bear face filled with worry. "Are you OK? Are the kids OK?" He looked past me to the door of the room where the little ones were sleeping.

I sniffed and wiped at my face. "*No*, you idiot. You were late!"

He looked confused. "What? What does that have to do with anything?"

I shook my head and threw up my hands. "I swear, you are the dumbest smart person I have ever met. You are never this late. You are always home for dinner. The kids were worried too. But I was terrified. What if something happened to you? What am I supposed to do then?" I stormed over to the sink to wash my face.

He made a noise in the back of his throat. It was the noise he made whenever he thought I was being dramatic. He let out a sigh of relief and walked over to where his plate waited for him. "I am sorry, sweetheart. I didn't mean to worry you. Next time I am going to be late, I will send word over." His tone was very calm and sensible. It made me want to hit him in the head.

There were whole days when I hated him. He was so damn reasonable about everything. He rarely argued. He would sit patiently and listen to the arguments, rants or disputes people threw at him, and then he would be all fucking rational and suggest solutions. This made it hard to disagree with him or find any fault in his logic, and it did *nothing* to relieve the anger or frustration.

I was still angry when I sat down next to him and asked, "Are you going to tell me what was so important that you had to scare the shit out of me?"

He sighed and leaned forward to kiss me. "I am sorry I scared you. I was thoughtless." He settled in front of his plate and picked up his fork. "I was helping with the power," he said casually as he put food into his mouth.

I counted backward from ten so that I wouldn't punch him. For a birthday one year, I had been gifted a collection of warning-label buttons: "Cute but crazy," "Beware, I bite," "Hugs and punches," things like that. I had been known to show my displeasure with fists, though not hard. In general, no one ever took it seriously. As I'd gotten older and had to worry about things like assault charges, I had decided to curb this behavior. But some days it was hard not to just ball a fist and express myself.

I looked at him, and my expression must have shown how irritated I was.

He shrugged at me. "What? I know it bores you when I go into details."

I crossed my arms and continued my glare.

He squirmed a little and sighed. "OK, I was working with the techs, as you know. We are trying to get the main hub for this section of the grid rewired. Do you remember when I told you about the old Mil-net?"

I honestly had only some vague recollection of the name, but I didn't really retain any of the details. He had told me something about a network of connections from the college.

I shrugged and nodded. "I think so—something about the old wires?"

He nodded as he ate. "MILNET was used to securely connect some of the original computer systems. It used a series of heavy copper wiring for its infrastructure. Well, the MILNET won't work for communications because the old RGs were cut out to use fiber optics. When they switched the communications over to fiber optics, they left the old metropolitan network in place. With it being old-style copper wiring, it can handle some current. Not much. We are talking about get lights on. But the wires are already there and if they grounded-out the terminals when they switched over, the lines should have survived."

I poured myself a cup of coffee from the percolator. "I thought the LT wanted to keep the lights limited so that we don't become a massive beacon. You know if we get the power on, then everyone and their brother is going to try to come and take it."

He waved a hand unconcerned. "It will be fine. Most of the lights are fried anyway, we just don't replace the external lights."

There was no point in debating this point with him. He was focused on solving the power issue. Any possible consequences would be lost on him. This is how his brain worked. I had to let him finish solving the problem. Any problems that arose from that solution would have to be handled later. It was very frustrating sometimes, but he seemed to always get the job done.

I decided to change the subject. "I had a chat with the LT today. The lieutenant wants me to do more recon and gather supplies. He said I was doing a good job. He also said that there are a lot of people in the valley and groups holed up in the city. He wants to try to make some allies and get prepped for a hard winter."

Albert frowned down at his plate. "I thought he would be pissed about you leaving without permission."

I smiled a bit. "I am sure he was, but we found some important stuff out there. You can't argue with results."

He gave me an expectant look. "Like what?"

"We found that there is a train station at the fairgrounds and at least one of them is working. I think it might be an old coal train. It is being used to slowly evacuate people out of the fairgrounds. There is also a faction of police who have fortified and blockaded a section of downtown. There are a couple of different factions, and Lieutenant Brick wants to work with some of them."

He nodded a little and started talking in a hushed tone. "I overheard some of the techs talking about the storm. We know it was a low-frequency, high-intensity geomagnetic storm caused by a solar flare, right?" he said that like I would know what all that meant. Which of course I didn't but I nodded anyway so he could continue.

"Ok, and these storms are rated by levels. Well, apparently, there were some areas that got hit by at least a level 6. We are talking cars exploding and light bulbs turning into mini fireballs. Anything metal would have heated up, melted, or burned anything it touched. At those levels, it wouldn't even matter if the metal was inside your body. I can't even imagine what Las Vegas must have been like." Sometimes Albert's brain was a horror filled nightmare. He chatted on about some other horrible scenarios as he finished his food. I knew it wasn't because he didn't care what happened, but his morbid fascination with power of electricity was worrisome.

My stomach clenched as memories of that huge grave came unwanted into my mind. I tried not to imagine what a city full of dead people would look like.

"Leo said that some places were almost completely untouched and are already back online. Can you imagine? I miss my computer." His voice sounded wistful.

I frowned at him. "How do they know any of that is true?"

Albert grinned mischievously at me. "I listened in on the radio chatter. One of the radio girls is a bit of a gossip. She talks to other radio-relay people to get info on areas where the units' families are located. The stronger we get the signal, the better the reception, and the further out she can talk to people. The other day she managed to pick up a radio signal from a military vessel at sea. They were in touch with someone overseas. China was hit hard too." Albert sighed and shook his head. "According to the radio chain, most of the world is blacked out like us, but with little shielded places, mostly due to natural rock and land formations."

I nodded. "Like how we were protected in the mountains. That doesn't bode well for us—the United States, I mean, with random places completely dark or sent to the steam age, with all the infrastructure damage and fear. There is going to be a lot of unrest. Even if DC had power, how would they get information out to the people? Even if they could, how many do you think would listen right now? The president is probably safe in some bunker. Even if the military does nothing but focus on getting power restored, it will take months to get communication working cross-country."

He nodded at me and finished eating as I continued my train of thought.

"That's just the logistics of repairs. We aren't even talking about the geographical and political obstacles. Think about how divided everyone was over the elections. All the anger and resentment, all the protests and riots. All those angry militia groups and folks preparing for the end of the world. You know they have already dug in deep wherever they were. And who is going to listen to authority figures at this point, so why cooperate?" I considered the idea a bit. It was my turn to sound strangely energetic and apathetic regarding horrible scenarios and possibilities.

"There will be power struggles and gang violence, and some places will just be in full rebellion. I won't be surprised if Texas closes off and goes independent again. California too. With their land formations it would be easy to shut off traffic into the Southwest. There could be a split right along the mountain and river lines. There could be a complete power shift with this."

Albert laughed and stood up, kissing my cheek on his way to the sink and only slightly distracting me from the rabbit hole my brain was going into. "That's my girl, always thinking. Why would the country fall apart? Don't you have any faith in the people?"

I shook my head. "None whatsoever. I am a student of history. What keeps this country together is the idea of one nation. States, cities, countries—it's all just a bunch of invisible lines someone with more power than everyone else drew up. The only real boundaries that matter are the ones that a person can physically touch and see."

I pondered the implications of some places having less damage than others. My mind went to history lessons. I thought about countries that had lacked resources or leadership in comparison to their neighbors. I had trouble thinking of a time when the neighbor didn't exploit or commit some huge violent act against the weaker party. That could happen here. If the government didn't reestablish itself quickly, the illusion of America that everyone had bought into for so long would fade. People's hunger, fear or desire for something someone else had would grow too great, and they would lose the idea of a nation. They would eventually realize that there was no law because there was no way to enforce it. Without government the only enforcement anyone had was their own might.

Then there were those who would prey on the fear, the hope, and the desperation of people. It would not just be warlords promising protection, but those who promised more, like salvation for obedience. During times of plague or famine, there were often wellsprings of zealots, full of God's wrath or ideas of pacifying God through a purge or cleansing. How many people had died in the course of history due to superstitious ignorance and blind faith?

My mind went to the glass man, the preacher, the way he seemed to distort things around him. When I was a child, my mother had this smooth, polished glass paperweight. It was a half-circle dome with a flat bottom. It felt cool and slick to the touch. It was so crystal clear that you could look straight through it, but when you did, whatever you were looking at became distorted and exaggerated. I liked to put it over a book I was reading and make the words look big and stretched.

That preacher was like that glass paperweight. He seemed clear and transparent, but things around him had seemed distorted and exaggerated to me. After what had happened, I knew he was dangerous. Then there were those different factions and the so-called Crazies we had seen. There were all these sections and groups splitting into little tribes. I started to panic as I considered all the implications, my mind whirling with disasters.

Suddenly, Albert was an inch from my face. I blinked and gasped in a breath that I hadn't realized I was holding.

He grinned. "Ah, there you are. I wondered where you'd gone." He kissed my cheek and finished cleaning up from dinner. "I worry about you out there. Mouthy mentioned you had one of the top snipers in the country escorting you, Keyan Mikoto. He said that guy is one of the best snipers the marines have ever trained. I am sure that is an exaggeration, but it made me feel better. I want you to be safe. I went and had a chat with Mikoto at lunch today. He seems smart, serious, and reliable. Interesting fact: he is Native American and Japanese. He thought it was interesting that I was Polish and African American..." Albert was still talking but I had started tuning him out.

The sniper made me nervous. The LT had told me his name, but in my head, he was still The Shadow. If I started calling him by his name it would make him more personal to me. It would make him more real. It didn't feel safe to do that.

"Mikoto said you and Zyada have been taking care of his spotter at the infirmary. What does she call him? Mr. Sunshine? Yeah, he is Mikoto's spotter. Is he doing better? Oh, don't forget you have hospital duty."

I had almost forgotten about the infirmary rotation tomorrow. Mr. Sunshine and the Shadow: that was quite a pair. My mind bounced their nicknames for a moment, and then suddenly "sunshine" turned to "moon," and before I knew it, I was humming the melody to the Cat Stevens lyrics: "I'm being followed by a moonshadow, moonshadow, moonshadow."

Albert started humming along with me, and before long, I was singing the almost forgotten lyrics. "Oh, if I ever lose my hands, lose my plough, lose my land, oh, if I ever lose my hands... oh well ... well, I won't have to work no more."

I found myself grinning as we sang. It was funny that I could remember the "Moonshadow" lyrics even though that song was written long before I was born, but I couldn't remember very many songs from a month before the blackout. It seemed sad. I hoped artists had their songs saved on more than just digital copies.

"So tomorrow you work at the hospital, and then the extra baking day for the Halloween, the party itself, and laundry day. Meanwhile, I have to work with the techs. We have tracked the lines connecting the neighborhood and the college. We still need to open the ground terminal. We are expecting there to be a lot of melted metal. We will then have to set up a switchboard at the generator and the destinations—and then run lines from the destination switchboard to the individual houses."

I frowned as I started processing what he was getting at. "Who is watching the kids while we do all this?"

He smiled and touched the tip of his nose.

I sighed heavily. "We will need to find someone to keep an eye on them." I rubbed the aching spot on my neck. I absolutely hated the idea. I noticed Albert watching me with a little smile. Some days I really hated him. He was too smart and knew me too well. "Shut up and tell me who you have in mind," I grouched at him as I got myself a cigarette from the drawer.

He sighed and followed me onto the porch to share the smoke in the cold air. "Well, there is Grandpa Silas. You know he would watch them," he said as I lit the smoke and took that first beautiful and terrible drag.

I shook my head as I handed him the cigarette. "No, Jeri is working with me, and that would leave Grandpa alone with the two of them, and Victor's a handful on his own." I took back the cigarette as Albert slowly released his smoke into the air.

"Well, I would be more worried about what Silas would teach Zyada," Albert said. "I'm not sure we need her to swear and spit just yet."

I nodded.

"What about Michael's wife?" he said.

I shook my head. "She has a little baby, plus she is working at the school."

He crossed his arms, and we passed the smoke back and forth a few more times.

"We could always ask Mouthy," he said finally with a hint of hopefulness.

I rolled my eyes. "Seriously, weren't you the one saying that his job is made up or something?" I took one last drag. It was so close to the filter that the heat was burning my lips. I let Albert take the very last drag.

Albert smiled and said, "I said creative logistics is not a thing. But a logistics specialist is. I never said he wasn't good at his job, just that the way he describes it is misleading. Besides, aren't you the one who says he is the guy to go to when you need something? Well, we need a babysitter. Let's see him work some magic on that."

I gave Albert a look as he put out the cigarette and put the butt into a closed can we had hidden on the porch. I shrugged, and we went inside. I didn't know who else to ask. All the people I trusted were either working with me or as busy as I was. The local church group had offered childcare to everyone, but I had seen what their den mother was like, and I wasn't leaving my children with that jackal.

We got ready for bed. Overnight, I dreamed of warm ocean waves. My eyes stung from the bright sun. I felt the surf rush in to cool my feet from the burning sand. I dreamed of dipping my baby girl's toes in the water with my mother and sister.

I woke to the sound of pounding rain. It was a steady medium rain, not so much that you couldn't walk with an umbrella, but enough that you needed rain boots. I was humming along happily. The rainy days never made me gloomy. The rain was cold, a strong sign that fall was well underway. It meant that outside work would be limited today. Albert's crew was going to wait till the rain stopped to try to lay the wire, which meant Albert could watch the kids while I went to work. I was needed at the nursing station. Then it would be an extra baking day for the party. Later I would be making costumes for the kids.

Albert took Nathan to his class as I got Zyada and Victor up, fed, and dressed in rain gear. I put a tarp on the back of the wagon so Lucky could ride without getting soaked. Albert met me at the common room, which was basically the big area where most of the kids hung out with the little day care. We were running late because the little ones had danced and played in the rain. When we arrived, Albert took Victor and Lucky to play with all the little kids.

Zyada came with me to the hospital so she could visit with Mr. Sunshine. He was awake and doing much better. He was even able to walk now. He had gotten very lucky. That infection had nearly killed him. It had left him with an ugly scar. I bet it hurt like hell. He was out of the woods, though, and they had switched him to a basic anti-inflammatory for pain because of some military protocol about rationing. I thought this was a bit harsh, but I understood. It wasn't easy, but you could heal with pain, and sometimes it was actually faster. People don't push themselves too far if it hurts.

We stopped at Mr. Sunshine's room first. His real first name was Jordan, but he wouldn't tell us his last name. It was some game between him and Zyada. When he had first woken up, she had been with him, calling him Sunshine. Now he refused to be called anything else. We got to his room, and taped to the door was a cheerful, almost annoyingly bright yellow sun colored on a piece of paper. "Sunshine's Room" was written underneath the sun in a kindergartner's scrawl. I smiled and knocked twice as Zyada just charged past me, opening the door.

"Good morning, Sunshine!" she sang in a voice so loud that it actually hurt my ears.

I winced and instantly made a mother's shushing noise. She bolted toward the bed. I missed her by an inch and stepped in to follow her.

Something blurred into my peripheral vision on my left, the side blocked by the opening door. It was so fast that I let out a gasp and grabbed for the blur with one hand. I lunged in between it and my daughter. My heart was in my throat, choking off whatever noise I was making, and my blood pounding was all I could hear. My hand was grabbed before it could make contact. It all happened in a blink of an eye. It took a moment for me to make sense of what had physically happened. As Zyada had bolted in, the door had swung open almost hitting someone, that person had dodged the door, causing them to move further into the room. I had tried to grab that person and put myself between them and my daughter. This left me in a very awkward starting position, of an unexpected Tango.

I found myself staring at a familiar set of fatigues and dark eyes. Those strange eyes looked down at me. In that moment everything seemed too bright, too close, too clear. His skin was clean, and I could smell his soap. His breath smelled like peppermint, but the candy, not the toothpaste. His hair was slightly wet from being washed, and I could still smell the flower and citrus of his shampoo or conditioner. I could smell other things in the room too, coffee, powdered eggs, and toast. The harsh scent of the stuff we cleaned the floors with was still there as well, but the smells of blood and infection were gone.

Mikoto, the Shadow, was calm. He didn't even seem surprised, but I could see the start of a little side smile. I realized the awkward positioning and felt a blush creeping up my neck. For the span of three heartbeats, I just stared and watched as his eyes dilated, ever so slightly. His lips pressed into a firm line, and he stepped back. Again, I had completely misjudged the amount of space between us.

I had hold of his wrist with one hand, having grabbed it away from Zyada, and he was holding the fist of my other hand, which I had brought around to hit him with. I dropped my arms and turned just in time to see Zyada climbing up onto the bed.

"Hey, my shining star!" Sunshine said, barely managing to catch Zyada as she hurtled toward him. He even managed to hide that it must have hurt a little.

She turned and looked at me with a big smile. I tried to act normal as I walked up to the bed. She tilted her head and frowned. "Are you OK, Mommy?"

I smiled and nodded as I gave her a kiss on her head. "I am fine, honey. You just scared me. I was worried you would run into him. We don't want to hurt Sunshine, now do we?"

She shook her head quickly and looked at Sunshine. With a gentle pat on his hand, she looked up. "Are you OK, Sunshine? Did I hurt you?" The giant eyes she gave him ensured only one answer.

"Of course not, Starshine! Never!" He grinned at her and winked.

The Shadow leaned against the wall as if he had been painted there.

I set down Zyada's bag of stuff and looked at Sunshine. "Starshine?"

He grinned and nodded. "Little Z here mentioned that her name means 'shining star.' And I explained that a star is just a sun that's really far away."

Zyada took over the explanation at this point. "Oh yeah! So it means we have the same name. Because our sun is a star, and it's shining. So a sun that is shining is the same as a star that is shining. But we can't both be called Sunshine, 'cause that would be confusing. So I will be Starshine since I am for the stars far away." She nodded very enthusiastically.

I could honestly say I was a bit taken aback but impressed all the same. I smiled. "OK, so do I need to call you that now too?"

She grinned and shook her head. "Nah. You're Mommy. You can call us whatever you want."

Sunshine grinned and nodded. "Oh yes, whatever you want."

I laughed at the blatant flirting. I rolled my eyes at him and checked his chart.

"I don't think your mommy thinks I am as charming as you do," he said to Zyada.

"It would be much more charming if you hadn't already flirted with everyone who has come into this room," I said as I checked his temperature and bandage. "Dr. Fisher said that at his age he will take whatever attention he can get but warned all the other nurses to be careful."

Sunshine just grinned. "Aw, that silver fox ruins all my fun."

Zyada perked up. "What silver fox? Dr. Fisher has a silver fox?"

"See what you did?" I nodded to Sunshine, who was looking at his buddy.

He turned to Zyada with an excited smile. "You want me to tell you a story about Mr. Fish and the silver fox?"

"Oh yes!" she exclaimed, beaming and shifting to sit more carefully.

I decided to make my exit. "Well, I am going to get to work." I pointed to Sunshine. "You, behave yourself, and Zyada, don't let him play rough, or he will tear those stitches."

She waved, too busy waiting for her story. To Sunshine's credit, he sat up and pointed a finger to her and then to me. "Hey, your mom's leaving. Say 'see you later.'"

It made me smile when she turned with a huge grin and said, "See you later, Mom! I love you!"

I stepped through the doorway. After watching for a moment, I turned and found that the Shadow had moved and was leaning against the wall in the hallway. His eyes tracked me as I walked to the makeshift nurse's station. It was intense and uncomfortable. I hadn't seen him leave the room.

For a moment I thought he was trying to intimidate me or maybe check me out. My face flushed, and my stomach fluttered, and suddenly my hormones thought I was sixteen again. To be fair, this guy was tall, dark, handsome, dangerous, intense and smelled like candy. And just like when I was sixteen, I hid my awkwardness with a temper flare. My chin went up, and I glared at him with narrow eyes. "You know, I am getting really sick of this staring contest. I know I didn't put my eyeliner on crooked because I am not wearing any. Now you have exactly five seconds to say something before I kick you as hard as I can, which is pretty damn hard."

About three words in, my index finger had started doing the angry-mother wag, and by the end I was poking him in the chest as if he were exactly my size. I would love to say that I was bluffing and knew exactly what I was doing. I would love to say that. The truth was that my mouth just took over in these moments, and suddenly I was ten feet tall and bulletproof. I had no fear and no limits. He looked at my finger and then back at me. He smiled. It would have been less devastating if he had punched me. I thought I had seen him smile before while on our supply run, but no. No this was different. This smile performed a kind of magic spell on his face. It took all the hard planes and sharp edges and shaped them into something beautiful. Not handsome, not hot, not attractive, fucking beautiful. With easy grace he moved slightly, motioning me past him. His dark eyes seemed to twinkle with laughter. "Sorry I startled you," he said, his voice smooth and deep.

I was startled by his calm voice. I tried to pull myself together and act my age. I stiffened my spine and nodded a little, trying not to get lost in the lines of his smile. "Well, I am sorry I tried to hit you," I said, as if it didn't matter anyway. I straightened out my sleeve a little and took a breath to calm down.

Before either of us could continue, Dr. Fisher called from down the hall. "I am terribly sorry! I was stopped on the way. Hello, Mrs. Sales." The Doctor huffed and puffed as he carried a chair down the hall.

The Shadow just smiled and nodded. "It's all right. I know you're busy. Thank you."

Dr. Fisher smiled, his face rosy from the workout. The Shadow easily took the chair out of his hands and stepped to one side. Dr. Fisher gave a brief nod and continued down the hall for his rounds.

He was standing there because there wasn't a chair, you idiot! He was probably looking at you because you're on shift and he was waiting for you to notice there wasn't a place for him to sit. And now you look like a total crazy person. Oh, wait that's because you acted like a total crazy person.

The Shadow's smile disappeared, and he looked serious again. "I like your husband."

The jarring sentence came out of nowhere and helped end whatever hormone-induced madness I was suffering. I shifted to a more neutral posture and gave a smile. "He seems to approve of you too. Albert is a good judge of character. I hope that means I can trust you." My voice sounded strange to my ears. I was relieved when I heard someone call my name from down the hall. I didn't say anything else, just pointed toward the call of my name. I didn't look at his face as I turned to leave.

His voice followed me down the hall, like smoke on a breeze. "You can."

It was a weird moment that I didn't have the time to dwell on. As it would turn out, it wouldn't be the weirdest thing to happen that day.

friday, 9:20am

THERE WERE FEWER PATIENTS NOW. Most of them had been helped enough to be moved elsewhere. The main tasks were keeping things clean and maintaining care. I helped get the laundry ready for when the rain stopped. A couple of hours passed before I returned to get Zyada. Sunshine was walking with her down the hallway, heading for lunch. Between Zyada begging and Sunshine giving me big green puppy eyes, I caved.

"Fine you can go to lunch together, but you have to help with the decorations after. We are setting up in the student center next to the kitchens." I pointed my mom finger at Sunshine, and he gave a quick salute and replied. "Copy that Ma'am." Zyada mimicked his salute. "Copy!" she chirped and took his hand. Yes, it was as painfully cute as you imagine it would be.

I headed over to the kitchen to work on homemade treats for Halloween. We were carving pumpkins for tomorrow night, I had old recipes for making candy, and there would be cookies and cupcakes too. I went to gather ingredients from the big storage area set up for the community kitchen. The community kitchen turned out three square meals a day. Many people still didn't have a way to cook for themselves. It was surprisingly efficient. Nothing ever went to waste. I walked past the bags of flour and sugar we had collected for baking and on into the back, past the cans of beans and other nonperishables. There were cases of lima beans on the furthest shelves, and I had my treasures hidden behind them: large bags of dollar-store candy I had found. I had put them back behind the cases because they were hard to see there, and no one would look. Whoever *looked* for lima beans? I was still going to make little candies, but I thought the kids would be happy to get things they recognized when they trick-or-treated too. Getting to my stash meant I had to get down on my hands and knees and crawl in behind the cans.

So, no shit, there I was, on my knees behind huge stacks of bags, crawling on the lowest shelf of a storage pantry behind some cans of lima beans, to pull out the secret stash of candy, when I first realized we were in deep shit and would need an escape plan by winter.

I am fairly sure my ass and feet were the only things showing while I pulled out huge bags of lollipops and Sweet Tarts. I heard a scuffling sound and voices coming from the door of the storage room. I was in the far corner, not visible from the door. I froze. I hoped if I held still, I wouldn't have to explain why I was hiding candy, especially since I had a lollipop in my mouth at the time. I realized they were moving farther into the storage room, so I carefully pulled up my feet. I moved as softly as I could, shifting behind the cans of beans. It is moments like this I am glad of my short legs. It was so ridiculous; I was trying not to laugh at the whole situation. I grinned like an idiot as I thought about Albert's expression when I would tell him about this.

"Shh!" someone said in a harsh husky whisper. I almost snickered at the irony and moved my lollipop from one side of my mouth to the other.

"Will you relax? No one saw us," a different voice said. This voice was higher, spoken with a more nasal accent. The light shifted as someone opened the door a little and then closed it again.

"You can never be too careful. We have to be certain. Things are moving along quickly, so we can't afford any sloppy mistakes." The husky voice answered in an irritated tone.

"Don't worry. If we play our cards right, all this will be ours." The nasally voice replied. My mind imagined a third-rate villain in an old b-movie. They should be standing there; one rubbing his hands together while the other twirls his tiny pencil-thin mustache. *Who actually says, 'play our cards right'?*

The husky voice hissed out angrily, "Don't get cocky. We don't have the right cards yet. You are taking too long. We need that equipment if we are going to get this done."

In between the sounds of munching, the nasally voice spoke again. "Don't worry. I have got it handled. They aren't working today because of the rain, so I will get it then. No one will even notice it's gone."

At this point I wasn't smiling anymore. They could have been talking about a lot of things, but it seemed like a very bad conversation no matter what. I moved a can of lima beans, so that I could try to see the door. All I got a look at were feet. Well, their boots and pant legs. There were three pairs of boots, and they all looked like the boots passed out by supply. Heck, I was wearing those boots.

A third voice spoke. This was a woman's voice. It sounded familiar but I wasn't able to place it. The accent was soft and gave the voice a gentle quality. "This is good work, brothers. God bless you both. We will prevail, for we are the righteous, and we are the chosen. Be strong. Our time is coming. Be vigilant and steadfast."

"Praise the light," they all said together.

I watched their feet as they left one at a time.

I didn't know what they were talking about, but I didn't like it. My mind whirled as I tried to decide what to do next. Who did I go tell? What would happen if I did? I didn't know who was speaking. They could be right outside. What if I go and act suspicious and they saw me? What if the LT didn't believe me? After a few minutes of contemplation, I decided that I would pretend I hadn't heard anything till I could talk to Albert and we could make a plan.

I gathered up the candy and put the lima beans back. I waited a few more minutes before stepping out.

I took the candy to the staging area where we were building a little haunted house. We had a bunch of games for the kids to play, including a sandbag toss, bobbing for apples, and even apples on a string.

One of the gathering groups had found a few apple trees and local backyard gardens. We now had some fresh root vegetables in addition to the fruit. We were leaving some on the vine, and the rest had been put into cool storage to save for next month, Thanksgiving. We had set up decorations and a bunch of stations for trick-or-treating. We were going for a haunted-hallway feel. There would be lots of food, and hopefully everyone would have fun.

For a moment I just stood holding the candy, trying to pretend that what I had overheard had never happened. Paranoia made it hard to decide what to do next. I was saved from having to make that decision when someone noticed me with all the candy. A cheer went up, and people helped me get the candy to the tables. There were Sweet Tarts, Tootsie Pops, and Nerds. There wasn't much in the way of chocolate candy, but there was lots of sugar. The kids would be thrilled.

I was working with a big group of people, and Alice and Vera were at the heart of it. The lieutenant thought this project would be good for the morale and bonding between the civilians and the military. The army boys were working hard to help set up for the party. They had even volunteered to dress up and be scary in the hallway. Everyone seemed to be in a good mood, talking and laughing. My kids were with all the others, making costumes. They were painting masks, everything from tiger faces to green goblins. It was going to take weeks to get all that glitter cleaned up. It was nice to see everyone so happy. Sunshine was helping Zyada with her mask.

The teenagers who were watching the kids seemed pleased to have him there. Lucky was sleeping under the table. There was no one acting any differently than before I went into the pantry.

I focused on my tasks: painting a scary ghost-filled graveyard scene and making sure there was enough candy at each station. There were now about thirty kids in total, of varying ages, and about 170 adults, including the military guys. There should be enough candy for all of them to have a nice little bag.

The clandestine storage-room meeting kept replaying in my head. I wanted to leave to go find Albert, but I didn't want to act suspicious. Questions swirled in my brain. What cards did they need? What was the guy going to take that no one would notice? Even if I told someone and they believed me, what could be done about it? I wanted to go find Albert, but Alice was keeping me busy. Every time I would try to excuse myself, she would call me over to do something else. She had me painting, scrubbing, stringing, and moving. When Albert came to get the kids for dinner, I still had about an hour of work left to do. There were still many people around and the kids were eager to leave. I barely got to kiss him before he had to leave again.

The rain had kept up a steady rhythm all day. Grandpa had promised to bring up some fresh meat for the party, but with the rain I wasn't sure he was going to. I finished my share of the decorations and help set aside the food in record time. I went as fast as I could without looking like a crazy person. Lucky rode home in the wagon, covered by the tarp. I was happy to find all the kids washed and dinner ready when I arrived.

Albert greeted me at the door. He kissed my cheek and whispered, "We need to talk later."

I nodded, a little surprised since I was about to say the same thing to him. "Yeah, OK," I said and headed to the table, which was alive with noise.

I didn't have to say a word the entire meal. The kids talked a mile a minute about the party tomorrow. Lucky ate his dog food and anything that fell off the table. Amid all the noise, it was easy to get lost and forget about the day.

People used to ask me all the time, "How could you forget something so important?" When I would miss appointments or forget to put gas in the car, I would just shrug and say, "How can you remember? Three kids all trying to get your attention at once, it's honestly amazing I remember anything." It wasn't until the kids were down to sleep and I was washing dishes that I remembered about the storage closet. I also remembered that Albert had wanted to talk about something. I put on some coffee. When he stepped out of the bedroom, I looked up and smiled while putting some powdered creamer into his mug.

Lucky found himself a comfortable spot and relaxed. It wasn't like Albert to say things like "we need to talk." He would just tell me things. He was such a creature of habit and routine that the sudden shift had me nervous. He sighed heavily and sat down. I sipped my coffee, waiting on edge.

"There is something weird happening," he whispered softly. "I think someone is diverting power from the grid and routing it somewhere."

"Who?" I asked as quietly as I could.

"I am not sure yet, but I checked the numbers, and the power is going somewhere. I haven't been able to tell where yet. Either the engineers know about it and are covering, or someone is hiding it from them."

I raised an eyebrow and nodded as he continued.

"If the army were doing it, there would be no reason to hide it. It is their power; they can use it however they want. So the questions are, one, why haven't the army guys noticed, and two, where is it going?" He took a sip of coffee as he thought about his own questions.

I frowned as I considered them as well. "I heard something strange in the storage room today." I briefly repeated what I had heard, and we both sat in silence as we considered the situation for a moment.

"You think they are connected?" he asked softly.

I shrugged. "There are fewer than two hundred of us here. The chances of these things not being related are pretty slim. I mean, how many secret groups could there be running around here, stealing shit? You think we should take what we know to the lieutenant?"

His answer came quickly. "No, I don't want anyone to know I found anything yet. Whoever is hiding the power will hear about it, and that always ends up bad for the guy who discovered it. No, I need time to figure out where the power is going. If it looks like it's part of the military's operations, we act as if we never saw anything. If there is some group running a private show, we need to find out who, and we need to be prepared for the worst."

My gut tightened. I didn't want to know what the worst was. I didn't want there to be a worst. I liked this little house. It was warm and welcoming, and it could keep us safe and cozy in the winter. I liked Mouthy and Samara, Alice, and the others. I didn't want to think about what the worst could be. I realized that somewhere along the way, I had let myself get attached to this place and these people.

"What exactly are you thinking?" I tried to sound neutral, like he hadn't just punched me in the gut, like I didn't want to just sit down and cry. He knew me too well not to know.

"I like it here too, sweetheart. But if there is something happening here and it goes bad, we can't afford to be caught flat-footed. We might have to bolt. I will talk to Grandpa and Jeri. We will look at exit strategies. Maybe the train will be running. We need to pick a couple of spots and stash supplies. Make sure the spots are out where people won't look. You can take the supplies out on one of your runs. We will see what we can find and see who we can trust. If nothing happens, we will go out and bring the supplies back in if we need them."

He put his arms around me and hugged me tight. "I know you've made friends. I like them too. Don't think of it as abandoning them. They might need us to be prepared. If bad things happen, they are going to need someone with a plan. We can plan to help them too if you want."

I nodded and tried not to worry. I had never been good at that. But I tried. That night I lay awake for a long time. I was awake when the rain stopped sometime before dawn. The air was very cold.

The sun was out and bright the next morning. The world sparkled on that October 31. Grass and leaves were edged in fairy dust, and it was lovely. Everything glistened and shimmered, but not with the morning dew or even with the rain from yesterday. Everything was covered in frost and bits of sparkling ice. Winter was on its way. Our time was running out.

Halloween had arrived. The morning was hectic and happy, filled with a jittery excitement. The kids couldn't wait for the fun to begin, and the adults were racing to finish projects before the designated time. Albert had been called away before breakfast to work with the techs on some electrical thing I couldn't pronounce or remember. I finished the stitches on Zyada's costume literally moments before she was supposed to put it on. She had an army hat with a sparkly rhinestone princess tiara on top of it. She wore a pink and black superhero mask and cape and an army fatigue jacket and pants, over which she wore a pink tutu. When asked, she said she was a superhero soldier ballerina. Nathan had diligently put together a Batman outfit, including a cardboard mask with bat ears, a black sheet for a cape, and black pants, and we painted a yellow bat symbol on a black T-shirt. Someone had tied a towel around Lucky's neck to make a cape. Victor had been tough. Mouthy had told me he would come up with something, so we got everyone else dressed, and Victor was happy to chase after Nathan and Zyada in their capes.

I had always been a die-hard Batman fan myself. He was idealistic and all about justice, and he was just a man. He didn't have superpowers, and he was flawed. However, I would never want my sons to be that dark and lonely. After having sons of my own, I realized that I wanted them to be more like Captain America. He had hope, he strived to be his best, and his biggest strength was his courage to face the odds and do what was right. That was what I liked best about Captain America. I believe that what makes a person good, or evil isn't really a single action. We are all a little good and a little bad. The small choices we make every day are what make us who we are. We have to look at ourselves and say, *I am going to try my best to be as good as I can.* Some days are better than others. But most boys liked Batman. He was pretty awesome.

We made sure everyone was dressed appropriately, with a couple of extra layers underneath. It was much colder today. Zyada wanted to ride in the wagon instead of walk. I loaded up the wagon with Zyada and our donations to the potluck party. Victor wanted to run; he had no interest in sitting. It was late in the morning by the time we arrived, but the sun had barely warmed the air. I feared the LT was right. Winter was coming fast. There was so much to do. We needed to preserve all the fresh vegetables and fruit we could find. We needed to smoke the meat and make sure we had enough fuel and wood for fires in case the generator broke down. We needed to do more runs and get missing supplies. Now there was even more for me to do. I needed to set up stashes. That meant I had to find extra supplies.

The community room was already buzzing with activity. The decorations looked wonderful. The pumpkins were on display, with more ready to carve. Nathan took off to hang out with the big kids. Zyada wanted to go join the kids who were coloring. I was trying to keep Victor from running off when Sunshine came over to sit with us.

"Hey there, Mom. I figured you could use a second pair of hands."

I smiled. Zyada waved excitedly at him. "You want to color with me?" she asked brightly.

Sunshine grinned and said in an excited voice, "Do I ever!" It was cute.

I let go of Victor and stood up to chase him around. He was so excited that he didn't know where to go, so he ran back and forth for a while, and I followed behind, making monster noises. About ten minutes into this, I saw Mouthy waving us over. I chased Victor in Mouthy's direction. It wasn't a Captain America outfit, but it was still pretty darn cool. With help from the rest of the crew, Mouthy made Victor into an adorable G.I. Joe, with all the trimmings. They even painted his face in camo. The only thing missing was a pair of combat boots.

I didn't really have any free time during the festivities. I was always busy watching and laughing with the kids or helping with some aspect of the day. I was fixing some dish or decoration or making sure things were on schedule. Albert was finally able to join us as we sat to have a late lunch with everyone. Lunch was stew and rolls, and it was very good.

Lucky was popular with the kids, so he spent his time receiving love, pets, and treats. We had a scavenger hunt for the kids that took a while. In the end some of the adults dressed up as ghosts by dusting ourselves with leftover flour. I was wearing a white shirt and light tan pants that I also dusted with flour. We made silly ghost sounds as we took the kids through the haunted house. Zyada was in front with Sunshine. He had decided to go as an injured soldier, with extra bandages and everything. Lucky trotted along with them.

There was a wide variety of costumes. There were folks dressed as farmers with straw hats and overalls, people dressed as cops, and one lady who came as a Grande dame from early twentieth century. It was creative but odd. These weren't like other costumes. People were dressed in other people's clothes, things found in strangers' closets. It wasn't a nurse's scrubs costume; it was a nurse's uniform.

This was very disquieting to me. They were just clothes. Whoever had owned the clothing before wasn't here to use it. It should have felt like finding something on the side of the road. But it wasn't the same. These weren't costumes, and the circumstances weren't pretend. The previous owners were real people somewhere. The partygoers were wearing someone else's life. I seemed to be the only one who even noticed.

People's perceptions of things had changed. The invisible lines that society had built to keep order had slipped away. My mind went to the beginning, when I had scouted and scavenged with the kids. One of the places had been a jewelry store that had burned down. We had spent hours carefully searching through charred rubble, collecting the sparkles and shines, as Zyada called them. Even Victor had helped find little bits of rings and some pearls. Someday they would have value again. We had our sparkles and shines hidden carefully, buried in the rubble of our ruined home. If things ever turned back on, we could try to rebuild.

I originally had felt very guilty about this. It didn't bother me anymore. If the owner of that store was even around, and the world returned to a point where it even mattered, his insurance would write off everything as a loss. I supposed I could feel guilty about the principle of it. But principles couldn't be eaten, couldn't keep you warm, couldn't protect you, and couldn't buy supplies.

I stood there watching people pretending to be someone else. It made me think of people all over America, other little pockets of humanity untouched by this disaster while some had been destroyed by the power of the sun. Imagine all of humankind's so-called achievements undone by the oldest thing in our solar system.

Somewhere there were people still going about life as if nothing had changed. But everything was different now.

Soon those with technology would figure it out. Those in power would figure out a way to exploit people who were in a weakened state. This was a chance for those at the bottom to change their place, people like me, like Grandpa Silas, like Alice and Michael, the struggling have-nots. We could carve out a niche for ourselves—find a way to rebuild and dig in deep so that no one could take it. Not here but somewhere. Somewhere better.

I shook my head, trying to clear the thoughts away. It was tempting to just stand and let my mind float off on a tide of random thoughts, but I didn't want to think about the future too much. I couldn't plan too far ahead; that was a way to get trapped by ideas and expectations. The world was hard and had only gotten harder.

I needed to focus on the here and now. There was danger here. Unseen things were moving, and I had to be ready, not daydreaming about a little house on a hill. I needed to find Grandpa Silas to talk to him about helping set up an escape plan. We had arrived here together; it was only right we leave together. Focusing back on the now, I finally found Grandpa Silas sitting off to the side of the party with Old Man Harris. They were passing a bottle back and forth, some brown liquid that I assumed was not kid-friendly. They were chatting as I approached.

Old Man Harris nodded to me, and Grandpa gave me a smile. "Hey there, Momma. What's got you in a twist?" he said in a warm, gruff voice.

I smiled and huffed. "Who says I am in a twist?" I assumed that was a bad thing.

"You have that look you get when you got something twisting around in your head. Seen it before." He gave me a sly grin as he took his turn at the bottle. Neither offered me any, Grandpa because he knew I'd say no and Old Man Harris because he wasn't the sharing kind.

I shrugged. "All right, well, I will cut to the chase. Hubby and I think we might need to pull a Steve McQueen."

He raised an eyebrow but gave a grunt of understanding. As usual, he was razor-sharp. He smiled and nodded again. "Well, it would have to be done before New York's old lady shows up. Once she gets here, it's nothing but the cold shoulder and long nights."

I glanced around as if looking at the crowd, mostly to see if anyone was watching us talk. "Well, I guess we should make sure we have some presents waiting. Wouldn't want to be caught empty-handed when she gets here," I said in a cheerful voice.

Old Man Harris snorted and snatched up the bottle. "What's with this James Bond shit? Who exactly do you think has ears on ya?" he grumbled into the bottle.

I gave him a small smile. "Not a hundred percent on that. But I am avoiding the Kool-Aid. I suggest you do the same. The wind is shifting, and we need to make sure our lines are drawn and our sail is trimmed." I waved as I turned and headed back to the crowd.

I had given Grandpa Silas a heads-up. I would find some other place and time to talk to Alice and Michael. They would need to be convinced. They were here seeking shelter for their newborn. They would need to plan ahead, or they would be trapped here. I needed to talk to Samara too. I hoped that I was just being paranoid and that we wouldn't need to leave.

seventeen
saturday,
5:00pm-ish

Halloween
Trick or treat!

I WASN'T sure how I was going to convince anyone. What proof did we have? Almost none: a weird conversation and some diverted power readings. But I felt it crawling under my skin, an uneasiness, a foreboding. It made the haunted house trick-or-treating a surreal experience for me. We knocked and yelled "Trick or treat!" as we went from classroom to classroom. The kids laughed and squealed at scary masks. Victor shouted as loud as he could at every door. Lucky barked and lifted a paw to shake hands. It was quite a trick. Even he started getting candy, which was split among the kids. The kids were exhausted by eight thirty. By the time I got costumes stowed, kids in bed, and dishes washed, Albert was already asleep.

With a duffel bag over my shoulder, I took Lucky on a night walk. The air was cold and crisp. I could smell the smoke from chimneys. Lucky ran ahead of me, and I could just make out the black and white pattern of his fluffy curled tail. We took a path down to the creek between the edge of the college grounds and the farthest and oldest edge of the graveyard. The creek flowed down the hill and into a sand-filter reservoir at the bottom. There was a park where you could walk past the lovely waterfall it created. We stayed up at the top since I was too tired to make a trip down and back up. Even in the cold air, I could smell the moss and vegetation surrounding me. The leaves on the floor were still soft underfoot, like a thick carpet.

If it had been daylight, I might have been able to see some of the tombstones and ancient brick work. The rocks and granite were smooth now, the names and carvings mostly covered with moss. This far up the hill, the tombstones were little more than lumps in short rows. The foundation of an old church remained hidden deep in the heavier woods. A small set of rough, hand carved stone steps followed the gentle curve of the hill. The path was easy to remember. Even in the dark it was hard to miss. The path led through the graveyard and beneath an archway made of granite wedges. It looked like an ancient mystic portal. Where magical creatures would show up and steal you away. When I had hiked here before I was sorely disappointed by its lack of supernatural activity. What interested me tonight was a small old mausoleum that lay beyond the archway.

It was half-crumbled from time and weather. Just past the doorway, hidden by some of the fallen roof, was a set of stone shelves. I stowed the duffel bag of supplies there. There was plenty of room in the bag to add to it later. For now, it was just a small amount of emergency supplies: clothes, first aid, food, water, and ammunition, all carefully sealed and contained. It wasn't a long walk. It had taken less than ten minutes, plus just a few more to stow the gear and move the rubble back to hide the bag.

I didn't use a flashlight. It would have ruined my night vision and given away my location. I moved slowly and carefully along the footpath. The forest had many sounds between the droning of night bugs and the other creatures. Clouds had rolled in and were covering the starlight, and the moonlight was thin. Lucky stayed closer now, helping me find our way back. I had just returned to the paved road when a tiny whisper of my name brushed against my ear. My body froze as my heart leapt into my throat.

The night-world sounds from before suddenly seemed very loud. Lucky's breathing next to me, the breeze through the rattling leaves, the sound of my own heartbeat. It was all thunderous as I waited and looked at the world of shadows and scattered moonlight.

There had been a study about dyslexia and how it affected people. The disorder had made it very hard for me to learn to read because I didn't process individual letters well. The idea of individual letters combining together to form words just didn't translate to what I saw when I looked at them. My eyes processed patterns, groups of letters. I would recognize "cat," but "c-a-t" would get all messed up in my brain. However, according to the study, this supposed disability wasn't really a disability at all. It was actually a trait that evolution developed to help humans with survival. For example, consider those puzzles where one word is hidden in a page full of letters. It could take some people forever to spot the word. I could do it in a matter of seconds. This translated to the real-world situation of camouflaged predators: the cheetah hidden in the tall grass, the shadow among other shadows. I believe that was why these things popped out to me. It might be the only reason I actually spotted him at all: the Shadow, Sergeant Mikoto.

He was so perfectly aligned with the stack of logs that I couldn't make out his legs. I saw only his arms and shoulders. The rest of him just melted away. Once I realized it was him, I felt the clench in my stomach loosen. I was about to rip him a new one for scaring me when light flashed across the ground ahead of me. On instinct I hid. I stepped back into the woods and pulled Lucky up behind the base of a large tree. We sank low into its knobby, gnarled roots. The dirt was soft and cold, but it helped us blend into the lumpy shadow. The light flashed again, and now I could hear the sound of footsteps. Lucky growled low in his throat, and I shushed him. He settled as I petted his ear. The sentries were on a strict rotation, and they were not set up near us. That meant that whoever was walking this way was not on duty.

In my youth, hiding in the woods while watching people had not been that odd of an activity for me. I was a weird person with weird hobbies and even weirder friends. But usually it would have been for a prank or a game of some sort. There in the dark, suddenly I was my old self again, full of curiosity and lacking in self-preservation.

The footsteps were hurried, and I heard voices. I tried to see where the Shadow was hiding for a signal, but at this angle he had disappeared again. The moon peeked out from behind a cloud, and the path was illuminated in grays and whites. There were three men walking, and two of them were carrying what looked like a stretcher between them. Whatever they were carrying wasn't a person. It looked like boxes. I scrunched down lower as a woman ran up along the road from the opposite direction.

"Finally. You're late." The woman's voice was low and angry.

The lead man, who was not helping carry the stretcher, waved her off. In a snarky tone he said, "It was a late night. There were people out and about till half an hour ago, ya know? For the party. I decided not to tell them to get the hell out so I could take this stuff and meet you here. Sorry." He didn't seem particularly pleased either. The voices sounded similar to the ones from the storage-room meeting, but I couldn't be certain. Maybe they were just stealing supplies. Not great, but not as dangerous as we had thought. They headed to a house that looked like it had been abandoned even before the storms. It was an old-style colonial with a big porch and lots of windows, all covered with plywood. The door creaked as they stepped in and shut it behind them.

Before I had a chance to think like a rational, sane human being, I followed them and crept as quietly as I could to a side window. There was just the tiniest of cracks in the plywood. I was able to find it because their lanterns glowed through it. They were obviously not paranoid enough. I put my eye to the opening and saw a brown coat hanging on the back of a chair. I could hear people talking as they moved things around the room. Chairs scraped against the hardwood floors. I could smell dust and kerosene.

"It's fucking cold in here," a different male voice complained.

"Quit your bitching. We'll be warm when we get back," said the snarky man from before.

The woman spoke again. "Quiet down, both of you. Now did you bring the parts from the list?" Her voice sounded pinched and hurried.

There was the sound of a match being struck and a sigh, which was actually an exhale of smoke. I could smell the menthol. The craving for a cigarette tingled in the base of my jaw, hooked under my ear, and crept along behind my neck, coming to rest at the base of my skull. I swallowed and clenched my jaw to focus on what they were doing. The hole was narrow and awkwardly located. I couldn't see much more than the coat. I pulled back to see if any of the other windows were giving away little slivers of light. When I didn't find any, I put my ear to the hole and tried to hear them clearly.

"I wasn't able to get everything yet. I told you, some of that stuff is under lock and key. It's going to take some time," the snarky man said around his smoke. I recognized the speech pattern of someone talking with a cigarette in their mouth.

There was cursing, and then the woman spoke again. Her voice was soft and calm, but it had all the warmth of a reptile living in the arctic. "I understand it's difficult, but we need those parts. Without a working radio, we cannot coordinate. Without that, all this will not really help us, will it?"

The smoking man spoke quickly, obviously realizing he had poked the cobra. "I get it. Seriously, we are working on it. The kid here has an in. He is making nice with one of the girls, and he will get it here by tomorrow night, or the next at the latest."

There was a slam of something hard against the floor and a grunt of pain.

"Do not fail. Jacob is counting on us. This is the start. We must be ready and complete the tasks he has set for us, so we can finally set ourselves free from the tyrants who seek to oppress us." She spoke with a chilling conviction. "It's their wickedness that brought God's wrath down on us. Their guns and power have been used for evil for too long. We will take it from them so we can make a better tomorrow for your children. They are trained killers. They aren't here to protect us. The only reason they are here is for that radio tower. We will take what we need to protect ourselves. This is the chance of a lifetime to change the whole world. And we will be the first step. Don't forget that. We are making history here."

The voices all joined together in a prayer ending with "Praise be."

I felt ice slide along my spine and encircle my chest, squeezing me tight, as I thought about all those people at the train station chanting "Praise be" in response to the glass man's speech. I wanted to take off running, but I was afraid to move. I stayed crouched by the side of the window and waited for them to leave.

A hand covered my mouth, and an arm wrapped around my body. I thought I would burst right out of my skin from the fright. I sucked air to scream, and my muscles coiled to fight like a crazy person until I caught the scent of peppermint. It was enough to bring my mind back to reality. Lucky wasn't growling, and the hands weren't hurting me. I took a moment to calm my breathing and heart rate. Slowly, I was able to relax my muscles. As I focused on trying not to panic, I heard it, the sound of footsteps on the hardwood.

"Did you hear something?" The young man's voice was very close, just on the other side of the window.

The hand that was over my mouth tensed. We froze, neither of us daring to breathe. The moment was suspended as we waited. The night sounds filled in around us.

"I don't hear anything. You are jumping at shadows," the smoker said dismissively. "Maybe ... well, anyway, we should get back before someone misses us." The young man's voice drifted farther away as he spoke.

The hand over my mouth let go and moved to my shoulder. I felt the heat of his breath against my ear as he spoke so quietly that I wasn't sure if I actually heard him. "Be still."

The scent of peppermint was so strong that I could almost taste it. I gave the tiniest dip of my chin to nod. I didn't see or hear him move. I felt the warmth of his body shift from one side of me to the other. A black shadow that didn't have the shape of a man moved to encompass me. The light from the hole disappeared, and my eyes had to adjust to the darkness again. I heard footfalls on the porch. I felt something heavy and warm press me against the house. Lucky was pushed up onto my lap. I was finally able to make out the edges of the world in the dark again. Even then, it was the heat of him that told me where he was. This close, I could see some of his strange outfit. It was like a netting filled with leaves and twigs and such. His hands were over my head. He curled above me completely, blocking my view of the people leaving. His strange curving made me think he was pretending to be a bush or a pile of leaves up against the house.

The time between breaths stretched and seemed to take forever. The moment lasted and lasted as I waited to hear my next breath. I was in slow motion and hyper aware of things around me. The air was full of smells, wood and dirt and peppermint. There was something jabbing into my left butt cheek. It was so dark inside the dome he created that I could barely make out the line of his face, which was distorted by camo paint. Heat seemed to radiate from him in waves. I felt sweat trickle down the side of my neck. He wasn't looking at me. His eyes were following the people

I couldn't see. There was just a little bit of that black hair hanging down by his collar.

My neck started to ache from the funny angle I needed to see his face. Being this close to him sent butterflies swarming around inside me again. I dropped my gaze to the strange outfit he was wearing. In movies they had shown lots of different stuff for snipers to wear. I had never seen this outfit in person. It was impossible to decipher how he was wearing it. The moon had gone behind a cloud again, and all I could make out was a single leaf. I couldn't tell if it was a maple or an oak leaf. I kept trying to focus on it. Staying focused on it seemed to help me calm down. I leaned in to get closer and closer. Finally, I reached out to touch it.

Now I would love to explain why this leaf was so important to me, but I have no idea. I just had to know. So I reached out and touched the leaf. It turned out to be a maple leaf. Yep, a maple leaf. Neat, right? Well, now I knew. And what followed next was a wonderful example of cause and effect.

I touched the leaf and apparently startled the hell out of Mr. Cool and Composed, because he jumped and stepped on Lucky's tail, which made Lucky yelp out loud and kick me in the stomach, causing me to gasp out for breath. All this ruckus got the attention of the people who had made it down the street, and they pivoted and shone their lights in our direction.

That's right—all hell broke loose, and we were spotted because I fucking had to know that it was a goddamn maple leaf.

His eyes were suddenly right in mine. "Run" was all that he said. An instant later, I was forcefully yanked to my feet.

"There! Get them!" an angry woman's voice hissed from the road.

Lucky was off like a bolt ahead of us. I tried to keep up. Although I could ride a bike very well, I was *not* made for running. The long-legged sniper man seemed to have had enough of my short-legged sprint and shifted from holding my wrist to doing a weird martial artsy, kung Fu move I couldn't see. Next thing I knew, I was up and over his shoulder as he ran. It had been a long time since I had been carried around.

I might have screamed at the sight of the ground suddenly rushing past, but his shoulder in my diaphragm prevented me. The way he moved across the ground made me think of those deer I had seen recently. He was so fast! He moved as if he could see perfectly and with complete confidence in the dark.

I couldn't make out people chasing us. I could see the beams from the flashlights bouncing and shining wildly behind us. I didn't see Lucky but heard him up ahead. I tried to catch a glimpse of the men chasing. Before I got a chance, I was whirled through the air again. I landed hard on a wet, muddy patch of leaves. All the air was pushed from my lungs on impact. It left me dizzy and winded and barely able to move as he pressed me into the leaves and dirt with his weight. He was breathing hard but somehow quietly. The buckles on his equipment dug painfully into me. I didn't even squeak. I prayed that Lucky had kept running. I heard people moving past us on the gravel road. Once the sounds of them had faded, I could breathe again.

"Be still. Wait here," he said, his voice barely audible in my ear.

I tried to swallow, but my throat was dry. Between one blink and the next, his warmth was gone, and the only sound was the wind blowing through the leaves. No crunching steps, no rustling, not even the shift of his clothing. Just the fucking wind through the goddamn trees, as if he had never been there. I considered the very real possibility that I was in more danger from him than from the people chasing me.

My body shivered at the temperature change. I tried to pull my galloping heartbeat back to a steady pace. My adrenaline was still racing, and the flush was hot on my face. If it had been colder, steam might have risen off my skin. I looked up into the trees at the sky above. Stars peeked out, twinkling in the gaps of night clouds. I realized I was smiling. It was ridiculous to be smiling, but I couldn't stop it. It was just so far-fetched to be chased by a group of people who were planning some secret overthrow of our little government and be saved by a guy I was almost certain could turn into a ghost or something.

I mean, really think about it, for fuck's sake. The world had fallen to shit. Modern society was slagged. We were completely on our own out here. We were staring down the barrel of winter with only about half of what we needed to survive it. But instead of trying to find a way to work together, these assholes were worried about who was in charge of the fucking radio! Wasn't that just like people? And to top off the whole shitty cake, they were doing it for religion!

History has repeated again and again, over and over, and still we've learned nothing. A star winked down at me from far above, and I winked back at it, barely holding back a case of giggles.

Adrenaline was weird. As I got my breathing under control, my mind seemed to speed up. I thought of what would happen next. They knew they had been discovered. They would have to assume the worst. What would their next step be? I tried to imagine what I would do if I were a religious zealot, and I knew someone had discovered my plot, but I wasn't ready to enact it. The only options would be to either kill the person who had discovered me or discredit them, maybe frame them, then hide the evidence or set the plan into motion before someone could stop me.

I guessed everything depended on whether they had seen me or Lucky. They would probably move their hideout. Their stuff would have to be moved, and they'd need a new location for meetings. I wished I had seen their faces. But the fact that I hadn't should mean they hadn't seen mine either. My mind continued through these terrible thoughts till it spun out, and I just stared up at the sky.

It seemed like I waited forever. It was cold, and I was shivering when Lucky found me. He was warm, so I hugged him tight. It was only a moment later that Mr. Shadow arrived, materializing out of the darkness; it was like watching a ghost form out of nothing. I could hear the sounds of the world around me, so I knew I wasn't deaf, but even straining, all I could hear from him was the faint sound of his clothes shifting.

His strange outfit was gone, and now he wore jeans, a knit shirt, and a thick lined coat. For a moment I thought I was having a hallucination, one of those dreams were everything is realistic and right, except suddenly everyone is left-handed or the sky is green. I must have looked bad because after one look at me, he took off his coat and put it around me, forcing me to my feet. The coat was so warm it almost hurt. It was far too large for me, which made it fantastic. It fell to my knees, and my hands didn't come out the sleeves. My legs and hands were filled with pins and needles, and my teeth were starting to chatter. The strange dream continued, and for a confused moment I couldn't figure out why he was touching me. He began to vigorously rub my arms and legs. It wasn't pleasant, but it helped bring warmth back into my limbs.

He made sure the coat was closed and did something with my hair, then took a moment to look me in the eye. I was trying to figure out how he had gotten all that stuff off his face so fast or where he had found a leash for Lucky. I was still a bit unsure about the dreaming thing. He turned me and gently started walking me down the road.

We took the long way around and walked at a leisurely stroll. He draped a large warm arm over my shoulders, keeping me tucked close to his body, as he held the leash. I was confused, but my brain fog kept me from protesting. We had been walking long enough for me to finally feel my toes and fingers when I figured out what was happening: we were pretending.

We were pretending so that if anyone saw us, they would see a couple walking a dog in the cold air. It was clever. We did see some people walking around, but if any of them were the group from before, they too were disguised. We passed guards on duty and a group of teens sitting outside the common room, sharing smokes and a bottle. It was almost one in the morning when he walked me to my porch. My limbs felt like they were made of lead. My nose was cold and felt like it was going to run off my face. I climbed the steps and stopped at the door. He looked at me for a moment. I was so tired, I felt like I could sleep forever. I had to tilt my head back to look at him. I might still have been in shock a little.

"Well, that was one hell of a night on the town, right?" I whispered. I had to smother the giggle fit that tried to begin again. I did not want to wake anyone. I felt weird and a little light-headed. "Wow, you are really tall," I said, still looking up, "like basketball player tall." I did laugh that time and quickly put a hand over my mouth. I found the whole situation hysterical.

He reached up and pulled a leaf from my hair. It was a maple, another fucking maple leaf. I sputtered around my hand and giggled for a moment.

"Why don't you keep it?" I said. "A way of saying I'm sorry for, you know, getting us spotted." I did manage to keep quiet, but tears pricked my eyes. The slight stinging helped me calm down a bit. Seriousness crept back over me, and self-preservation returned as I began to think of what all this could mean for the kids. "Do you think they know it was me?" My smile was gone as I looked out at the street.

"No, they would have been here waiting." He patted my shoulder and nudged me toward the door.

My brain tried to process that, but could only manage it in a strange, disconnected way. "Wait, is that why we were walking around for so long?" I said as I stopped at the door. After all the walk to the stash was less than ten minutes and we had been walking a long time. Finally, I asked what really mattered. "What are we going to do?"

"You? Sleep. Pretend this never happened. Me? My job." He smiled at me, casting that magic across his face again. There in the cold, in the shifting moon-cast shadows, he was more dream than man. He was as mysterious and intriguing as music at midnight.

In response to his sudden mythic transformation, I sneezed. I am not talking about some cute dainty sneeze, but one of those awful, loud wet ones that makes your whole face hurt. I couldn't be certain, but I was pretty sure he was laughing at me when he nodded toward the door again and walked away. I was going to give him the coat, but he had already made good distance, him and those legs.

Fuck it. I needed a new coat anyway. I took Lucky and the coat inside. The house was warm and inviting. I could hear the snores in the bedroom from the doorway. I searched the coat pockets and found a small wrapped red-and-white candy.

Peppermint, my favorite. "Happy Halloween, trick or treat," I whispered as I ate the candy.

sunday, morning - too early

THE NEXT MORNING, I wouldn't describe what I tried to do as waking up. It was more like trying to pull myself out of sleep sludge. I could hear Zyada, and I could feel Victor crawling on me. I opened my eyes and felt the weight of the air on my skin. I was shivering from the cold, but I could feel the dampness from my sweat. I groaned and tried to call out to Albert. I don't think I managed to make any noise before Victor was lifted off of me. Without the pressure of his weight, suddenly everything hurt.

Albert's voice seemed too loud as he spoke and brought me a cup of water. "You have a fever, honey. You need to take these right now." He handed me some pills, and I took them just to get the water.

I drank the whole cup and then a second one before I felt like all my strength was sapped. I finally managed to lift my arm enough to look at my watch. It was past noon. I drifted in and out of sleep for a while, floating on the edge of consciousness. Dr. Fisher came to check on me. He took my vitals and examined me. He believed it wasn't an infection but a virus. He took some blood samples and put me on bed rest. Albert dug out one of the bottles of cold medicine we had hoarded away, and I nursed it. Vera came to help take care of things while I was sick. She made food and helped me change after the sweats. I had chicken soup and tea and sleep.

The pain was horrible, and I felt cold all the time. I couldn't read or write, and it hurt to talk. I was always thirsty. Everything seemed to transpire through a haze. It took so much energy to accomplish anything. I was aware of my little ones and people coming and going, but it was more an impression than full awareness. The next time I opened my eyes, Sunshine was there, sitting on the floor teaching Zyada to play cards. Zyada was cheating. Albert was there with some soup and more medicine. It felt like every joint was bruised. Every muscle ached. I could smell the menthol from the vapor rub on my skin. It hurt to cough, to sneeze, to breathe, to move; it hurt to be. Oh, the joys of the flu.

I had no real way of knowing how much time had passed. It could have been a day or a week. It was a very serious case of the flu, or at least that was what Dr. Fisher assured me. There were a few people at the infirmary who had it. Amazingly enough, my children hadn't caught it. The kids were having fun camping out in the living room. Sunshine was also staying over, though I wasn't sure why, until Dr. Fisher explained that since there were so many folks with the flu, the infirmary needed all the beds.

"What about me? Should I go to the clinic? I don't want to make anyone here sick."

He smiled and shook his head. "If the children were going to get this, they would have at this point. From what I can tell, none of the kids are getting sick. I'm thinking we got lucky and this is one of the strains of flu that we vaccinated for. They might have received the shots at their checkups. Looks like we dodged a bullet here. I always say get your flu shot." He smiled and patted my shoulder. "You will be fine. We just need to make sure this doesn't turn into something more serious, like bronchitis or pneumonia. Stay inside, stay warm, and drink your fluids. You should be back to your old self in no time."

As my fever spiked, I dreamed. I dreamed that I was running in the woods, following the Shadow. I almost caught up, my hand outstretched. Then suddenly I was a deer, and he was a wolf chasing me. Then I was in the stars, swirling up over the hill as if I were flying. One moment I was on fire, and the next I was lying in icy snow. Most of my dreams consisted of broken bits that left no real memories.

The only other vivid dream was the last one. I was looking down at myself lying on a bed of leaves. I looked like I was sleeping, but as I watched, I started to rust. It was a time-lapse view of a robot me slowly falling prey to the passing of time. I tried to struggle, and suddenly I was no longer looking at myself but *was* myself. I squeaked and groaned as I moved my rusted limbs. It hurt. Dreams weren't supposed to hurt. I woke slowly from that dream; it was hard to shake off.

I finally came back to life when I heard Zyada laughing. Mouthy was in the house talking, telling some story I couldn't follow. The haze was gone, and though I felt shaky and weak, the pain was less. The room didn't seem freezing or boiling. It was dark but warm. Lucky slept at the foot of the bed. I wondered how long he had been there. I shifted to a sitting-up position and could have sworn I heard my body squeak. I let my legs dangle off the edge of the bed for a moment as I waited to stand up.

I let myself take a step toward the door. I leaned there and blinked, squinting as the light hit my eyes. Mouthy was sitting at the table with Victor, Zyada, and Albert. They were playing something with dice. It was a rousing game, and apparently Zyada was winning. Nathan was playing chess with Mr. Shadow. Sunshine was chopping a vegetable that I couldn't see, but I could smell spaghetti sauce. The garlic smelled amazing, and my stomach growled. The house was full of life, noise, happiness, food, family. I wanted to stand there all day, just watching.

I got only a few minutes. Victor had his back to me. I don't know how he knew I was awake. He suddenly threw his dice, very quickly got out of his seat, and ran over to me as fast as he could.

He didn't cry, didn't babble, didn't make any noise at all, and just hugged me tight. It was then that the others realized I was there. I squeezed him close and petted his head. Zyada and Nathan were quick to follow suit. They all tried to hug me at once. Zyada was asking me questions, and Nathan was stuttering, trying to get all his thoughts out at once. I just closed my eyes and held on.

After a few minutes Nathan finally finished what he was saying and went back to playing. Zyada backed up and smiled. "I am glad you're feeling better, Mommy."

Albert came and helped free me. Sunshine helped keep the kids distracted while I went and showered. I felt more like myself. I sat and had a little spaghetti. It tasted awesome.

I would like to pretend that I was some badass who got right back up on the horse and got back to work. To be frank, I completely forgot about anything other than food. I barely spoke as I lumbered to a chair at the table. I stared blankly ahead until a bowl of food and a mug were set in front of me. All I could think about was how good that sauce tasted. I just sat eating and drinking coffee as if this were the only occupation in the world. Cookies seemed to appear by magic next to my plate. I have no idea how long I sat there completely engrossed before I noticed that not only were their humans around me, they were talking.

Albert was speaking low. "I think I have finally found the trail for the energy drain. It's being siphoned off at an outlying junction box, then out of the grid."

"Any idea where it might be going?" Mouthy said, taking a cookie.

Albert shook his head. "I found the cords, but I was worried that if I tracked them then and there, I would be followed. I'll go back later when there are fewer people around."

"Well, any ideas on what it might be used for?" Mouthy asked in a hopeful tone.

I was suddenly struck by lightning. Like an overeager student in class, I bounced in my seat and practically choked myself trying to answer. "Radio!" I exclaimed, finally getting the word out around my mouth full of garlic bread. "She said that they needed the radio. There was some part they needed."

"Radio?" all three men said in unison.

Their surprise confused me. "Yeah, the woman who was ordering people around said they couldn't get the radio working. Something about trying to coordinate... Didn't you tell them?" I looked at Mr. Shadow with a "what the fuck" look.

He sipped his coffee and seemed unphased. "Wasn't at the hole. Couldn't hear them."

I gave him an annoyed look and took another, smaller bite of my bread dipped in sauce. I snatched a couple of cookies to make sure I actually got some before Mouthy ate them all. I continued my thought. "I don't know who they were, but I think she is part of the religious group we saw at the market."

Albert looked over at me, but Mouthy beat him to the punch. "Why?"

I shrugged. "The stuff she said. She talked about God's wrath and being chosen for this task. Then there was that chanting 'Praise be' at the end. I have heard that before, from that preacher at the fairgrounds. He gave me the creeps." I shivered thinking of The Glass-man. "I think they called him Father Jacob." I looked at the Shadow. "Did you check out the house?"

He nodded but said nothing.

Mouthy somehow managed to speak even as he shoveled food into his face. "Yeah, it was empty. We missed whatever party was happening there. The dust on the floor was all walked in, there were cigarette butts everywhere. A bunch of stuff in inventory got legs and took off. Nothing big, tools, small equipment, and some other supplies."

I looked at them. "Do you think they might stop now since they know we're looking for them?"

Albert rubbed one of my shoulders, and everyone gave me the

"aww, isn't she so innocent" look. I did not appreciate their patronizing bullshit and made no effort to hide it.

After a moment of silence, I asked, "What's the plan then? Just follow the cords?"

They all seemed to take a moment to think about that.

Mouthy shrugged slightly and was the one to finally answer. "Well, Mama Mouse, we have to wait for them to make another move. We investigate and try to figure out what parts they took and why. You want to help play detective?"

Albert looked a little worried as I nodded and gave Mouthy a fist bump. "You know it!"

It might have been the cough syrup, but I was feeling pretty optimistic about finding the bad guys and saving the day. I needed to read those warning labels a little closer. *Warning: May make you believe you are smarter, tougher, and cleverer than you actually are.*

I had been down with the fever for three days. The fourth had been spaghetti night. That made my first day out Thursday November 5. I was probably the only one bothering with days of the week right now. But then, I also had the watch. Someone had gone to the trouble of fixing the clock in the infirmary for the sake of the doctors and medicines, though.

I bundled up with extra layers because the air outside was so cold. Vera said that snow would be coming soon. She didn't tell me how she knew; she just said she had been here long enough to know. She predicted that by the middle of next week, we would have our first snowfalls.

I walked Victor and Lucky out in the backyard. I threw a ball for Lucky to chase while Victor played in the leaves. Zyada and Sunshine had gone to the infirmary to cheer up patients with their new and improved comedy act. Nathan had gone with the teens to gather vegetables from the local gardens they had found. Albert had gone back to work. We all were pretending everything was fine.

The first step to investigating a secret organization that had infiltrated your group was to pretend you didn't know that a secret organization had infiltrated your group. From my vast knowledge of espionage from TV shows and movies, I knew that the first part of dealing with spies was to not let the spies know you know they are there.

We had stayed up late talking about what might be happening and what we should do. Taking over a place wasn't easy, even in the best of times. However, the biggest obstacle was the people. You needed to convince the people to go along with it. I figured that was the reason they'd had people infiltrate us already. In all the shows, the infiltrator was supposed to whisper and plant seeds of doubt. They weren't just here to sabotage equipment. We had to figure out a way to try to keep track of that whisper campaign and maybe even counter it.

Vera Wilson helped with that. She was a nice elderly woman, with plump rosy cheeks and a quiet pleasant disposition. She volunteered with the kids, and in the kitchens. She was in the church group. She was a Unitarian, but she had been going to the prayer meetings because it gave her comfort about her husband. He had died in the storms when his pacemaker killed him. She had stopped by shortly after our spaghetti dinner to make sure I was taking my meds and to help clean the room.

"It's not that they are saying anything wrong exactly," she had whispered over coffee with us late that night. "It was more the way they were saying it. Like when they said, 'These hard times are a test of our faith' or that 'we have to overcome our weakness and find strength to lead the world into a new day.' There isn't anything wrong with it, but somehow when they said it, it gave me shivers. Like they mean something else underneath." She looked worried.

She nibbled a cookie. "We have the sewing circle where we have been working to make winter clothes for everyone. It's the same as with any social group, there is a pecking order. Just like back at school, the gossips, the popular ones, and so on. Little groups form up of people who get along. But recently things are shifting, and the little groups are being gobbled up into one big group. Alice and Samara and we older ladies are being separated out. A couple of other ladies, Edith and Susan, have started sitting with us. They said the big group was just too political for them. I don't know what that meant, but it made me nervous."

I smiled and held Vera's hand. I tried to reassure her that we would be OK. We made plans to have a baking circle, before she had left that night. The social gatherings getting more political was never a good thing.

Erica came to check on me and brought me some stuff she had picked up from a small pharmacy she had scouted last month. She helped me wash the sheets and hang them in the house to dry. We pulled out my tea, a mix of green and black tea with a wonderful, strong flavor. It was soothing and warm. In soft voices, we spoke about what was happening in camp. She was worried too. She said she was Wicca and didn't like the idea of any religious group running things. Erica was putting a log on the fire in the little woodstove when the knock on the door came.

I quietly tiptoed to the door and looked out the peephole. A private was standing there, looking around nervously. I opened the door just enough to smile at the private.

"Hi, Private Fowler. How can I help you?" I said in a soft voice. "The little one is sleeping."

He gave me a small smile and took off his cover. "Afternoon, ma'am. Sorry to bother you," he said in a soft voice. "I have a message to deliver to you from Private Benjamin. He said to make sure you got it right away." He held out a small wooden bushel crate, like the ones I had seen at the farmer's market.

I frowned and looked at it as I took it. It was heavy with fruits and veggies. "This is from Private Benjamin?"

Fowler smiled and shook his head. "Oh no, ma'am. A group of men brought it. They were Amish or Mennonites; they had a little buggy. They said that they had traded with you before and that they had a delivery for you. We asked if they wanted to speak to you, but they said it was just a delivery. Then they left."

I was confused but pleased. "Wow that was really nice of them."

He nodded and smiled. "They're good people."

He worried his hat a little in his hand and shuffled. "I am glad you're feeling better, ma'am. All us boys were worried about you. Take care, and don't push yourself too hard. Mouthy said to make sure you have everything you need. A couple of us will be by later to make sure you have enough wood." He stepped back and waved, eager to be away, obviously a little embarrassed.

"Thank you. That would be wonderful," I said.

I waved as he walked away. It was a nice feeling to have people care about you, to have a community. I held that word, "community," in my brain as I closed my front door. I locked the door and walked back to the counter. Erica looked at me curiously. I set the small box on the table, and slowly we started sorting out what was inside.

"Well, it can't be the end of the world if there is still mail." I laughed a little and continued talking. "Hey, I loved that movie with Kevin Costner, The Postman. I think it was a civilization's ability to communicate that made it a dominant power. It is such an interesting concept. Massive empires had to prioritize how to communicate with their people long distance." I said in an excited tone.

Erica held up a hand to prevent the history lesson that was about to ensue. "I mostly just like Kevin Costner."

I closed my mouth and nodded. "Yeah, he was great in that movie." I tried not to be disappointed and focused on the delivery.

In the crate were potatoes, carrots, onions, two big rutabagas, and a small bunch of apples. I picked up a small jar of preserves. It wasn't labeled, but it was dark, and I thought it might be raspberry. The crate also held a small block of butter, six eggs, a chunk of smoked bacon, and a small bag of milled flour. There was even a little bag of sugar. Everything was in little burlap sacks or wooden boxes. It was like looking into the past. I was oohing and awing over all the contents when I saw that underneath everything was a Bible.

We were still speaking in hushed tones and sorting out the goods. It was such a thoughtful, kind gesture.

I suddenly felt a clench deep in my chest, and it became hard to breathe. I felt disjointed and out of sync with myself. My mind pulled me away from Erica and the box of goodies. I was suddenly looking out my old kitchen window. I was standing in the kitchen that no longer existed gazing at the backyard as I listened to the children play in the next room. I was tired, grumpy, and about ready to pull my hair out. If I got one more whine from Zyada or blank stare from Nathan, I would burst. I was ready to scream at Albert that there was an entire family that needed him while he was lost in one of his notebooks, projects, or computers.

The moment shattered as the vision in my mind caught fire. The last few months rushed in at my brain like a tidal wave. It was so huge. It was all gone—our house, our car, the money at the bank. The job, the college. I had been working so hard to get those degrees. Who cared now if I had a bachelor's degree and had been working on a master's? No one. I didn't want to have to struggle for survival over winter. I didn't want to fight some bizarre, mysterious cult. I wanted to watch Netflix. I wanted my house, my life, even if it had been poor and stressful, even if we had been desperately trying to make it better. It was my life. Tears threatened to spill over as I tried to keep from bawling like a baby.

I tried to pull my head out of the sudden wash of helplessness and loss. I took a deep breath to refocus on the present. *I still have my life and my family. Everything else was just stuff.*

I wiped my face as Erica rubbed my shoulder. "Sorry, Erica. I don't know what that was. This is just so kind and generous that I got overwhelmed."

Erica smiled and nodded. "I know. It can be surprising. But you do nice things all the time. It's OK to accept some kindness in return. Besides, with everything that is happening, we all need a good cry now and then. I could also use a glass of wine and a good book." She snorted a bit. "Now all I have are books. I am all out of wine."

I smiled and laughed a little. "Yeah, I don't drink, so it used to be ice cream and Netflix for me."

We spent about an hour going over different shows and the best episodes of our favorites. Erica cleaned up our coffee cups as I reached over and picked up the Bible. It was a lovely copy with very nice binding. I opened it up because I was always impressed with that super thin paper that Bibles had. Tucked in the front was a small, folded slip of paper. Written on the inside cover was the name Margaret. Was that the full name of my mom friend, Margie down in the valley? Why would Margie send me a Bible through the Amish? How did they even know each other?

Maybe she had bought this for me and asked them to deliver it. I thought a little further through this theory. Had I told her where the hill was? How had the guys in the buggy found us? I opened the note. Written in neat handwriting was "page, paragraph, line, word," followed by a series of numbers. It was a book code. I had seen something like this on a detective show.

Erica was turning back around from the sink as I carefully tucked the paper into my pocket and turned the book over. She sighed and shook her head. "Those religious types are always trying to push their God down your throat, but at least these guys give food baskets with it, right?"

I nodded and laughed a little uncertain. "Yeah, I know, right?"

I didn't show the note to Erica. Maybe it was because she hadn't questioned how they'd known we were here. Maybe it was because she didn't seem to question anything. I didn't know why I didn't trust her. I couldn't point to anything as a reason. I just didn't.

I just went on talking and smiling. Erica headed out when Victor woke from his nap. I gave her some of the food, so she left happy. Once she was gone, I gathered Victor, Lucky, and the little harness. I took both Victor and the dog outside so they could practice walking together. Today Lucky was pulling the empty wagon. As Lucky grew stronger and more comfortable with it we would add more wait, a little at a time. Victor walked with him and helped call commands. Eventually, we practiced with Victor in the wagon. As we worked, "Moonshadow" popped into my head again. So Cat Stevens it was.

nineteen
thursday, early afternoon

After Receiving the package.

EVENTUALLY, I had Lucky start the walk to supply. It was more like a meander than a walk. It was a slow, easy pace that felt good on my healing aches. The air was clean and crisp. As we came closer to the center of camp, we passed many faces I didn't know. Some of my friends in uniform smiled and waved as we went past, but everyone walked with purpose today. I seemed to be the only one taking it easy. When I made it into the common area, Sunshine found me and took over the task of entertaining Victor.

I stopped by the kitchen to make sure bread day was going well. Nothing was on fire, and there were plenty of loaves. I told everyone what a good job they were doing and put our ration of bread in the wagon. I reassured them I would be up and ready to help by the next bread day. Sunshine and Victor were kicking a little soccer ball around and chasing it through the leaves when I passed them on my way to supply.

I was supposedly heading there to catch up with Mouthy and find out whether there was someone to help me with laundry. But that was not my real reason. I needed to tell someone about the message, and I had some questions. I wanted to know how the hell the Amish had known where we were. I wanted to know if all these new folks had arrived on their own. Did the LT know about the threat that this cult posed? Maybe this was their backup plan after we found out about them. I must have had a dozen half-formed questions running circles around my brain.

I tried to keep my paranoia to a minimum as I walked into the supply area. I rolled the wagon inside, and Lucky followed me happily. Sunshine brought Victor. I was surprised at how busy it was. Normally, I came early in the morning or late in the after-noon. There was a low din from people speaking to each other and the moving of the machinery.

One of the privates we knew, Fredricks, smiled and walked over. He had line duty. "Hello, ma'am. It's good to see you on your feet." He leaned forward and whispered softly, "The bread is terrible this week."

I laughed and nodded. "Yeah, they are cutting corners. I will set them straight when I get back to it."

He smiled, and I motioned to the line. "Guess I always come at a different time. I've never had to stand in line before."

He sighed in resignation. "Yeah, it's a bit long today. We had a big group come in yesterday. They came up from the south along some side roads. The infirmary is full up too. A bunch have the flu, and there was a lady who had a baby yesterday. I am going to go check up on her after my shift."

I nodded and looked sympathetic. "Take some extra linens for her—and baby formula. Don't forget to tell Alice and Michael. If she has extra milk, maybe she can do a little wet nursing."

He nodded and smiled. "Always full of good ideas."

I laughed. "Not always. Do you know how they found us? Or were we spotted?"

He shook his head and leaned into whisper. "They got direc-tions from a guy on the outskirts of Amish property. He has a working shortwave radio. He heard us and figured out where the signal was coming from." His face screwed up into a grimaced. "The lieutenant wasn't happy about that part but said it was our duty to help them. He wants to increase our supply gathering. So, it looks like you and the other groups will be going out more than before. He was even talking about sending some of the marines too, but I think he is worried about defenses."

I raised an eyebrow and nodded. "Is someone going out to talk to the guy with the radio? Find out who he is and what he is doing?" I tried to sound casual.

He winked. "Ask your boys Shadow and Sunshine. Heard a rumor they are being sent to find out who he has been talking to."

I nodded and shuffled forward with the line.

Fredricks looked around. "Hey, did you want me to get Mouthy so he can get you taken care of and out of here?"

I smiled brightly. "No, thanks. It wouldn't be fair to all the other people here. It's no big deal. I can wait my turn. We don't want to be showing favorites right now, especially with so many faces I don't know."

He nodded, then promptly ignored me and went and told Mouthy I was in line.

As I stood in line, I tried hard to keep the paranoia at bay. I could feel it pressing in on me. All these unknown people. The gym was suddenly cavernous to me, with every voice echoing ominously. People talked in line or in small groups as they cluttered around. The voices were a pulsing thing that thrummed around me. The hairs on the back of my neck rose, and heat radiated on my shoulder blades. Someone was watching me. I felt the person's gaze, hot and burning.

Now I don't want to hear any of that bullshit about how there is no way to know someone is looking at you. Everyone has felt it at least once, walking in the halls of high school or at a store or restaurant. You feel it, that tickle that strange, eerie feeling that makes you turn, and suddenly you're looking right back at someone who is staring at you. It is how, when moms glare at their kids, the kids know to look up and stop doing whatever they're doing. It was probably something like pheromones or electric waves, but it was real. So, when I say I felt someone glaring at me, I mean I *felt* someone glaring at me.

This glare was burning with fury. Someone was *not* happy to see me. For a moment I thought Albert's ex-wife was nearby. I forced myself to breathe slowly and evenly, kept my back relaxed, and played with Victor in line. We started singing "You Are My Sunshine." Sunshine sang the lyrics as "I am your Sunshine," and Victor did his happy dance and sang along, as best as he could anyway. His happy voice was off-key and not really keeping the beat, but he enthusiastically shouted the words he knew and danced with me happily as we waited our turn. This drew the attention of our neighbors in line and plenty of smiles. Lucky gave some happy yips and made little circles, trying to dance with us. The burning eyes were still there, but after a moment more they shifted away. Or at least the joy seeping into the moment helped shield me from them.

Mouthy gave us a high-pitched whistle and summoned us over. All three males abandoned me and ran over to him. I followed along more sedately for a number of reasons. As I gathered my things, I used that time to look around. I saw a few faces I recognized, and I was pretty sure I knew who had been looking at me with hate. But all I saw was her back now. Little Miss Holier than Thou was discussing something with some of the new ladies. Yeah, it had to have been her. I tucked that into my mind's pocket and headed off to see Mouthy. When I arrived, he was talking a mile a minute about finding something important for Victor and Zyada.

As Mouthy led us back to the little impromptu office he had made for himself, I couldn't get a word in edgewise and tried to follow what he was saying. It seemed like idle chatter. I walked into the office, and the door shut behind me, too fast and with a snap, like a trap.

I nearly jumped out of my skin, and even Lucky gave a surprised growl. Shadow was standing on the inside of the door, having closed it from where no one could see him. Victor jumped and laughed; he loved a good startle. Sunshine grinned, having known about this meeting from the start.

My head got a little woozy from the sudden shift in blood and adrenaline. My heart was in my throat, and there was a thudding in my ears. It took me a moment to remember how to get air back in my lungs. Mouthy never missed a beat. Once the fear had left, I felt like all my muscles were a bit watery. I glared at the Shadow. He just gave a tiny head nod toward Mouthy, and I returned my attention to the talkative sneak.

"What was that Mouthy? I couldn't hear you." My voice did little to hide my annoyance. I planted my fists on my hips, elbows sticking out.

Mouthy grinned at me and shook his head. "OK, so I know we need to tell the Brick that we have infiltrators, but now we can at least present some evidence besides what you may or may not have seen in the woods. There is nothing he can do with that. But this … this he can't ignore."

"And thankfully we can be sure he isn't part of this cult. Though if what Vera observed is any indication, they are gathering support." I said.

Mouthy nodded and sighed. "Yeah, as much as I am for leaving the brass out of things, this seems too big to play out without his knowing. Especially if things go south. So we have to get him on board and up to speed."

Shadow interjected. "How bad is it?"

Mouthy winced and shook his head. "It is worse than I first thought. Whoever it was took more out of our inventory than I expected. Some of the items were things they should not have known about or had access to."

I frowned and shivered a little. That meant whoever it was had been here awhile and had been given trust. Who could it be, and who else was working for the glass man? All these new faces only added to my paranoia. "We need a plan if they attack or take over," I said.

Mouthy and the Shadow both frowned at me like that didn't make sense.

"We need an escape plan," I said seriously.

Mouthy laughed and waved his hand. "Oh, come on. We may be a tech unit, but we have all had weapons training, and we can fend off a couple of nuts with guns."

I shook my head in earnest. "No, you are thirty guys with guns against two hundred or more civilians in a religious surge of faith. Seriously, I have seen this movie. It didn't end well for the thirty guys. Are you really sure your guys are going to be so happy to shoot if it's Betty? Or Mr. Erickson?"

Mouthy sighed and gave me the look people always gave me when they thought I was being overly dramatic. I was used to dealing with it, but it still pissed me the fuck off. The only person who took me seriously was Albert. He was an upbeat pessimist; he believed that we should plan as if the worst was going to happen, because it would, but we would be prepared.

I was more of a grimly eternal optimist. I believed we should plan as if we were going to survive the worst happening. Our ten-year plan had included the purchase of a remote five-acre partially wooded plot of land, on which we would build a self-sustaining farm with a pond and an on-site recycling and fertilizer station, though the latter had been Albert's department. He had even been going to a university to study sustainable energy. I had found there were many things that it was better to have and not need than need and not have; for example, things like condoms, guns, first aid kits, booze, gas cans, coats, and a pencil.

Mouthy stared at me and sighed, obviously deciding the argument wasn't worth it. "Fine. We will make an escape plan. I will let you be in charge of it and help you set it up. I don't think we will need it, but we'll have one." He laughed and smiled at me. "It can even have a codename and secret passwords if you want. I know how you're into that stuff." Sometimes that patronizing big brother shit I get from men has its uses. It didn't mean I didn't want to kick him in the balls, but it got me what I needed. He shook his head again. "OK, who is going to tell the LT?"

There was a sigh from Shadow. "Me. My recon briefing is in twenty. Give me the list of missing inventory. Any missing hardware?"

Mouthy shook his head. "No, all weapons have been accounted for. Those get checked daily. As of now it's mostly electronics and kitchen supplies, though some people are saying they are missing tools." He shrugged and looked down at the list before handing it over to the Shadow. "It seems almost random. I mean, some of this I understand. If I didn't know better, I would think they were trying to start a meth lab."

My face must have reflected my thought of "what the hell?" because Mouthy gave a sheepish grin and waved me off with a laugh. "It's not like I would know about that or anything. But they aren't taking the right chemicals for meth."

"Well, I guess that's good," I said as I peeked at the list of things taken. Mouthy and his team had used some kind of shorthand to list things, so I had no idea what the items were. I noticed a tagging marker on the majority of the items: 23B4, 23B5, 23B6. Everything seemed to be near that 23B. "Hey, Mouthy, what does this part stand for?" I asked, pointing to the 23B.

He glanced over and pointed as he explained. "That's where things are stored. We have areas sectioned off so we can find things a little better. Section 23, column B, row 4."

I took the list as the guys talked about what could possibly be made with all these things. Once again, my dyslexia came in handy. To get my dyslexia diagnosis, I had to take a bunch of assessment tests. In one case, I had to match lists of number and letter combinations in a timed test. It had been a lot like this, with the numbers and letters in columns and rows. I noticed there were clusters, all just a single digit different from each other. If this was their stowed position, it meant the items were right next to each other. I didn't know what this meant, but the pattern kept jumping out at me every time I looked at the page. It could be really hard to un-see something once your brain made the leap.

I wondered if other people felt ideas tingling inside their own skulls. I imagined that this was what the dirt must feel like when a seed grew, like in one of those time-lapse films. Sometimes I thought about that slow shifting and wiggling of a tiny seed, the little spark of life, of creation. Maybe it was just me.

I took a pen and wrote down all the numbers of things taken. I was just getting to the last of them when there was a crashing sound from where Victor was standing. Everyone jumped. He had pulled on the cord of the phone long enough that he had pulled everything on that side of the desk to the floor. He had scared himself with the noise and now was starting to cry.

I smiled and said, "Oh no!" I put my hands on my cheeks in an overly exaggerated display of surprise.

He made a little sniffle sound and said, "Oh my!"

I picked him up. "My poor giant little man. Oh my."

As Victor hugged me tight, I gave Mouthy an apologetic smile.

He waved it off. "Don't fret. It's not really my office anyway."

I took my copy of the numbers and handed the list back to the Shadow. I looked him in the face while I swayed and slightly bounced with Victor. "I need to be heading back, but when you talk to Lieutenant Brick, you tell him I need to get started on the winter stockpiling. I need an office and an assistant, and we are going to make a detailed inventory of all the supplies we have, then figure out the things we need for winter. I will coordinate the other finders and send them out on specialized runs for things we are missing."

Mouthy frowned and then laughed. "Brilliant. For this you

will need detailed lists of everyone you are planning for and everything here. Anything missing will have to be accounted for. It puts them on the defensive."

Mikoto frowned at me. "Wouldn't that make you a target? They might realize you are the one who overheard them."

I grinned and shook my head. "It's related to the job I was already assigned to help with before now. And me ordering people around and demanding to do it my way would just be me being me. I'm the bossy bitch who thinks she owns the place. Besides, you don't catch rats by chasing them; you have to lure them out, and for that you need bait."

He gave me a scowl, which I ignored.

"You just make sure he agrees," I said. "Mouthy, you better get your best Machiavellian on. We both know there is going to be a lot of resistance and hoarding."

He nodded with a smirk.

I turned to the Shadow again. "I can do this. I am not afraid. I just have to keep my babies safe. You give me your word that nothing will happen to my kids. You keep them safe, and I got this."

He seemed a little surprised. He let out a slow breath and nodded. "You have my word. I will not let anyone hurt your children." He said it solemnly, his eyes steady.

I knew he meant it. He would keep them safe. This gave me a sense of peace; it helped my courage flourish. I knew Albert would fight to protect our kids. But neither of us was a marine-trained, Special Forces badass. We didn't have the skill set these men did. Maybe it was wrong to use the Shadow to protect my kids. I didn't care. Morals, ethics, dignity, pride—these were things that a society cared about. They wouldn't feed you, clothe you, protect you, or shelter you. They were the luxuries of civilization. Until civilization was restored, they were of no use to me.

I nodded to the room as I carried Victor out of the building and hooked Lucky up to the wagon. I was exhausted by the time I made it back to our little house. I put things away and began cooking dinner. It wasn't until I wiped my hand against my pocket and felt the paper crumple that I realized I still hadn't shown anyone the note.

thursday, evening

Day of Package

ALBERT GOT HOME WELL before dinner was finished. He gave me a smile and a kiss. He was followed in by Nathan, who proudly carried his sack of vegetables into the house.

"Hi, Mom!" he said cheerfully.

It was the happiest I had seen him in a while. It was nice to see. I smiled at Albert, who was also visibly pleased by the change. Nathan rattled on at full steam about all the things they had dug up, how he had been trusted to carry and go with the bigger kids.

There was a happy cheer from the door as Sunshine brought in Zyada and a basket of something that looked like leaves. My little shining star ran in and jumped up for a hug and to show me her little basket of treasure. There were leaves, acorns, rocks, snail shells, and of course, magic sticks. She went over each one. She got her army bear—a little bear in an army coat she had been given by the FEMA people when we first got here—and set him on top of the basket. "He is on guard duty," she explained to me.

I went back to making sure my rice didn't burn. The corn bread had finished baking, and the chili was done. I made Zyada a bowl of rice and some warmed-up beans. Sunshine hung out for dinner. I expected Sergeant Mikoto, the Shadow, to arrive, but he remained absent—not that I had time to notice.

Sunshine and I had something in common. We loved to chitchat. That wonderful ability to talk and entertain was a lost skill really, like the talents of poets and traveling minstrels. People like Sunshine had wonderful anecdotes and stories that might or might not be true. Those stories had morals and lessons in humility but always a humorous and delightful end too. In another time or place, Sunshine would have been a bard or a jester to a king. For now our humble table was his ancient hall, my daughter his beautiful princess, my husband his king. In my imagination I could even see the lute in his hand.

While Sunshine kept the laughter at the table steady, I gathered dishes and took them to the sink. I wondered why our bright and shiny guest had joined the marines. However, there was an unspoken rule among us chatty ones: if we didn't bring up a topic, it was a topic we didn't want to talk about.

I put coffee on the stove to perk and retrieved cups from the cupboard. I began the routine of getting kids to bed. They'd had a busy day, so they fell asleep in rapid succession. I only had to sing twice before everyone was drowsy-eyed or completely out.

The coffee wasn't quite ready, so I went to the bookshelf and pulled down two books. One was the newly arrived Bible. The other was the complete works of Arthur Conan Doyle. I had thought I was being very clever and ironic when I had hidden the note in the second book. Maybe I was just being pretentious. I took the note and the Bible to the table and set them down before going to get the sugar, powdered creamer, and mugs. I brought all of that to the table and fetched the coffee pot. I carefully poured out three mugs and fixed mine.

As Albert waited for his coffee to cool, he looked over the note. He began using the numbers to find the page, the line, and the words listed in the Bible, writing them down to create the message we had been sent. I had considered trying to decode it after Erica left but Albert hadn't been home. If it was important enough to encode and send in a care package, then it was important enough to involve Albert. However, if it was time sensitive it probably wouldn't have been sent in the bottom of a food box delivered by horse and buggy. I decided that I didn't want to have to deal with it alone and it could wait for Albert to come home.

Sunshine fixed his mug with a big smile. "Thanks. This is so much better than the brown water they serve up at the cafeteria."

I nodded and smiled, blowing at my steam. In the quiet of the moment, we could hear the sound of the wind against the roof. I thought back on what Vera had said about the first snow of winter coming. Winter coming early could be a good thing. If it arrived early enough, it would mean that whatever the conspirators were planning wouldn't be able to happen. A heavy snowfall would make travel almost impossible up this hill. It wasn't likely to happen, though. Heavy snow didn't usually arrive until after Thanksgiving. The last couple years, it had barely snowed before Christmas. But the weather was getting more and more unpredictable. However, a heavy snow or even a light snow also could make escape difficult.

Sunshine looked up and with a serious face said, "Mikoto said he talked to the lieutenant. He is going to make the announcement tomorrow. You are going to be in for quite the workload. We are up to almost two hundred people up here now. The lieutenant is hoping that we are overestimating the threat and that he has roped you into doing a ton of work for nothing. I don't think we are. I feel it, like something is moving just outside of my sight. It puts my teeth on edge."

I nodded at him and took a sip of the hot, precious caffeine. Oh, what a fabulous thing a hot cup of Joe with two spoons of sugar was. It was enough to make you believe that not only was there a God, but he loved you too. I didn't know how the human race existed before coffee. People thought I wanted to live in some distant past because I was into old things. Nope, not me. I loved espresso, pizza, 657 songs on my smartphone, vaccinations, antibiotics, indoor plumbing, streaming movies on my laptop in bed, and did I mention espresso? As a woman, having rights was a great thing. Being a historian, I had a very profound gratitude for the fact that I had been born in this time period, even if a major solar storm had ruined my smartphone.

I let the heat and the caffeine warm me up inside as I answered, only half-thinking about my response. "I know, right? Like it's going to rain or something, but you can't see the clouds, even though you can practically taste the ozone. I feel like something is …" I floundered for a word, trying to find the right one.

Sunshine was on my level. He pointed at me as it suddenly came to him. "Stalking?" he asked quickly.

I gasped and tapped the tip of my nose.

He continued, "That's it exactly. I feel like any second I am going to smell smoke, and all hell is going to break loose." His expression turned serious again. "It's nice to not be the only one. I felt a little crazy."

I shrugged. "It's OK to be crazy; it's a sign of genius."

He laughed and nodded. "Yeah, well, I want to help with the escape plan. Routes, logistics—whatever you need, I'm your guy Friday. I know all the fastest ways to get out."

I frowned slightly. "No, what we need is to figure out where we are going. We have kids with us and older folks. We can't just run out into the bush. The kids, Albert, and I just wouldn't be able to keep up. Fast is out of the equation as long as we are on foot." I took another sip, the caffeine lubricating my brain. Some things in life needed to be looked at like riddles. It was hard to figure out a riddle if you looked at it as a whole; you had to break it down into parts and sort out each part as you went. This was like that: figure out parts, then put them together.

"So if we must go slowly, then there are only two ways to go, slow and quiet or slow and protected, like in a tank. But since we don't have a tank, it's slow and quiet, like mice. We move quietly and find hiding places along the way. The big question is, where we are heading?" I was speaking but not really to Sunshine. Sometimes it helps me keep my thoughts organized if I hear them out loud. If I keep them in my head, I tend to get lost in tangents. I took my pencil in hand and began absently drawing little three-dimensional boxes stacked up on each other. I don't know why, but it was how I doodled.

"The end goal is someplace safe and secure. That means modern civilization. The only place we know of that is even remotely like that is over seventy miles away. Realistically, we wouldn't make it with everyone. So, walking to the base is out." I continued the verbal play by play of my train of thought. I was no longer looking at anyone, just watching the three-dimensional boxes appear on the paper under my pen. I took a long pull from my mug as I began another stack of boxes. Sunshine was watching me intently but was silent.

"Which leaves the train. It's a few hours by bicycle. Even if we all had bikes, I know I can't haul gear and the kids in the wagon. Albert can't pedal, and if it starts snowing, we are done for."

I blew out a breath in a silent whistle and let my fingers continue their idle shape-creating as my mental gears turned and shifted the problem around. I wished we had a functioning car. My mind went to that Mustang by the fire hydrant. It wouldn't run now, but maybe we could fix it, if we had the time. It wouldn't fit everyone, but maybe we could tow something. A truck would be better. The army truck would be best. It was huge and armored. But the military would want that.

I sighed and shook my head. "We haven't even taken into account the people out there. We have the cult that's got its base near the train camp and those people holed up in the big department stores or the prison downtown, not to mention the Crazies."

Sunshine gave me a surprised look.

I pulled out my notes and passed them over. "There is this group out there that was tagging things, and it looks like they might be killing people. All I know is when we were about to be caught by guys chasing us from the train camp, these people showed up all painted and acting like wild animals. We heard the guys call them the Crazies. Maybe it's all for show, but it was sure as shit scary. It's way to *Lord of the Flies* for my tastes."

Sunshine nodded. "Yeah. We have some recon about this group going all Mad Max in the area. Too many video games, as my mother would say." He took a moment to look over my notes and grinned. "These notes are detailed. You make a good Scout there Marlene." Sunshine said with a smile.

I just shrugged and continued my thoughts. "The end goal is to get to a place with some civilization," I said. "Like Fort Bragg or a city that wasn't hit as hard. For that we need the train ... or vehicles. But I guess that depends on whether the military is taking the trucks, which is what I am guessing will happen. If we aren't running with them, we have to plan something else." I began making the boxes that would connect my two stacks. "For the train we need a route that will let us get to the station by either walking or biking, so we can make it without losing people. We need to make it there before winter hits. We need a vehicle or a horse and wagon."

We sat in silence as we tried to figure out the solution to our problem. I wanted to have as many plans for escape as I could think off. Like I said, it was always better to have something and not need it than to need it and not have it.

Albert suddenly cleared his throat. "Got it." He shifted forward in his chair and pushed the paper in front of us. "Sorry. The words were all spread out."

We all stopped and looked at the message: "Flee, He comes with his swarm before thanksgiving."

Despite the Old Testament taste to the words, the message was clear. Whatever the group was planning was going down before Thanksgiving. We didn't have much time to figure out what the hell to do about it. I missed the good old days when the biggest thing you had to worry about was the in-laws at the holidays.

Hours later, after we had gone round and round, the house was silent as everyone else slept. I sat smoking in the rocking chair on the porch. I was bundled up in a blanket to keep the cold from reaching me.

My mind was in that space between dreaming and remembering. It was warm, sweltering really. The sun was intense and bright as it reflected off the sand and hard-packed dirt. Heat waves rose up, giving the world around me a shimmering effect. Scrub brush and cactus broke up the brown, gold, burnt red, and dusky rose hues. There it was, my beloved desert sky. There was no shade of blue that matched that color. It was a shaded mix of azure to cornflower, with just the faintest wisps of horsetail clouds to decorate it. I could hear the cry of a desert hawk as it soared high above me.

I shielded my eyes as the hot wind whipped my hair about my face, cooling the sweat on the back of my neck. There in the distance, I saw my mountains. I could see for miles in all directions, across the rolling hills and boulders; nothing blocked my view. No creatures were visible but me and the hawk above. The heat chased most living things into shelters of shade, looking to escape. Warmth penetrated deep into my bones. It hit me from above and seeped into me from below.

I knew it was because the light bounced off the sand, but still I imagined that I was in a wonderful, huge oven. I could smell the sand, the scent of mesquite, and the heated rocks. I began to move. The heat of the ground rose through my hiking boots. I pulled my bandanna over my mouth to keep dirt out and moisture in. I climbed up the rocky ridge. It was a path made centuries before I was born. The history of the land was etched in the rock, painted in the layers of shifting sediment. The trail traveled along the side of the mesa. The wind grew louder as I finally reached the top. The sun almost blinded me. Blinking, I waited for my eyes to adjust, tears stinging as they cleared away the dust. Finally, I could see down into the hidden valley that rolled out at my feet.

Down below, I watched the dry, hot world sway in the wind. Dust devils swirled and disappeared. I spotted a shadow slinking into the scrub brush. I followed its progress along the trail. I watched as he approached me, his tail low and his ears up. His muzzle was clean and his fur short. Coyotes were slightly bigger than dogs but smaller than wolves. They were lean with big ears and eyes. He sat panting in the sun, waiting. I moved without moving and touched his side. The sun had made his fur hot.

Suddenly, I heard it. I would know that sound anywhere. That sound had been taught to every child of the desert. That was the sound of the bogeyman in the sand. It was called a rattle, but that didn't really describe it. It was more like a buzzing, a terrible sped-up buzzing, as if it were a motorized maraca. Panic rose in my throat as my body froze. I was afraid to look, but my eyes were drawn to the sound.

There it was just under a bush, the diamondback rattlesnake.

I locked eyes with those gleaming chips of coal. Its black, indigo tongue darted out of its triangle head and flicked at the scents in the air. I knew it could sense my heat, feel my vibrations and smell my fear. I forced my breathing to slow, and it took a concentrated effort to keep my panic under control. I shifted my weight away from it. The huge rattle danced on its tail, bragging of the snake's age. As I shifted away, I saw its coils tense. It was pulling itself tighter, getting ready to strike. This was the night-mare of my childhood. Even on my fastest day, I couldn't ever beat a diamondback. I was so focused on putting distance between me and the deadly fangs that I didn't see the other shadow move. I had forgotten the world around me. I felt the air shift suddenly, and a blur of feathers flashed in front of me. I screamed and threw myself as far away as I could, landing on the dusty hard-packed earth.

The screech of the hawk called back to me. The snake was dead. The tail lashed and twisted in angry dismay, but the head lay useless, a foot away from my hand. The hungry hawk tore into the flesh of the snake, greedy and messy. I turned away from the disturbing sight and came face-to-face with my own reflection. I was reflected in the eye of the coyote, and then I was the coyote, watching my human self. I stared at myself, looking deep into those amber eyes until the eyes turned to look down at my hand. I followed the gaze and gasped in horror. I watched, paralyzed, as a scorpion crawled out from under a rock and climbed up onto my hand. I growled at it. I yipped and barked, trying to warn myself. The scorpion clicked its claws and whipped its tail with its huge stinger up and over its head. Then it stabbed deep into my hand.

I let out a yelp in pain. I blinked the sleep out of my eyes trying to figure out what happened. My cigarette had burned down to the ember and fallen on my hand. I put out the ember and shook my hand. The sting passed. I grumbled a few curses under my breath and sighed. I missed home, not just my house here, but *home*. I missed big skies and open landscape. I missed feeling like I belonged. The sad part was that it wasn't even the disaster that had kept me from it.

I hadn't been there since I was a teen. My mother had remarried a navy man, and he had taken us from El Paso to San Diego. Most people would see that as a major step up—California dreaming and all that. Yeah, there were beaches and surfers. But I had never been a strong swimmer. I was short and curvy, which made me fat by California standards. I was teased and became terribly insecure about wearing a swimsuit. I didn't really like the beach. The sand was all wrong. The sky was the wrong kind of blue. It blended away into the blue of the ocean. Though the sun setting over the water was beautiful, it wasn't the painted sky of my home.

We lived in navy housing, where I made friends with other navy kids, a hodgepodge of misfits. Our core group was a Goth emo guy I could lift over my head; my best friend, an overly aggressive, overprotective punk rocker; and me with my cowboy boots and sundresses. We were the core, and then we later added a few other kids who didn't fit in anywhere. We got a computer media geek and a really nice but quiet poet. We all played Dungeons and Dragons and stayed up too late. It made high school a pleasant memory for me.

I was the country Pollyanna. So much went on that I never knew about. I only saw the good in people then. No matter how scary or strange they appeared, I accepted them as anyone else. I would just smile and say, "People are people." That meant I missed a lot of subtext. I didn't notice a lot of the darker things happening around me. Because I only saw the good, the bad slipped past me.

My best friend helped make sure it did. He used to say, "She is just happy to be here." And I was. What I didn't know was that he went to great lengths to make sure I stayed happy to be there. I was never harassed or treated as anything other than a little sister by almost anyone we knew. I was never offered anything more than a cigarette till I was almost twenty. I had no idea it was because my friend had threatened and scared anyone who might have tried. I was the group's "happy," and apparently all of them wanted to keep it that way.

If I had found out back then, I would have been hurt. It would have made me mad that my friends hid things from me. I would have been upset that they didn't trust me or think I could handle things. Now I was glad I had never found out. Maybe that was selfish of me, but as I looked back at that time now from my thirties, I understood so much better what he did for me. He let me keep an innocence he had lost. For that he would always be a hero to me. I got to have happy memories of crazy times with my friends. I must have seemed so naive, with my attitude and optimism, but maybe that's what they needed. I hoped I was that for them. They had meant so much to me. Being one of the pack, being so happy-go-lucky, and being protected—it gives you a confidence to be yourself. Everyone should have friends like I did. I wished they were here now.

Things wouldn't be any safer if they were here. Life wouldn't be any easier. But I wouldn't feel so out of place. I was a desert critter lost in the forest. Here was a beautiful place, full of life, everything green and wooded. I loved the bright sunny summer and the colors of spring and autumn. I even loved snow, though Albert assured me that at some point that would go away. But I still dreamed of wide-open sky, hot desert sand, and my great open land.

If we were there now, I would know where to go and how to get there. I knew all the tricks for surviving in the heat and dryness. I knew which cactus you could eat and which you couldn't. I had been taught how to find water in the desert when I was a little girl. I knew how to spot animal tracks. I knew how to hide my tracks and where to find shelter.

But here ... here I was lost. I felt like a coyote trying to outsmart wolves in their own forest. I didn't know which plants were safe to eat or touch. I didn't know what poison oak looked like. I wasn't able to navigate without a map or compass. Half the time I couldn't even see the sun. I was worried; I didn't want to think about what would happen if I picked the wrong place to hide.

I exhaled slowly, and the steam rose up around my face like dragon's breath. Lucky sat next to me, unaffected by the cold. His thick coat would keep him much warmer when the snow came.

An owl hooted somewhere in the distance. As I looked out toward the college dorms, I couldn't stop myself from wondering where they might be. Were they sitting up in anticipation? Were they waiting for the signal to carry out whatever nefarious plan they had set up? Or were they fast asleep, confident as true believers tended to be?

I wondered what would happen if we remained, if we tried to just stay and get along with whoever came up. Some part of me just wouldn't let the idea form up. Zealots could not be reasoned with. If they were true believers, they wouldn't want nonbelievers there. Over and over again in history, this had played out. Whenever group A was taken over by group B, group B always made sure group A was either severely crippled or brought under the control of group B, usually through acts of violence and abuse. If the group plotting here managed to overthrow our little band of military brothers, any of us who were in tight with the military would be either eliminated or brought to heel. I had too much to protect and too much that could be used against me.

I still believed that there was good in everyone. But now I knew there was just as much evil. People were people, no matter where you went. From the very rich to the very poor, from the strong to the weak, any race, creed, or gender, at our core we were all the same. We all loved, hated, hoped, feared, dared, believed, doubted, and struggled the same. We all needed the same things: food, shelter, security, companionship. We were all fundamentally the same. We were all capable of the most tremendous acts of courage and kindness; we were also all capable of murder and torture. It all depended on the environment we were in. If you took away the civilization, then people would behave in an uncivilized way.

The only reason anyone listened to Lieutenant Roberts, or Brick, was because he wore a uniform. People had been raised to recognize that as symbol of authority. However, he had no more authority over us than we allowed him to. We outnumbered him and his men. We followed because we wanted the order, the security of rules.

In times when there was no law and no way to enforce it, the only truth was "might makes right." Power belonged to those who took it and kept it. If the glass man had any real numbers or weapons, the lieutenant and his men would be screwed. We were at the mercy of whoever was the strongest.

I shivered from the cold and ruffled Lucky's head. I smiled down at him as he grinned his happy grin at me. If you weren't the strongest, be the smartest. "You know what my daddy says?"

Lucky just tilted his head at me as I spoke.

"My daddy says you can't be lucky all the time, but you can be smart all day." I stretched my spine and arms as I stood up. "And Mama would say, 'Staying up worrying won't do anything but wear you out before trouble arrives.'"

I locked the house as I went inside. I checked and banked the fire before crawling into bed. Lucky took his spot next to the fire. I dreamed of school friends and happier days.

twenty-one
saturday, 8am

First day of new job.

THE MORNING WAS GRAY, and the clouds were heavy. The air was cold and still. I was up early and made an effort to make myself presentable. After my coffee, I felt fairly human. A little breath mint, and I felt downright chipper. It was good to have a goal. The excitement helped curb the worry. Knowing that Sunshine and the Shadow were protecting the family lifted the fear like a heavy blanket. I felt light and ready to take on the world.

My mood seemed to be infectious. Everyone was smiles that morning at our breakfast of oatmeal and scrambled eggs. I braided back my hair and put on the heavy coat. I gave everyone hugs and kisses, and Lucky walked with me as I stepped out the door.

Albert kissed me at the door and said, "Have a nice day at the office, dear," as if he were some 1950s housewife, and I was the husband heading off to work.

I grinned and played along. "Have a nice day with the kids, dear. I'll be home at five," I said in my best baritone voice.

Zyada fell into hysterical laughter. "You're weird, Mom!"

Albert smiled and put the flip knife in my coat pocket. "Be safe," he whispered.

I nodded and smiled. "You too."

Having a plan filled me with confidence and purpose. I felt like I was finally standing on solid ground. That feeling lasted for the first hour of work. By the time the second hour had passed, I realized I was in the shifting dunes of some bureaucratic hell.

At lunch I was pulling myself out of a sorting jungle quicksand pit. *Whose terrible plan was this anyway? I was tricked, I tell you!* It was nothing like working in an office. No amount of inventory work at a restaurant could prepare anyone for this. How was anyone supposed to do this without a calculator? Everything had to be done by hand. We found some clickers, those things where you press a button, and it ticks over another number. The clickers worked, but I had only three people to help me. We had to have people count the physical objects by hand. Then I had to do all the math to figure out how many such items we would actually need for the number of people we had.

That was just supplies, not counting people or medicines. I diligently recorded the number of boxes of mashed potatoes and cans of corn we had. It was hard and tedious. Three poor souls ran up and down the storage shelves, counting each item, then reported back. It was slow and painful. I was so grateful when my little watch showed me it was noon. I called a lunch break and pulled out my little can of fruit salad.

I sat in the quiet of the office room. The lights didn't work in this room, so the blinds were open, and afternoon sun poured in over the desk. This helped keep the room at a pleasant temperature since it was getting quite cold. The massive generator was going, but we were on a conserving ration. Only certain places got power for certain periods. It was about saving fuel. There were solar panels, but as the days got shorter and the light weaker, less power was generated from that.

I pulled the little metal tab and popped open the can. Lucky sat up at the sound, looking to see what I had. I grinned and pulled out his little can of food as well. I plopped his on a paper plate and set it on the floor. He munched happily as I sipped the juicy light syrup from the can. I ate slowly while staring out the window. I thought back to the last time I had eaten lunch in an office. It was before Zyada was born. I'd had a lot of different jobs. This had been a little part-time office gig where I basically answered phones and backed up the computers every day. It was good money, but it had the mental challenge of finger-painting. In the afternoon I had a good job where I walked other people's dogs. It was fun, and I spent all afternoon outside with dogs—best job I'd ever had.

I remembered sitting in the cubicle, waiting for my shift at the office job to end, staring out at the trees as sunlight filtered through the green leaves. I had been eating a sandwich, saving my fruit cup till the end. I hated my cubicle. I had been counting the minutes, desperate to get outside. I had been so happy to quit. It had been a blessing to become an at-home mom. The work was harder, but I wasn't trapped in some stupid cubicle. I looked around the present little office and heaved a sigh. *I hate offices.* I ate my fruit cup first and then the sandwich, which was homemade bread with peanut butter and jelly. I had a big container of water. I drank a cup and filled a little dish for Lucky. I stretched and yawned.

I decided not to go out and smoke since it was going to be a long day. Instead I stood up and stretched, doing some of the yoga poses I knew. I worked on my deep breathing as I raised my arms to the ceiling. Lucky watched me curiously but stayed where he was.

Have you ever experienced moments that seem too ridiculous to be true? That seem like they belong in a movie or are part of a bad joke? Like you're already having a bad day, so of course, that's when your tire blows. Or you're bent over with your butt up in the air, trying to stretch, and of course, you're facing away from the door, so you don't notice when someone walks in. Then when you are balanced precariously in your full stretch pose, the person coughs or grunts or stifles a laugh, as the case may be. What do you do? You try to jerk yourself out of your pose, trip over yourself as you get up, and then try to act like you weren't doing anything. Well, at least that's what I did. Fate loves to mess with you when you are already down.

It was none other than Mr. Shadow himself. He had his arms crossed and his head slightly tilted to one side. He was laughing at me, I knew it. Of course, he had his usual stoic expression on his face, but his eyes gave it away. His lips were pursed, and I could tell he was trying not to smile. *Damn it. Marlene, why do you care what he thinks anyway.*

I coughed as my whole face burned all the way up to my ears. Lucky laid his head back down and yawned. I took a drink and pretended I was flushed from the stretch. "Yoga is good for blood flow," I said, even though I didn't owe him any explanations.

He stepped fully into the room. His presence seemed to fill up all the extra space. It wasn't that he was really so large. Some of the other marines were like walking, talking refrigerators. He just took up all the air between us. He was long and lean, with hard angles and sharp edges.

I sat down again and got my pen ready. "OK, ready. What have you got?"

He read off his report, and I added the totals to the roster of visibly checked items. Then I went to the whiteboard and carefully checked the lists, writing the missing items on the board.

"Is that the last ..." My voice choked out when I realized he was right behind me at the board. *Damn it, it should be against the law for a man to smell like that. It is just wrong.* I gritted my teeth and tried to ignore the flutter in my stomach.

My mother had told me once that there were just some people that you would never get along with. She called it chemistry. There was something in their DNA or pheromones, and you just couldn't get along. Even if you didn't do anything to aggravate each other, there were just some folks you couldn't be near without it bothering you. But the opposite was also true. There were just some folks that, no matter what you did, you were attracted to, even if they were the wrong person for you. Something in their DNA called to yours. Biology was stupid. I did my best to ignore it and went back to the paperwork. But it was hard to focus. He didn't say anything but just stood there looking at the list.

"Looks like you were right about the cluster pattern of the stolen items," he said with a nod. "These things are missing by location."

It was like someone had gone to the shelves knowing exactly what they wanted, taken it, and then stolen a bunch of other things in the area to hide whatever their target was. I nodded at him and looked at the cluster lists. "Yes, but we still don't know which of these items is the focal point. Some of this stuff seems important, but then some of it is so weird that it's hard to imagine they would grab it at random."

"I mean, I can understand why someone might want to steal the copper wire, but I don't get what they need all those cotton balls for," he said calmly.

I grinned and shrugged. "Maybe they need to take off makeup or do their nails. I can't think of a lot of things I would use cotton balls for."

He leaned back against the desk. He was too close again. I could feel his heat radiating.

I was chewing on my fingernail in frustration. This was worse than being on a diet and seeing that someone had obliviously brought éclairs to work for the whole office, but because they don't know you were on a diet you can't be mad at them. Yep, it was that kind of frustration. I focused my eyes on the numbers on the page and stared at them as hard as I could. I was doing this trick where I forced my vision out of focus and back in. It helped slow my pounding heart and the blood rushing to my head.

Meanwhile, he must have been talking to me because he snapped his fingers in front of my face. "Hey, you with me?"

I blinked and gave a yawn to cover my stare. "Sorry, what was that?"

He continued giving his report to me, and I finished writing it down. He walked over to the wall and opened a window. He then nodded and headed back out.

I sorted my stacks and began getting ready for the next phase. We had a complete inventory of what we had and what was missing. We had a complete head count of all the people. The rest, I could do at home with Albert, my resident math genius. I gathered up the papers and headed out. I was walking down the hallway, with Lucky following close behind, when I heard her voice.

"You must think you're pretty clever." She spoke from a chair in the waiting area. It was the church woman, the one with the bread problem. She had a book in her hand. I didn't remember her name.

"If we are being honest, yeah, I do actually," I said, matching her tone. I had never liked bullies. I was always the kind to fight back. I really didn't like this lady. I didn't know what I had done to her, but we didn't mix. Maybe it was that pheromone thing again. Stupid biology, always getting me into trouble. I decided to continue walking.

She rose to her feet and moved to intercept me. "I don't know what you did to get this job, but I know you're up to something. Don't think you have me fooled. I have seen you sneaking around with those marines. I don't trust you. If I don't trust you, then there is a big group of us that are going to do everything we can to ruin your little plans." Her voice was calm and even, one might say pleasant, as she spoke. Her proper smile firmly in place.

I considered the possibility that she was with the cult but figured she was just an entitled rich lady who didn't like taking orders from a commoner. I didn't have her skill for pretending, so I just laid it out. "OK, princess, what's the deal? Hmm? What did I do? Make a loaf better than you? Not say enough hallelujahs? I don't know why you have such a problem with me, but if it's really that big a deal, then how about tomorrow you come help with the actual work? The only reason I am the one doing this is because I am the one willing to work."

Her smile disappeared as she crossed her arms. She looked down her nose at me. She was taller than me by a few inches and had a willowy figure that so many women wanted. I felt stumpy standing there. I smiled and lifted my chin a little, making my stance a little wider.

"You are more conceited than I thought if you think you matter to me at all," she said. "But I have worked too hard for too long to let something like this destroy my position." Her voice was ice-cold. She smiled, but the smile made my skin crawl. There was something not right about her eyes. She was definitely a new kind of crazy. As she continued talking, her tone changed back. "Since you so generously offered, I will be here bright and early to assist you in your endeavor. After all, it's for the common good, right?" She had changed so suddenly. Her whole persona shifted to a warm smile and humble posture. It was creepy. I took a step back from her as a few more people came down the hallway. They smiled at her and nodded as they passed. She was like a chameleon. It was scary to watch.

"Right. See you then, I guess." I turned quickly to leave. Even if she was part of the infiltration, the whole point of the plan was to bring them in close and observe them. But she gave me a weird vibe. I refused to look over my shoulder, though Lucky kept a wary eye on her as we both left. I was relieved when I made outside into the brisk air. I wrapped my coat tighter and pulled my scarf around my face to protect against the biting wind. I stuffed my hands into my pockets and looked at the sky. It was still clear and bright, but I felt the storm was just out of sight.

I spent the afternoon helping with bread loaves. The team had indeed been cutting corners, and I didn't like it. I decided to go over all the steps again. The work seemed to get easier every week. New equipment was always being found and brought in. The ovens were working as well as the mixers. It was nice to be in the warm oven area, so there were plenty of volunteers. I was mostly supervising and giving instructions now. After just a few hours I was able to leave, with three loaves to take home. There was still plenty to keep me busy until Albert got home to go over the numbers with me.

Sunshine brought the kids back from day care. He was great company, and we chatted back and forth about the day. He laughed hysterically when I told him about the yoga incident. He told some hilarious stories himself, including one about being caught with a girl in a broom closet on an air force base.

He laughed and said, "The best part is that it was the general's daughter."

I groaned and shook my head. "No! I am surprised you didn't get in big trouble."

He grinned and waved a hand. "I did, but it was worth it. I'm just glad that it was not the day before when I was in the same closet with the governor's son. He was stationed there and is probably still in the closet. Metaphorically speaking."

I choked on my coffee, I grinned and tried not to laugh. "Well, I certainly hope he isn't still in the broom closet. You should always clean up after yourself." We both laughed, and he helped me make dinner.

Albert got home, and soon we were all laughing over one of Albert's navy stories. I had heard it hundreds of times, but it was always funny. When there was a knock at the door, I went to answer it while Albert talked. I opened the door to the Shadow, Mikoto, who had a bag in his hands.

I smiled brightly at him and said, "Hey there, stretch! Come in. You're in time for dinner."

He looked at me funny, but I was in such a good mood that he didn't get to me.

I just made a face at him. "What, did I grow a second head?

Get in here. It is cold, and you're letting the heat out." I reached out and yanked him in so I could shut the door.

He stumbled forward and stopped just inside. I shut and bolted the door behind him. He stood there staring into the dining room. He seemed tense as I looked at his back. Maybe because I was relaxed, it was easier to notice things like this. He seemed scared, like a cat trying to decide if it was going to run. I considered that maybe I had been reading him wrong. His way of watching, his strange speech—maybe they were actually aspects of social awkwardness. It wouldn't be uncommon for military person to have social anxiety. It could be a symptom of his PTSD.

I am going to tell you what I told myself. This is my answer, no matter what anyone says. I did it because he was a protector of my family, because he was a friend. And I wanted to let him know it was safe. I reached up and gently laid my hand on his shoulder. He twitched like I had given him a static shock. I kept my hand there and gave him a small smile as I motioned into the room.

"Come in," I said. "You are welcome here." I had learned something a long time ago. If someone was acting shy or withdrawn, I would say things in a really formal way, with very specific instructions. It would sometimes make the person feel better. It was different enough to break through the social wall. It would also provide a very clear set of tasks to follow giving them something to focus on.

I ushered him to the table and fixed him a plate. Everyone greeted him warmly, and he said polite greetings in return, though they were a little mumbled. Sunshine told him how lucky he was to get there just in time for a great story.

When the children had all fallen asleep, we all sat around the table and went over the numbers and discussed what was needed— for the whole camp and for the escape. Finally, we discussed the missing items. In the end I told them about the creepy church group lady. We decided that having her help was good. It was very late when we finally went to sleep. Everyone stayed over. Sunshine slept on the couch after winning the coin flip with Mikoto. It was almost midnight when I closed my eyes.

I am not sure what woke me at about 3:00 a.m., but I was completely alert when my eyes snapped open. I tried to identify what was wrong. All seemed quiet. I figured I might as well pee. I slipped out of bed with a shiver and put on my slippers. I made sure not to wake anyone as I tiptoed into the bathroom. Once I was done, I washed my hands in cold water and went to check the fire. It was still banked, and I put another log in. I was still on high alert, so I got a drink of water. The restlessness wouldn't fade. I paced back and forth in the kitchen. When the tension didn't ease, I decided to head outside.

I could see the figures sleeping in the front room. Lucky looked up from his place by the fire. He yawned and followed me as I slipped on the big thick coat. The Shadow still hadn't asked for it back. I pulled out my pack of smokes and counted them. I already knew exactly how many I had left and how many packs remained in the hidden spot in the basement. I also knew how many were in the bags I had hidden. I counted them anyway.

I pulled one out as I stepped onto the porch. I shivered when a gentle breeze blew up my leg, just as I lit the smoke. That first drag was always the best. I took it long and slow. I pulled it in deep and held it for a moment with my eyes closed. In my head I heard a horn play. It was wonderfully slow and low. Then a piano played gently, and a bass kept time. I began to hum along softly as I let the smoke out. The little tinkling piano played along with the brass horn. In my mind I heard Louis Armstrong singing in his wonderful rough voice.

I smoked while softly singing "La Vie en Rose." Lucky didn't seem interested. He went to the bathroom in the yard and came back. I didn't sit. I just sang to myself in the dark, humming the refrain as I took the last few drags.

"You shouldn't be out here alone." Mikoto's voice came from

the doorway, and I jumped. Lucky gave his hand a lick and headed back inside through the open door.

"I wasn't alone. Lucky was with me," I said back quickly. I always felt like I needed to argue with him. I knew he wasn't doing anything wrong. It was me. My reactions came from my attraction to him. It made me feel like I was getting pulled toward him. My first instinct was to struggle against everything he said or did, even when I knew he was right. I was being childish. I shrugged and put out the smoke. "You're right, of course. I will go in."

I turned to head in, but he was right there, filling up all my space again. I sighed and leaned back a bit to look up at him. He looked down at me for a long moment. His gaze was intense, and he leaned closer.

"What are you doing?" I said in my iciest tone, even though my face flushed and I felt my heart rate pick up.

"Be still." His voice was low and soft as he leaned forward. His impossibly big hand darted out and snatched something from the left side of my jacket shoulder. "Got it." He pulled back his hand and tossed whatever it was toward the yard.

I couldn't tell what it was, but my embarrassment was very real. Again. "Thanks," I said, barely managing to squeak out the word.

He nodded, giving me a small smile. I felt really stupid and started to laugh. Here I was, acting like a teen with her first crush. I was too old for this nonsense. The look he gave me only made me laugh harder.

"Sorry," I said finally. "Look, I know I act really weird with you. I don't mean to. It's just been a while since I was actually attracted to anyone besides Albert, and I haven't handled it well. I realize it's a bizarre thing. Sorry if I made you feel awkward. I will try to stop." I looked out at the trees. It felt good to be honest about it and let it out. Now maybe I could let it go.

He was silent for so long that I eventually looked back to see if he was still there. I found him staring at me. "What?" I said, brushing hair out of my face.

"You are attracted to me." He said it like a statement, not a question. It was like he was telling me something he had just learned.

I tried hard not to be too self-conscious. "Well, yes, though that wasn't supposed to be the takeaway. Don't get a big head about it. I wasn't trying to come on to you. Albert and I are solid. It's no big deal. I just wanted to let you know why I was acting strange." I found myself doing that fidgeting thing where you suddenly need to rub your neck and forearms.

He didn't say anything, and I decided it was time to go inside. I didn't even see him move, but suddenly, he had ahold of my wrist. His grip was not tight, not painful, and just firm. His hand was huge. His fingers engulfed my not-at-all-dainty wrist. His hand was hot against my skin. I stopped instantly. My heart kicked hard against my ribs. I turned to look at him. He was still facing the tree line. His expression was unreadable in the shadows and moonlight. His voice was quiet but deep. "So am I."

For a moment I didn't understand what he had just said. It wasn't that I didn't understand the words, but my mind couldn't seem to process them. My brain had shut off when he touched me. I stood like a deer in headlights, trying to figure out what he meant. I am embarrassed to say I didn't catch on until he moved closer and looked me straight in the eye. I forgot to breathe.

"I am patient," he said, his face very close to mine. *Again with the peppermint.* "Good night," he said as he let go of my hand. He gently pushed me into the house.

I was about halfway to my bed when my brain rebooted. I was so flustered that I was worried my fever might be coming back. As if there weren't enough things going on. The last thing I needed was this romance novel bullshit. I shook my head and climbed into bed. I wished I were one of those calm, composed women who could have shrugged it off and put him in his place. I did not feel calm or composed at all. I pushed him out of my thoughts. I curled up tight next to my husband. Albert shifted a bit in his sleep. I kissed his shoulder and closed my eyes.

I was sound asleep in no time and didn't notice when the first snow of winter began to fall.

sunday, a little after 8am

IN THE MORNING the sun seemed content to sleep beneath its heavy gray blanket. The sky remained dim as little snowflakes dotted the air. They didn't fall. Instead, they drifted lazily from the invisible source above. The air was cold but not unbearable. Everyone put on their long underwear. All the kids got snow pants with gloves and boots. We weren't messing around this winter. We all bundled up and headed to the community center. The kids bounced excitedly through the snow. Lucky bounced along with them, his thick fur coat keeping him warm. It was fun to walk in the quiet hush. I loved watching the snow fall. The trees were almost bare of leaves now, so they didn't block out the sky. I looked through the gnarled skeleton fingers of branches, reaching upward into the glowing gray clouds above.

As we walked down the road toward the main buildings, the snowfall was turning the path from gray to white. It was like powdered sugar dusting the top of cookies. It made the whole lane seem magical. The black fingers of the trees twisting into the sky began to gather the white dust, a sharp white outline against their dark bark. Ahead there was a tree that looked like it hadn't lost its foliage girth. It took me a moment to realize it was full of crows, as was the next tree and the next. There must have been easily over a hundred crows sitting silently as the trees were covered in snow. The heat from their bodies prevented them from receiving their own white coat. Icy fingers crawled up my body. It unsettled me to see them just perched, watching us walk by. I didn't dally. I kept up with everyone, but I kept my eye on those black birds.

Mikoto and Sunshine were walking with us, so I knew we were safe. I hadn't liked it the last time I saw this. I liked it less now. The sight still had horror-movie vibes. How many crows did it take to go from a murder to a massacre? I tried to push away the dark feeling that clung to me. I looked first at Sunshine and then at Mikoto. Our eyes met. I tried to act casual. It didn't feel casual. He looked at the crows, and one side of his mouth turned upward just a tiny bit.

"They are sheltering," he said and nodded to the sky. "A big storm is coming."

Sunshine looked at him and then at the trees. "Wow that is a lot of fucking crows." He grinned mischievously. "You are looking a little bit nervous, Mouse. Let me guess—you're a Hitchcock fan."

I made a face at him, and he laughed.

Albert laughed and said, "It's creepy. It doesn't matter if you like Hitchcock or not."

I shrugged defensively; I knew they were teasing me. "Yeah, well, you would make us turn around if they were doves."

Albert shivered and cringed visibly. "Doves are evil, and they hate me," he said, and we all laughed. He smiled and poked me. "I don't know why you are worried. Crows have always liked you. Remember that one that kept leaving you gifts?"

I laughed at the memory and nodded. "Yeah. I saved those beads. They are in the bag with the baby stuff."

He grinned at me and put an arm around my shoulder. I felt better. "Well then, don't worry," he said. "Obviously, they are here to just keep an eye on you."

Sunshine leaned forward eagerly. "Evil doves? Crow's beads? What is all this?"

I grinned and told them the story. "I fed this crow that lived near my house. One day it landed so close I could feel the air off its wings. It squawked a few times and then flew away. It left behind this little set of shiny black Buddhist prayer beads."

Sunshine and Mikoto looked dubious.

I smiled. "I still have the beads and witnesses."

Albert smiled and nodded his assurances. "I was there for this particular delivery. It was quite a sight. This crow brought her many shiny little things. It was odd, but Mouse here has always been a weirdness magnet."

That seemed to make Sunshine's day. He laughed hard and had to wipe his eyes. "Weirdness magnet ... yep, I can totally see that!"

Zyada laughed and made a face at him, and they played a little game of chase down the road. I was finally able to leave the worry behind.

The noise at the main hall told us the meeting had already started. As we approached the auditorium, Mouthy spotted us and began heading our way. I knew my pleasant day was about to be ruined by the look on his face. Suddenly, there were shouts from the auditorium. People sounded really upset.

Sunshine turned and said to Zyada, "Hey, let's go to the infirmary. There are people who need a story told." Zyada cheered and took one of his hands. Victor claimed the other, and they headed off. "Come on, Nathan," Sunshine called over his shoulder. "You have never helped there either. Come along."

I nodded to Nathan, and he took off with them. I looked at Mouthy, who waited till the kids were gone.

"OK. What has happened?" I said seriously as we listened to the rise and fall of voices from behind the doors.

Mouthy made a disgruntled noise. "There was a stupid fucking problem last night. Just more dumb ass soap opera bullshit. To recap, one of the enlisted men was spending time with one of the civilian ladies. Her husband took exception to the interpersonal activities and tried to express his disapproval with a kinetic altercation. But seeing how the not husband is a heavy weapons specialist, and he was trained by the US government at expressing how many fucks he didn't give... So now the husband is in the infirmary, the wife is being scarlet-lettered by the Bible thumpers, and the civies have their skivvies in a twist since the specialist isn't in jail. It doesn't appear to matter that we don't actually have a jail, or judges. Fuck-heads."

I rubbed my forehead. "I don't get it. Why did he mess around with a married lady?"

Mouthy gave me a look I didn't understand. "People are stupid? And to be clear she was just as eager to be messing around with him. Just between you and me, the crows say she ain't that interested in being married no more. But seeing how we don't exactly have a divorce court; we can't do much about that either. I'd tell you the specialist sorted it out just fine, but I've been told not to promote that kind of behavior."

Grandpa Silas and Jeri had approached as Mouthy spoke, forming a small semicircle.

Albert frowned. "This seems a bit much for that."

"Yeah, seems we have a few folks feeding the fire," said Jeri. "People are quite upset about it." He crossed his arms. "We have rats in the walls."

I frowned as I tried to clarify what he meant. "Rats in the walls?"

He nodded and motioned to the auditorium. "They can't be seen but are constantly gnawing at the house, destroying it from the inside."

Albert almost growled. "Instigators. They showed up during the peaceful protests, trying to make the groups violent. Sometimes all you need to do is whisper discontent in the right ears, and suddenly you have everyone pissed. It only takes one person to cross the line, or throw the rock start a full-blown riot."

I sighed and looked at the men around me and then at the building. "This is their move. This may have been part of the plan all along." I said as I blew warmth into my hands. "I guess we will just have to counter it."

Mouthy looked at me like I was crazy. "Pardon? Why would we want to get mixed up in this dumb-assery?"

I smiled. "Well, if we don't do anything, everyone is going to be resentful at anyone in a uniform. Then it won't take much to tear this place apart."

Mouthy nodded in agreement. Albert smiled softly at me. "That's my mouse, always thinking. You got an idea?"

"Yep, time to do as the Romans do and give out bread at the Colosseum." I gave a big cheeky smile. It faded quickly as all the men just stared at me blankly, even Albert was looking confused. I shook my head. This is what happens when no one pays attention in history class.

I tried not to sound disappointed while I explained. "Why not pass out the supplies? We already figured out each person's portion for distribution. A large part of the resentment comes from feeling like the military controls everything. By making them in charge of their own supplies it lets them feel independent. It will free up people to work elsewhere. It will also make it harder for anyone to steal supplies." I smiled, feeling very pleased with myself. "Besides, the creepy church-lady was looking for a way to look all Mother Teresa for her flock. Let's give her a way to do that."

Mouthy cringed. "I don't think the LT is going to like it."

I shrugged and waved a hand toward the auditorium. "You think he will like this better?"

We hurried inside to find the LT. It was easy to see the tension in the room. People were standing and arguing back and forth. Well, arguing was a generous description. Mostly, they were just loudly insulting each other. Mouthy and Mikoto went over to

Lieutenant Brick to try to convince him of my little plan. I watched the lieutenant as Mouthy talked and Mikoto stood quietly nodding his agreement. As the idea was explained in detail, Lieutenant Brick's body seemed to become squarer. His shoulders seemed to hunch and tighten. His jaw clenched, and he looked down as he thought. I found myself watching the muscle in his jawline as it began ticking, slowly at first and then faster and faster.

I had a flashback to my childhood, standing in front of my father, next to my brother. We were in trouble for something. I remembered watching that muscle in his jaw twitch. I had used that twitch to try and figure out how mad Daddy was. Years later, my father told me that clenching his jaw was how he kept himself from grinning. He couldn't believe how cute we looked standing there with big sad eyes. I shook off the memory and stepped up to the Lieutenant.

"Lieutenant Roberts, I hate to break it to you, but you have to give these people something. Look at them. They are losing hope. They woke up to the same thing I did: snow and no ride out of here. There are more of them than us. You have to give them some feeling of control, or they are going to break." I moved closer to whisper to Brick. Everyone was taller than me, so Lieutenant Brick was looking down at me. I stared at him hard trying to make sure he understood. "This way everyone is responsible for their own roller skates. Not to mention, if the storm gets bad and it's a few days till we can shovel them out, people will have what they need."

He snorted and shook his head. "You know this won't pacify them for long," he said, his voice low.

I nodded. "It will buy us time. Then we can find out who is working everyone up and put a stop to it."

He huffed, obviously not liking it. "Fine. I will handle it." He walked away—well, not so much walked as angrily marched—and stepped up onto the stage. He really did have a presence about him. When his boot hit the wood of the stage the whole auditorium went silent. With just his walk and a sharp turn toward the crowd, he quelled the noise. It was impressive.

The lieutenant looked out at the crowd. "Let me make this clear, in no uncertain terms: I don't want to hear about anyone's personal business. Fighting won't be tolerated. Mrs. Sales and Mrs. Kerns, please come up. " His voice filled the cavernous silence of the auditorium.

I started toward the stage, as did creepy Church-lady.

"We have made a full inventory of all the supplies," Brick continued speaking while we approached, "and we will be distributing them later today. They will be divided as equally and fairly as possible. Please be responsible with rationing your supplies."

I winced. Today was going to suck.

He continued. "We want to make sure the supplies are all secured before the storm hits, since people might be shut in for a few days. Now if you are not one hundred percent sure that where you are staying will be secure and warm enough during the coming weather, we recommend you bunk up at the dorms. We will be using the generator for that building's heat as well as for the infirmary. We need volunteers to help Mrs. Sales, and Mrs. Kerns with distribution today. Please sign up with them as soon as possible. I want this done before the end of the day. Thank you."

Like a magician, he had made the anger disappear. He turned and left the stage and stopped next to me. "This is only for the supplies designated for civilians. Military-issue is for the enlisted. Understood?" he said quietly.

"Affirmative, Lieutenant. I will not distribute government property," I said with a salute.

Mrs. Kerns had not wasted a moment, as she took over and began organizing people and setting up her volunteer roster. People were already getting in line.

Lt. Brick gave a long-suffering sigh as he walked past Albert, he said something to quiet for me to hear. Albert laughed and responded with "You know it,"

I figured they were talking about me because Albert looked over and blew me a kiss. I smiled and gave him a wink. I was grinning happily when I turned, and my eyes met Mikoto's. The Shadow was watching me with a little smirk. I blushed and cleared my throat as I turned toward the office. There was some serious work to be done.

We worked at a breakneck speed. I found myself running full steam back and forth with everyone else, getting each group ready. The creepy Church-lady Mrs. Kerns, was actually really good at this. She also had a small army of volunteers to put to work. They had run a food pantry and charity at her church, so she was used to putting these things together. It was like watching a hive of ants work. I was sorting in the back when Sunshine returned with a sleeping Victor. We put him in my temporary office for his nap. He left again to go play board games with Nathan and Zyada at the infirmary. We somehow achieved a small miracle and were done by early afternoon. When the last rations were finally passed out, a cheer went up among the volunteers. Mouthy gave me a high five and fell over into a chair.

I went to go have a smoke. I stepped out behind the buildings, away from the main exits, because I didn't want people to know I had cigarettes. The wind had picked up, and the temperature had dropped a few degrees further. I found some shelter from the wind in an alcove. I shivered and pulled the heavy coat closer around me as I lit my smoke.

I was fascinated by the look of the snow falling around me. The wind was swirling flakes off the tops of the buildings, turning them into pixie dust. Those sparkles were swirling around the big fat flakes that were falling in wet puffs. I felt like I was inside a snow globe. The ground was crunching under my feet. Large white mounds were forming into drifts. It was strange to me how many different types of snow there were. I watched it fall down the hill into the ravine and saw the tree's branches become a dark underline covered in a white blanket.

I loved how snow didn't change just the temperature. It changed everything, the way the world looked, felt, even sounded. I took my time, watching my exhale come out as dragon's breath. A huge cloud of my smoke drifted and danced among the snowflakes.

The wind changed direction and brought an odd sound. It was a strange whirring noise. Since all the machines had died, the world was a quieter place. It was easier to hear now. The sound echoed against the rocky hillsides and was hard to place. I couldn't pinpoint the noise. I could hear the generator, and this was a separate sound. It took me a full ten seconds at least to realize that what I was hearing was a motor. *Engines.* I blinked and started trying to find the source.

Even in the muffle of the snow, I could hear it and it seemed to be getting louder. I moved out of my alcove to where the bridge connected one side of the campus to the other over the deep ravine. The stream that ran down below had started to freeze over, but a little water still flowed out into the open valley. Without the foliage on the trees, I could see out and down for miles. The view was clear from the bridge all the way out to the black scar mark where the fires had burned themselves out. Now, even that was being covered in white. From this vantage, I saw figures coming full speed toward the campus. They were on ATVs and four-wheelers. The sounds of their engines echoed off the hills. There were people on foot running along ahead and behind them. I stood frozen for a moment. They looked like a cross between rejects from a 1980s apocalypse movie and a bunch of cosplaying paintballers. But the weapons they were carrying looked real enough. Some had long rifles; some had bats and other implements. My heart started to pound as adrenaline dumped into my system. We were under attack. *They didn't use the road, so the lookouts didn't see them. They are inside the perimeter. Someone needs to sound the alarm!*

I don't remember what I did with my cigarette. I don't

remember making the decision, but the next moment, I was running. My legs were pumping as fast as they would go. The cold air hurt to breathe and made my lung cramp on my right side. I could have run to a guard post or the supply area, but I ran straight to the radio station. I burst through the door and startled the hell out of the woman in the front area.

"Under attack … south end … up the ravine!" I shouted with what breath I had left. I gasped for air, holding my side where the cramp had formed.

The woman at the desk didn't respond, but the men at the war table burst into a flurry of motion. They grabbed arms, and suddenly, a siren started to blare.

Brick was there, and he snapped out orders as he grabbed a rifle and a helmet. "Get the civilians to the infirmary! It's the most secure location."

I remembered that Zyada and Nathan were already at the infirmary building with Sunshine. But Victor, he was napping in my supply office. "My baby." The words escaped as fear clutched at my heart. I turned and ran out of the building. I heard someone shout my name as I hit the cold air again. The supply area was to the south. I was headed straight toward the attack. I didn't think about that. It didn't matter. I needed to get to my little boy. I knew Sunshine would keep Zyada and Nathan safe; they were already at the fortified location. I didn't know where Albert was.

I wasn't even halfway there when I fell. I hit hard, and the cold snow in my face made me gasp. The ground had begun to freeze and become slippery. There was yelling and screaming now. I could hear popping as guns were fired in the distance. The sounds of engines were louder as I clawed my way back to my feet. I kept moving even as my thighs burned. My feet felt like they were coated in lead as I moved them.

It seemed like forever since I'd heard a motor. They sounded massive, like giant lawnmowers. I tried to get control of my breathing. I sucked air in through my nose, trying to slow my racing heartbeat. The cold air seemed to burn as it entered my nostrils. I let out a shout as I reached the gymnasium building's back door and ripped it open. Bits of the wall overhead burst as bullets smashed into the stone siding. I threw myself at the stairs, scrambling away from the heavy doors. I didn't have enough air in my lungs to scream. I scrambled to my feet, trying to get down the hall. There was pandemonium in the main building as the civilian volunteers panicked and scrambled to evacuate. I didn't even slow down as I ran past them. I was so focused on keeping my feet moving that I almost missed the turn in the hallway and bashed my shoulder against a locker.

I gasped for air as I fell against the door to the office, pushing it open. Lucky was standing guard, hackles raised. Victor was rubbing his eyes from his nap on the office sofa. Thankfully, his shoes were on. I sucked in air as I hugged him tightly at the sofa. I started getting Victor's coat on as quickly as I was able. My hands shook as I tried to zipper it closed. He was so dense that my tired body groaned as I lifted him. He clung tight to me. I wrapped his blanket over him to hide his face and opened the door. I peeked out and started out slowly.

I knew they were coming, but I couldn't be sure if they were in the building yet. Lucky followed us, keeping close to my legs. When I heard shouts and footfalls, I pulled them both into the nearest room. We waited till the people had passed before starting again. I didn't know where Mouthy or Mikoto was, but I didn't have time to worry about that. We headed toward the northern exit. We went out the side glass door by the gym, and I tried to run as fast as I could. My legs were on fire, which helped keep the cold off me. My arms ached, and I thought my shoulder was going to come undone. But I hung on to Victor as tight as I could. I went to the nearest alcove to hide. It was so hard to breathe in the cold air. Lucky was growling low in his throat as he stayed close to me.

Victor knew something was wrong and clung tightly to me. He didn't make a sound. The ATVs were driving in every direction. I could smell the burnt odor of exhaust. Some of the riders came under fire. Some zoomed around different buildings. There were so many people running that it was hard to tell who was who. I was about halfway to the infirmary. There were at least a few civilians still running that way. One of them screamed as he was attacked by a group of men from behind. It was completely open ground from where I was hiding to the infirmary. I looked for some cover because I just wasn't fast enough or strong enough to make it. I couldn't stay here either; it was only a matter of time till I was seen.

I looked around and saw a small path toward the ravine, which ran along the length of the campus. It was steep and sheer and covered in snow at the moment, but it could get me much closer to the infirmary. I started around the opposite side of the building, which looped me around the cafeteria. I went slower now, trying to remain unnoticed in all the commotion. People were running and screaming. Many of the raiders had run into the buildings and seemed to be ransacking the place.

I sneaked along the huge woodpile that had been placed next to the kitchen where we baked, and I heard shouts from inside. Vera was yelling at some men who were putting as much food as they could into sacks. She was cursing at them in what I think was Italian. The old bird apparently still had some fight left in her. Her gray hair was askew, and she was holding a cooking pot. One man made the mistake of putting a hand on her and received said pot right upside his face.

He cursed as he held his bloody nose. "What did you do that for?" He shoved her, and she fell backward against the counter. They didn't pay her any mind and roughly pushed her aside as they moved to the food pantry. She slumped down to the ground.

"Vera!" I said as loud as I dared.

She looked up and saw me.

"Come on," I whispered, waving frantically.

She hurried out to me, and I grabbed her hand. We ducked

behind the utility shed. I whispered the plan, and she nodded, still holding her pot. We crouched and walked behind the woodpile till it came out next to the smokehouse. Then it was a few yards before the edge of the bridge, where we could sneak down the ravine. My arms were giving out, and since we were moving slower, I set Victor down. Lucky stayed close, keeping low and quiet. Vera let go of my hand and took Victor's other hand. I smiled at her and then at Victor, trying to show them that it was OK.

"We are fine. They want supplies. They won't even look at us," I said, trying to sound confident.

My idea was to peek around the edge of the smokehouse and then head to the ravine. It was a good plan, I thought. However, I had forgotten an important detail. I hadn't really included in my thought process what exactly a smokehouse was. A smokehouse was a small shed containing a handmade smoker. When put to use, the room slowly filled with smoke, and the heat from the smoke dried out and preserved the meat. This was important because preserved meats are in fact, supplies. The raiders weren't giving people that much attention, but the smokehouse—well, that was a big shiny target. I peeked around the corner and didn't see anyone, but as I stepped around, suddenly there he was.

He wasn't huge or anything, but he seemed to tower over me in my crouched position. He was filthy. His hair might have been brown, but it looked greasy and black. He was wearing goggles. His face was covered in a scraggly beard. A link of handmade s was half-hanging from his mouth. His clothes looked like something between redneck hunter and athletic store looter. There was a split second after we both had turned that he didn't see me. Fear dumped another round of adrenaline into me.

I hit the fight button on the fight-or-flight response. I pushed Victor back into Vera. I put one foot back as I shifted and twisted into a full-body fist punch into his midsection. I let my kiai out loudly as muscle memory from teenage martial arts training came back in a flood. I stepped forward, pressing my attack. I stomped my foot into the inside of his ankle and tried to punch him in the throat. He dropped what he was holding and brought up his hands to block. There was a coppery taste in my mouth as I brought my knee up into his groin. I shoulder-shoved him as hard as I could into the open door of the smokehouse. I slammed the door shut and dropped the bar that locked it. I heard his shouts of pain as he was singed on the coals and fought to get back up.

Suddenly, Lucky barked, and I barely got out of the way in time as a baseball bat swung past my head. It smashed against the wood of the shed, and splinters flew. I lurched back and stared at the scary man who was coming around the other side of the smokehouse. He was much larger than the one I had locked in the smoker. I could see his face, and there was something in his eyes that terrified me. He looked hungry, but he was looking at me. His eyes were blue and bloodshot. He dropped the piece of meat he had been eating and grinned as he started slowly moving toward me. Fear clawed up my spine. Everything inside me screamed to run. I glanced around and saw Vera holding Victor, who clung to his blanket, too scared to cry. Vera wasn't going to be able to carry him. I couldn't run.

I reached into my pocket. I pulled out the knife Albert had put there, and flipped it open. My heart was pounding; all I could hear was the drumming of it. Suddenly, the voice of my martial arts instructor filled my head. "You are short—that's a gift. Get close, get inside their power. Then they are yours." I had never been so glad for those years of after school, strip mall martial arts classes. I held the knife low and shifted my feet to get traction. He was moving closer, his bat held in one hand, the other arm extended like he was going to grab me. I counted my breaths, waiting for him to take another step. Lucky barked and growled, running up to snap at his arm with the bat. I thought about Victor and Vera. *He wants to hurt us.* I thought about Nathan and Zyada. *He wants to stop me from getting back to them. No. He won't stop me. Not today.* That thought kept playing in my head. *Not today... not today.* He growled and swung the bat at Lucky. As he did, I sprinted in as close as I could.

"NOT TODAY!" I screamed, thrusting my knife toward him. I had never tried to hurt someone before. I had been in fights, even some where I was really angry. But I had never intentionally tried to hurt anyone. I knew I was going to stab him. I knew that could kill him. It was madness.

I was inside his swing range, almost embracing him. I stabbed him—and stabbed him and stabbed him, as many times as I could. He screamed out and swung the bat at me. Pain exploded on the side of my body. I hissed out air as I let go of the knife. It was still in him. I brought my hand up to slam my palm into his nose. I felt it crunch under my palm. He grabbed me by the hair, yanking my head back as he grabbed at my coat with the other hand.

I jerked violently as my foot went out from under me, my boot losing grip on a patch of ice. I grabbed him as I went downward, pulling him along with me. His huge hands couldn't get a grip on me. Mikoto's coat was too large for me. It acted like a loose covering, so he couldn't get a grip on my body. I brought my knee up as hard as I could as he climbed onto me. He yelled in pain and fury. I felt the impact of his fist on my face, once and then again. The rush and haze of battle kept the pain at bay, but my vision was becoming blurry. One eye saw only red. I knew I was screaming now, but only because I felt the scream in my throat. I punched, kicked, and clawed like a wild animal. I finally got a hand up to his face and shoved my thumb into his blue eye. He howled as he finally grabbed me by the throat.

His hand was huge. It gripped so tight that I thought he was going to crush my throat. I reflexively clenched my throat muscles as he bared down on me. I didn't bother trying to breathe. There was no way that was going to happen. I tried to arch my spine, but his weight was too much. I clawed at his thumb, but it was useless. The knife. I needed the knife.

My brain gasped for air as panic took over. I flailed as I tried to search along his body. I punched at the bloody spot at his side. He growled something I couldn't understand. I was going dark as my fingers searched in earnest for the handle of the knife. With my good eye I spied Vera shouting and holding a crying Victor. Suddenly, Lucky lunged out and bit the man on the shoulder, forcing him to let go of my throat.

Air, sweet air. It burned like delicious fire. It hurt, but I sucked it in and coughed, convulsing, as the man tried to shake off Lucky. I pushed away from him, digging my feet into the mud beneath me. I twisted my body, scrambling away from him on my side. I saw the glint of a metal handle. *The knife.* It had fallen into the snow next to us. It felt like I was moving through invisible mud as I reached for it. I heard the sharp yelping sound from Lucky. I screamed as a desperate rage filled me. I finally got a grip on the bloody handle.

I could hear his grunting and panting behind me as he grabbed me by the back of my head. He was on top of me, growling like a beast. I roared back, just as animalistic. I turned the blade and tried to stab him again. I was in the middle of the maneuver when suddenly the weight of him disappeared. I lurched forward, pulled by my own struggle. I twisted around as I put distance between us.

He was lifted off the ground. He floated above me in the most bizarre manner, with his arms all akimbo and his head tilted at an unnatural angle, before he jerked like a weird ugly string puppet. Then he seemed to collapse into a pile a few feet away. My vision blurred as I sucked in cold, harsh air. Everything was in slow motion, and the colors were stark against the snow. The dark red stain of blood was so vivid, it was unreal. It seemed to take a lifetime to blink and raise my eyes to look up from the red that steamed and melted the snow into a grotesque puddle.

I looked up and saw *him*. Mikoto, the Shadow, was suddenly right over me. Seeing him sent a wave of relief over me. He was dressed in his full battle gear, his long sniper rifle hanging over his shoulder. He was very close to my face. He was touching me. I tried to push him away and tell him to stop. My body felt impossibly heavy. Moving my arms took such great effort, and my mind was floating. He ignored anything I might have said. The knife slipped from my fingers as I fell backward. I knew my legs weren't supporting me, but somehow, I wasn't lying down. I had no thoughts, just relief.

I couldn't run anymore. The last of the adrenaline had faded, and now there was only agony. I felt Victor hug me, and I tried to wrap my arms around him. I felt him against my chest and tucked my chin against his head, holding him close. Mikoto was there next to me. He was talking, but I couldn't hear him. The world dimmed. I heard my name, but all I could do was hug Victor as the world went dark.

twenty-three
sometime after the
attack

I WOULDN'T SAY I dreamed. A jumble of images flashed around like falling photographs, some in focus, some out. Lights, voices, and other sounds all mixed together like a bizarre collage of noise and color. I didn't even try to follow them. I was floating but not in air. It was more like I was drifting underwater in a dark pool. I looked up at the surface, trying to make out the world above. Sometimes I would begin to float up to the surface, but it hurt, and I would let myself sink again. I wanted to hide in the warm dark water. But when you're underwater, eventually your lungs burn and tell you that you need to surface. For me it was the quiet; I couldn't hear their voices. I didn't hear Victor's laugh or Zyada talking.

Any mother will tell you that nothing wakes you up faster than not hearing the sound of your children. Once I realized that I didn't know where my babies were, fear gripped me. I burst through the surface of the water, gasping out as agony slammed into my face and throat.

It hurt. God, did it hurt. I tried to open my eyes, and even that was painful. The left one refused to open at all. The room was dark except for a little stream of light coming through a covered window. I took a breath and grimaced at the pain in my throat.

The grimace caused me to gasp when I felt the pain of moving my face. It was a horrible little cycle of agony.

"Shit," I croaked out. It felt like the pain after Victor's birth but all in my face and throat. Had it hurt this much to get beaten up when I was a kid? I couldn't remember. Of course, the last time I'd gotten into a fight, I was seventeen, and it hadn't been a fight to the death.

"Be still." Mikoto's voice was low and deep. I was too tired to be surprised.

"Where's Al?" I whispered back. I tried to turn my face toward his voice. I barely made him out in the dark room. He moved so I could see him.

"With the kids," he whispered, and I sighed in relief. He brought over a cup and pitcher. One of those stupid bendy straws was in the cup. I felt like I was made of lead. I swear I could hear the sound of rusted hinges as I pushed myself up.

"Be still." His voice was still quiet but intense as he reached over and lifted me slightly. Oh man, that did not feel good. I was one big bruise. If you've ever had a cramp in your calf, you know that even hours later, the muscle feels sore. It was like my whole body had been one massive cramp and then had been hit by a truck, twice.

"Sorry," he said as he positioned me more upright and put a pillow behind me. He held out a little pill and the cup.

Then I realized why it hurt so badly: we were low on meds. I had an almost empty saline drip, but all the pain pills were oral. I took the pill gratefully and sipped the water. The water felt amazing, like I had been in the desert for years. It also felt like I had poured lemonade over a rug burn.

I took a moment to move my jaw, wiggle my toes, and flex my fingers. Though slow and stiff, everything moved. Nothing seemed to be broken. "Well, at least they don't need to wire my trap shut," I whispered as I raised my hand toward my face.

Mikoto reached up and grabbed my hand. He shook his head.

"Don't." His voice was different, and he kept ahold of my hand as he looked at me.

"Wow, it must be pretty bad," I said, trying to joke. "Did a number on me, huh?"

He made some noise in his throat, a sort of grunt, and reached up and gently touched some different spots on my face. I managed not to flinch, though that might have been exhaustion.

I tried to smile, but it turned into a pained smirk since only one side of my face could move and the other felt like I had stabbed it. It was probably better that the kids not see me until some of the swelling went down. I didn't want to scare them. I must have looked awful.

We sat silently as I sipped the water. His eyes seemed to watch all of me at once. It was a very disconcerting feeling, but how could I be angry? He had saved me. He had saved Victor. He had stopped that man. He had killed him, most likely. I wasn't sure how I was supposed to feel about that. I knew I felt grateful and relieved that the man was gone. Maybe it was wrong to be relieved that someone else was dead. I couldn't seem to bring up any other emotion regarding it. Should I have been afraid? He had lifted that full-grown man up like nothing, snapped his neck like a chicken, and tossed him aside. But as he sat there next to me, I felt nothing but a deep understanding that I was safe. I was grateful for it.

That's about when my curiosity kicked in, and till the day I die, I will claim it was the meds that prompted this rush of honesty. My voice sounded terrible and croaky. It was hard to get the words out.

"Normally, I would just ignore this ... but it's been a rough day ... and I am just not up to it. I think you like me, but ... I love my husband. You're ..."

I had to pause there because looking at him in that moment, I couldn't find the right word. My brain still felt sluggish, and things just didn't fit the way they were supposed to. He was handsome, but not in a pretty way. He was strong and powerfully built. His features were sharp and angled, but that wasn't the only thing that made him attractive. There was something else there, something beneath the surface, something that pulled me in. It called to me like some animal in the wild; it was deep, intense, and smoldering.

"Amazing." That was all that I could come up with. I had to look down at his hands after that. "What you did for me ... you saved me. Thank you. I am grateful. I can't repay you for that. But I love my husband. He is the father of my children. Please understand ..." Tears burned my eyes and blurred my vision. I watched his hand as it came all the way up to curve around the side of my face that wasn't as bruised. I looked up into his face. *God, I am such a cry baby.*

In his face there was an agony that I couldn't understand. In that moment I would have done anything to take it away. He moved closer and knelt next to the bed. I didn't know what to say. Tears slid out of my eyes and stung the scrapes on my face. He moved and laid his head on the curve of my lap with his face turned away from me, so that his hair spilled over my middle. I felt something in my chest twist with agony. This wasn't my fault! I hadn't done anything to provoke this. It wasn't fair. The air was thick and hard to breathe. His breathing was shallow, and the way he gripped the blanket spoke more than his words would have. I knew this tension. I had known men like this my whole life. It had been called PTSD, battle fatigue even shell shock. Whatever they'd called it, I was sure the knights from the dark ages had had it too.

The wounds no one can see always last the longest. He had killed that man today. He had killed men before. All the justifications aside, it was completely unreasonable to expect anyone to take a life and not feel agony over it. No amount of training stopped that. It left a mark on your soul, like a tattoo.

Tonight, his wounds were raw and bleeding. He was as beaten up as me. His agony hurt my heart, and I reached out and rested my hand on his head. He flinched, but I kept my hand there. He tensed and gripped the bed like he might be flung off the planet.

Slowly and softly, I started sliding my fingers along his hair. I let my fingers dig into his coal-black strands and hummed, just the simple tunes I sang for my babies.

"You are taken. I know this," he said finally, after a long while. "But my eyes always find you."

I paused for a moment, then continued stroking his head silently. "That's not fair. I can't help that," I whispered into the dark room, watching my fingers slide and dance of their own accord in that thick dark hair. It felt like we were in a shadowy bubble, in another world. "Don't expect me to compromise myself and give up all I love." I pulled his hair back from the bottom of his neck. I let my fingers rub gently along his scalp, continuing the massage down his nape.

His hands slowly loosened from tight-knuckled fists, and his breathing started to ease. I twisted locks of his hair around a finger and then let it slip away.

"You would not," he said in a surprisingly calm voice.

His hair was cool on the tips. But it was slowly warming as I stroked it. It felt good against my palm. "My family likes you, cares about you—you and Sunshine. Don't twist yourself into knots like this."

I felt the medicine taking hold, making me drowsy. I stopped making any noise then and just kept petting his head. I don't know how long we stayed like that. I was suddenly brought back to fully awake because he moved. He took my hand and pressed his mouth to my palm. His lips were warm velvet, and my fingers curled as the pleasure shot up my arm.

"I am patient," he said. "Don't worry, you are safe."

He slipped away as gracefully as smoke on the breeze. He paused briefly at the door. He looked back to me for a long moment, his face unreadable and intense. It stretched the moment, painfully, my heartbeat thunderous in the powerful silence of him. Then he was gone, like darkness disappearing before the light. The only proof he had been there at all was the scent of peppermint.

I drifted in the strange haze of that scent until the medic arrived to check on me.

When I was able to make it to the bathroom the next day, I stared at the face of a stranger. I could finally open both eyes. However, I wished I hadn't. The left one looked like a bloody marble with a brown pupil. The right looked streaked with red lines. The left side of my face was swollen, hot, and tight. I looked like I was wearing raccoon makeup. My swollen eyelids were surrounded in black and deep purple shadows. My lip was puffed and split on one side. Around my throat was a necklace of deep bruises. The rest of me had scrapes and bruises from fighting. Even through my heavy clothes, the contusions were neatly shaped. The man had left me feeling like I'd been run over by a car. It hurt to do anything.

I slowly washed myself and pulled on clothes. When I stepped out of the bathroom, Zyada squealed and jumped off my bed. I didn't make it more than a few steps before I was being squeezed. I slowly sank down and hugged Zyada, doing my best to not show how much it hurt. Nathan ran over and wrapped his arms around me from the other side.

I looked up, and there was Victor standing next to Albert. He was holding his blanket and gripping Daddy's leg. He looked at me shyly. He looked like he might cry. A completely different pain filled my heart. *What if he is scared of me now? What if this has stolen his joy? What if he stops running to hug me when he sees me?* I forced the panic down and pushed a smile onto my face, ignoring the pain. I held out my arms.

"Oh, are you hiding? You're OK. Who is a brave boy?" I said in the silly upbeat voice I used when he fell or scared himself. "See, Mommy's OK. I just need kisses to make it better. Ready, set ... charge!"

Even though he had tears in his eyes, he ran over and practically plowed me over. He kept whispering, "You OK, you OK." He rained tiny kisses all over my face. I was so relieved that they barely hurt. Something deep inside of my chest unknotted. I held him close and pulled my children into a huddled hug. My husband petted my hair as Nathan sat down and leaned against my back. I closed my eyes and for a few minutes completely forgot about everything else but the warmth and love.

Finally, I let out a sigh and looked up at Albert. "Help, I am stuck." I gave him a grin.

He laughed and picked up the kids one at a time and put them on the bed. Then he helped me to my feet. I was in agony, but I couldn't stop smiling. Everything hurt so much, but it was worth it to hold them close. I was good enough to walk, so I was checking out and opening up a much-needed bed.

The attack hadn't left many dead, which was the good news. The bad news was that many people had been injured. Looting seemed to have been the main purpose of the raid. The FEMA cots were set out where people were resting in the bigger rooms. I wasn't sure why I had been given a private room, maybe because I had lost consciousness. I went to the nurses' station to let them know I was leaving and the bed was free.

"Hey, maybe you should stay another day, huh?" said Barbara, one of the volunteer nurses, as she looked at me with concern.

"It looks worse than it really is, Barbara. All I am doing here is lying down. I can do that back home too," I assured her. "Besides, you guys are busy with real injuries." I nodded toward Albert. "I promise I will take it easy, and Albert will look after me."

She nodded slowly. "OK ... But keep an eye out for heavy swelling, excessive pain, or fever."

Albert held up his hand. "We will be vigilant," he said, giving her a quick salute.

I rolled my eyes. "You're such a dork." I grinned on the good side of my face.

We headed out of the infirmary and down the walking path toward our house. It took us past the cafeteria and the supply depot. There was some visible fire damage, and I noticed dark brown stains on the concrete and heavy tread tracks in the snow. Military and civilian personnel were boarding up windows and doors. There were people chopping down trees and dragging logs in the snow.

"What are they doing?" I asked Albert.

"After the attack there was an emergency meeting. It was decided that we needed to be fortified since people obviously know we are here. They are trying to build better fences, perimeter lines. There are all kinds of arguments going on right now." He shook his head. "Either way, I don't like how it looks. I don't think this was the attack we were warned about."

I sighed and shivered, thinking about the men at the smokehouse. My eyes darted towards it unconsciously. "I don't think it was either. These guys were just looking for supplies. They had this desperate, hungry look to them. They were very dirty and thin." I shrugged. "The glass man and his people were surprisingly clean and didn't look like they were going hungry."

Albert turned and gave me a funny look as we began to cross the bridge. "Glass man? Is that what he calls himself?"

I laughed and shook my head. "No. It's what I call him. They call him Father Jacob or something."

"Why the glass man?"

I shrugged a little as I thought about how to explain. "Because he reminds me of a glass paperweight, smooth, clear, and clean. They distort whatever you look at through them. They hold things down and keep them in place but aren't really good for anything else."

Albert looked at me for a moment and laughed before putting a kiss on top of my head. "You do that so well it's almost scary."

I wasn't sure what he meant, so I gave him a curious look. "Do what?"

He sighed as if I should have caught on. "You do this with everyone—Lieutenant Brick, Sunshine, the Shadow, Mouthy, Old Man Harris, Grandpa, the glass man. You give them names, but it is like a magic spell. You find some deep truth about them. Even the kids when you named them. Victor: he who wins. Zyada: a shining star. You were right about them too."

I laughed. "You're being silly. But some people say names have power. After all, Albert means the old and wise."

He grinned at me mischievously. "Oh, I am an old man, huh?"

I laughed, and he started poking me.

"Ow, ow, *ow*! Hey, no picking on the injured," I gasped out, holding my side.

He smiled and turned to make a groaning monster noise at the kids. They squealed and fled in all directions as he followed after them.

Nathan quietly stopped beside me and whispered, "I am glad you're OK, Mom." He said it in his slow, awkward way. I ruffled his hair with a smile, and a little grin appeared on his face. "I love you, Mom ... I was scared."

I smiled at him but felt a twist in my chest. "I love you too, Nathan. I am sorry I scared you. I am OK. Do you want a hug?"

He stepped toward me timidly, resting his hands on my waist as I hugged him, like he was afraid he would hurt me. It took a moment before he finally hugged me back.

"See, there we go. That's better, huh?" I kissed the top of his head as he pulled back and stuffed his hands into his pockets. He didn't say anything else as he walked away, following behind his dad. I followed along and watched as they all moved ahead of me.

Suddenly, I felt a presence behind me. I flinched as fear jumped up my spine, and agony blazed through my muscles at the quick movement. I sucked in air as Sunshine appeared next to me. He smiled at me like he knew a secret and draped an arm around my shoulders. He did not seem to care that I was in pain. I glared at him.

"Hey, good-looking," he said in a silly voice.

"Oh yeah, I am sexy pounded beef over here," I grumbled, but I didn't shake him off. I tried to keep my voice from giving away how startled I was or how much that had hurt.

"No, seriously, compared to how you looked when they brought you in, this is way better." Sunshine spoke in a low tone. "I was ... upset to see you that way."

I frowned as I looked at him. "Was it really that bad? Did the kids see?"

He shook his head. Though his smile was still silly, his voice had a hard edge. "No, the kids didn't see—except Victor, of course. In fact, Albert didn't see until after you were treated. Just me and Keyan."

"Keyan?" My brain was still a little slow. It took me a moment to remember that was the Shadow's first name. "Oh, you mean Mikoto?"

Sunshine's face hardened as he looked at my neck. He let out a laugh that didn't sound funny at all. It was bitter. The grin on his face was strangely feral. "Those bruises on your neck make me want to punch Keyan."

I frowned, confused and disconcerted by his reaction. "Why?" I said quietly, not sure that I wanted to know.

"He killed that bastard way too fast. We should have broken every bone in his body and left him in the ravine. If anyone had hurt my sister this way, they would have suffered for days before they died." The way he said it, with absolute calm, made me question Sunshine's mental stability. I didn't say anything, and Sunshine continued speaking.

"Albert told us you're the toughest woman he's ever known. He was very calm and levelheaded through all of this."

I groaned as I realized what story he must have told. "It was the C-section story, wasn't it?"

Sunshine laughed. "Yeah, it was. A day early up and out of the hospital. On your feet less than eight hours after surgery. That's nothing to sneeze at."

I rolled my eyes and waved at Zyada, who was doing cartwheels down a small snowy embankment.

Sunshine continued in his serious tone, but now there was more warmth in his words. "Keyan is not just my friend. I am his spotter; he is my gunmen. He has to trust me to keep him safe. I have to trust him to make the shot. We are a team. We know each other better than most brothers. He doesn't care who I sleep with, or how much I talk. I don't care how quiet he is, or how much of a knock head he is. So, you can believe me when I tell you, that he is not an emotional man. But when he carried you in ... he was a wreck." He sighed and for a moment his smile faded. "I told him falling for a happily married woman with kids was the worst kind of idea. The big moron didn't listen." He stuffed his hands in his pockets.

I wasn't sure how to respond but Sunshine wasn't looking for an answer. Somewhere in all this, he was coming to a point. He continued speaking.

"Part of me thinks I should just leave him to his fate of despair and misery. But I don't need him to be taking shots with a broken heart." He turned to look at me. "Whatever happens or doesn't happen, just do me a favor, will you? Be gentle. I know he is weird, but try to understand, he is like one of those big rivers, all calm on the surface, but down below, and its rapids." He groaned. "Ugh, I am using stupid metaphors."

He leaned in close enough that I could see flecks of green in his eyes. He laughed as he moved away. "You get what I am saying—though, if you ever need someone to cover for you so that you two have some alone time, just give me a holler. I am his partner after all. It's my job to cover his back. Just in case." He wiggled his eyebrows as he stepped away. My mother would have said, "That boy could steal the shine off a halo."

I tried not to think about what he had said. Albert was right—

I put names to people. It might have given them power, but it also took away from them. It made them less. As long as they were Sunshine and the Shadow, they were incorporeal. Sunshine would brighten a room, but it was always moving. Shadows might give you a hiding place or frighten you, but they were empty. Neither were things to be touched or felt. They were out of reach. That made them safer.

Or at least I had believed that right up until Keyan had reached out and touched me.

I thought about Vera as we passed the kitchen. It was still closed. No one had restarted the ovens or even picked up anything. The pantry was empty, and the place was trashed. It would take forever to clean up. My stomach ached as I looked into that room. It made this place seem scary and gloomy.

I did not look toward the smokehouse again. I kept a mental wall up and blocked it out of my mind. It wasn't as hard as you might think. You would be surprised at how good your brain is at denial. It would ignore things that caused you distress if you let it, like when your finger moved away from heat without your even thinking about it.

As we approached the gymnasium, we heard shouts from the large front area. A crowd was gathering as people yelled. Lieutenant Brick stood with his arms crossed as he listened to the angry voices shouting at him.

The loudest was Roger Tucker, a real blowhard of a man. Tall and balding, he had wide shoulders and had been some big-shot construction guy. He wasn't exactly a bad guy. But he was pushy and entitled and always believed he knew the best way to do everything. Honestly, I really couldn't stand the guy.

Tucker looked around at the crowd as he shouted. "We are in as much danger as anyone else. We don't have access to the radio or the firearms. We should have a militia so we can all protect ourselves. Who decided that we have to even listen to them? This is a college campus, not a military base. We don't even need them!"

There was a chorus of agreements from the crowd.

You know that voice in your head that tells you, "Hey, that's a bad idea" or "You shouldn't say that"? You may have noticed that I don't seem to have that voice.

"I didn't know you went through sixteen weeks of military training, Tucker. Is that where you were trained in automatics and close-quarters combat?" Not only did I seem to lack that inner voice of reason; I also had an outer voice that could project across a crowded room. I had no problem making sure everyone heard me. Really, go big or go home, right? I looked at Tucker as I strode forward. Sunshine was staring at me. Even Brick had looked up at me. People turned to look at me and then flinched back. My face made quite the impression. I was going to put it to good use.

I climbed up next to Roger on the bench he was standing on and looked at the crowd pointing to one of the men. "Hey, Bill, you know how to use an automatic rifle? Weren't you working at the wireless store? And Frank, you're a CPA, for God's sake. Seriously? You think you can do a better job of taking care of all the women and children here? You expect me to put the lives of my family in your hands? Have you ever even fired a rifle?" I tried hard to ask these questions in as sincere a voice as I could. Though I did mean to be a little insulting, I knew it would be better if they really asked themselves these questions.

"I am sure you have all been avid hunters your whole lives. But this isn't like hunting deer or rabbit. Those weren't deer coming up those hills. Those were people! Maybe even some you knew, people who lived in the same town as you, Americans. You are ready to start killing them? You are really ready to put yourself on the line for me, Tucker? You are ready to die to protect my kids?"

I glared at Roger. I was sure my swollen face and blue bruises looked horrible in the light. Some of the men looked away from me. Tucker glared back at me. He didn't like me butting in. I didn't think he liked anyone trying to take his spotlight in general, but especially not some silly housewife. I didn't back off. I turned and looked out at the crowd.

"These men saved us. It is because of their training we have made it this far. If it hadn't been for the things that came in that supply convoy, we wouldn't even have the few power sources we have now. No offense to Tucker and Bill—they are great guys, pillars of their community. But I would rather have a bunch of rough and rowdy marines and army men between me and what's out there any day. Someone who knows how to fire an automatic, someone who knows first aid, someone who has sworn an oath to defend this nation and its people."

I shifted my posture to a more relaxed one. "I know there has been a lot of talk going around about the military guys. Some people think they are being unfair or lying to us. People don't like that they have the guns or that they have the radios. That they are in charge. There has even been some talk about trying to change that." I could see some guilty faces. "I think that would be a very bad idea. We all know this sucks. I don't want to be here, but my house is gone. Without those men, my children and I would be out there right now facing God knows what. We have all heard the rumors of the gangs out there. There is no law here, no police, no hospitals, nothing. Without the military we would all be screwed."

I had taken a public speaking course in college. I had often given my speeches with as few facts as possible. My instructor had said I was gifted, but he didn't like that I didn't use verified facts. I told him that facts didn't persuade people. Facts bullied people, intimidated them. You used facts to convince scientists or to force authorities to take you seriously. To persuade everyday people, you needed to understand what moved them. The *fact* was that people didn't want to know facts; people wanted their hearts to be swayed. Facts could change policy but not sway hearts.

"Sarah, your husband was a computer guy before this, right? What about the others? We have car salesmen, some college kids, a couple of retirees, some folks who worked at Walmart. Ask yourself: are these the people you want to be responsible for your welfare? Who would you rather have standing on the perimeter, guarding our lives? So why don't we just let them do their jobs?" I was quiet for a moment while I looked at each person. Then I smiled and tried to lighten the mood a little. "I mean, can you imagine Mr. Ferguson out there with a rifle, working the gate? 'Hello, welcome to Walmart. Have a nice day.'"

Mr. Ferguson was a retired clerk from city hall. He laughed at that and in a grumpy voice said, "Get your shit and get out!"

There was a small chorus of laughter, and I knew I had them, at least for now.

"I am sure Lieutenant Roberts is looking for a way to up our security, to make sure this never happens again. I know people were hurt, but the majority of the injured were enlisted. If it had been civilians who were armed or in those guard posts, then they would have been targets. The only reason I was attacked was because I tried to stop some of the men from raiding the smokehouse. And even then, it was an enlisted man who rescued me and Vera. So please, let's depend on them. They will keep us safe."

I turned and smiled at Lieutenant Roberts, but I tried to make sure he saw in my eyes that he had better appreciate this. Right on cue, he stepped up to reassure everyone that the military was working overtime to keep them safe. He didn't miss a beat as he addressed how the civilians could help. I reached out, and Albert helped me down from the bench. My knee and hip were complaining. Sunshine grinned at me and gave me a thumbs-up. I gave a smile from the good side of my face.

We moved back to the outer edged of the crowd. Some of the folks watched me as I went by, but I wasn't bothered. The bruises would fade, and as my brother liked to say, "Chicks dig scars." In my case it would be Albert. I pretended not to notice the tall dark figure lounging like a cat on some of the empty crates. I had caught myself looking for him, and it pissed me off. Why the hell did he have to be so, so ... him? Goddamn it. Why did I have to notice that he was so damn tall? I didn't want to look for him, but my eyes just kept spotting him. Maybe this was what he had meant when he said his eyes always found me.

I felt something twist up inside me. *No, no, no.* I refused. *Hell no.* I took that knot inside and ironed it flat. I had always been such a stupid romantic. The world wasn't a romance novel. I had a family and a man I loved, who loved me. I didn't need tall, dark, exciting strangers. People like that were wildfires, hot and powerful but destructive. I had enough burn scars.

the day i left the infirmary, 11:16am

I STOOD at the edge of the crowd as the talks continued. Brick was asking for volunteers to be trained for additional security. They would work with the military men for the protection of the camp. Brick might be hard, but he wasn't dense. He understood that he needed to feed the mob. If he gave in and let them help with security, he kept control of them. It also allowed him to train them enough, that they weren't a danger to themselves. Sunshine made his way back to me and patted my shoulder. I made sure I didn't wince.

Brick wasn't the only one taking advantage of the golden opportunity. Tucker and creepy Church-lady were already hard at work, gathering donations to help those who had been hurt or robbed. The jackals were in full force. I looked around and slipped through the crowd. I was no jackal. However, there was something that mice and jackals had in common. We were scavengers. Scavengers didn't waste a good opportunity.

As I passed through the crowd, I paused to whisper in the ears of a few people I wanted to come with us, those people I had come to trust. We would meet later tonight after dinner. I gave Albert a kiss and sent him on ahead with the little ones. Lucky followed them for a moment before he changed his mind and ran back to me. I ruffled the fur on his ears. I waited until my family was out of sight before I approached Mouthy. He had just finished with the LT, discussing details of volunteers.

Mouthy grinned as I approached. He was the only one who hadn't winced at seeing my face. "Hey there. That's a good one. What's the other guy look like?"

I smirked back at him with the good side of my face and shrugged, even though the movement hurt. "Not so good since he is dead." I was worried by how little that bothered me. I took all those feelings and shoved them into a box and locked it up tight in my mind.

Everyone has a box like that, a place where they put things that they can't think about. It's where I had locked up that basement and that mass grave. It was where I kept the sounds of those Crazies. It must have been getting crowded because it was hard to shut the lid.

I forced myself to focus on Mouthy, who talked pleasantly to the air until I returned. The nice thing about Mouthy was that he understood. When I went inside my own head, he didn't pry or question it. He just kept talking till I came back.

I smiled and looked around. "Well, seems like your workload is a little less now."

He snorted and shook his head. "For now, but we both know they will find some other way to fill up all my time." He groaned and rubbed his neck. "This unit would fall apart if I weren't here, I tell you." And then he did tell me. He started telling me all the things that would fall apart if he didn't take care of them.

Then slipped into all that talking, he said, "Speaking of which, I was really concerned that our favorite tall, dark sniper would break in half when you went to the infirmary. He didn't look so good. Seriously." Mouthy gave me a sideways glance and stretched his arms above his head as he grinned. "But I guess something must have made it OK, because this morning I heard him talking with Sunshine. He even smiled, and I swear I heard a chuckle."

I could only imagine what my face looked like. My eyes stung as they involuntarily went wide. My skin tightened and ached as a blush forced more fluid into my swollen cheeks. My lip pulsed as my heart gave a kick. At that moment embarrassment really hurt. "What?" I managed to get out.

It didn't matter. Mouthy was still talking. I was actually a little grateful. I knew he was teasing me, but at least he wasn't cruel about it.

"Really, now I am not the kind to pry, and I don't judge. I am not gonna ask and don't wanna know what may or may not have gone on. I will say that I am glad that whatever happened, happened. Keyan Mikoto is a good man and great soldier. We are all lucky that he is here. In times like these, we need men like him in tip-top shape. So I hope for all our sakes that whatever it was keeps happening."

Mouthy didn't look at me, but the ache in my cheek increased. I could feel the heat rising off my ears.

"Never mind that," I said, trying to act composed. I was too old for all this blushing. "I have something I need to ask you about."

He raised an eyebrow. "Oh? What is on your mind there, Mama Mouse?"

I gave him a serious look. "I want to know about the prisoner."

He blinked and gave a very convincing ignorant look. "What prisoner?"

I wasn't fooled. I knew him well enough to know that nothing happened within the enlisted that Mouthy didn't know about. I crossed my arms and gave an unfriendly grin. "The one I locked in the smokehouse. Considering people are still pulling meat out of there, my guess is he isn't still in there. Someone would have flipped, considering he would be cooked by now."

Mouthy looked a little green around the gills at that idea and sighed. "Come on, you know they ain't gonna tell you nothing. Just let us handle this."

I lost the unfriendly smile and replaced it with a glare. "I am not kidding. I want to know everything, or I go out there and tell all those fine folks everything I know."

Mouthy winced and looked me over. He seemed to see something in my body posture and sighed. "Man ... why does it have to be like that, Marlene?" he said, his voice grumpy.

I put my hands on my hips. "You know I don't want to be like that. But if you guys are gonna try to treat me like a mushroom, I am gonna throw that bullshit around."

His irritation dissolved into a laugh as he shook his head. "You really are something else, Mouse. Were you always this interesting?" He started walking and motioned me to follow.

I walked with him and tried not to smile. "I think the word was strange back then."

Lucky obediently trotted along with me. I steeled my resolve. I knew it would be hard to see this man again. But I didn't open the box. I focused on controlling my breathing, clenching and relaxing different muscles. It helped me stay calm and relaxed as we approached the building where they were holding him.

"The college campus had a small security station on the grounds," Mouthy explained. "It has a holding cell inside. It's the closest thing to a jail we have."

Private Davis and Private First Class Fredricks were guarding him. They both hopped to attention when we walked in. Lucky stepped in like he had been here many times before and claimed a spot in the corner to lie down.

Davis smiled at me. Fredricks looked at me, his face filling with anger. "Excuse me. I need a smoke," he said to no one as he stormed out.

Confused, I looked to Mouthy, then Davis. "Is he pissed at me or something? I mean, I know I am not supposed to be here. But I didn't think he would be so mad about it." My feelings were a little hurt since I thought of us as friends.

Davis looked at me like I had grown a second head. Mouthy

looked stunned and then burst into laughter. "Holy shit, Albert is right," he managed to say between laughs.

I got that he was making fun of me. I just didn't know about what. "It's Albert. He is usually right. He is also right about how I kick really hard. Want to find out?"

Mouthy didn't stop laughing, but he moved out of range as he explained. "He said the way you see the world is really odd, like you look at the world from a different angle. You will see things everyone else misses, but because of that, you miss the completely obvious." Mouthy composed himself and managed to finish his thought. "He said that's what led to you being called 'happy to be here.'"

Davis smirked but contained his laughter. "Marcus isn't mad at you," he said, finally clearing it up for me. "He took it real personal that you got hurt. He was on watch duty at the time of the attack. He was on the northern gate. He couldn't see where the men attacked from, but he blames himself."

I felt a pang in my chest. "Damn, it's not his fault. I was running around all over the place. I was being stupid. If I had any sense, I would have stayed in the office room, barricaded the door, and waited for someone to come and find me. It was really stupid to try to run around like that."

Mouthy crossed his arms and shrugged. "Probably, but if you hadn't, who knows what would have happened to Vera? They roughed people up pretty bad. She told a bunch of folks how you saved her."

I smiled and shrugged. "I guess. I am glad I did help her, but that doesn't mean it was smart."

Davis grinned and nudged my shoulder. "Smart doesn't always equal right. Don't worry about Marcus. We are all a little upset that you got hurt."

I tilted my head, a little surprised but flattered. "Really?"

Mouthy nodded enthusiastically. "Yeah, you're our mascot. Besides, you make the best bread. So we are all glad you are OK."

I felt some of my tension ease away. "Thanks, that makes me feel good. So tell me, what have you all learned about this guy?" I said, motioning to the man in the holding room.

Davis shrugged. "Not a whole lot, actually. The guy was sedated for a day due to the burns. He didn't get found right away. Since he woke up, he's just been staring off into space."

"Oh Lord." I walked over and peeked in the window to the holding cell. A man rested on a cot. He was cleaned up. He didn't look much like the movie reject I had seen before. He looked like a sad, skinny, ordinary man. His skin was red and blotchy and bandaged. "He looks younger than I thought. Can I talk to him?"

"No!"

I jumped at the sound of both of them forcefully answering at the exact same moment.

"Yes," another voice answered from the doorway.

It was Mouthy's and Davis's turn to jump as they came to attention. The voice belonged to the lieutenant's right-hand man, Senior Sergeant Adams. The way he walked in reminded me of Clint Eastwood in *Heartbreak Ridge*. I hadn't been this close to him before. His eyes were a faded blue, like the gray from his hair had seeped into his eyes. Faded or not, the look in those eyes was sharp and precise.

"You go on in and talk to him," said the sergeant. "See what you can get him to say. Just get the words coming. Be careful." He handed me the tray of food he had brought with him. "Take this." It was not a request.

I found myself following orders without even thinking about it. I had wanted to talk to this guy. I couldn't explain why, but I needed to face someone. I had to look my fear in the eye. I needed to do this. The sergeant opened the door of the holding cell, let me in, and then shut the door behind me. I flinched when it clanged. The man jerked at the same instant as the door, awake and alert. He was a live wire, vibrating with tension and fear. I stood there watching him watch me. I took deep, even breaths, letting them out slowly to a soft count of five. He reminded me of Nathan during a panic attack.

I tried the same technique I had used with Nathan. I said, "Calm ... Breathe with me. In ... one, two, three. Out ... one, two, three. In ... out..." I spoke in a low, soothing voice while I did the breathing. I maintained my distance and watched his face until he was unconsciously breathing with me. Then slowly, I shifted forward and to the side. I gently set the tray on the table before moving away from it. I held my hands away from my body at waist level to seem less threatening. "It's OK. I am not here to hurt you," I said softly.

"Liar! You are the one that locked me in the meat cooker!" He spat the words at me, his voice rough and hoarse.

I nodded. "Yes, that was me. But I didn't mean for you to get stuck in there. I was just trying to get away."

He glared at me but wasn't able to maintain the angry look. His eyes took in the bruises, and his expression shifted as he looked away. "He did that to you." It wasn't a question.

I reached up and touched the bruises on my neck. For just a second I could feel the man's hand around my throat again. I had to throw all my mental weight against the lid of that box. I needed to stay calm, focused.

My voice shook slightly. "Yes. He did. He is dead." I wasn't sure if I was telling him or myself.

The young man nodded. "I know. I could see bits through the cracks in the door." He looked down at the bandages on his hands. "I hurt my hands trying to get out of there. We were hungry. I would have tried to stop him ... when he went after you. He's dead." After a pause, he continued. "That old lady was screaming so loud." He looked up at me accusingly, his voice full of resentment. "His name was William!"

I looked him straight in the eye and responded, "My name is Marlene."

He blinked as if he didn't know what to do with that. Words

started to fall out of my mouth as I held myself together as best I could. "The old lady's name is Vera. The little boy's name is Victor, my son. Your friend, William, tried to strangle me to death in front of my three-year-old son." I barely recognized my own voice in the metal room. It was cold and low and full of anger. "You attacked us. You came here to take whatever you wanted. We both know what he was going to do to me if he got the chance."

The man flinched as if I had struck him and looked away. I was getting off-track.

"Was he your friend?" I asked softly, trying to bring the conversation back.

He looked at his bandaged hands. "He was a truck driver. We were on the same road when it happened. He helped me. The gangs wouldn't have brought me along without him. He could get the motors running." He clenched his fists. "He saved my life. You don't know what it's like out there. We had to stick together, no matter what. We were starving already, and then the snow hit. We had to get supplies before it was too late. We had all been traveling down from Albany. We needed to beat winter." His voice strained, but the cork had been pulled, and everything came out in a rush— the violence he had witnessed, the death of his wife from what seemed to be infection, how William had been the last of the people from his original group. He went on and on about how William *had* to do certain things. Every time, it was "had to." He wasn't even looking at me anymore. I was not sure he was even talking to me.

His story didn't follow a timeline exactly. It hopped back and forth between the beginning and the end. It revolved around a middle point. I assumed it was the moment when he himself finally "had to" do something. His moment had come when he killed a man during a raid. The man had surprised him, and by the time he realized it was his friend Jeff, it was too late. Jeff had been his friend for a long time.

"I didn't know it was him ... I didn't see him. He came running out of the building. I just jumped and squeezed the trigger. I didn't even realize until he said my name. He died right there in my arms. I killed him ..." His voice broke as he sobbed.

The sergeant came in then. I stood to leave, and the prisoner grabbed my wrist. "Wait ... please ... you have to understand. Please, *please!*"

I knew what he wanted, even if he didn't. It was why he was telling me all this. I forced a gentle smile on my face, even though it hurt. I patted the hand on my wrist. "I understand. You only did what you had to. It's OK. I forgive you," I said as soothingly as I was able.

The sergeant pulled him away from me. My words seemed to crumble the young man, and he fell into heavy sobbing.

I stepped out of the holding room and shook slightly as I took in air. Mouthy touched my shoulder. "You serious with the 'I forgive you' shit?"

I let out a breath as I looked at my wrist. "Honestly I don't know. Maybe... Either way it doesn't cost me anything. And he needed to hear it. Besides, the world fell apart. People lost their minds. Who am I to judge him?"

Mouthy looked at me for a moment. "Yeah, I get it. Don't worry, I got you. I will judge him plenty for ya'."

I nodded. "That sounds fine to me."

Davis chimed in from where he was eating his lunch. "Are you all right? That looked rough."

I nodded as I looked back into the room. The sergeant was talking to the young man, who was answering now. "Yup." I looked over at Davis and smiled. "Just sending a mental thank-you to the man upstairs, I guess."

Mouthy shook his head. "I didn't take you for the religious type, Mouse. You gonna start going to the prayer group?"

I gave a smirk and waved a hand. "No way. God knows, and that's enough for me. I talk to him when I need to but try not to pester him. He keeps an eye on me. It works out fine. We don't make a production out of it."

Mouthy laughed harder. "OK, that does sound like you."

I tried to make a face at him and winced at the pain. I flipped him off instead. "Jerk," I mumbled as they both laughed.

I felt the tension in my chest ease as I realized that I could forgive them—even William. Whatever had made him attack me, he had someone who mourned him. He was a human, not a monster. I was ashamed of how I had felt about his death. It left a blackness in me that I didn't want. I forgave him for what he had done, and I hoped he forgave me for hurting him back. Then I forgave myself for how I felt. We were all human.

After I had listened to the prisoner, Matt, for an hour or so, it was clear that neither he nor his gang were part of the religious group that was making plans against the camp. His group was a roaming gang, headed south and raiding along the way. They had gone through an abandoned FEMA camp and two quarantine zones. It was clear they were mobile and wouldn't bother coming back for anyone who fell behind. The picture he painted was grim and violent, full of humanity's worst. He confirmed that there was a bunch called the "Crazies," mostly made up of teenagers and young people that was running around raiding all the stores and city refugee groups. Matt said his group had lost a bunch of people to them as they passed through the city. They had been able to negotiate some trade and gather some news about the area. There had been a massive gang war over at the Walmart almost three weeks ago. Dozens of people had died. The building had been looted and burned to the ground. He talked about how his groups kept forming together and splintering apart. After a while he just didn't care anymore. He had stuck with William, and they had stuck with whoever had the most food.

I listened for as long as I could before heading out the door. Lucky quickly followed me down the ramp and ran ahead to attend to his business. I pulled out a smoke and braced myself against the frigid air as I started back toward the campus. I wanted to talk to Brick. The cigarette smoke hurt my throat as I took it in. The burning ache felt oddly good. All the aches felt good. The icy air felt good against my swollen face. I looked at the brilliant blue sky. The white snow had become sparkling mounds of sugar on the ground. Everything was a little brighter, sharper, and more vivid.

I was alive. If it hadn't been for Keyan, that might not be the case. I drew a stinging and delightful pull of smoke into my lungs. My thoughts floated in my mind as my feet followed the runner's path toward the main campus. All I wanted was to keep my children safe. I wanted us to find a place where they could grow and be happy. But where was that? Not here. The quietness was an illusion. Even now dangers were sleeping in disguise as friends.

All feminism aside, I just wasn't strong enough on my own to protect them. There were other Williams out there, men losing their humanity, including some men who hadn't had much humanity to begin with. I just wasn't enough to keep myself or my children safe. Albert loved me and would die to protect us. But could he have stopped William? Could he stop the next one? What if there were more than one? How many could he take?

The idea of something happening between the civilians and the military scared me. It was hard enough to look after my little ones here, with a house and military presence, but what would we do if the military was gone? Could I trust the civilians? They didn't know how to ration food, build shelters, and defend a perimeter. It wasn't the civilians who had saved me. It wasn't that long ago that I had been worried about school grades. I had worried about what to make for dinner. Now I worried about whether we would catch dinner or whether there were enough supplies for winter. Now everything was about the basics—food, shelter, safety.

My thoughts drifted to my childhood, to my father working in our barn, hammering or sawing. I used to sit in the sawdust with my little tack hammer, nailing scrap pieces of wood together as he worked. As I watched his hands, I thought they were full of magic. I worked with him in our little backyard garden, weeding and planting. The garden had seemed huge to me. He showed me how to check the corn, how to help the beans grow straight. I had learned early how to hoe a row, push a wheelbarrow, milk a goat.

My grandmother had canned peaches. I remembered sitting in our kitchen as my mother and grandmother turned bowls of peaches into pretty jars of dark golden sweetness. I remembered the kitchen being hot and steamy as the jars and lids boiled and bubbled. I remembered us sitting around shelling peas or pecans or shucking corn. We would sit and talk as we worked. And when all the work was done, it was transformed into some delicious food. It was magical to me.

There had been sad times as well, like when we killed the chicken and I had to help pluck it. I remembered that I had stood a few feet away as my father picked out the hen we were going to kill. I was so upset. Every morning before school, I came out and fed those clucking biddies. I gathered their eggs. I had secretly named each and every one of them, even though Dad had told me not to. I stood there trying not to cry as he picked up one of the fat hens that had stopped laying eggs. He carried her over to a stump that we used to chop firewood. He spoke softly to her, petting her head as he walked. She clucked at him and closed her eyes. He turned away from me so I couldn't see what happened, but I heard that terrible noise.

He broke her neck quickly and easily. When he turned back around, she was limp and still. My father looked over at me and sighed. He set the body of the hen down on the stump and walked over to me. He squatted down in front of me. He never sat on the ground or knelt, just did that squat where he bent his knees and sat on the back of his heels. He smiled softly and took hold of my hands. I was crying a little and sniffling. His voice was calm and firm.

"Now listen, Pookie Sparkle, I know it's hard to think about, but everything that lives on this earth has a purpose. It's OK to be sad when things die, but remember that things die so other things can live. We grow plants so we can eat them, and because we grow those plants, other plants don't get to grow. There is a cycle to life. You respect what lives and dies. Life can be sad and messy and even mean, but as long as we respect it and do our best, things will work out. Now we are going to eat chicken tonight, and that meant I had to take Bessy."

I was shocked that he knew her name.

He took my face in those big magic hands and smiled. "She didn't suffer, and I think she would be happy knowing that she is gonna help you and your brothers and sister grow big and strong. If it makes you feel better, we can say a thank-you to her at dinner."

I wiped the tears off my chin and nodded. It was still really hard to watch him clean and dress her. Grandma was much less sympathetic when it came time to pluck the chicken. She was a rough old woman; she'd had a hard life. She didn't give much slack for sentimental feelings. She just cuffed the back of my head and told me I was being silly, crying over a chicken. She put me back to work plucking the bird. But she turned that raw bird into the most amazing chicken and dumpling stew. She snorted when my father gave thanks to Bessy for feeding his family. It wasn't so hard after that. It was tough growing up on a farm. It involved hard work and tough experiences, but when I thought about my childhood, I couldn't help but be grateful.

I released another puff as I thought about my grandmother. Such a tough old bird. I put out my cigarette and looked up. I looked out at the perimeter fence that the enlisted men were patrolling. They were training some of the civilians, who looked awkward and slow compared to the military men. The fact was, I didn't trust them. It wasn't that I thought they would turn tail and run. I just didn't think they were strong enough. They wouldn't be able to stand up against a real attack. What could I do? How could I keep my children safe?

My mind flashed to a vision of Keyan as he snapped that man's neck. Keyan Mikoto was very strong, physically and mentally. He was extensively trained and skilled. I was not stupid. I knew that if I were to use his attraction, he would keep me safe, me and my children. Right or wrong, I couldn't ask for a stronger guardian.

But I loved Albert. It was not about wedding vows. I loved him. He was my home. He was my peace, my quiet happiness. He always pulled through for us. During the recession, he had been prepared and kept us in a house and fed. Even when our income was almost nothing, he kept pushing me to pursue my schooling. Albert had always supported and encouraged me. I wanted to keep us together. I felt the bite as tears leaked out of my swollen eyes. The cold air made the wetness on my cheeks sting. If we couldn't find a safe place to stay, we would have to keep moving. How long could Albert do that? He would leave me himself before he put us in danger.

He has already planned for this. The thought popped into my mind. *He always plans ahead.* I rolled that around in my skull for a moment. I was sure of it. He would have thought about his limitations. If he had made some deal with Keyan, I was going to kick both of their asses. I wiped my face and called to Lucky as I headed down the hill toward the last place I'd seen Keyan. I had questions that needed answers.

I asked some of the lingering crowd and eventually was told that he had headed over to the radio building. I went around the corner from the far side. No one was there at the moment. Staff was minimal with so many repairs and other work being done. The inside was also restricted access. There was a little alcove protected from the wind, tucked away against the retaining wall at the tower's base. It was cozy and had built-in seating, so people used it for a smoking area.

I never saw him. I never saw the motion. A hand was just

suddenly over my mouth, and I was pinned against a wall, looking at those bottomless eyes again. *Keyan.* I recognized him almost instantly, but that didn't stop the adrenaline. My heart was pounding, and I could feel the rapid beating in my face. The hand over my mouth hurt my split lip. My blood roared in my ears. He held me up off the ground. My feet dangled and were not able to find purchase. I was pressed against the wall from my neck to my hips. The stone of the wall was cold against my back even through the thick coat. I dug my fingers into the shoulder of his coat and gripped tight to his wrist at my mouth.

"Be still." His voice was barely a whisper.

What the fuck do you mean, be still? I thought. How the hell was someone supposed to just "be still" in a moment like this?

But like the last time we'd done this dance, I fell right into step. I stilled my body, and one of my feet found a perch on a piece of cinder block. I tried to slow my breathing and calm my heart so I could listen. My face ached where he pressed on the bruised side, but I didn't move. It was so damn quiet in the alcove that all I heard was our breathing.

His face was turned to the side, his eyes focused on something else. Even lifted, I was still so much shorter that I was eye level with his collarbone. His hand slowly came off my face and moved to the wall beside my head. He shifted his body closer. My nose was stuffed against his jacket. The fabric was cold against my warm face. He must have been outside for a long time.

My heart was still racing when I heard the static from the radio.

"This is station 4-8-5. Come in, relay 26." The voice was low and quiet, but in the silence of the alcove, it seemed to vibrate through the stone. I tilted my head and pressed my ear to the wall to listen to the voices.

"This is relay 26. What is it, station?" I knew that voice. It was Junior Sergeant Bethany Sergio. She was in charge of the radio. She was a tough lady, not easily intimidated and almost six feet tall. Her voice was firm as she spoke to the person on the other end.

"Reports from refugee camp. Factions fought over supplies, and rioting broke out. Some group called the Sol's Apostles has taken control. Majority of civilians have evacuated. Lookouts report that the fairgrounds are empty. We are awaiting visual confirmation of their current location. Current data shows them heading along the freeway in a southern direction, possibly passing your location in forty-eight hours. Orders remain as standing, but under no circumstances is the radio to fall into hostile hands. The relay is to remain in our possession or to be slagged."

Bethany gave an affirmative response and then read off a series of code numbers. Then she asked, "ETA on relief or reinforcement?"

There was a pause. "That's a negative. No personnel or supplies will be allocated at this time. Be advised, there is a massive weather front headed your way. Should be there within seventy-two hours. It's expected to be a hell of a blizzard. Make sure you are buttoned up tight."

"Yes. Received. Understood. Confirmed." There was a static sound followed by an angry thump. "Sons of bitches, leaving us out here with everything that is going on. Dicks." Then I heard a door slam shut.

I waited to hear anything else as something hard dug painfully into my right thigh. He might have been happy to see me, but I thought it was probably his survival knife. I tilted my head to look up at him and whispered in as low a voice as I could manage, "Keyan?"

His eyes snapped down to me, pressed between the wall and him. He seemed startled to see me there. I think it was the first time I had ever used his first name. "Oh," he said. He didn't move away. I felt like time had stopped. It was hard to breathe. *Is he getting closer? Where did the rest of the world go?* He filled up my whole field of vision. In that moment between moments, he was all

I could see. A hummingbird was trapped inside my chest, trying to get free.

He was carved of living stone. It pissed me off. There I was, a bundle of exposed nerves ready to fly apart, and he was completely unaffected. He stared at me, his face composed. His eyes narrowed till they were almost closed. His thick lashes curled up slightly. I had opened my mouth to spew something angry at him when I saw the vein on his neck. It was pulsing wildly, in almost the exact same rhythm as my heart. I became aware of the tension in his body. The place where my hand gripped his shoulder could have been made out of steel cables. The hand next to my face moved, and the tip of his thumb traced a line across my face to the corner of my mouth. His thumb pad was rough and calloused as it barely caressed the cut on my lip.

Chills ran along my skin while my insides caught fire. I couldn't remember how to breathe. I tried to speak, but my tongue was dry and clumsy. I was trapped, pinned by those eyes. They reminded me of the snake from my dream. Or was he the hawk? Either way, I was currently trapped by someone who looked very hungry.

There are moments in life that remain with you, painted on your soul. When you're old, and memories start to fade to shades of gray, there will be these little snapshots in your mind that remain. The sights and smells will stay. Memories you never realized were so important—swinging at the park in the sun, fireworks from some long-ago summer, a kiss that tasted like lemonade, rain on windows—will stay with you, strange little moments that the mind captured with perfect clarity. These moments in life seem more vivid. They become more real than the rest.

I knew I would never forget the exact shade of black of his hair, or the way the white snow behind him glittered and glowed in the sun, outlining him, or the shape of his lower lip. For the rest of my life, the smell of peppermint would always bring me right back here.

I had a thought that I might just burst. For a moment I felt completely weightless, and all the aches and pains from my injuries were gone. He lowered his face toward me, and my lips tingled in anticipation. I felt myself stretch toward him. I felt his warm breath on my lips. The strength of my longing frightened me. I was drowning. Pain in my neck and fear brought reason, pulling me out of the fog just in time. I turned away. His lips hovered just above my bruised cheek. My guts hurt as if I had been punched. My breathing was ragged like I had been running. It was so hard to calm down.

His voice was different, ragged around the edges. "What ... are you ... doing ... here?"

Some mean little part of me was happy that he was as troubled as I was. *Why had I come here again? What was I doing?* "Albert." I said his name like a magic spell, and I remembered why I had come. I was able to think. I forced my hands to release Keyan's shoulders and pressed against the wall of his chest. His eyes looked darker, like storm clouds. He radiated heat under my palms. He didn't move.

I kept Albert in my mind as I spoke. "Did Albert talk to you? Did he make some kind of deal with you? Is that what this is?" My voice was gritty and rough, like I was about to cry. Maybe I wanted to cry. I didn't like the idea of losing Albert, and I really didn't like him arranging a replacement. There were so many reasons this upset me—fear of losing Albert, the indignation of not being consulted, and some deep-seated insecurity that the only reason someone like Keyan would be interested in me was because of a deal with Albert. Everything was tangled up in a ball inside me. My rational mind said that it would be a good plan, to make sure that both the kids and I would be safe. But my heart was full of rebellious rage. I wrapped myself up in the anger. The fury became my protection against the heat of him. I stoked the feeling and used it to distract me from the ache in the pit of my stomach.

"We spoke," he said finally as he pulled back from me.

Speaking of Albert seemed to put him physically in between us, and Keyan moved away. Chills ran along my body as cold air rushed in to fill the space he had put between us. I became more myself.

"What did he say?" I asked, since it seemed those two words were all he was going to say.

"Ask him," he said and turned away from me, shoving his hands in his pockets.

"I am asking you. What did you say? Is this why you came to sit with me in the infirmary? Is this an obligation because I helped Sunshine? Do you owe him or something? Was all this just part of the deal you had with him?" I knew those weren't the things to ask or say. My insecurities made me ask them anyway. What did I want him to say? Wouldn't it be better if he were only doing this as a favor—if he wasn't really interested at all, and it was just some obligation, and all this chemistry was one-sided?

You would think at my age I would have been past these doubts. But just because wounds heal doesn't mean that the scars don't ache on stormy days. Man, I really hated this high school bullshit. I clenched my teeth and forced myself to stand up straight. "Poor man's pride" was what my father called it. I glared at Keyan, chin tilted upward. I was pissed as hell. They both made me so mad. I felt transparent and exposed. I had been working so hard to ignore this attraction, and meanwhile, they were talking about me behind my back.

He turned and stared at me with his fists clenched. He looked angry, but my dams burst and words poured out.

"You know what? Fuck that and fuck *you*!" I shouted at him. My words echoed in the little alcove. "I don't know where you two get off thinking this is OK. And don't worry, I will be chewing his ass out as soon as I get home. As if we don't have bigger fucking problems right now. Both of you can just kiss my ass. It would serve you right if I just ran off with Mouthy!"

His eyes widened a little, and his jaw clenched. I pointed my finger at him. "But *whoever* or *whatever* I choose to do or not do, it will be my choice. Period." I blew out the last of my steam. My hands shook as I tried to get myself back together. "Now ... can we please deal with what is happening right now?" I motioned to the window.

He stared at me, and for a moment I felt the urge to run. I had a flash of recognition. Once when I was twelve, I had been walking down a street when a massive dog had come charging around a corner, panting and growling, his hackles raised. I knew to never run from dogs. It was in their instincts to chase, and you couldn't outrun them. Holding my ground in that moment had been one of the scariest and hardest moments in my life. Holding my ground while I watch Keyan wrestle with himself was only slightly less difficult.

He turned his back to me and cursed in a language I didn't know. I pretended to not notice as he took some time to calm down. Knowing that he also was struggling to regain his composure helped the last of my anger fade.

In my mentally unguarded moment of exposed emotion the dark inner thoughts decided to pounce. My mind flashed to the woman at the fairgrounds. A sickening feeling filled me with dread as I thought of her and her children. *Were they OK? How was the baby? Was it warm enough? Had the formula lasted long enough? Where were they now? Had they made it onto a train? Were they walking down the freeway right now?* My mind spun with horrible possibilities. The lid on my mental box tried to open as I bit my hurt lip and stopped my thoughts. *I did everything I could. I helped her as much as I was able. I can't save everyone*, I told myself over and over. I struggled with my emotional upheaval and hugged myself tight. *Your job is to protect your children first. Help where you can but focus on your family first.* I had to repeat that to myself a few times before I was able to settle my thoughts. I looked upward at the clear sky. Dark puffs of clouds in the distance marred the blue background. The storm was gathering. When I looked back at Keyan, he was looking at the radio tower.

"They are coming before the snow." His voice was low and ominous.

We both looked at the tower in silence. In history class, we had discussed that over the centuries the reasons for war had changed very little. Humans made war for resources. Someone had something you wanted or needed, and they wouldn't give it to you, so you went and took it. Excuses had been used, such as religion or ideology, but those were just ways to convince people to fight. The reason for the war was always the same.

"Come on, we need to tell the others. They are meeting in the music practice room. It's soundproofed," I said as I grabbed his arm to drag him along.

He barely stumbled as his long legs shifted quickly, and soon he was pulling me. I really hated him. Lucky moved along beside us easily.

The piano room was a good-sized room. It was designed to seat about thirty students and still have room for a piano in the front. There were only fifteen seats set up, with one piano in the front of the classroom and one in the back. Sunshine was with all three kids in the back of the room, playing on the piano. He played it well. He was starting to freak me out a little. No one should be that good at that many things.

Albert was talking with Grandpa Silas and Jeri. Mouthy lounged at a desk in the front row. Old Man Harris dozed in the seat next to Vera, who was knitting quietly. Alice and Michael were sitting near Mouthy, taking turns playing and talking with their baby. Samara was sitting on the floor on a blanket with her son Vahid, who was practicing turning over. The light in the room was coming from large windows high up on the walls. Keyan Mikoto, the Shadow, followed in behind me and shut and locked the door. Everyone looked up and waited. Part of me was amazed that they had come. I had whispered my message to them on the fly—"Book club secret meeting, piano room 243, in two hours"—and had worried no one would take it seriously. Now that they were all here, I wasn't really sure where to begin. I moved to the teacher's desk and sat on it. My feet dangled. Keyan stood next to the door.

The silence was oppressive. I felt the butterflies churning in my stomach. I had given presentations before, for my work and in college for classes. But this felt so important. My skin was tight, and my mouth was dry. I looked up at the light streaming in from the windows and watched as dust fairies danced through the air.

"So here we are ... our very own little conspiracy group," I mumbled at the fairies. I took a deep breath. As I let it out slowly, I imagined all the butterflies flying away with it. That visual always helped me with my nerves.

I turned my eyes to the group. "Folks, it looks like our time is running out. I know we were planning on taking the long road to try to find out who was infiltrating our group. But I don't think it's going to matter soon. We had received a warning that the attack was coming before Thanksgiving. But the timeline has drastically changed. The fairgrounds are empty now. We overheard a radio call, and it sounds like they are headed our way. If they are somehow getting word from their sources here, then they know exactly where we are. They could be here in two days, before the major storm hits in three days."

People sat up in attention, even Old Man Harris.

Michael said, "Wait, how do you know that whoever sent the warning wasn't talking about the raid?"

I shook my head at him. "No, the prisoner Matt gave us intel. He was one of the raiders that had been trapped in the smokehouse. The raiders came from the opposite direction, while heading south for the winter. They were traveling from Albany, just raiding randomly. They saw some smoke from the chimneys. I think the warning came from a woman who lives in the valley. She got the information through her group."

Samara spoke up as she rubbed her baby's back. "Thanksgiving is in three days. What should we do?" She was always a cut-to-the-chase kind of girl.

"Well, we need to have a plan. If the military men can hold this place, that will be awesome, but we should be ready for the worst. We need to prepare to run."

Albert brought out the map of the area I had been using, and we started discussing possible evacuation locations.

Jeri stood up and pointed to a spot on the map. "We should have a place where we all meet up before we try to get out. This old public library should work. No one really goes there but me. And we can get there from back here, so no one will notice."

Grandpa grumbled as he started to point out some of the side areas on the map. "The ravines are great, but they can be a maze. Not all of them connect. We need to make sure we use the right ones. We should go down the steep side toward the valley. The scar is an easier climb down, but once you clear the hill, there is no cover. Everything was burned flat, so there isn't any shelter. The valley still has a lot of old buildings intact with a bunch of side streets that can lead toward the train tracks. I was thinking maybe we follow along those until we get somewhere we can catch the train to the refugee camps."

Old Man Harris shook his head. "No good. Maybe if the weather was OK, but once that snow comes, we will freeze if we don't have a place to find shelter, especially the little ones. They can't walk that far in the snow."

I looked at the two infants. "He is right. We need to figure something else out." I dug out my notebook. "Hang on." I flipped through the pages, looking at places I had searched before. "There was this old church. It was all stone and looked really old on the outside, but it had been renovated—you know, like they were trying to historically preserve the exterior." I finally found the page. "Here. It was all done, but there was still no electricity, so nothing burned. Everything was intact inside, but there weren't any supplies. I just looked around and left. It had a basement and a bunch of rooms, even one with a fireplace."

I checked the location on the map. It was really close to downtown. It would take a long time to get there if we went down the steep side. It would be a lot faster to take the scar. "If we take the ravines and the graveyards down the side of the hill to go through the scar, we could be there in a few hours. Otherwise, we have to hike down the steep ravines, go down to the valley side, and loop back around to take side streets toward downtown. That takes us right next to the freeway." I pulled out my pencil and traced a faint, easily erasable line on the map.

"I am worried about this weather," Mouthy said suddenly. "We need to make sure we have everything we need and everyone. I mean, we need to know exactly who we are taking with us."

I felt myself flinch. I didn't want to think about it. It was one thing to decide to just take care of your own and let everyone else worry about themselves. It was different to pick and choose whom you were going to try to help. It left a bad taste in my mouth. I hated it. When I responded, my voice came out hoarse and low, sounding far more serious than I intended. It contained all the bitterness I felt.

"There is no way we can take everyone," I said. I was telling myself as well as them. "We don't know how many people are involved in the cult. We don't even know who will listen to us. Most of them will want to stay here—which is fine, because whoever takes over will want the manpower. Every cultist wants followers." I turned away from the map and looked at everyone present. "But I know that no matter what denomination they claim to be, I can't be a part of that. I have already shown my loyalty to the military. There is no choice for me. I am not saying we leave people here to get hurt. We have all seen the camp splitting. The cult will try to win people over. If they want to stay here, we let them. We need to figure out who we can trust and who it would be safe to bring with us. "

Vera said quietly, "Maybe I should stay." She looked like she was going to cry. "I am an old lady. I will slow you down. I have lived a long time."

I reached out and took her hands. I had to blink back tears. "Hey, don't you talk like that. We can't leave you behind. We need you. Being old doesn't mean being useless. Look at Grandpa. There isn't a better hunter, and he is teaching Jeri to be a great tracker. Harris can rebuild engines in his sleep. Alice needs someone to help her learn how to knit. You have forgotten more things about baking than I have ever learned."

She gave a weak smile.

"And how could I break Victor's heart and not bring his favorite nana?" I sighed as I looked around at the rest of the group. "I am not really sure how many people will even want to come with us," I said sadly.

Alice piped up in a small voice. "What do you mean?"

I shrugged. "My daddy used to say that fear is like a sickness—it will pass from one person to the next, and the only cure is reason. But folks make an awful lot of money from treating the symptoms."

Jeri looked confused. "How would you make money that way?"

Grandpa took over for me. "She means that when folks are scared, they turn stupid and will buy whatever snake oil someone is peddling."

As I nodded, Albert stepped forward. "And after that raid," he said, "there are a lot of scared people out there. Right now the illusion of order is holding, but it won't take much for it to crack."

Alice looked at him. "What do you mean, illusion?"

I tried to explain. "Why does everyone listen to Lieutenant Roberts?"

Sunshine answered from the back of the room. "Because he is the highest-ranking officer here?"

I nodded. "That is why the soldiers listen to him. But why do any of the civilians? What authority does he really have here?"

Sunshine grinned, as if this was too easy. "He has the US government authority and the might of the US Army to back him up. Right now he has the only authority."

Sunshine, Keyan, and Mouthy all gave a grunt in unison. Yay for solidarity.

"What you mean is, he has guns and manpower. Right now there is no government. There is no president, no Congress, no Bill of Rights, no police, judge, or prison. None of that is here right now."

Sunshine wasn't smiling now.

"The reason police and the military wear uniforms is because it creates the illusion of unity. It is a show of force. And the only true authority is force." I tried to think of a better example. "Classrooms full of normal kids are good. The teacher tells them all to sit in their seats and be quiet until she comes back. How long will it be before someone starts talking? Once the first kid starts, how long till others follow suit? A leader's authority has only as much power as it is given by those who follow that leader. What would happen if someone walked up to the gates and said, 'I am a general with three times the men and resources this lieutenant has. Now, come with me'? Who would stay behind? Seriously, would you hesitate to go with him? Are the rest of you so loyal to the lieutenant? Or would you go to the person who has the means to protect you?"

There were a couple of small sighs and some downcast eyes. I continued speaking.

"I wouldn't really have a problem with someone coming up and taking over. To me it is not about who is in charge. However, the man who is coming isn't trying to lead us. He is coming to convert us. He wants followers. He wants disciples, and he is using fear to sell the new cure-all savior. People will buy anything if they think it will save them. The glass man is coming with his shiny bottle of instant salvation. We need to be ready to leave when people start buying."

Mouthy seemed lost in thought. "Even if we're fully armed, there are only thirty of us. If he has any weapons at all, we are looking at a rough fight if he comes up here hot."

I looked around. People were starting to nod.

"We need people to start moving their go bags to the meeting spot," I said. "Also, let's get our list together of who all is coming." I went to the whiteboard and wrote down our names.

We then spent the next few hours putting names up and taking them down. At the end we had our list and our plan.

the night of the radio transmission, 8:35pm

THAT NIGHT, after I finished putting the kids to bed, I found Albert going over the list of missing supplies, yet again. The light was getting dim. He was deep inside his own mind, figuring things. I loved how brilliant he was. He could always see so far ahead. I never had to worry. I knew that I didn't see things the way others did. I had always loved that because it meant I knew things they didn't. However, like Mouthy had said, I missed things that were obvious to others. Albert covered those blind spots for me. I trusted him.

"So you talked to Keyan Mikoto about looking after me and the kids if you die?" I said in a casual way as I poured myself some coffee.

He froze for a second and looked up as I put in sugar and powdered creamer. He sighed and went back to writing in his notebook. "Yes," he finally said. Albert never lied. Not ever.

"Hmm, well, I guess he is an OK choice. However, shouldn't the stepdad be fun? I think Sunshine would be way better for the kids. Zyada just adores him. She would be calling him Daddy in no time. Also, with his sexual preferences, it could be a lot more fun for me too." I knew that was mean, but fair was fair. I did get a small degree of satisfaction when Albert's hand clenched. I decided to twist the knife a little just to remind him that rational thinking came with a cost. "I mean, there are several promising candidates. It really depends on the criteria we are going with," I said in a flippant voice as I licked the spoon clean.

He took a deep breath and set down his pencil. "I get it. You're angry. I thought about talking to you first, but I knew you would just worry. I also thought that it might change the way you behaved around them. I just needed to make sure you and the kids had options. And those three were the best candidates."

I nearly choked on my coffee. I had thought he'd talked to only Keyan. "*Three*! What were you doing, *shopping*? Which three?" My voice was much louder than I meant it to be.

He flinched when he realized I hadn't known about the others. "Shit. Just Mikoto, Sunshine, and Mouthy." He held up his hands in a placating motion. "I am sorry. I just needed to know that if anything happened to me, someone would protect you and the kids."

I glared at him and slapped the spoon down on the counter. "Fucking humiliating!" I hissed. I moved forward to punch him a couple of times in the shoulder. He winced but took it without comment before wrapping his arms around me.

"Marlene, we have known each other for over twenty years. You know I am not going to give up, but I know you too. If something happened to me, you would take a long time to move on. You would push people away because of my memory. With the world the way it is now, neither you nor the kids can afford for you to be without someone who can protect you." He took my face in his hands and put a kiss on my forehead. "I know you love me and will always love me. I love you. I want to know you will be safe and happy. So yes, it was high-handed and even primitive for me to go discuss this with other men. But even you have said that we are facing a primitive time. I would have asked you, but you would have gotten angry and refused. So I asked them not to say anything."

He hugged me tight. "Sunshine and Mikoto are marines. I wasn't asking them to marry you, just look after you either way. Mouthy is married and has like six kids. He agreed to look after you anyway because he has like four sisters."

I groaned and shook my head. "Jerk ... such a stubborn asshole."

He laughed at my irritation and stroked my head. "A stubborn asshole, yes, but a jealous idiot, I am not. I will do whatever it takes to protect my family. I would die for you and the kids, but physically, I am not able to protect you. Those marines can, and will be able to protect you better than almost anyone." He sighed softly. "Doesn't mean I like it or want it. I would hate the way Mikoto looks at you if it didn't mean he would protect you." He nuzzled my neck as he squeezed me tight and then nibbled my ear.

I wasn't fooled. I knew he was trying to distract me. It was working, but at least I knew. "You are just trying to distract me from what you did. You know I love you, right? And that I don't want to lose you?"

He nodded against my neck, where he continued to put little kisses.

"So mean ... this is serious," I said, a little breathless.

He whispered low, "So am I, Marlene. I used to have nightmares about when I was in the navy." His fingers were digging through my hair, tangling it up and twisting it around. He buried his face and nose in the strands, breathing deep and rubbing his cheek on it. "Now all my nightmares ... have your face. I can't let you or Zyada ... Nathan ... or Victor ..." He suddenly clenched tight down onto me, his whole body tight with pain and fear of whatever horror he imagined.

I tightened my arms around him and sighed. "OK ... I promise. You hear me? I promise. Whatever it takes to keep them safe, I will make sure we are protected." I wasn't sure if he could hear me, so I held him tight and put kisses on his shoulder, his neck, anywhere I could reach since he was still holding my head by the hair. I rubbed his back and rocked back and forth, bringing him along with me, swaying us as I hummed one of our favorite songs. I sang it softly to him. I made it to the chorus before he started singing it with me, coming back from wherever the darkness had pulled him. He smiled at me and went back to kissing me.

I kind of hated the fact that it was true, this horrible crisis, this terrible place, the world falling apart. Yet somehow Albert had never been so confident. I wondered if this was what he had been like before the navy took his hip, before it broke his back and showed him something that scarred his soul. He was a wonderful husband and father. If he had an anxiety attack like this before the solar storms, he would have withdrawn and gotten lost in his computer and notebooks for the rest of the night. He recovered so much faster now.

I smiled and danced slowly with him in the quiet kitchen as we sang our song. We cuddled and spent time together in the warmth by the embers of the fire. We climbed into bed, and he fell asleep quickly. I checked my watch. It was only ten. It seemed so late. The winter nights came early and stayed longer. I watched the moon-cast shadows dance across the ground. Back and forth they danced, twisting and swaying in different directions.

The next day was cold. The sun was out, and it made the frost that had formed on everything sparkle with frozen diamonds. The wind was bitter and cut through my clothes to my bones beneath. Mikoto kept a lookout somewhere out of sight. Ethan and John were searching the buildings across the street. We were at a small shopping center between neighborhoods. It was just a group of small shops, but it was enough. I finally managed to crowbar the dry cleaner's door open. No one had bothered this place yet.

Michael was helping out today. Once the door was open, he

asked, "Why are we here? There isn't going to be food in a dry cleaner's."

"We aren't looking for food. We will look in the other stores for food. We are looking for clothes and blankets. The babies need warmer wraps. But honestly, I am surprised this place didn't go up like a torch."

As we dug through all the different shelves, Michael laughed. "Did people really wear this stuff?"

I grinned and shrugged from where I was looking at dozens of prom dresses. "They must have, right? Can you imagine? What do you even wear a tangerine strapless poofy dress to? It must be a wedding." I smiled, but there was something sad about all this. No one was ever going to come pick up this dress. Had they already gone to the wedding? I looked around at all the clothes hanging in their little plastic coverings, snippets of people's lives, all diligently waiting for someone who was never going to come and get them. I made it to the coats and pulled anything thick and heavy or made of wool.

I gave a crow of victory at what I found in the far back. "Oh, wow! People still have them!" I pulled out a couple of puffy brown hangers.

Michael had his arms full of smaller bags. "This looks like baby stuff—blankets and even some snow gear. What is that?"

I grinned at him. "If we are lucky, it's genuine fur. Even if it's fake fur, it makes a nice lining. But real fur would be awesome."

We went back outside, put the clothes into the wagon, and went to see what the boys had found. The little veterinary clinic had been ransacked, with all the drugs taken. Thankfully, all the pens and kennels were hanging open. I was relieved. Walking in to see a bunch of dead animals would not have made this a good day for me. I found a good harness and leash in the reception area. I pulled out bags and cans of dog food. Lucky wagged his tail furiously as I collected tennis balls and treats. Grinning, I tossed one of the tennis balls down the street, and Lucky tore off after it at full speed.

Ethan and John soon took over playing fetch with Lucky as we checked the last few places. The corner store was a mess. It looked like a fight had broken out. Things were scattered all over the floor. We carefully sifted through the debris and found cans of beans and corn, chips, and other things that didn't go bad. Most of what was left was either junk food or power bars. We gathered up water bottles and the cans of juice that were scattered. I burst out laughing when I spotted what had fallen into the pile of car accessories. I went to gather them all up. The bright yellow sponge-like quality remained unchanged. Oh yes, boys and girls. I had found Twinkies, a dozen little gold bars of joy. I hid them away and searched around in the fallen shelving for more. I found those chocolate cupcakes and some other preserved junk food and filled my bag. It was there between cheese poofs and high-fructose corn syrup–filled baked goods that I saw the polished brown wooden handle. The metal had a dark gray dull gleam. Someone must have lost it in a fight. I casually picked it up and slipped it into the pocket of Mikoto's coat. It was an old-fashioned six-shot revolver. I kept looking around and found a small box of ammo, which I put in the other pocket. Then I hit pay dirt and grinned wide. "I should buy a lotto ticket!" I cheered as I started pulling up what had fallen from the storage area above.

Ethan laughed and called back, "A dollar and a dream, right? What did you win?"

I popped up from behind the register area like a jack-in-the-box. "What every road trip needs! Smokes, jerky, and booze!"

I hoisted up a couple of those weird clear plastic boxes that used to sit up on display next to the register. One was full of little bottles of booze. The other was full of big slabs of different flavors of jerky. I also found the refill stock cartons of smokes. There were even chocolate bars and candies. We found a display that had a bunch of kid toys, so we took those too. We also took every roll of toilet paper.

"Looks like Christmas came early, huh?" John laughed as he helped me load the wagon outside.

Back inside, I spotted a back-to-school display. It had stacks of spiral notebooks and boxes of pencils. I grabbed a bunch and shoved them into a backpack. I took pens and superglue I found in another section. I found some boxes of matches and took those too. The mess from the fight had hidden many of the more important things. We found some cold medicine and even some aspirin. I took all the tampons and condoms from the personal aisle as well. There were a lot of things that both could be used for, believe it or not. Lucky was happily watching over the wagon. He was getting too big to ride in it now. He was filling out so quickly. He wagged his tail at me as I came out and knelt down to love up on him. He licked my face happily and pressed against me, almost knocking me over.

"Well, we got almost everything on the list. We did really well. I am surprised it went so smoothly. I was really worried," I said quietly and stood up. "It's about that time. We should—"

Caw! Caw! Caw! Flap, flap.

The air was suddenly filled with screeching black creatures bursting away from the bare limbs of winter trees and over the rooftops. They swirled into a black vortex toward the sky and screeched their protests as they flew away. The wind that chased them was so cold it took my breath away. I hadn't learned how to breathe in the winter yet. I could never manage to suck in any air. I always had to tuck my face down into my coat. This could make it hard to see, but since the cold wind hurt my eyes, I guessed it didn't matter. I watched the birds as an ominous feeling slinked through me. They shifted around randomly, swirling and moving in massive clouds of black feathers. When the massacre of crows disappeared from view, I looked at the others.

"Let's get back," I said, my voice serious and quiet. I didn't want to find out what they were running from.

The following day, the only sound inside the dim library was that of my own movements mutedly echoing back at me. I hid the supplies behind the bookshelves, in the storage bins, and shifted the wooden bookcases back into place. The air was cool against my skin but stagnant and stale. Dust drifted and collected on every surface. I wiped my face as I diligently put books back on the shelves. Streams of weak silvery-gray light filtered through the windows on the western side of the building, but the books and shelves soaked up what little light came through. Everyone else had left about an hour ago—well, almost everyone. He never really left me alone, my shadow, Keyan Mikoto. He was currently putting countermeasures in place to make sure that if anyone came looking for what we had hidden here, they wouldn't find it.

I kept out a couple of the little bottles of booze and some of the jerky. I had to figure out a way to talk to him and sort this out. We didn't have time for this, whatever this was between us. This emotional quicksand made it hard for me to focus. When I was finished, I took my peace offering and headed over to where he sat. He was relaxed in a reclining chair, reading something from the mystery section. Lucky was lying down on a big couch section. I fought the urge to get him down. Keyan was in full battle dress, but his lips were turned up softly as he read.

"Jeez, you don't fight fair at all, do you?" my mouth blurted before my brain could stop it.

"No. Do you?" he replied. His deep voice rumbled in the quiet space.

I shrugged and sighed. "No, I guess not." I sat down in a chair across from him, and started chewing on the jerky as I looked around at all the books. I smirked a bit, thinking about all those people who had claimed e-books would take over and ruin libraries. Here we were, surrounded by the greatest achievement of humankind, the written word. Books were the very essence of creation. Inside a book was a whole world unto itself, filled with heroes, villains, survivors, and victims. The good, the bad, and everything in between truth and lies—it was all right here on these shelves.

"Someday, we are going to get the lights back. They will get the cars and machines operating, and all this will be back up and running. People will come back and start checking out books again. But I wonder if it will really be the same." My voice sounded small.

He closed the book and slid it into a pouch as he stood up. "No, not the same." He walked toward me. I felt again the strange tension in my limbs that told me to run. The pull of him made it hard to tell if I should run toward him or away.

On a side topic, I loved the zoo but hated it too. I always wanted to see the animals, but it broke my heart to see them in cages. I once watched a panther walk from inside his cave out to the fence where we were standing. "Walk" was the wrong word. He moved slowly and easily, almost lazily, but you could see all the power and grace he didn't need flowing with every ripple. He strolled up to the fence and looked at us. Then the panther rubbed himself along the fence before finding a sunny spot in which to bathe. That was how Keyan walked, lazy and slow, with grace and power. Even when he was wearing all his gear and equipment, it looked like he flowed across the floor.

"It must be a crime. And if it's not, it should be." Once again, my mouth had decided it was going to speak without a filter today.

He raised one eyebrow slightly as he reached out and took the beef jerky I had been eating. "What?" He put the jerky in his mouth.

I was trying to think of how to explain when my mouth took

care of it for me. "The way you move. It should be a crime." The blush that crept up my face and neck still hurt but not as much as before. *What the hell was that, mouth? Bad pickup line. Ugh.* My brain panicked as it scrambled for some way to recover.

He suddenly looked away from me and put the back of his hand to his mouth, as if wiping something away. But I saw it: he was grinning.

My mischievous nature began to take hold more firmly. "Like harassment in the third degree. Or maybe it would be a moving violation. They could give you a ticket for creating a health hazard because women keep having heart attacks." I pretended to give it more thought. "I suppose if they did make it a crime, then stop and frisk would suddenly take on a totally different meaning. I bet there would be more female officers." I grinned as he started to chuckle. I summoned my best serious chick-cop voice. "Freeze! Now assume the position!" I laughed at the absurd conversation.

He laughed and sat down on the table next to me. "You are so …" He seemed almost at a loss for a moment before he reached over to tuck some of my hair behind my ear. "Strange."

I smirked. "Oh yeah, that's just what every girl wants to hear."

He shrugged. "I like strange."

I nodded. "I know … Look, I am just trying to sort it all out for now. We need to figure out how to work together. It would help if you talked to me. I want to trust you, but I don't know anything about you at all."

He looked at me and took another bite of jerky. "My mother is from Nebraska. She is part of the Santee Sioux tribe. My father is Japanese. His family comes from Okinawa. They were relocated to the camps in Wyoming during World War II. After their release they settled near in Nebraska. My folks met as teenagers there."

He shifted around till he could lift his shirt and show me a tattoo on his chest. It was a strangely drawn turtle in black ink. It almost looked like a Hawaiian-style tribal tattoo, but not exactly. "Keyan … means turtle. My middle name is Eddie."

I sat there for a moment in silence as we went back to eating jerky. I had expected it to be much harder to get him to talk about himself. I hadn't expected him to tell me about his family. "My middle name is Mae," I said. "My mother named me Marlene after my great-grandma." I smiled a bit and shrugged. "After I was born, she picked Mae as the middle name. I think I would have preferred something like Turtle. Zyada means 'a shining happy person.' Victor means 'he who wins.' I figured those were pretty good names."

He nodded, and we fell back into companionable silence for a few minutes.

"Turtle, huh?"

He shrugged and sighed. "Not exactly cool, is it? But it could have been worse."

I snickered as things popped into my head. "Like Squirrel?" I tried to stop my laughter but failed.

He gave a smirk and rolled his eyes. "I had a cousin named Squirrel. It's not like you have any room to talk, Marlene Mae Mouse."

I laughed. "Mice are awesome! However, I guess I can see the turtle thing. You have a hard shell and all." I reached up and ruffled his hair. The look of surprise on his face was priceless.

I grinned as I picked up my stuff. "Come on, Turtle. It's time to get back."

He tilted his head and looked curiously at me. "Just like that? No more fear?"

I shrugged. "It only takes the light of a single candle to dispel the darkness, or something like that. I was never afraid of you hurting me. I just couldn't figure you out. People fear what they don't know. Now you have a family, a mother and father, a home. Now you're a person. I can connect to a person."

He frowned, looking a little offended. "I was always a person."

I slung my backpack on. "True, but you were a mystery to me.

It's like a roadrunner meeting a hawk. They might both be birds, but that doesn't mean they understand each other."

He stood up slowly. "Should I be offended? Just because my mother is Sioux doesn't mean you should use those kinds of analogies."

I drew a blank and scratched my head for a second. "What do you mean, those kinds of analogies? What kind?"

He frowned as if I were teasing him. "Animal analogies. The roadrunner and the hawk."

I frowned as I thought about that. "I guess I didn't think about it. Though to be fair, just because someone says something about hawks doesn't mean it has anything to do with Native Americans. I guess I could use Roadrunners and chickens for the analogy. Jeez. What if I talked about rattlesnakes and jackrabbits? Up here people talk about bullfrogs and deer. Back home there were so many roadrunners, they should have been my state's bird. I don't understand why they picked the mockingbird."

He gave me a weird look. "Where are you from?"

I laughed out loud. "Sorry, I thought you knew. I am from El Paso, Texas."

He frowned even more. "Is that a desert?"

I knew my smile must have practically glowed with pride. "Yeah, it's in the Chihuahuan Desert."

He nodded and smiled. "You are from Texas. No wonder you seem so crazy."

I stuck my tongue out. "What's the state bird of Nebraska?"

"No idea. I was born and raised in California. My folks moved to Laguna Beach just before I was born. I am a surfer. We would visit relatives in Japan every other summer, though." He grinned and tossed the last bite of jerky to Lucky. He smirked at me. "Though this does explain why you are such a country hick. Do you miss your cowboy hat?"

I glared at him but didn't deny it. I did miss my hat.

twenty-six
the day of the storm, 4:27pm

HAVE you ever wondered if you could make God laugh? Don't worry, I have it on good authority that whenever you make plans, God chuckles. Grandma said that is why plans go off-course, because God is looking for a laugh. God must think I am fucking hilarious.

I have often said that being prepared would save my family. Closer to the truth was that you should prepare for your plans to fail. Trust me, make all the plans you want. Have as many backup plans as you like, but the world would still find a way to ruin them. People had all kinds of plans when the solar storm hit. However, when the radiation from the sun slapped like giant galactic waves against our poor blue marble, none of those plans mattered anymore. Plans didn't matter because you never know where you will be when disaster strikes. If my family and I had been at home when the storm hit, we would have died, either in the fire or in the following chaos. We had gone up to the Adirondack Mountains to camp for a fishing trip. It was just a bit of dumb luck that we were shielded by the mountain.

So let that be the lesson. Make your plans, and prepare for as much as you can, but understand that when you are standing there staring at the tidal wave of an oncoming disaster, you can't cling to plans as a lifeline. They will not save you. Be prepared to flow and change with the current. This was something I had almost forgotten. I was so confident in my plan. I thought I was so clever. For the second time, it wasn't the plan that saved us, but just a bit of dumb luck.

Keyan and I were walking back together. Lucky was running ahead slightly, playing in the falling snow. I had just asked him what Laguna Hills was like. He was telling me about his surf club. It wasn't as hard as you might think to picture him as a surfer. I tried to picture him on a sunny beach, looking out at the crashing ocean waves with his intense stare. I felt heat rising up my cheeks and felt embarrassed and shy.

I turned my eyes away from him to regain my composure. I looked at the darkened knots and gnarls of the winter trees. The shadows of the early winter evening were thick now, heavy in the weakening sunlight. The orange light danced against the low grim curtain of storm clouds above us. As we passed one of the empty houses, I looked out at the valley below through a small break in the tree line. Snow had accumulated, covering the ground in a white blanket. I blinked as the light played tricks on me. I stopped walking and rubbed my eyes. As I looked again, dread crept up my chest. It looked like something was writhing, shifting, and throbbing just down the hill. I flashed back to the fireman, his skin throbbing and pulsing from whatever was crawling inside.

"What is that?" I whispered, the fear circling around my heart. I felt a hand on my wrist and gasped out loud.

Keyan pulled me toward him, making me look at him. "Get the others. It's started." He pushed me down the road. "They are here. They may be past the gates."

The realization of what I had seen filled me with terror. Those were people sneaking up the hill, hundreds of them. They wore brown and were being covered in snow, and they were climbing. I took off running as fast as I could. Lucky was hot on my heels. Seeming to sense that something was wrong, he ran along silently.

I should have thought a little better about where I was going, but the first place I went was home. I burst in the front door, out of breath and panting. I could feel my heartbeat in my face. It throbbed with a dull ache. Fear made it easy to ignore. I called names, but no one answered, and the house was dark. There was a note on the table from Albert: "We are with Mouthy and Sunshine, putting together some equipment. Come when you can."

I ran in and grabbed the go bags, along with the shotgun and ammo. I shoved all of it into the wagon with the supplies we had set up for escape. I pulled it along behind me toward the campus as fast as I could. The snow had started up now. Big fat flakes fell lazily around me. I made sure my coat was zipped and my gloves were on. As I approached the campus, I pulled my wagon into the graveyard. I hid supplies in the old mausoleum, covering them quickly. I used a tree branch to hide my snow tracks in and out of the graveyard. What disturbance I left disappeared quickly with the snow. I ran back towards the campus as the desperate silence seemed to oppress the last rays of daylight.

The construction teams had been hard at work finishing the new fence around the main camp. It was only about three feet high, but it went around the natural slopes of the campus. It formed a circle around the main buildings, generator and radio tower. Which meant I couldn't cut through the tree line and down the walk anymore. I had to go all the way around to the main road and pass through the gate.

As I jogged up, I realized the little guard house at the gate was unmanned. I slowed down and sucked in cold air as I tried to look calm and composed. There was something very wrong with this scene. None of the gates were ever supposed to be unmanned. Lucky stayed close to me. He was hunched as we walked forward.

I moved slowly toward the little guard house. My hackles raised, and I heard Lucky growl. My heart tripped painfully in my chest. The movie theater inside my head played an eerie piano tune. The version of me that was seated in the theater screamed at the screen: "Don't! You need to be *running*! Don't look!" But just like every character in every horror movie ever made, I moved forward and looked. When I couldn't get my feet to bring me any closer, I leaned. I didn't see the body, just the blood that oozed out of the open doorway. It was dark and thick as it froze. My heart pounded against my ribcage, and I felt tears prick my eyes. I thought of Davis and Fredricks. *Please be someone else. Please be someone else.*

Horrible, right? I didn't wish anyone to be dead, but I couldn't stop the thought that I just didn't want it to be one of my friends, someone I knew. Selfish, cruel, horrible. But true. I desperately wanted it to be the face of a stranger. But now I had to know. I took one step after another until I had a clear view into the guard hut. I almost choked out a scream when I saw that it was Private Thomas Brown. His face was turned toward the door. His neck was sliced deep, and his eyes were glazed over. His lips were blue and his face gray. I had spoken to him only once or twice. He was from Florida or someplace like that. Thomas had been nineteen. All he had talked about was his mother. Tears burned and stung as they spilled out of my eyes. I moved away trying to swallow my sobs. I put my hands gently against my swollen cheeks and wiped away the tears. The wetness was making my skin sting. I looked around and didn't see anyone. I needed to sound the alarm. The urge to get to Albert and the kids was almost overwhelming, but the alarm had to come first. Thomas's walkie-talkie was gone, as were his weapons and ammo.

I moved as quietly as I could down the side path, up and around the service entrance, to where the prisoner was being held. I knew the generator was still running because the lights were still on. I peeked in the window, and to my relief I saw Davis and Fredricks playing cards at a table. I quickly opened the door and stepped in. Lucky ran inside and did a quick run around the room before starting to pace. I must have looked as terrified as I felt because the second they saw me, they were on their feet.

"What's wrong?" Davis said as he moved over to me. Fredricks grabbed his gun and looked out the window.

I gasped for breath as I tried to speak. "They are here ... the gate ... they killed Private Brown!" I clenched my fists against my stomach and sucked in air, forcing the panic down.

Davis grabbed his walkie-talkie to radio in, but I held up my hand. "Be careful," I warned. "They already have Brown's radio. They had infiltrators."

Davis nodded. "Hey there, Tower. This is Davis on patrol on the eastern edge. Checking in with all's well."

A man's voice came over the line. "Roger, Davis. This is Tower. Please return to main station and report in."

Davis and Fredricks looked at each other, and then Davis picked up the line again. "Hey, Tower, did Brown already beat us back?"

Again the mystery man's voice came over the line. "That is an affirmative. Brown has reported in and is already having some chow."

Fear ran along my spine as I looked out the window. Fredricks gathered his stuff, his expression dark. Davis killed the lights. We stood there in the dark for a minute.

Davis spoke with a calm that helped me focus. "OK. I don't see anyone approaching. The lieutenant kept it need to know about the prisoner. Maybe they don't know anyone is here. We keep it that way. We need to alert security that an attack is underway. They have the radio, which means the generator is already theirs."

I rubbed my neck, it was aching terribly. "It's too bad all the speakers blew on the PA machine. We need something that everyone can hear at once." I tried to think of something the invaders wouldn't have thought of yet. I remembered how the Saxons used to ring church bells whenever seafaring invaders were coming. "I wonder if the church bells still work. It's a pretty old-looking church. What do you guys think?"

Davis seemed to give it a thought. "It's better than nothing. We should go and ring the bells. Hey, Marcus, where did you put those bottle rockets that we confiscated from the teens?"

Fredricks grinned. "I kept them in the backpack. Otherwise, the sergeant would have found them during inspection."

Davis nodded. "OK. So we ring the bells and shoot off the bottle rockets. That should be enough to alert people that something is wrong. Then what?" Davis looked at Fredricks and then me. Fredricks responded after half a heartbeat. "We should mount a counteroffensive. Help take back the radio while civilians evacuate. That means finding a couple of our fighters, maybe some of the other patrols or off-duties."

I looked at them. "Some of us have set up a rally point off-base."

Fredricks nodded and checked the ammo for all of us. I still had ammo and the little snub revolver in my pockets, along with the shotgun. Davis gave me his lighter. Fredricks gave me three bottle rockets.

"You go to the church, ring the bells, and shoot these off," said Fredricks. "Then you start your escape and go to that rally point. Don't come back until you hear an all clear over the walkies. Code word snickerdoodles. We are going to gather up a few more people and see what we can do about a counteroffensive."

Davis gave Fredricks a confused look. "Snickerdoodles?"

Fredricks nodded and smiled. "It's my safe word."

I gave a little nod, grateful that someone else had a plan. "I will set off the rockets and bells and go meet up with Albert and the kids. Are you sure you will be all right? We saw a bunch of people coming up the hill. It looks like a full-fledged invasion."

Davis smiled and patted me on the head. "Hey, it's our job. We have to keep you guys safe. We defend this country, and the people are this country, right?"

I nodded, even though we both knew that was not really how it worked.

Both Davis and Fredricks took a turn asking me questions. It took me a minute to realize what they were doing. They were keeping me calm and making sure I could handle the task. I felt like a little kid. It was weird since both of these guys were younger than me. It did make me feel better. Davis took something out of a locker. It was a flak vest. He strapped it on me underneath my coat. It was super heavy and pinched me in places I didn't like.

"Keep it on, no matter what," he said, slow and calm. However, something in the back of his voice sounded strained. It scared me. I nodded.

"Let's move," Davis said to Fredricks.

They nodded at each other and quickly exited out the door. I stood in the dark and felt like I had grown roots. My heart thudded against my ribs. I wanted to cry. Suddenly, I heard a sound. I looked around and realized the prisoner Matt was pounding on the cell door, in the dark. I grabbed the key off the wall and without thinking opened the door. He must have been surprised because he nearly jumped out of his own skin.

He looked at me with wide eyes and whispered, "What's happening?"

I held up a hand. "The camp is about to be overrun. The attack could break out any second. You should go and hide. When it's over, you can try to join them if they don't seem too crazy for you."

I undid his leg cuff. His hand clamped down on my shoulder like a vice, and I froze. Fear clogged my heart, and with my free hand I reached into my pocket where I had the gun. I looked up at his face. His eyes were so wide with fright that I could see their whites, but behind that there was confusion, hope, and no small amount of desperation.

"Why?" he choked out. "Why would you risk letting me go? I could betray you and even hurt you. My friend tried to rape and kill you. Why wouldn't you just leave me here?" He shook me a bit as he demanded answers.

"You're right. All those things, you could do. I'm hoping you won't. I don't know what you will do. The only thing I do know is that dehydration, starvation, and hypothermia would all be really awful ways to die. If I left you here, it might be days before anyone checked this building. If the snow is really heavy, it could be even longer." I looked at him seriously. "Whatever you have done, whatever you may do in the future, that's between you and your soul. I couldn't live with being the one to sentence you to a death like that."

We stared at each other for a long moment. He didn't seem so scary now, just a guy who was as lost as the rest of us. I took my hand off the gun and patted his hand on my shoulder. He jerked away as if I had burned him.

"Well, that's the dumbest naïve bull-crap I have ever heard." he said finally in an annoyed tone.

I stood up and nodded. "Yes, but I guess I am just not quite ready to give up on humanity. So be grateful and keep yourself safe. The people taking over are religious nuts, so if you choose to stick around, be careful." I turned and started toward the door.

He moved quickly and reached the door at the same time I did. "How about I go with you?" he said suddenly.

"What?"

He must have heard the surprise in my voice, because he spoke quickly. "Look, I don't expect you to trust me, but seriously, I can't join a cult, and the military will put me back in the prison. All I want is to stay alive and not be a captive. I will do whatever I have to."

"Fine, let's move," I whispered as I opened the door. I knew it was a bad idea, but sometimes you just had to make the best of it with what you've got. To tell the truth, I was terrified and didn't want to go out there alone.

We moved out into the dark night. I didn't use a flashlight.

The heavy snow clouds made the light from the moon disappear. The white snow made what little light there was glow. I was able to lead us to the church. The air was heavy and still as huge flakes fell in big clumps. The snow was falling so fast that it was already up to above my ankles.

We swept into the church quickly. At some point there might have been a way to ring the church's bell from the ground floor, but that was gone. We had to climb up three flights of rickety stairs and then up a ladder to get into the bell tower. The air was cold as we pushed open the small trap door and made it to the bell. The wind whipped shards of ice and globs of snow at us. Lucky waited down below, unhappy and whining. I shivered as we tried to figure out how to ring the bell. It had a strange lever system.

Matt grabbed the handle and nodded. "OK, I'll ring the bell. You set off those fireworks."

I pulled the Zippo from my pocket and got the bottle rockets out. I flipped open the metal case of the Zippo and got the first rocket pointed out toward the campus and the courtyard. I ran my thumb over the flint on the Zippo, and just as advertised, a little flame illuminated us in the wind. I put a hand up to protect the tiny flame and lit the fuse. It flared and sizzled as it burned up toward the bottom of the rocket.

If you have ever set off a bottle rocket before, then you know the next part of the story. Fireworks were strictly regulated and harshly punished in West Texas due to the high risk of fire. Because of that, I had never actually used a bottle rocket before. I had no idea that the reason these fun little firecrackers were called bottle rockets was because you needed to place them in something nonflammable, such as a bottle or can, before lighting them.

So no shit, there I was, holding the long stick end of a lit bottle rocket. I screamed in surprise as superhot sparks and fire shot out the bottom toward my face and hands. I managed to hold the rocket steady until it went screeching off into the night sky to explode with a flash of light and a loud crack that echoed in the sky. I had fallen on my ass at some point. I screamed as I frantically tried to put out the hot little embers that were burning my outer layers. Matt was laughing so hard that he almost couldn't ring the bell.

"Fuck you!" I shouted at him, breathless and freaked out. He was laughing too hard to speak. Hysterical laughter burst out of me as I finished putting my clothes out. Looking back, it was not really funny, but at that moment the adrenaline made everything sharp and edgy. I caught my breath and stood back up. I looked around and spotted a cigarette butt can. I used the can to hold the rocket end of the next bottle rocket and set it off far away from my face. Matt kept ringing the bell as I got the last rocket off. We heard shouts and muffled gunfire in the distance.

"We need to get the hell away from here," Matt said as he scrambled down the ladder.

I followed behind him as quickly as I was able. He paused at the bottom of the ladder to help me down. We both took off at a run out of the church. The wind had picked up. The big globby flakes had been replaced by tiny balls falling and swirling madly through the air. The snow crunched under my boots as we crossed the campus. Matt followed me as I chose my steps more from memory than from sight. I heard shouts in strange echoes off the buildings, but they were muffled because of the snow. I could hear my panting. Steam billowed out of my mouth and nose, as if I were a human locomotive. Lucky was just ahead of me and seemed to know exactly where we were going.

I saw an orange glow growing somewhere behind us. I realized that someone had set a fire. I could see white smoke rising up against the dark sky. I ran until we came to the side door of the supply office. As soon as we were inside, I shut the door behind us and pressed against it, trying to suck air. We took a moment to get our breathing under control. I strained my ears to hear if anyone was in supply with us. The sound of our breathing seemed impossibly loud.

"Fuck it. It's too late to move quietly. Let's just get there fast," I said, realizing there was no way to calm my breathing.

He nodded as he sucked in air just as raggedly. "Lead the way, boss lady," he said and then grabbed what looked like a pipe.

I nodded and headed to the supply office, where Albert's note had said they were working. We ran down the hall, and I hit a wall as I tried to make the sharp turn to the right. I got to the door and gave a frantic 'Shave and a haircut' knock. Two bits came back, and the door opened. We fell inside and shut the door behind Lucky. I was quickly hugged by my two smallest. I practically started crying right then and there.

Albert relocked the door quickly before looking at me concerned. "What is happening? Are you alright?"

I just squeezed Zyada and Victor tight and looked up at Sunshine and Albert. Before I answered I noticed someone was missing. I looked around the room and began to panic.

"Where is Nathan?" The worry and fear squeezing my throat made my voice squeak.

Albert moved closer to me and rested a hand on my shoulder. "Nathan is with Silas. They needed an extra set of hands. Don't worry he will be safe. What's happening?" He asked.

"The attack... It's started! Keyan told me to get everyone to the library. We spotted people climbing up the hill. Some are already in camp. I don't know where Keyan went. Where the hell is Mouthy?" Albert scowled as the words poured out of my mouth in a loud rush.

He turned away and quickly packed equipment and tools into a duffel bag as he spoke. "Radio central called all hands to report in person." He was doing that thing he does in a crisis, where he reverts to his naval training. His movements were filled with purpose and focus. The pain I had come to know in his face eased. Even his speech changed, the sentences were condensed and precise. I was always surprised at how much confidence it gave me when he did this. I was able to let go of the panic and get my children ready to move.

I noticed that Sunshine was putting on the last of his gear.

"Why didn't you go, Sunshine?" I asked.

The smile on his face was almost as frightening as the weapons he was loading. "I don't give a fuck. I take my orders from Sergeant Mikoto, and he said to protect your family. I will join Keyan when I get you all to a secure location." He seemed almost... excited.

Both Albert and Sunshine looked at Matt who was panting heavily against the wall beside me.

Sunshine looked at him with a deceptively pleasant smile. "You're the guy from the smokehouse. Boy, are you lucky. You should thank that little girl right there. I don't want to traumatize her. That is the only reason I am not putting two in you now." His voice remained happy and pleasant, but I saw the look in those cold blue eyes. He meant every word.

Sunshine looked at me and sighed. "You are way too soft." He grinned as he shook his head. "Then again, you have me, so I guess it's OK. I have absolutely no problem taking care of this. So, buddy, let us be crystal clear. You make even the smallest move like you might hurt or betray these folks here, and I will make you wish she had left you to starve in the prison cell. Got it?"

Matt nodded with a worried smile. "Got it. She's the boss. No problem."

Zyada let go of me and looked at Sunshine worriedly. "Where are you going?"

He smiled and patted her head. "I am going to make sure you and everyone else get out of here safely. So stay close to your daddy and mommy. Everything will be fine. We will meet you on the road."

I stood up, holding Victor's hand. Sunshine whispered to me, "I will meet with Keyan, and we will keep an eye on you guys as you head out to the library. Head that way and then continue with the escape. Don't look around, don't look back. Just go."

I nodded, and we all started out from the room, moving quickly down the hall.

Albert carried Victor, and I held Zyada's hand and kept her close to my body as we stepped out into the bitter wind. It blew hard, whipping little shards of ice and tiny razor flakes at us. It was hard to see, but the blaze of some of the buildings down the road gave us light. It was a strange red glow. The wind howled against my ears, bringing screams and gunshots. We headed toward the back walkway that led to the library, past the empty guard house and down the street. We saw shadows ahead and crouched down low in some underbrush. Dozens of men ran by holding firearms. They stormed the supply building, going in the door we had just left. I looked at Albert. He wore a grim expression. We stayed low and took back alleys and backyards till we got to the library. We snuck in quietly, barely making a sound. I heard whispers and looked around. I saw first Samara and then a few others. They were all sitting in the far back of the library, down low, so no movement could be seen from outside. I hurried over and found Nathan sitting between Silas and Jeri. He gave me a worried smile and a little wave as I knelt and hugged him tight. "Hi mom." He whispered as he hugged me back. I looked over Nathan's head to Grandpa Silas and Jeri. "Thank you." I said quietly. Jeri nodded but Silas waved it off.

I frowned as I looked around. "Not everyone is here," I said, keeping my voice low. We were missing not only Mouthy but also Old Man Harris and Ethan. Vera looked to be holding back tears.

"It's OK, Vera. I am sure Harris is on his way. He might be old, but we both know he is a tough old buzzard," I tried to use a soothing tone to reassure her. "Don't worry. I won't let us leave without him."

She grabbed my arm and shook her head. "We had a fight! What if he doesn't come because of me?"

I patted her back. Everyone looked a little shaken. I didn't want to leave until we had everyone. Suddenly, there was a weird sound out on the street, cutting through the howl of the wind. All eyes focused on the front of the library. I realized there was bright light streaming in the window from outside. I got up slowly and moved to peer out into the street. The snow was making the light stretch farther than it normally would. I realized there was a glow from campus. "They turned on all the lights," I said. "They must be running the generator full-force!"

Everyone moved to look out the window.

"I didn't realize we had so many working flood lights," I whispered.

Michael frowned. "Why would they turn on all the lights like that?"

Grandpa Silas cursed as he ducked low out of the light. "They are searching. They turned on the lights to help make sure they find everyone. They have a lot of people. If they start a full grid search, they will be able to cover this whole hill in no time. We can't afford to wait."

Vera shook her head. "No! I am not leaving without Harris. And Ethan isn't here either."

People started bickering, and I frowned as I looked out at the lights. "It won't work anyway."

Everyone fell silent at that.

"Those are serious lights. They were designed so that if we were under attack again, we could see into the ravines and the forest area. We won't be able to sneak out with those lights running."

I looked at Zyada and Victor sitting on a couch. They were looking at books with Alice and the baby. They couldn't move fast. None of us were fast enough. Fast, fast, fast. Man, I wished I had that Mustang from the valley; that thing could have flown us out of here. Hell, I would have settled for my little four-door economy car.

"A horse, a horse. My kingdom for a four-wheel drive," I grumbled at the window.

Jeri laughed, but it sounded more like a caustic snort. "What we need is a tank. Those people came here with guns. They aren't here to keep the peace. I saw them packing lots of rifles. They aren't playing around."

A tank. Where are we going to find a tank? I rested my chin on the windowsill. My eyes fell onto the cheery stained wood, which softly shone in the glow from outside. The delicate texture of the antique wood was visible because of the unusual light. I idly let my fingers trace along the grain until they came to a deep groove in the polished wood. It was like an old wound, long healed but forever scarred. Even the wood around it was stained darker. My finger slipped along this indent as my mind's eye flashed to a different scar, this time in steal.

That bullet scar...I had expected it to come back smudged, but the burn was set into the metal.

I thought about all those bullet scars in the side of the marines' equipment truck. The bullet hadn't gone through the metal, just dented it. The truck was armored. I frowned as I thought about it. *The key.* The key to the truck was under the gas pedal. I doubted anyone else had found it. They would see us and hear us, but they wouldn't be able to shoot us. We could outrun them. That sounded almost like a good idea.

However, I thought about the first time I had seen the truck, filled with bloody marines full of bullet holes. It was armored, but that didn't make it safe. The attackers would chase that truck forever. But if you wanted to sneak away from someplace, there was nothing like a big noisy distraction that everyone was chasing instead.

If this had happened a few months ago, what would I have done? I would have left without regrets. Now I couldn't leave the others here. It was my job to keep my children safe. More than that, my children needed a place. How could we have a place without people in it? We might be small, but we were a community. This was my tribe. I needed to protect all of that.

I clenched my fists and stood up. My voice filled the quiet library.

"I have a plan." I did *not* have a plan. I had most of an idea, at best.

"Don't worry. I know what to do." I had *no* idea what I was talking about.

I smiled and patted Vera on the shoulder. "It is going to be alright." I did not think it was going to be alright.

I nodded confidently. Really, convincing people to do things was all about confidence. If you acted as if you knew what you were doing, people would respond accordingly. But as Mouthy would say, between you, me and the crows, I was completely full of shit. I took off my backpack and helped them get the supplies out of the hiding place. "OK, folks, here is what's going to happen. I am going to create a big distraction. When I do, you guys follow the plan and make your way to the next point on the map. I will meet up with you there."

Albert grabbed my arm and whispered urgently, "What the hell are you doing?"

I smiled and touched his face. "I am making sure my family is safe." I leaned my forehead against his. "I need you to keep the kids safe, honey. I need you to help these people stay quiet and move carefully."

He frowned and shook his head. "What is your plan? What are you doing?"

I grinned and tried to reassure him. "The truck. I know where the key is. I am going to start it up and rig it to drive out of town. It will just plow over everything. They will think we are in that and chase it. That way, we can all escape easily."

He frowned and shook his head. "No way. That is a stupid plan. I won't let you. We should wait till Sunshine or Mikoto comes back, and we can have them do this. Or I will go."

I shook my head. "Hell no. For one, when was the last time you drove a stick shift. Your hip is already killing you. There is no way you could crouch and sneak in without being spotted. I know where the key is, and I know how to get in. We don't have time to wait for Mikoto or Sunshine." I smiled and held his face in my hands. "I love you. I am not going to do anything crazy. I can do this. If I couldn't, I wouldn't even try." I looked at him with a stern expression. "I can do this, Albert." See? It was all about presenting with confidence.

He sighed and shook his head. "I know you can. It's not about that."

I grinned. "Is this the whole 'you're the man and husband' thing, so you should go do the dangerous stuff?"

He glared at me. "Don't pull the equality of the sexes shit. I love you and don't want you doing something dangerous. I hate that you go out by yourself. I hate that you are in danger, and I can't protect you. You really think I am going to let you go off and do something like this?"

I glared back at him, my jaw tightening as I felt myself growing roots. I knew how stubborn I sounded and how it could work against me. I took a breath and tried to remain calm. "Albert, think of this rationally. We are a team; we do the jobs we are best suited for. The reason I go out isn't just because your hip and back won't let you. I am also really good at it. If not me, then who? Alice and Samara need to be here with their babies. Grandpa Silas? I know he could do it, but then who is going to lead everyone down the ravine. Maybe John or Jeri—they are young. Oh, but neither of them knows where the truck is parked or how to drive a stick."

He closed his eyes, grabbed me in a hug, and squeezed me tight, whispering fiercely, "I can't lose you."

I hugged him back just as tightly. "Never. You couldn't lose me if you tried." I kissed him. "I will be back before you know it. You need to keep them calm. Make sure they stay hidden until I give the signal. They are our family."

He gave me a nod. "Go. I will take care of this. Don't worry about us."

I stood on my tiptoes to give him a big kiss. John made a whistle sound, and Jeri laughed. The kids giggled because we didn't normally do more than hugs and little kisses in front of them. Nathan made a silly face and looked embarrassed. My heart raced for a moment, and I laughed. The fear was gone. I could do this.

I smiled and gave my children kisses and hugs. I even gave Nathan a kiss on the cheek. He tried to pretend he didn't like it but hugged me back. "OK, you little munchkins. I want you to stay here and help Daddy."

Zyada nodded and whispered, "Yes, Mommy."

Victor clutched his car in his hand and in his little man voice mimicked Zyada. "Yes, Mommy," he said as he touched Alice's baby's feet.

Nathan gave me a very grown-up look and nodded. "Be careful Mom."

I took a moment to watch them.

Grandpa Silas patted my shoulder. "I will make sure they get down the hill. Don't worry. They may as well be my own." He turned and looked at me with intense eyes. "You hear me? You understand?"

I smiled and nodded. He meant that if they were his own grandkids, then I was his daughter. I hugged him. "Don't worry. I am coming back."

In a gruff voice he huffed, "Of course ya are."

Michael walked up, looking as if he wanted to say something. I cut him off before he could speak. "Stay with Alice," I said. "She needs you. Make sure Albert doesn't push himself too hard."

He sighed and shook his head. "What did you do before all this?"

The question caught me so off-guard that I laughed out loud. "What?"

He grinned and shrugged. "I was thinking military nurse. But some thought maybe CIA or trans-dimensional time traveler."

I smiled at him as I moved toward the door. "The last real job I had before my daughter was born was as a pet care professional. I helped train and care for dogs and other animals. But I was a navy brat most of my life, and I did train to work as a nursing assistant. So you were kinda right."

He blinked. "Wow ... you are weird."

I nodded in agreement. "Yep. Totally bizarre. Besides, if I were a spy or a trans-dimensional time traveler, I wouldn't be able to tell you, right?" I winked and tapped the side of my nose.

The glow from the campus reflected off the snow and the night trees, giving the world strange shadows. Albert checked my gear. Then he showed me a compass and map before sticking them in my pocket. "Come home soon," he whispered fiercely before kissing me softly. His voice was rough. "Find those two and make sure they bring you back in one piece."

No more dawdling, I told myself. Time was running out. I looked at Lucky, who was waiting for me by the door. I looked at the new guy and gave his shoulder a shove. "You help carry supplies and don't give them any trouble. If you do, Grandpa will hang you upside down and gut you like a deer. You understand?"

Grandpa gave him a scary smile. Matt nodded quickly. "Yes, boss."

I screwed my courage in place, opened the door, and stepped out into the icy wind. The storm whipped the snow down, then blasted it up again. I pulled my scarf up and my hood down. Lucky followed close as we moved as swiftly as we could toward the glowing light.

i am in the middle of an attack during a blizzard. who fucking cares what time it is?!

THE AIR HURT TO BREATHE. Icy fingers kept trying to find ways into my clothes like some bizarre frozen pervert. When the wind blew hard enough, it found ways to sink right into my skin. I kept my nose down into my scarf. The snow was so rough that it hurt where it hit against me. Little crystal shards flew at my face. I kept my legs moving. My boots were a heavy double-lined pair from last Christmas. They were warm, but they were heavy. I couldn't move fast, but they gave me steady footing.

I made good time to the edge of the light. I slowed down and went around to the far end of the fence. The ground was even there. I didn't have to worry about the snow hiding ditches or holes. I decided to slip through the science buildings because they were not in use. They had suffered major fire damage from the storms. The other end of the science buildings let out at a service exit by the gymnasium. This put me in sight of the door to the supply area. I saw people gathered in the quad. Even with the shelter of the surrounding buildings, it was cold. The lights were burning brightly. People were shouting and cursing. The wind carried only bits and pieces to me. Up on the open ground, where the flagpole rattled in the wind, the soldiers were kneeling, with their hands on their heads. A few were lying down. It looked like almost all of them were there. Behind them was a massive group of people aiming a wide variety of weapons at the soldiers.

It took a moment, but I spotted Fredricks holding his head and Davis laid out next to him. There were shouts as two rather large men dragged a struggling Sunshine along. He was bound and gagged, and even then, the men barely got him to the group. Both the men escorting him were bloody, and behind them two more men were helping an injured third. My fear grew as I scanned the crowd. My eyes didn't find Mikoto. Lieutenant Brick stood at the flagpole. It looked like he was tied to it.

I looked at the group of people standing as an audience to this display. Most of them were the faces I had looked at during all our community meetings. They looked afraid and angry. They held each other and stood huddled against the wind. That's when the glass man walked out of the armed crowd.

He drew everyone's attention. He moved with smooth, easy steps to the center of the light. He seemed calm and serene even as the cold wind blew. I eased my way along the edges of the crowd. I needed to get to that door. The ATV was parked inside at the supply depot, but the only way in was behind this crowd. Slowly and easily, I made it to the door.

My hand fell on the door handle as the glass man's voice filled the night air.

"Wait... Be still... Listen... Do you hear it?" He put one hand to his ear. I froze in place, panicked that he had spotted me. My eyes darted to him as he raised his arms up to the snow-filled clouds above. His clothes were clean and neat, and his hair was parted perfectly. He wore a heavy winter coat that hung open. The crowd hushed. There was a strange texture to his voice. It had the confident ring of someone who often spoke in front of a crowd. There was something else to it too, a rough edge that rubbed against your ear just enough to draw attention. It made me feel as if he spoke just to me.

"That is the sound of God's will delivering us to salvation!" He tilted his head backward as the wind rushed past him. He was smiling. I wondered if other people found this comforting or pleasant. To me he looked like an evil Ken doll brought to life. His smile was painted in place. He looked over the crowd with his painted-on smile and waved one hand in the air.

"Now I know ... I know you are scared. We came up here unexpectedly. I know you are worried. You are tired. You are cold. I know. However, do not fear. We have not come to harm you. We are here to save you. We have come to release you from this man's tyrannical rule." He pointed back to Lieutenant Brick and then looked around at the crowd. Everyone was watching him carefully.

"This man is sworn to protect the people of this nation, but does he really? Or is he using you as a shield to keep his precious radio safe? Think, if he really had your best interests at heart, why didn't he use his radio to help you? Does he listen to you? Does he respect you? Did he keep you safe? No!"

There was an amazing cadence to how he spoke. It was rhythmic. His words throbbed with the beat of my heart. He spoke with the soft, drawling accent of a southeastern minister. I knew what he was doing. Hell, I had done this. He was appealing to the mob.

"He lied to you. He made you gather supplies and work to fix up this place. He didn't do that for you. No, it was for his own men. They serve an uncaring and cruel master. They don't care about you. You are just workers, shields, their cooks and cleaners. When they are done with you, they will just send you to their internment camps. Soldiers have been rounding people up and taking them to concentration camps. You think they will protect you?"

He paused for a moment, giving the crowd just enough time to wonder about it, to process the accusation. "Don't be fooled by their uniforms. These are not your saviors. They are your overseers. They are here to make sure that their master remains in control of you! He and his men are the soldiers of the past. Their corrupt and ungodly leaders have been struck down by the light and purity of

God almighty! This is the reaping! They are the last throes of a dying snake!" His voice pounded against the wind, pulsing with righteous fury.

"Instead of a great flood, God sent fire from the sky. Nevertheless, we have been spared like Noah in the ark. We have survived. We shall inherit the earth. First, we must throw off the shackles of sin and part from those that would hold us to those evil ways. Their corruption and greed led to their own demise. We must turn away from those false idols and cleanse ourselves of their tainted beliefs." The wind seemed to whip in time with his rhetoric. The impassioned madness flowed from his mouth, a poisonous smoke riding on the icy wind.

"We, who have been baptized in the holy fire of his glory will raise a new kingdom here on earth. We will send our message out into the wilds and call out to the believers. We will be the shining beacon in this dark night. Our light will burn away the evils of this world. Won't you join us? Won't you stand with us in the light of our creator?"

Fear ran along my spine. He was turning the mob on Lieutenant Brick and his men. If the glass man killed the lieutenant, then people could blame him or rebel, claiming coercion. However, if the mob killed the soldiers, they would have no one to blame but themselves. There were murmurs in the crowd. The followers behind him gave up a loud "Amen." Some of the camp's more religious types looked pleased and were nodding.

The glass man smiled as he walked back and forth in front of the crowd. His posture was easy and relaxed. He reminded me of a cat, or a snake swaying back and forth. He was almost hypnotic in the way he spoke and moved. "Even if you don't realize that God has blessed you, surely you have chafed under the oppressive thumb of these militant dictators, forcing you to slave away like ants. Look at my people, well-fed and cared for. We don't need these oppressors to survive. We will work together and all share in the bounty. We will help you throw off your shackles and rise up. Rise up, my brothers and sisters. Stand up for your freedoms."

A few people nodded as a few others said, "Praise be." There might have been more infiltrators than I thought, or maybe he was winning people over. He reminded me of a black-and-white movie's snake-oil salesman. There was always an assistant disguised in the crowd who would come forward to be healed. The glass man was clever. He had planted his assistants like a magician. They had been here the whole time. I was only a little surprised when I recognized faces, I had seen on bread day and at the meeting halls. They came forward and made their cases for why they should follow the light. Like all great magicians, he wowed the crowd with his sleight of hand. I looked around at the faces of followers at the edges of the quad. Yes what clean, well-fed, well-armed followers he had. Why hadn't people seen them? They had us completely surrounded.

"I understand your fear, your trepidation," the man continued. "It's frightening to step away from what we have known to something new. I too was held back by the shackles of the past. That was until *GOD* showed me the way. He burned away the trappings of my old faith and filled me with the fire of his divine light. In this holy flame my sins were cleansed, and I proved my worth to my beloved father. He showed me the way with his light, just as I will show you. I will lead you, and together we will walk in the light of the beloved father. We will bask in his glory and build our own heaven on earth. We will be free of their dark greed and corrupt ways. We will be free to make our own choices and make our laws that serve God instead of destroy him! Join me, and we shall prosper together!"

People started shouting and agreeing to join with him, caught up in the passionate speech, fear giving way to the desperate euphoria of salvation. More of my father's words echoed in my mind: "Fear is the greatest salesman. If people are scared, they will buy anything." I grimaced and once again grabbed the door handle to go into supply. In the past when people had mixed religion and law, they had burned women at the stake. In some places they still stoned women like me. It was time for me to get the hell out of here.

"This is wonderful! Praise be!" the man said with a loud cheer. There was a thunderous sound as everyone around him repeated "Praise be!" in unison.

I said my own prayer under my breath. I slowly turned the handle and had opened the door just enough for Lucky to slip in ahead of me when the glass man spoke again.

"Now! All those that wish to join us in this new age, we must first clear away the old regime. Erica, bring them."

I froze and was suddenly very glad that I was only five feet two; it was easy for me to duck and be hidden behind the person in front of me. I was shocked to see Erica—*our Erica*—walked up wearing a smile and made a waving motion to others. Several people were brought out of the crowd. The crazy church-lady, Mrs. Kerns, had a bloody nose and looked like she had put up quite a fight. Several of the loudmouths who had given the LT a hard time, along with Ethan, the Fishers, and an unconscious Keyan, were dragged out before the crowd.

Mr. Glass walked up to Mrs. Kerns and looked her over before dismissing her. He looked over the group in question. Then he seemed to search the crowd before turning toward Erica. His smile faded, and he gave Erica a hard look. "Where is she? I don't see her anywhere."

Erica flinched and looked nervous. She answered him in a voice I hadn't heard before. Her accent and speech were completely different. "We haven't found her yet. However, people are searching as we speak. If she is still on the hill, we will find her. Don't worry. Marlene isn't important."

He glared at her hard for a moment, and Erica seemed to shrink as he took hold of her chin. "I have plans for her and her family. Find her, now," he said in a pleasant tone.

Erica shook visibly and nodded. "Yes, Father ... Praise be." As those words came out of her mouth, I realized I had heard that accent before.

My stomach twisted into a knot. Erica was the woman I had heard. I had thought it might be Mrs. Kerns. It had been Erica the whole time. They were looking for me. I didn't want to know why. I slipped into the building and headed down the stairs to where the trucks were parked. It was dark, with only the glow from the lights outside shining in. There was no one here now that the supplies were kept elsewhere.

My heart raced as I replayed what he'd said about clearing out the old regime and sending out their message. They were going to use the radio tower to spread their cult. They had gathered anyone who had shown any leadership or rebellion and had them kneeling there. He was going to have them killed. I had to act now. There was no time. I had to do something right now, or all those people were going to die.

My heart was jackhammering in my chest as I ran to the truck. They were looking for me. Did Erica know about the library? I didn't know. *Oh God, what if Ethan told her?* But there was no time to think about that. I ran up along the side of the truck and was almost to the cab when I tripped on something in the dark. I landed hard on my hands and knees and realized I'd tripped on someone's legs. I gasped and almost cried out but managed to swallow it in time. It was Old Man Harris. *Oh God, don't be dead!* I was about to burst into tears when he suddenly grumbled. Lucky licked his face a few times, trying to help him wake up.

"What's all this then?" His voice was slurred and grumpy. He reeked of alcohol. He dropped his empty whiskey bottle and looked at me, confused.

I helped him sit up and started trying to get him into the cab of the ATV. Lucky jumped inside easily, but it took a lot of heaving to get Harris in. He grumbled and groaned the whole way. Once he was finally in, I reached under the gas pedal and found the key with a sigh of relief.

"What are you doing, girl?" Harris asked as he finally looked around. "Why are the lights on outside?"

I groped around and found the gun that had been strapped here before. I made sure it was loaded. I looked at him and tried to sound calmer than I felt. "Harris, Vera says she is sorry and was crying because you didn't come to the library. The attack happened, and they have everyone rounded up outside. We need to find a way to distract them before they kill all the military men." I took in a deep breath and gagged as I realized there was some horrible stench in the cab. I coughed and waved a hand in front of my nose as I rolled down the window. "Oh God, what is that smell? What were you drinking?"

He snickered. "That's the biofuel I's makin'. The back of this-here truck is where we stow it, to refill dem trucks and the generator. We're stockin' up fer winter. I also got's my still in here, so I get my moonshine going here too."

I suddenly remembered all the copper tubing that had gone missing. I glared at him.

He gave a snort and said, "We could start a fire."

I shook my head. "No, there are already fires going." Ideas rattled around in my skull. "The radio. They want the radio. They can't have too many people over there right now. This is an armored truck, so it could easily go through that little brick shed."

Old Man Harris looked at me for a moment, his old blue eyes glittering excitedly. "Now you're talking, little Lady. I am way too drunk to drive this truck, but I can help ya!" He strapped in and told me how to start the truck.

The engine growled like an angry monster and came to life. I slammed the clutch down and put the truck into gear. I felt like I was trying to ride a dragon. The cab was up high, and I had to sit on the edge of the seat to reach the pedals. We roared out of the stadium docking area. I heard shouts as people heard the racket. I drove at full throttle around the building and honked the horn repeatedly as I drove through the quad. People screamed and ran in all directions. I made sure that I didn't hit anyone. There was so much chaos that at first no one fired at us. As I drove past the quad, I looked out the windshield, and my eyes locked with his cold glassy eyes. He was still smiling, as if he knew something I did not. My skin crawled as he puckered his lips and blew me a kiss. Fear raked my heart as I turned my eyes back to the path in front of me. We roared up the hill toward the radio tower. I hoped that in the chaos the military men were taking the chance to escape.

I felt like a pea in a tin can. Old Man Harris was hooting and howling like a madman. I heard the craziest-sounding laugh as I bounced on the hard seat. It took me a moment to realize the laugh was mine. I looked ahead and saw lights from the radio room and, not too far off, the generator.

"Hey, girly, I got's me a god damn plan! After we run over the radio, hit that- there generator and then the tower. We will set the whole fucking thing on fire! That way they can't use them parts to fix up a new radio!"

I nodded and pressed down hard on the accelerator. I laid on the horn the whole way, to make sure anyone who was in there got out. People scattered, and shots were fired at the truck, a few cracking against the bulletproof glass.

"Oh shit!" Old Man Harris gasped as a bullet left a perfect circle in the glass right at his face. "Drive faster!"

I nodded and gripped the wheel tighter as I pressed down as hard as I could on the accelerator. I screamed and shut my eyes as we impacted the building. I really expected to be launched through the windshield. But the truck barely slowed! It rammed in one side and came out the other. I screamed and laughed. It seemed unreal. I had the very distinct feeling of none of this being real, like it was some crazy adult version of Mr. Toad's Wild Ride, including the mad voice telling me to go faster. I turned the wheel, and we almost toppled over making the wide circle to pick up speed and hit the generator. We hit it hard, pushing it into the tower, before we were deflected.

There were cracks and pops, and I was blinded for a moment by the white-hot arcs. We were rocked by an explosion, but I kept my foot down on the gas. I blinked repeatedly, but it took me almost a full minute to realize it wasn't just that I had been blinded, but all the lights had gone out. People were screaming.

I grinned. Lights were the first line of defense against fear. Let them be afraid of the dark. Let's see his fucking divine light shine a way out of this. With the lights out Albert and the group had a better chance of escaping. I wanted to make one more pass by the quad, to make sure the military men were free. I flicked on the headlights of the truck, including the high beams.

"Hey, girly!" Harris barked. "We are on fire!"

I looked over at him. "What!?"

He pointed behind us. "The back, it's on fire."

I had lost my rearview mirrors and had to turn my body have way around to see the flames licking the back of the truck. "What do you expect me to do about it, Harris?" I shouted in desperate frustration and to be heard. It was hard to hear anything over the sound of the engine, the gunfire and Lucky barking wildly.

He shrugged and spit. "No idea, but we better do sump'ten before all this fuel catches, or we will be riding this bitch to the promise land in a blaze of fucking glory."

I screamed at him, "Well then look for a fucking fire extin-guisher!"

He rolled his eyes and grumbled as he unbuckled and climbed back to where the cab connected to the storage area.

I drove back into the quad. In the darkness of the storm, the truck's headlights and fires casted mad shadows. People were running everywhere. I pulled around so I could pass by the flag-pole. The lieutenant wasn't there. He and some of the soldiers had weapons and were forming a firing line. I slowed and pulled the ATV alongside them, so they could use it as a moving barricade.

We slowly moved out of campus, toward the tree line. I rolled down the window to shout at Mouthy, who jumped up to hang on to the driver's door.

"Let us in!" he said urgently.

"No. The truck's just a big target. It's a death trap. And it's still on fire. The others should be leaving the library already. Get to Albert and the kids, get them off this damn hill! When we pass the tree line, use the ravine. I am going down on the valley side. This thing is filled with biofuel. We are going to burn it. Go!"

Mouthy glared and shook his head. "Hell no. I am not letting you do that. You can't do this alone." He tried to open the door.

Suddenly, Keyan was there. He grabbed Mouthy and pulled him back. The truck was creeping along at five miles per hour as the gunfire became more earnest. We weren't far from the tree line now.

"You heard her," said Keyan. "Get them moving. Sunshine, get to her family and make sure they get to the safe house. I have to pick up our package, and we will meet back there. Go! There is no time."

Sunshine grimaced and nodded. "Don't be late!" He grabbed Mouthy and pulled him along with the others as they fell back into a practiced formation.

People were shouting, but Keyan ignored them and looked me in the eye. His voice was hard as he spoke to me. "Drive!" He said as he reached inside to open the driver door and with surprising easy climbed in past me.

I slammed the clutch down, and my dragon roared again. We flew down the road toward the hill. It was going to be a steep descent. As soon as we were out of range of guns, I slowed down. As we came to the gated road, Harris flung open the back door and started throwing out fuel containers, which were quickly catching fire. As the containers caught, they exploded out the back, one after another. He was cursing and hopping around, trying to put out the fire as it went near his still. "No! No! Damn you!" he screamed at the flames till he finally found a fire extinguisher.

Grinning, I pressed the accelerator again and started down the hill. I looked at our speed, and that's when I noticed the gas gauge. I couldn't believe it! It was hanging past the red line. I reached out and tapped it a few times. "Oh shit, guys. I got bad news."

Keyan, who was doing something in the back, looked up. "What?"

"The gauge says we are out of gas! Why isn't there any gas in this thing?" I shouted at Harris.

Harris yelled back, "It runs on diesel. They took it out for the generator. The generator runs on either diesel or biofuel. We hadn't converted the truck yet."

I groaned. "We need to get farther if we are going to get away."

I used the hill to pick up speed so we could coast for a while. It wasn't long before my roaring monster coughed and sputtered out of gas. The wind was howling, and the snow was heavy. I could barely see the road ahead of us. We grabbed everything we could out of the truck. I climbed down and saw Harris leaning over the seat to grab something.

"What are you doing?" I asked as I put the handgun in my pocket. We used Harris's duffel bag to gather the few things we could take from the truck.

"Radio!" He pulled out the little CB radio. "Now we have one, and those assholes on the hill have nothing but slag!" His cackling was lost in the howling wind.

Keyan grabbed my arm and leaned into my ear. "We need to move," he said. "Storm's getting worse!"

Holding on to him and hiding in the little break his body provided, I pulled out the compass and map. I carefully put them in his hand. He tied a leash onto Lucky and studied the map for a moment before he began to move. We formed a chain, holding on to the person in front of us.

It was a long walk to safety.

twenty-eight
still in the blizzard

WHEN I WAS FIVE, we packed up the car and drove up to Pennsylvania to visit my grandmother at Christmas. It was the first time I had ever seen snow. The snow was already piled high when we got to Grandma's house. I was bundled up in my heaviest winter coat. I would never forget its bright shade of red. I felt like I was a maraschino cherry. I loved that coat. I also had a little white scarf and mittens. We all went sledding that day. It was so much fun. Over and over, I squealed as we went down the hill and then hauled that little wooden sled back up.

Eventually, everyone else got tired of it, but not me. I remember everyone heading back, but I kept saying, "One more time, Daddy! Just one more!" Then I would slide down and race back up the hill. But the last time I came to the top of the hill, I couldn't see Daddy anymore. In fact, I couldn't see anyone. I couldn't even see their footprints in the snow. I realized that new snow had started to fall, and I couldn't see the house anymore. I tried to follow the road. Then I was somewhere I didn't know, looking at an old church. Its wood had turned black with age, and it looked scary against all that white.

I sat down on my sled, my arms tired from pulling. I kept brushing the snow off my coat so that my daddy could see me. I was afraid of being buried in the snow so deep that he wouldn't see my bright cherry-red coat. I remember being so scared and cold. It just kept snowing more and more, and eventually, I couldn't even see the black church.

Then my daddy came over the hill. It was as if he just materialized out of the white world. He hugged me and gently pulled me on the sled the rest of the way home. I don't remember it, but I am sure he chewed me out. The only thing I remember about the trip home was being relieved. I never took my eyes off his strong back as he pulled me along behind him. I do remember the hot chocolate that my grandmother made me when we got back. It was thick and creamy with a candy cane in it. I sat with my feet in a little tub of warm water. It stung horribly, but I got to have little ball-shaped cookies. I'd never had cookies like that before. I have never had them since. That experience is the only thing I remember from the visit.

That snowstorm was nothing compared to this one. Icy fingers clawed at the seams of my clothes. Frozen fists beat against me and tried to shove me back and forth. It was hard to breathe. I could barely see. I was so thankful for my big-ass boots. The salesman had said they were rated to negative twenty degrees. I believed him. I just wished all my clothes were the same. My eyes hurt as the snow whipped into them. My breath steamed into my scarf. I held on to Keyan's coat. I couldn't have seen ahead even if I'd tried. Old Man Harris was holding on to my jacket. How he was staying so steady, I didn't know. Maybe all that moonshine meant that his blood couldn't freeze, like vodka.

I wished I had a sled to ride now. The area was so dark. We had glow sticks to help us, but they didn't do much. We walked through this frozen hell for what seemed like forever. I checked my watch just to make sure time was still passing. We had been walking for almost two hours.

Suddenly, I felt a huge tug on my jacket, and I was almost pulled down to the ground with it. I held my footing mostly due to my hold on Keyan. Old Man Harris had fallen behind me. Keyan and I lifted him between us. I pulled his arm over my shoulder and grabbed ahold of his waist band. Keyan had to bend awkwardly to lift him. We moved fast and it took a moment before I realized we were cutting across a road. I couldn't see where we were going until Keyan pulled snow-covered boards off the doorway to a building and pulled us inside. I was so glad. I didn't think I could have helped carry Harris for more than a few minutes. Once inside my vision cleared a little. It looked like an old house. It was still cold inside, but at least I was no longer being attacked by ice giants. I pulled Harris into what looked like a living room. Keyan was closing the doorway behind us before he went through the house.

I stumbled over to the fireplace to see if we could use it. I heard the wind and felt cold air coming in from the flue. Keyan came back into the room and looked at me for a moment. He walked up and put a hand on my shoulder as I was placing some wood in the fireplace. He shook his head. "It's gas." His voice was low and calm.

I looked back at him. All I could think of was trying to get warm. "So?"

He gently pulled me away from the fireplace. "It means we can't burn wood in it."

Even as he said that I still couldn't figure out why that would have been an issue. I just nodded. *Well, don't I feel stupid?* So much for that idea. I felt the cold air seeping into me. My breath steamed the air around my face. I checked on Harris. He snored loudly, but I was worried he would get cold. I dug into my backpack and pulled out a couple of chemical hand-warmer packets. I cracked two, put one in each of Harris's armpits, and then tucked a blanket around him. Lucky moved in and laid his body over Harris's chest, helping to keep him warm. I then used two packets for myself. It wasn't enough, but it felt good.

Keyan seemed to be destroying the house. My mind was blank

as I watched him. Everything was a fog. He climbed up the stairs and pulled down a metal duct. He seemed to be constructing something. I couldn't figure out what he was doing, and I was too cold to ask. I huddled next to Harris, trying to keep the warmth of my packets, and listened to the wind howl.

I watched my breath steam around my face for a few more minutes. With Keyan hard at work with whatever he was doing, I pulled the ham radio and the battery over to me. I didn't know a lot about radios. That was usually Albert's job. But I had always done well in shop, and the radio turned out to be fairly user-friendly. I ran the connectors from the back of the ham radio to the battery. The front panel of the radio lit up, and the little speaker buzzed. I carefully and slowly moved the dial and listened for any sound. When I didn't hear anything but static, I picked up the little mouthpiece, pressed the button, and spoke as calmly as I could.

"Hello, can anyone hear me? We need help. Please, if you can hear me, respond ... Is anyone out there?"

I just kept talking, asking if anyone was out there, over and over. I watched as the dial moved from one side of the little glass display to the other, then back. Keyan finished building a makeshift fireplace with the duct and some other pieces of furniture. We began burning anything we could find to add some warmth to our little room. A wooden bed leg was glowing nice now in our strange fireplace. Harris was still snoring loudly when Keyan sat down next to me by the fire and checked his gear. My throat was dry, and I was so tired. The only good thing about the cold was the bruising on my face and neck had gone completely numb.

I closed my eyes, trying hard not to think about anything. Were my children safe? Were they warm? Where were they? Had they made it to shelter? Had they gotten away? Were they scared I wouldn't come home? Pain radiated throughout my chest. It was hard to pull air into my lungs. My heart was being squeezed. My stomach was being wrenched out. My poor babies. I had left them with capable people, and their father was with them. My head knew that. My heart didn't care. I couldn't hold them. I couldn't sing them to sleep. I couldn't touch their hair. I hated myself for leaving them. I was happy I had saved folks. I was glad I'd stopped those crazy bastards. But again, that was my head. My heart just wanted to hug my babies.

I clenched my teeth together. I curled into myself as I fought against stupid, pointless tears. I struggled to pull myself out of my what-ifs and if-onlys. I told myself these thoughts were stupid and pathetic. They had supplies and their father, and Sunshine and Mouthy were with them. Alice and Samara would make sure they were OK. I didn't regret my decision, but that didn't make it any easier. Lucky whined and licked my face. I reached out and hugged him tight.

I wasn't used to having these kinds of self-hating thoughts assault me. It was the cold. I am sure of it. It was the kind of cold that ground you down. It seeped into your skin and made your bones ache, as if it were gnawing on them. I didn't mind the snow, the sudden bursts of sharp-edged cold, the hard-blowing winds that made your whole-body tremble, or that stabbing cold that awoke every nerve ending. It always made me feel alive. However, this seeping damp was torture. It numbed you and sucked away your will.

I groaned and slowly forced myself to get up. Trying to stand on my frozen feet felt like trying to stand on icy bricks. I shifted closer to the fire, which helped. I rubbed my arms. I looked around and didn't see Keyan. I started walking in place to get my blood flowing again.

"What are you doing?" His voice reached me from the darkness at the edge of our firelight. My heart forgot what it was doing for a moment, which gave me the strange sensation of excitement and terror that came with heart palpitations. This guy was either really good for my cardio or really bad for my heart, but it helped me forget the cold.

"The cold was getting to me. I thought moving around would help."

I didn't hear him move. I wasn't really sure where he was in the room. His voice came from multiple places at once. The echoes gave him an eerie quality. I was rooted to the spot as my eyes and ears played tricks on me. For a second time my heart stopped suddenly, then skipped ahead a few beats, as if trying to make up for the time lost.

You have heard of something melting into a shadow? Well, he melted out of it, as if he was forming up out of the darkness, and it was gently pushed aside from his body. It was fascinating and way too much like something out of a movie. His cheeks were flushed from the cold air. His hair was ruffled and slightly damp from the melting snow and ice in it.

I was staring again, I knew that, but I couldn't stop. I was trying to figure out if he was a temptation sent by the devil or a test. Either case was not good for me. I swallowed hard and turned my body back to the radio. "I was thinking of starting again with the radio calls. We know there were other people out there with radios. Someone is bound to hear us. Maybe even one of the walkie-talkies that the others were carrying will pick us up."

Keyan shook his head. "No." He crouched down next to the fire to warm his hands. He added a broken piece of table to the fire. "Save the battery."

I sighed and nodded. He was probably right. He was experienced with this sort of thing. It was just my fear making me want to keep busy. I rubbed my arm in an effort to release my worried energy.

"How close are we?" I asked quietly as I looked out one of the small gaps where the window wasn't covered. Snow whipped past at alarming speeds. The sounds of the wind could be heard over the crackle of the fire. The house creaked and groaned as it clung desperately to the earth, trying to shelter us as best it could. I put a hand against the wall and was shocked at how icy it was.

His hand covered mine on the wall as he made a noise low in his throat. I nearly jumped out of my skin as my heart tried its best to pop right out of my mouth, which of course made it impossible to scream.

The sound that came out of his throat wasn't a growl exactly. There is apparently some big scientific debate about whether big cats can purr. It is said that out of the biggest cats, only the cougar and the cheetah are 100 percent able to purr. I even got to hear a recording of a cougar purring. If I hadn't been able to see his hand and arm, I would have bet money that there was a purring mountain lion lounging right behind me, breathing hot breath against the back of my neck.

My hand was completely covered by his on the wall. The heat of his skin seemed burning hot in contrast to the cold wall. I couldn't look anywhere but his hand over mine. My heart was a tiny bird fluttering wildly inside the cage of my throat, with that cougar behind me gazing in at it. My blood rushed to my head making me woozy. I felt nothing but the heat and cold on my own hand and the heat of his breath on my neck. He didn't touch me anywhere else. My vision blurred as my eyes stung. I felt something sting my cheeks and realized I was weeping.

What was I doing? Why was I trembling? When had I become so weak? My mind swirled with so many emotions. Just like when I had worked at the ER, now that the emergency had passed, and nothing remained to do, I was having my breakdown. I was so raw and restless. I was all twisted up inside. I wanted to lean back. I wanted to lean back and take his comfort and warmth.

I swayed, even as my mind tried to reason all that excitement away, tried to tell me to calm down. It didn't matter. I was reacting, and there wasn't a damn thing my head could do about it. I leaned back against his chest. *Oh!* His body was so hot! I had known he wouldn't be just warm. He wasn't a nice hot bath or being toasty by the fire. I had known he wouldn't be that. No, he was wildfire, burning infernos, and glowing lava. He was that red-hot glow of the inside of forges that melted iron till it ran like water.

The heat filled me, and my knees melted. I was so dizzy. The world tilted, and suddenly my feet weren't touching the floor. He seemed to be holding me up somehow as he looked down at me. He was talking, but I couldn't hear him over the sound of my own heart. I knew he was speaking because his lips were moving. His mouth was so close. The world seemed to narrow till his face was all I could see. I felt myself stretching toward him. I was so close I could practically taste his breath. I tried to swallow the bird in my throat. His heat seemed to scorch my skin. It was a little painful. I craved the heat and tried to move closer. His face was so close to mine. It would have been so simple to kiss him. My hands betrayed me, seeking the heat of him. I felt like I was slipping. Then in a panicked attempt to save myself from burning, I shoved away from him and fell back against the wall. Agony sliced up my body as I fell against some horrific jagged blade of frozen death.

I flailed forward in pain and terror as I tried to escape the icy claws of doom. Lights exploded behind my eyes and pain burst through my nose as my face collided with his chin. To his credit, as we fell, he made sure I didn't hurt myself further. I cried out, holding my face in one hand and my back in the other. The injuries on my face came back to life with a vengeance. All the numbness provided by the cold now caused additional agony with frozen needles. Pain helped me come back to myself as I learned how to breathe again. The brain fog lifted slightly, and I could see a little more clearly now. Lucky tilted his head from where he was resting near the fire.

The culprit was a small electrical switch box that wasn't set into the wall. The metal had fried and at some point burst outward. The sharp edges were frozen razors. It hurt so bad that I just laid my forehead against the floor. My nose was bleeding slightly and throbbed in pain. However, my back hurt so much worse.

"Let me see," Keyan said quietly as he moved behind me. I just kept my face to the floor. "Damn," he said under his breath as he lifted the back of my coat and shirt. Either he was admiring my tattoos, or my back wound was worse than I thought.

"As I thought. You're hypothermic. We'll keep you close to the fire. I will bandage this." he said quietly. I shifted to a more comfortable position as he pulled out the med kit. He cleaned my back with some disinfectant and put something over the cuts that stung like a son of a bitch. He had just placed a bandage on my back when the radio chirped. I looked up from where I was lying. Keyan grabbed the receiver. I sat up slowly, gingerly covering my back and zipping up my coat to recapture my warmth.

"This is the cavalry. We were sent to pick you up. Give us your location."

He hesitated to reply, and we waited for a moment. Finally, he said, "No, tell us your location, and we will come to you."

The voice over the radio sounded a little amused. "Sunshine said you would be mistrusting. He said to tell you, 'Code 427832.' Oh, what was that other thing? Oh, tell Mouse that Wombat needs a cheesecake? I don't know what the hell that means, but he was very specific. He made me repeat it a bunch of times."

I started laughing as relief flooded me. "It's OK," I assured Keyan. "Tell him where we are. Albert sent them too."

Keyan nodded slowly and gave our location.

He sat down next to me as I took an aspirin. He didn't say anything as he added more wood to the fire. The air was cold but not as bad as it had been. Even outside, the snow seemed to be falling less heavily. Maybe the worst of the storm was over. I felt relief sink in, and I began to relax. My eyelids grew heavy as I started to doze off.

"*Pumpernickel!*" screamed Harris as he suddenly bolted upright.

I screamed in surprise and fell over, groaning in agony. "God-damn it!" I cried as I slowly sat up. I glared at Harris, who blinked sleepily and scratched at his head and belly. Lucky had yipped and huffed awake and now licked Harris's face before lying back down.

Keyan was trembling slightly as he forced himself to put his pistol away. He rose to his feet and picked up his gear. "I will spot," he said tightly as he stepped outside.

Harris watched him for a moment and let out a little chuckle. "The boy is going to pop a blood vessel one day. He really needs to blow off some steam." He grinned at me and winked.

I looked away embarrassed and a little guilty. "I wasn't doing anything..."

Harris patted me on the back and pulled out a flask that I didn't know he had. He took a drink and sighed. "I know. I know. Don't get all bent out of shape." He ruffled my hair and handed me the flask.

I took a sip. Whatever was in there, it hurt. It was like pouring molten glass down my throat. I tried to cough, but that only made it worse. My eyes watered down my cheeks as I tried to breathe. The agony of my throat made it easier to forget my other pains.

Harris laughed and slapped me on the back. Then I felt a burning heat spread from my throat to my chest. "What ... the hell ... is ... this?" I choked out.

"That's my own moonshine. This will keep the winter from touching ya!"

And damn his eyes if he wasn't right. I didn't feel the cold at all now. Hell, I didn't even feel the pain in my back, my legs, or my face. However, I could barely talk after he pushed two more sips down my throat. By then all of Old Man Harris's stories were hilarious. The fire was warm and toasty, and the worries about anything were all gone. Moonshine was a very effective mood-changer. I lost track of time listening to Harris's stories. Honestly, I couldn't tell you half of them, but they cracked me up.

I was laughing my ass off when in walked Keyan with absolutely the last people I expected to see. OK, maybe not the last. I guess Bill Murray would have been the very last person. But these guys were a close second. It was Wolf-man, the scarecrow, and the tattooed giant, the three prison guys I had spotted downtown! They weren't wearing the jumpsuits anymore. My jaw fell open as I looked at them.

They looked back at me, and the scarecrow broke out into a huge toothy smile. "Oh, someone has a drink! It's like Christmas!" He plopped down next to Harris, who was only too glad to share a drink.

Keyan looked irritated as he walked over to me. "What is that?" He pointed at the flask.

I shrugged. "Staying warm?" I said lamely. I wobbled as I got to my feet. "Are these the fellas coming to our rescue?" I tried to say it nicely, but I must have failed because Wolf-man was glaring at me.

"Yeah, your husband sent us, but he might have thought twice if he saw you. I wasn't exactly thrilled to be coming all the way out here to get you, but maybe we should just leave you to your drinking party. I don't need a sloppy drunk in my truck."

Moments like this were why I shouldn't drink. "Hey!" I yelled. "Who the fuck do you think you are, Wolf-man? As if you any judge to right me!" So yeah, me plus alcohol equaled no brain-to-mouth filters. "Don't you worry about my man! He never thinks twice! He gets it right the first time!" I almost toppled. It was very hard for my legs to hold me up. My mouth just continued running, without any real thought to the words. I yelled at Old man Harris. "Come on, you smelly old coot! Let's go. My babies are waiting!" I glared at Wolf-man and pointed a finger at him. I wasn't able to regulate the volume of my voice. "Talking about my man like that ... He is a genius! You bad-mouth him again, I'll punch your lights out!"

Keyan easily captured my arms as I tried to shake a fist at Wolf-man and maneuvered me toward the door. Old Man Harris thought it was funny as hell and laughed as he stumbled to his feet.

I followed our rescuers out to the snowplow truck they had running. Wolf-man was shaking his head as he led the way. Everything had a pleasant, fuzzy feeling. People were talking, but I didn't hear them.

I didn't feel the cold outside. The wind had finally stopped. The snow was thick and heavy, falling in big fat flakes. It was beautiful. The light from the truck gave our surroundings a golden hue and caused golden sparkles to glint over the surface of things. It was a deadly magic. Christmas music filled my mind as I climbed into the seat. Someone had to buckle me. The warmth from the heater hit me, and the alcohol sent me spinning. I was asleep before everyone was loaded.

I didn't so much wake up as I became aware of the thrumming in my head. The light was impossibly bright. Half of me felt like it was pressed against a furnace, while the other half was lying against an iceberg. At least the bruises on my face and hip had stopped hurting. In fact, most of the pain from the bruises had left and found their way to my head. My mouth was dry and tasted like I had tried to eat a bale of hay. I tried to roll away from the light but found I was trapped. It took a Herculean effort to pry one eye open.

The sight made the pain from the light worth it: Victor and Zyada curled up together next to me. They were a mess of arms and legs all thrown on top of each other, with little hands gripped together. *Could this get any cuter?* I pulled one hand out and brushed my fingers through Victor's curls and then along Zyada's long hair. I looked at my hand and tried to figure out what was wrong with it. There were red patches and blisters. My thumbnail was slightly discolored. I looked at the other hand and saw similar marks. *Did I touch poison ivy hidden under the snow? Or did I fall in the fire?*

My head was pounding. I lifted an arm to cover my face, but the ache made it impossible to fall back to sleep. I looked across the room at the steel sink. I was so thirsty that I considered whether it would be worth the battle. I decided it wasn't and instead looked around the room. It was a very small room, more like a storage closet. High on the wall, there was a very small barred window, and a little steel toilet sat beneath it.

I lay there and tried to figure out why someone would build a toilet in a closet. I had not been able to think much past that question when Albert walked in. He had a bottle of water and a cup of coffee. I whole-body reacted to the smells. "Oh, I love you so much," I said. The sound of my own voice hurt my head.

He grinned and sat down next to me. He set down the coffee and held out a couple of aspirin. He then opened the water bottle and helped me take the pills. My hands didn't seem to work the way they were supposed to. They were stiff and still a bit numb. He assisted me to an upright position. I was so thirsty that I drank the whole bottle all at once. Some of my exhaustion abated. He then handed me the coffee, and I started nursing it. It was warm and sweet and perfect. I was in the middle of my third drink of coffee when I started to cry. He took the cup from my hand, and I latched onto him. I just hugged him as tight as I could, sniffling. He held me close and rubbed my back gently as he waited for me to compose myself. Everything still hurt.

I finally sat back and smiled sheepishly as I took the coffee back. After another sip, I whispered, "I feel like shit. This is way worse than any hangover I have ever had."

"I am not surprised. Between your previous injuries, hypothermia, frostbite and the moonshine, you probably feel like roadkill." he said as he began looking over my hands.

I winced a little as I became more aware of other aches and pains. "I am fairly sure that whatever Harris was drinking no longer counts as moonshine."

He gave a quiet little chuckle, keeping his voice low. "Guess you are lucky you didn't get alcohol poisoning."

I looked around and felt worry rise up in my chest. "Where is Nathan? Why isn't he here?"

Albert continued to gently reassure me. "He is with Jeri. He is fine. You have been sleeping for almost a full day. These two munchkins keep coming back in here. Nathan will meet us for food in a little bit." I held my cup and considered the effort it would take to go to the sink and wash my face. "This is such a weird room."

He looked around and gave a sort of pained smile. "Yeah, I guess so ... Honey, you ready for me to catch you up?"

I turned my attention back to him. I was still so foggy, but I nodded as I drank my coffee. He scooted closer. The moment felt cozy, and the pounding in my head seemed to have eased to a dull ache.

"We aren't at the church," Albert said in a low whisper. "When we got there, it was already burned down. They burned it before they ever got to the hill. We think Erica told them."

I frowned into my coffee. He gave me a reassuring smile and brushed my hair out of my face. "We tried to use the walkies to reach you or Keyan," he continued, "but we reached a group of scouts instead. They were out looking for one of their own people. The lieutenant convinced them to come get us. It was amazing. They came in and rescued us in this big old prison bus." He shook his head and gave a small laugh. "I was a little apprehensive when we first arrived here at the penitentiary."

I looked around, and the realization hit me. This was a cell of some kind. "We are inside a prison right now?" I whispered back to him, almost dropping my coffee.

Albert carefully steadied the mug. "Yeah. It's the Evansville Correctional Facility." My face must have shown how thrilled I was about this because he rubbed my shoulders gently and smiled. "Don't freak out. Drink your coffee. We are fine. See, none of the doors are even closed. This was a minimum-security facility. The men who were here were here because of petty crimes. Violent offenders go north."

I sat up more fully and frowned at him. "Were here? Where are they now?"

He gave a sigh, obviously trying to stay patient with my reaction. "They were released after the storms. The warden decided that he couldn't maintain the prison. He decided to use it to help refugees instead. Those who stayed and are helping run the place will have their sentences commuted when order is restored."

I wasn't exactly thrilled with this idea, but I settled down a bit. "Do you think it's safe?"

He nodded. "It's safe. All the cell doors are open, and everyone is just walking around. They have been very welcoming and helpful. We have about an hour, then food is ready. All of us are going to meet with Lieutenant Brick after we eat." He smiled and sat back now that I was calmer. After I finished my coffee, he helped me get out of the bed without waking the little ones. He helped me wash my face since my hands hurt so much; the water was warm. It stung my skin, but I didn't care.

"It isn't a bad plan," Albert mused, more to himself than to me. "Penitentiaries are already set up for large numbers of people. There are plenty of beds and bathrooms. They have big cafeterias and eating areas—not to mention the built-in security measures." He looked around as he gently petted Zyada's head. His expression was distant and distracted.

I frowned as I leaned over towards him. "What's wrong?"

He shook his head. "Oh, nothing. I was just thinking about the structure. Was it the old iron in the concrete or maybe the layout of the buildings? Something in the design maybe." He was doing that thing where he shared only half of his thoughts. I didn't bother pushing. He would come back when he was ready. Instead, I started checking my bags in the room. It took only a few minutes for him to continue speaking.

"Some parts of the prison were completely intact after the storms, and other places were badly damaged. I was just trying to figure out why." He leaned forward, excited about the topic. "But so much is still functional. They have power, heat. The LT is talking to the warden about setting up the radio tower."

I felt tears coming again, and I moved over to hug him tight as I cried. The waves of relief hit me as I sat in his lap. He held me close and stroked my head. "It's going to be OK. We will figure it out. We always do."

I nodded against his shoulder and laughed. All the plans had fallen apart, I had been so reckless, and somehow we had come out of it. My new little tribe had escaped the hill and the storm. It hurt to cry at first, but I just let it out anyway. I don't know how long I cried. But I know that by the end of it, I had to wash my face in cold water to take down the swelling in my eyes.

We got the kids up from their nap and went to go meet Jeri and Nathan at the main cafeteria. I seemed to be the only one to notice a little chill in the air. All the windows and doors had bars or wire cages on them. Having all the doors open did make it a little less frightening. As we passed out of section 43D into a main hallway, there was a big décor change.

All the walls were covered with scrawled artwork. I don't mean graffiti. It was as if a kindergarten class had come in with paintbrushes and had been told to just go for it. Flowers, stars, hearts, people, suns, and animals that defied description were painted in a rainbow of colors. The walls were cheerful and bright as we made our way to the main cafeteria. In other places adults had painted words and verses on the walls, everything from Bible lines to song lyrics. It helped dispel the gloom that clung to the place.

In well-painted script someone had written a few segments of lyrics from Johnny Cash's "Ring of Fire": "Bound by wild desire, I fell into a ring of fire ... The taste of love is sweet, when hearts like ours meet ... It burns, burns, burns, the ring of fire."

A flush flooded my face and neck. *Get a grip, Marlene. You just got caught up in a crazy moment. Nothing happened. Let it go.* I realized I had fallen behind, so I continued down the hall, trying to catch up with Albert and the kids.

As I rounded the corner, I saw Keyan standing just outside the cafeteria doors, speaking to Albert. I wanted to avoid him, but my feet kept moving forward. I tried hard to keep my face neutral as my insides twisted in embarrassment. *Act natural. Calm down. Say something, you weirdo!* My brain shouted, but my mouth remained silent. They seemed to be having a ridiculously relaxed conversation.

Keyan looked at Albert and in an annoyingly calm voice said, "Mind if I steal her for a moment?"

Albert smiled and nodded. "Sure, no problem. I will get the little ones started inside."

I nodded and gave Albert a smile. I needed to make sure the boundaries were still clear, for myself as well as Keyan.

Keyan waited till Albert had stepped inside and then moved away from the cafeteria doors, just out of sight. Without even realizing I was doing it, I followed him.

He was suddenly very close to my face, and for a wild moment I thought he was going to kiss me right there in the hall. I gasped and leaned back as he put a hand on my forehead. Then he grabbed my hands and turned them over.

"What are you doing?" I squeaked out.

He examined my fingers for a moment longer. "I am checking your injuries. We need to watch for frostbite. Hypothermia is no joke. All the swelling made it impossible to judge how bad it had gotten." After a moment, he seemed satisfied and nodded. "Good, we don't need to worry about losing fingers. Your boots were good, so you don't have it on your toes. Doesn't look like any permanent damage."

I watched him with confusion and no small amount of irritation. I wasn't sure which of us I was irritated at. "Is that what you wanted to talk to me about?"

He still held my hands. He lifted my right hand to his face, and instead of answering me, he whispered against the skin of my palm, "I just wanted to take care of you." His eyes remained on my hand resting in his.

My heart thudded heavily. I took a deep breath and pulled my hand away. *Come on, Marlene. Get it together. You have to set boundaries. If you are going to be firm with him, you must be firm with yourself.* I took a small step back, trying to put some space between us. I needed breathing room. I pressed my lips together tightly, afraid of what might come out of them. My hands were clenched close to my body as I looked up at Keyan. "I know," I said as I tried to form coherent thoughts. "Thank you." The words fell out of my mouth suddenly, and I winced at how dumb they sounded. "For saving me," I finished weakly. I felt so completely stupid. "I mean ... the snow ... and everything." I flushed again as I tried hard not to think about how close I had come to trying to kiss him.

His brow was furrowed in thought as he looked at me for a long moment. Then his mouth tilted into a smile. He gave me a nod and turned and walked away.

I groaned and hung my head. *Smooth. Real smooth, Marlene. You really showed him where the boundaries are. I am sure he is clear on where you stand, crystal clear.*

I took a moment to collect myself before I went into the cafeteria to find Albert.

The cafeteria was a loud and bustling place. Voices overlapped with the clinking of silverware and trays. It was a massive area, and there must have been close to 150 people in there. Though for the most part my headache was gone, the noise was almost overwhelming.

The first person I noticed was a massive man covered in tattoos. Even his bald head was tattooed. He was still wearing his prison jumpsuit. He was sitting at a table, facing away from me, and he had a spoon in one hand and a bowl in another. He had caught my attention because he was feeding a baby. The infant couldn't have been more than a year old. The man was even doing the airplane noise. There seemed to be several such men positioned around the room. They were all feeding people who were unable to feed themselves, like nurses at an assisted care facility. I just stood there for a moment, watching these men tend to the helpless.

A vaguely familiar voice whispered in my ear, "Almost restores your faith in humanity, right?"

I jumped a bit as the Wolf-man came up right alongside me. I looked up at those blue eyes. He stared at me seriously for a moment, like he had something to tell me, but then he just looked away. It unsettled me.

"Though I suppose we shouldn't judge others," he said. "Everyone deals with the disaster in their own way." His tone sounded flippant and sarcastic. He gave my back a pat and in a friendly tone said, "We have AA meetings here every Thursday, if you need one."

My mouth dropped open. "I beg your pardon?" I said in a startled tone. The fucking nerve of some people. Albert started to laugh from a few feet to my left. I hadn't seen him when I came in. But I found him easily enough now. I snapped my glare to Albert instead.

Albert just shrugged. "Oh, you lush ... can't get you off the sauce!"

I was not in the mood today that was for sure. There were whole days when his sense of humor made me want to murder him. "Are you serious right now? Alcoholism isn't a joke." When Albert didn't show even a moment's remorse, I growled at him. "You can be such an ass."

Wolf-man looked at Albert like he was nuts. I decided that these men were not worth the aggravation at the moment. I stepped over to Albert and took ahold of the kids' hands. We headed toward the food line. Over my shoulder, I snapped, "You know better, Albert Preston Sales Jr.!"

Zyada gasped and looked at Albert with wide eyes. "Ohhh Daddy is in trouble; Mommy used all your names."

Albert grinned happily as he followed along behind us. "That's right. Daddy's in trouble for teasing Mommy!" he said in a pleased silly voice. I did my best to ignore him. I heard Albert say to Wolf-man, "She actually almost never drinks."

Wolf-man laughed a bit awkwardly. "Ah, I see. My bad. No offense."

"Your face will stick that way!" Sunshine said to my frowning face. He seemed to have materialized out of nowhere beside me. He immediately picked up Zyada. "There is my beautiful princess," he said as he twirled her around. He took her to the lunch line and got her a tray.

The bruises on my face were starting to ache again, but I blew out a breath and followed with Victor. As I grabbed a tray, I felt some deep tension start to ease. I couldn't figure out why I was so relaxed. I thought perhaps it was the good cry, or maybe it was exhaustion. But there I was, standing in the food line in a prison, feeling more secure than I had in weeks.

Once we were at a table, Mouthy joined us and started eating like he hadn't eaten in years. The food was powdered eggs and canned ham, with biscuits. Albert took over the job of making sure Victor ate his food. Zyada was seated between Sunshine and Mouthy, content to eat what was on her plate.

I stirred powdered creamer into my coffee. I licked the spoon clean to taste if it was right and put it back in my mug. I idly continued to stir the now brown liquid, watching light dance across the top of my cup. The liquid moved in little ripples and tiny waves. I found myself completely fascinated by the look of my coffee in the cup. It was still hard to keep myself alert. It wasn't that I was tired; it just felt like thinking took so much more work.

I sighed in pleasure, wrapping my fingers around the warmth of my coffee mug. I recalled a photo I had entered into a contest. I had pointed my camera down into my coffee cup, with the light reflecting from above. It had made a neat shape, like a rippled circle. The light had made the coffee look a weird red. I had thought it looked so cool. I watched the shadow of my head dance across the coffee's surface.

I finally registered that there was a *shadow* inside my cup. I froze for a moment and just stared into the cup. I looked at the edges of my shadow, with the light filling in from behind. We were inside. I turned my face upward and stared in amazement. Light bulbs blazed overhead.

Albert and Mouthy laughed at the same time. Sunshine grinned at me from across the table and whispered, "They were wondering how long it would take you to notice."

That was it. I was relaxed because the lights were on. I'd had no idea how much of a difference it made to me until that moment.

Sunshine continued talking around his ham. "Some places here the lights barely flickered. When the storms hit, there were fires and such here. But after they got that under control, the guards left. The prisoners brought their families here because it seemed safe. After a while they started bringing in other locals and set up a refugee camp."

I looked at him over the rim of my coffee cup. "How do you know any of this?"

Sunshine grinned and shrugged. "Hey, a spotter's job is getting the lay of the land. That's not just about geography."

Zyada nudged his elbow. "You're not supposed to talk with food in your mouth."

He smiled and nodded. "That's right, princess. My bad."

We ate slowly as I watched a few more of our little band come in and stand in line. I started looking around the room to see if I could spot any more. Maybe it was just instinct, but those from our camp sat together in a cluster. I was concerned about how few I saw.

Sunshine caught me trying to do a head count. "Four-two," he said. "There are twenty-four servicemen and eighteen civilians.

Everyone else stayed behind." He saw my distress and gave me a serious look. "Hey, you did everything you could. If it weren't for you, none of us would be here. I for one am grateful you are so damn crazy. Thanks for saving my dumb ass."

I gave a smile and nodded. "Yeah, it was pretty crazy. I don't know what the hell I was thinking."

My hands were still stiff and clumsy. I was focused on trying to get my eggs from my plate to my mouth when a roll was placed on my tray. I looked up, and Mrs. Kerns was standing there holding a tray as she looked down at me.

"I can't decide if it is that the Lord looks after fools or the devil takes care of his own. But in either case, thank you." She somehow managed to look both disgusted and pleased at the same time. "I suppose we are all in this together now." She smiled and sat at the end of our long table.

I sat there staring at the roll a moment and then smiled. *Together. My little tribe made it.* I looked around and saw that Harris was nursing a hangover and being fussed over by Vera. Jeri and Silas were seated next to them, eating large helpings of eggs and bacon. Nathan waved at me from his spot and seemed to be trying to beat Jeri. Samara was seated with Alice, and they had the babies in highchairs while they ate. Michael was talking animatedly with Dr. Fisher. Roger Tucker was seated at a nearby table with a bandage on his head.

Davis and Fredricks walked up and sat down at the table next to ours. They looked like they had lost a brawl, but both were smiling. As people came in for food, they would pass me and pat my shoulder or say good morning or thank you. I received an orange, some cream to put on my frostbite, and a new pair of gloves.

The last person to approach me was the old sergeant. He didn't smile, but he picked up my hand gently and put a medallion key chain into it. A stone castle was beautifully pressed into the medallion, from which hung a strange-looking key. "Good work,

Mrs. Sales. At ease," he said. He then took an empty seat not far down the table.

I was still overwhelmed by the responses when Lieutenant Brick came in, followed by Mikoto. The lieutenant had a bandage wrapped around his head. Both men sat down at our table, wearing carefully blank expressions. Mikoto sat on the opposite side of the table from me, farther down. I tried not to notice him.

I felt a shift in the mood. I thought maybe it was just in my own head. No one else seemed to be responding to anything. I felt a strange tightening in my shoulders. I looked at Mouthy, who gave me a little smile that seemed to mean something and then took another big bite. He said nothing. I knew something was wrong at that moment. Sunshine smiled and pushed my coffee toward me, but there was a tension now. It was like everyone was suddenly playing poker. The ease I had been feeling evaporated.

I was thinking about how to broach the topic when a tall older man stepped into the cafeteria. He looked to be in his fifties. His gray hair was clean-cut and brushed back. He wore a heavy sweater over a button-up shirt and slacks. As he walked toward the front of the cafeteria, the noise in the room died down. By the time he reached the front, the whole room had settled into obedient silence. He stood there for a moment, and I noticed that he had everyone's attention.

"Good afternoon. As you may have noticed, we have some new faces today. Let me be the first to welcome all our newcomers to the Evansville Correctional Facility... I am the Warden. As you may have noticed, it is not currently operating as a detention center. Right now we are working as a safe haven and refugee camp. We are trying to make sure people have a place to be safe until they can be relocated to a more permanent location."

He smiled as he looked around the room. I felt a nervous energy. Almost everyone was relaxed and smiling. The lieutenant and sarge seemed as hard as always. Mikoto was silently staring at the warden. I tried to push a smile onto my face as I continued looking around. I saw the scarecrow, Wolf-man, and their giant leaning against the kitchen counter. I probably wouldn't have noticed if Wolf-man hadn't been looking at our table instead of at the warden. I couldn't tell which of us he was looking at, but he had a strange expression on his face.

"I know our newcomers will be a great help to us. The lieutenant from the Army Corps of Engineers has explained that his men will be building a working radio tower for us. It will work as a relay station for the military as well as help us connect to the rescue efforts. Those who are not working on the radio will even help by joining work rotation here. This will begin after they take a few days to recover from their ordeal." The Warden looked over to where the LT sat at our table. "I want everyone to make sure they feel welcome and be sure to help them learn the ropes. We like to keep things orderly around here, right?"

There was a chorus of agreements and chuckles.

"We are happy you made it and are glad you are here. Enjoy your food. That's it." He turned and spoke to someone on his left.

Out of the corner of my eye, I saw Wolf-man again. He looked disgruntled as he headed into the kitchen. The warden headed out the far end of the room quietly. His boots made a scuffing noise on the cafeteria's tiled floor. I listened to the sound as he walked away. He had a long, even stride.

The ambient noise of conversation and eating started again. I hadn't realized how quiet it had gotten until the sounds returned. It was like someone had pressed pause on a sound machine.

I whispered to the table, "Did anyone else think that was weird?"

Sunshine nodded and looked at Mikoto. "I did. Any thoughts on it?"

Mouthy opened his mouth and then took a big bite of an apple.

The Brick leaned forward and gave a smile. "Leave it alone,

people. We are safe, the lights are on, and the food is warm. Everything else can wait."

So, no shit there I was, beaten up, frostbitten, and having breakfast in a prison cafeteria. I looked at the friends and family surrounding me and smiled. I took a deep breath and nodded. "Yeah, whatever comes along, we will figure it out. Together."

epilogue

I HAVE TRIED to record here what I remember of my time after the solar storms. I thought it was important to write everything down, as much as I can remember anyway. Someday historians will look back at this time and want to know what it was like, to learn from what happened. I have tried to be honest and keep to what I knew at the time.

The snowstorm we had to travel through to escape the hill lasted for three days. It took almost five days before I was completely recovered. It was during my recovery that I decided to make notes about what had happened, what we had seen, and how we had survived. I wanted someone to know what it had been like for us. Someday, I want people to know that the world didn't end. As long as people continue to try to build a community and work together to survive, it won't end.

Our community is thriving. We have learned from the mistakes of the past. We work together to find solutions and work to protect each other. I know some other towns are further along. Some big cities are opening up again. The landlines are being rebuilt. It will be a while before we can get any of the fancy tech up and running again, but people are working hard on it. Things are getting better every day. The wind traps that we put together have really been working great, so we haven't had a power shortage in a long time. Three months ago, we were able to get the mail running, not just for our town but for the whole district. It takes about a week, but now a letter can reliably travel from several states over. The biggest news is that the train lines are running. It's great that we can count on regular shipments now. I can grow things now just because I like them. I have a whole area just for flowers.

Next week we are holding an election for our regional governor. It's exciting, and I am trying to decide who I will vote for. Victor's seventh birthday is next month. It has been a lovely summer, so we are going to grill outside and have a big outdoor picnic with all our friends. We managed to get a bike for him. Our whole neighborhood is planning a big birthday party.

Those beginning months were so chaotic for everyone. There were so many struggles that first year. It will take a long time to tell you how we got through it and finally managed to find our new home. I wasn't sure we would ever find a safe place to be. Even after we finally got here, it took work to get to a sense of normal. It is different than it used to be. It might never go back to the way it was. Maybe that's all right. It takes a long time to rebuild the world. I just hope we do a better job of it this time around.

about the author

Jesse M. Harvey debut book is 'Motherhood at the End of the World.' She writes many types of fiction, including science fiction, space fantasy, supernatural, thriller and mystery. She graduated from Syracuse University with a Bachelor's degree in history

Jesse currently lives in Syracuse NY. She is married with three school age children. Her family comes from a military background, and her husband is a veteran.

Through all her work, Jesse includes underlying themes of hope, compassion, courage and determination. She believes that fiction shapes the future. Jesse wants to help inspire a more diverse and inclusive world.

https://jessemharveybooks.wordpress.com/